Praise for *The Seven Year Slip*

"I ADORED this book. Ashley is such a talent. The worlds she creates are so warm and specific and beautifully rendered. *The Seven Year Slip* is a gorgeous love story from one of the finest romance writers out there. I laughed, I cried, I didn't want it to end. Consider me Ashley Poston's greatest admirer!"

—Carley Fortune, *New York Times* bestselling author of
Every Summer After

"Ashley Poston has again created a world that is off-kilter, romantic, and irresistible. If you love *The Lake House* but also want some top notch make out scenes, this is the book for you."

—Emma Straub, *New York Times* bestselling author of
This Time Tomorrow

"Warm, funny and heartbreakingly hopeful, *The Seven Year Slip* is a magical love story, a devastating portrait of grief, and a loving ode to what it means to grow, evolve and blossom."

—Sangu Mandanna, bestselling author of
The Very Secret Society of Irregular Witches

Praise for *The Dead Romantics*

"It's *While You Were Sleeping* meets *Six Feet Under*, and I need to yell to everyone about how good it is. . . . The result is an antidote for despair, a romance that is frank about the fact that life ends and time marches on but that nevertheless insists: We aren't a gothic horror novel. We're a love story. This is a book to make you laugh during the funeral scene and cry when the dance party begins."   —*The New York Times*

"We could all use a good summer ghost story, and you can't get much better than Ashley Poston's adult fiction debut."

—*Entertainment Weekly*

OTHER TITLES BY ASHLEY POSTON

The Dead Romantics

THE SEVEN YEAR SLIP

ASHLEY POSTON

BERKLEY ROMANCE

New York

BERKLEY ROMANCE
Published by Berkley
An imprint of Penguin Random House LLC
penguinrandomhouse.com

Library of Congress Cataloging-in-Publication Data

Names: Poston, Ashley, author.
Title: The seven year slip / Ashley Poston.
Description: First edition. | New York : Berkley Romance, 2023.
Identifiers: LCCN 2022054539 (print) | LCCN 2022054540 (ebook) |
ISBN 9780593336502 (trade paperback) | ISBN 9780593336526 (ebook)
Classification: LCC PS3616.O8388 S48 2023 (print) |
LCC PS3616.O8388 (ebook) | DDC 813/.6—dc23
LC record available at https://lccn.loc.gov/2022054539
LC ebook record available at https://lccn.loc.gov/2022054540

First Edition: June 2023

Printed in the United States of America
1st Printing

Book design by Daniel Brount

For all the food lovers out there who burn popcorn in the microwave:
we'd be too strong if we could cook, too

THE SEVEN YEAR SLIP

My Darling Clementine

"THIS APARTMENT IS MAGICAL," Aunt Analea once said, sitting in her wingback chair the color of a robin's egg, her hair twisted up with a silver dagger hairpin. She told me with mischief in her eyes, as if daring me to ask her what she meant. I had just turned eight and thought I knew everything.

Of course this apartment was magical. My aunt lived in a century-old building on the Upper East Side, with stone lions on the eaves, half broken and clinging to the corners. Everything about it was magical—the way the light poured into the kitchen in the mornings, golden like egg yolk. The way the study seemed to fit more books than possible, pouring off the shelves and piled against the far window, so high they almost blocked out all the light. I charted foreign maps in the brick face of the far living room wall. The bathroom, with its perfect high window and frosted glass that reflected rainbows against the sky-colored walls and ornate claw-foot tub, was the *perfect* place to paint. My watercolors came alive there, pigments dripping from my brushes as I imagined far-off places I'd never been. And in the evenings, the moon looked so close from her bedroom windows I could almost catch it.

The apartment was indeed magical. You couldn't convince me otherwise. I just thought it was my aunt who made it magical—the way she lived, wide and wild, that infected everything she touched.

"No, no," she said with a wave of her hand—the one holding a lit Marlboro cigarette. The smoke wafted out of the open window, ruffling the two pigeons cooing on the sill, and into the cloudless sky. "I don't mean *metaphorically*, my darling Clementine. You might not believe me at first, but I promise it's true."

Then she leaned closer, and her mischief turned into a smile that shone in her glittery brown eyes, and she told me a secret.

1

Publishers Lunch

MY AUNT USED TO say, if you don't fit in, fool everyone until you do.

She also said to keep your passport renewed, to pair red wines with meats and whites with everything else, to find work that is fulfilling to your heart as well as your head, to never forget to fall in love whenever you can find it because love is nothing if not a matter of timing, and to chase the moon.

Always, *always* chase the moon.

It must have worked for her, because it never mattered where she was in the world, she was home. She waltzed through life like she belonged at every party she was never invited to, fell in love with every lonely heart she found, and found luck in every adventure. She had that air about her—tourists asked her for directions when she went abroad, servers asked her opinion on wines and fine whiskeys, celebrities asked her about her life.

Once, when we were at the Tower of London, my aunt and I accidentally found ourselves at an exclusive party at the Chapel Royal of St. Peter ad Vincula and managed to *stay* with a well-placed compliment and a knockoff statement necklace. There, we met a prince of Wales, or Norway or somewhere, moonlighting as the DJ. I didn't remember much of the rest of that night since I overestimated my tolerance for too-expensive scotch.

But every adventure with my aunt was like that. She was the master of belonging.

If you aren't sure which fork to use at a fancy dinner? Go along with the person beside you. Lost in a city you've lived in for most of your life? Pretend you're a tourist. Listening to an opera after never hearing one ever before? Nod and comment on the chilling vibrato. Sitting in a Michelin-starred restaurant drinking a bottle of red wine that costs more than your monthly apartment rent? Comment on the body and act like you've tasted better.

Which, in this case, I had.

The two-dollar bottle of wine from Trader Joe's tasted better than this, but the delicious small plates made up for it. Baconwrapped dates and fried goat cheese drizzled in lavender honey and smoked trout fritters that melted in your mouth. All the while sitting in a charming little restaurant with soft yellow lightning, the front windows open to let in the sounds of the city, vines of pothos plants and evergreen ferns hanging from the sconces above us, as central air brushed across our shoulders. The walls were trimmed in mahogany, the booths a supple leather that, in this early June heat, would peel the skin off my thighs if I wasn't careful. The place was intimate, the tables spaced just far enough apart that we couldn't hear the hushed conversations of anyone else in the restaurant over the constant soft murmur from the kitchen.

If a restaurant could romance, I was utterly enchanted.

Fiona, Drew, and I sat at a small table in the Olive Branch, a Michelin-starred restaurant down in SoHo Drew had been *begging* to go to for the last week. I'm not usually one for long lunches, but it was a Friday in the summer, and to be fair, I owed Fiona, Drew's wife, a favor, since I'd had to bail on a play last week that Drew wanted to see. Drew Torres was an editor and hungry to find unique and talented authors, so she'd dragged both me and Fiona along to the weirdest concerts, plays, and places I'd ever been to. And that was saying a lot, because I'd been to forty-three countries with my aunt and she *excelled* at finding weird places.

This, however, was very—*very*—nice.

"This is officially the fanciest lunch I've ever been to," Fiona announced, popping another bacon-wrapped date into her mouth. It was the only thing we'd ordered so far that she could eat—the rare wagyu slices were out of the question for a person seven months pregnant. Fiona was tall and waifish, with dyed-periwinkle hair and pale white skin. She had dark freckles across her cheeks and always wore kitschy earrings she found at flea markets on the weekends. Today's flavor was metal snakes with signs in their mouths that read FUCK OFF. She was Strauss & Adder's best in-house designer.

Beside her sat Drew, spearing another wagyu slice. She was a newly minted senior editor at Strauss & Adder, with long curly black hair and warm brown skin. She always dressed like she was about to go on an excavation in Egypt in 1910—and today was no different: supple tan trousers and a pressed white button-down and suspenders.

Sitting with them, I felt a little underdressed in my free Eggverything Café T-shirt from my parent's favorite diner, light-wash jeans, and red flats I'd had since college, duct tape on the soles because I couldn't bear to part with them. I was going on three days without washing my hair, and the dry shampoo only did so much, but I'd been late to work this morning, so I hadn't thought a lot about it. I was a senior publicist at Strauss & Adder, a perpetual planner, and somehow I had not planned for this outing in the slightest. To be fair, it *was* a Summer Friday, and I hadn't expected anyone to be in the office today.

"It *is* really fancy in here," I agreed. "It's much better than that poetry reading in the Village."

Fiona nodded. "Though I did enjoy how all of their drinks were named after dead poets."

I made a face. "The Emily Dickinson gave me the *worst* hangover."

Drew looked incredibly proud of herself. "Isn't this place just so nice? You know that article I sent you? The one in *Eater*? The author, James Ashton, is the head chef here. The article is a few years old, but it's still a great read."

"And you want him to do a book with us?" Fiona asked. "For—what—a cookbook?"

Drew seemed genuinely hurt. "What do you take me for, a plebeian? Absolutely not. A cookbook would be wasted on someone who is such a wizard with words."

Fiona and I gave each other a knowing look. Drew had said the same about the play I narrowly avoided last week as I moved into my late aunt's apartment on the Upper East Side. Fiona told me on Saturday, while I heaved a record player into the elevator, that she would never go swimming in the ocean again.

With that said, Drew did have a fantastic eye for what a person *could* write, not what they had already. She was brilliant at possibilities. She thrived on them.

That was what made her a unique sort of powerhouse. She always took in the underdogs, and she always helped them bloom.

"What's that look for?" Drew asked, looking pointedly between the two of us. "My instincts were right about that musician we saw on Governors Island last month."

"Sweetheart," Fiona replied patiently, "I'm still getting over the play I saw last week about a *man who had an affair with a dolphin.*"

Drew winced. "That was . . . a mistake. But the musician wasn't! And neither was that TikToker who wrote that amusement park thriller. It's going to be phenomenal. And this chef . . . I *know* this chef is special. I want to hear more about that summer he turned twenty-six—he alluded to it in *Eater*, but not enough."

"You think there's a story there?" Fiona asked.

"I'm sure there is. Right, Clementine?"

Then they looked at me expectantly.

"I . . . haven't read it, actually," I admitted, and Fiona *tsk*ed in that way of hers that will end up making their future child incredibly contrite. I ducked my head in embarrassment.

"Well, you should!" Drew replied. "He's been all around the world, just like you. The way he relates food to friendship and memories—I want him." She turned her hungry gaze toward the kitchen. "I want him so badly." And whenever she had that kind of look in her eyes, there was no stopping her.

I took another sip of too-dry wine and picked up the dessert menu to scan it. While we usually took lunches together—it was a perk of having best friends who all worked in the same building as you—we mostly stayed around Midtown, and the restaurants in Midtown were . . .

Well.

I'd eaten more sandwiches and lobster mac and cheeses from food trucks than I cared to admit. Midtown in the summer was tourist central, so trying to find a lunch spot anywhere that wasn't a food truck or the greens at Bryant Park was nearly impossible without a reservation.

"Well, when you get him, I have a question about this dessert menu," I said, pointing to the first item there. "What the *hell* is a deconstructed lemon pie?"

"Ooh, that one is the chef's specialty," Drew informed us as Fiona snatched the menu from me to read about it. "I definitely want to try it."

"If it's just a slice of lemon sprinkled with some granular sugar on a graham cracker," Fiona said, "I'm going to laugh."

I checked my phone for the time. "Whatever it is, we should probably order it and head back. I told Rhonda I'd be back by one."

"It's Friday!" Fiona argued, waving the dessert menu at me. "No one works on Fridays in the summer. Especially not in publishing."

"Well, I do," I replied. Rhonda Adder was my boss, the director of marketing and publicity, and copublisher. She was one of the most successful women in the business. If there was a bestseller to be had in a book, she knew exactly how to squeeze it out, and that was a talent in and of itself. Speaking of talent, just so Fiona and Drew knew the situation, I added, "I have three authors on tour right now—and something is *bound* to go wrong."

Drew nodded in agreement. "Murphy's Law of Publishing."

"Murphy's Law," I echoed. "And Juliette cried herself sick this morning because of her boyfriend, so I'm trying to lighten her load today."

"Fuck Romeo-Rob," Drew intoned.

"*Fuck* Romeo-Rob," I agreed.

"*Speaking* of dating." Fiona sat up a little straighter, and put her elbows on the table. Oh, I knew that look, and I inwardly suppressed a groan. She leaned in to look at me, arching her eyebrows. "How're you and Nate doing?"

Suddenly, the wineglass looked very interesting, but the longer she stared at me waiting for an answer, the less resolve I had, until I finally sighed and said, "We broke up last week."

Fiona gasped like she'd been personally insulted. "Last *week*? Before or *after* you moved?"

"While I was moving. The night you all went to the play."

"And you didn't tell us?" Drew added, more curious than her distraught wife.

"You didn't tell us!" Fiona echoed in a cry. "That's *important*!"

"It really wasn't that big of a deal." I shrugged. "It was over text messages. I think he's already dating somebody he met on Hinge." My friends looked at me with utter pity, but I waved it off. "Really, it's fine. We weren't that compatible anyway."

Which was true, but I didn't include the fight we had before the texts. *Fight* was a strong word for it, though. It felt more like a shrug and a white flag tossed onto an already-abandoned battle-field.

"Again? You have to work late *again*?" he'd asked. "You know this is my big night. I want you here with me."

To be fair, I had forgotten that it was the opening night of a gallery with his work. He was an artist—a metalworker, actually—and this was a big thing for him. "I'm sorry, Nate. This is important."

And it was, I was sure of it, even though I couldn't remember what the emergency had been to make me stay late.

He was quiet for a long moment, and then he asked, "Is this how it's going to be? I don't want to be second to your job, Clementine."

"You're not!"

He was. He absolutely was. I kept him at arm's length because at least there he wouldn't be able to see how broken I was. I could keep lying. I could keep pretending I was fine—because I *was* fine. I had to be. I didn't like people worrying about me when they had so many other things to worry about. That was my allure, right?

That you didn't need to worry about Clementine West. She always figured it out.

Nate let out that heavy, body-heaving sigh. "Clementine, I think you need to be honest." And that was it—the nail in the proverbial coffin. "You're so closed off, you use work as a shield. I don't think I even really know you. You won't open up. You won't be *vulnerable*. Whatever happened to that girl in those photos? With watercolor under her fingernails?"

She was gone, but that much he already knew. He met me after she was already gone. I think that might have been why he didn't just dump me after I canceled plans on him the first time, because he kept trying to find that girl with watercolors under her fingernails that he saw once in a photo in my old apartment. The girl from before.

"Do you even love me?" he went on. "I can't remember you saying it once."

"We've only dated for three months. It's a little early, don't you think?"

"When you know, you know."

I pursed my lips. "Then I guess I don't know."

And that was it.

I was at the end of this relationship. Before I said anything I'd regret, I hung up the phone, then texted him that it was over. I'd mail his toothbrush back to him. God knows I wasn't going to take a trip to *Williamsburg* if I didn't have to.

"Besides," I added, grabbing the too-expensive bottle of wine to top off my glass, "I don't really think I want to be in a relationship right now. I want to concentrate on my career—I don't have time to mess with guys I might end up dumping in a text message three months later. The sex wasn't even that good." I took a large gulp of wine to wash down *that* horrid truth.

Drew watched me in awe, shaking her head. "Look at that, not even a tear."

"I've never seen her cry over any guy," Fiona said to her wife.

I tried to argue that no, I actually *had*, but then closed my mouth again because . . . she was right. I seldom cried, anyway, and over some guy? Absolutely not. Fiona always said it was because all my relationships had boiled down to calling them *some guy*—a person not even worthy of a name in my memory. "Because you've never been in love," she once said, and maybe that was true.

"When you know, you know," Nate had said.

I didn't even know what love was supposed to feel like.

Fiona waved her hand. "Well, *whatever* to him, then! He didn't deserve a financially stable girlfriend who is kicking ass at work *and* owns an apartment on the Upper East Side," she went on, and then that seemed to remind her of the *other* thing I really didn't want to talk about. "How is it? The apartment?"

The apartment. She and Drew had stopped calling it my aunt's apartment back in January, but I still couldn't kick the habit. I shrugged.

I could tell them the truth—that every time I walked through the door, I expected to see my aunt there in her wingback chair the color of robin's eggs, but the chair was gone.

So was its owner.

"It's great," I decided.

Fiona and Drew both gave each other the same glance, as if they didn't believe me. Fair enough; I wasn't a very good liar.

"It's *great*," I repeated. "And why are we talking about me? Let's find this famous chef of yours and woo him to the dark side." I reached over the table for the last date and ate it.

"Sure, sure, we just need to flag down our server . . ." Drew muttered, looking around to see if she could catch anyone's eye, but she was much too polite and too meek to do anything more than give them a meaningful look. "Do I just raise my hand or—what do you do at expensive restaurants?"

Drew had been a lot more proactive about finding authors to build her list over the last few months, but I had to wonder if some of these excursions—the concert on Governors Island, the play I regrettably couldn't make, the opera last month, the TikTok influencer we met at a bookstore in Washington Heights, the gallery exhibit for the artist who painted with their body—were to help distract me. To pull me out of my grief. Except it had been almost six months and I was fine now.

Really, I was.

But it was hard to convince someone of that when they had witnessed you sobbing on your bathroom floor at two in the morning, blackout drunk, the night of your aunt's funeral.

They'd seen the worst, rawest parts of me and they didn't delete my number from their phones. I wasn't always the easiest person to get along with, and the fact that they stuck around meant more to me than I could ever actually admit, and being dragged on these field trips the last couple of months had been refreshing.

So the least I could do was flag down a server for Drew.

"I got it," I sighed, and raised my hand to motion toward our server as she turned away from another table, and called to her. I wasn't sure if this was how you were supposed to get their attention at a fancy restaurant, but she quickly came over anyway. "Could we have the, uh—" I glanced at the dessert menu.

Fiona piped in, "The deconstructed lemon whatever!"

"That," I said, "and also could we perhaps talk with the head chef?" Drew quickly pulled a business card out of her purse to hand to the server as I added, "Please tell him we're from Strauss and

Adder Publishers, here about a business opportunity—a book, actually."

The server didn't seem surprised at all by the request, as she took the business card and tucked it into the front of her black apron. She said she'd see what she could do and quickly left to put in the dessert order.

Drew clapped quietly to herself once the server had gone. "Here we go! Ooh, do you feel that thrill? It never gets old."

Her excitement was infectious, even though I felt very little about this chef. "Never," I said, and suddenly my phone began to vibrate in my purse. I took it out and glanced at the email notification. Why was one of my authors emailing me?

Fiona leaned over to her wife. "Ooh, how about we set Clem up with that new guy who moved into the apartment next to us?"

"He's cute," Drew agreed.

"No, thanks." I opened my email. "I'm not ready to jump into another relationship after Nate."

"You said you were over him!"

"There's still a mourning period—oh, shit," I added as I finished skimming the message, and popped up out of my chair. "I'm sorry, I have to run."

Fiona asked, worriedly, "Is something wrong? We haven't even gotten our dessert yet."

I took my wallet out of my knockoff Kate Spade bag and set down the company credit card since this was, technically, a work lunch. "One of my authors on tour just got stranded in Denver, and Juliette's not answering her emails. Put lunch on that and I'll see you at work?" I said apologetically as Drew took the card.

She looked stricken. "Wait—what?" She darted her eyes to the kitchen, and back to me.

"You got this," I said as my author sent another panicked email. I hugged them both and stole one last fried goat cheese ball, chased it with the rest of the wine, and turned to leave—

"Watch out!" Drew cried. Fiona gasped.

Too late.

I collided with a server behind me. The dessert he held went one way, and he went the other. I shot my hand out to grab it as he went to grab *me*, and pulled me back upright. I stumbled and he steadied me, his grip strong on my arm.

"Nice save," he said warmly.

"Thanks, I—" And that was when I realized my other hand was on his very solid chest. *"Oh!"* I quickly handed him back the dessert and stepped away. "I am so sorry!" A blush rose too quickly on my cheeks. I couldn't look at the guy. I had definitely just put my hand on a stranger for longer than necessary.

". . . Lemon?" the man asked.

"Yes, sorry, sorry, that's our dessert, but I have to go," I replied in a hurry. My face felt as red as a cherry. I quickly dodged around him, mouthing to my friends, "Good luck," as I left the restaurant.

Two calls to Southwest Airlines and four city blocks later, I had the author on the next flight to their final tour stop. I descended into the subway to make my way back to Midtown and to work—and tried to get the feeling of that man's strong grip, the solidness of his chest, the way he bent toward me—he *did* bend toward me, didn't he? Like he *knew* me? I wasn't imagining things?—out of my head.

2

Strauss & Adder

THE FIRST TIME I walked through the stone archway into the building on Thirty-Fourth Street and rode the chrome elevators up to the seventh floor, I knew there was something special about Strauss & Adder Publishers. The way the doors opened and let out into a small, white-shelved lobby filled with books, both ones they had published and ones they just loved, weathered leather chairs faced you, beckoning you to sink down into their cushions, open a novel, and drown in the words.

Strauss & Adder was a small but powerful publisher in New York City, specializing in adult fiction, memoirs, and lifestyle nonfiction—think self-help books and cookbooks and how-tos—but they were most renowned for their travel guides. When you wanted a guide to a far-off place, you went toward the little mallet-hammer logo of Strauss & Adder to tell you about the best restaurants in the most remote reaches of foreign cities, ones where you would still feel at home.

I could do publicity anywhere—and probably get paid better

doing it—but I couldn't get free travel books at a big tech firm, or in some PR-firm hellscape. There was something just so sure and lovely about walking down the hall every day, lined with books about Rome and Bangkok and Antarctica, the enchanting smell of aged paper like a department store perfume. I didn't want to write books myself, but I loved the idea of some long-dead or long-forgotten travel guide waxing about cathedrals of old and shrines of forgotten gods. I loved how a book, a story, a set of words in a sentence organized in the exact right order, made you miss places you've never visited, and people you've never met.

The office was an open floor plan, surrounded on all sides by floor-to-ceiling shelves of novels, the space clean and white and bright. Everyone had small half-walled cubicles, each desk with pops of color as people displayed their favorite odds and ends—artwork and figurines and book collections. Mine was closest to my boss's office. The higher-ups all got offices with glass doors, as if that were the same kind of lack of privacy as listening to Juliette in the cubicle in front of me sob over her on-again, off-again boyfriend of ten months, her *Romeo*, Rob. (Fuck Romeo-Rob.)

At least even in their tidy glass offices you could see them dissociating at 2:00 p.m. on a Monday with the rest of us.

And yet here we all were, because if we all loved one thing, it was books.

I managed to send out a few interview queries by the time Fiona came back to the office.

"The dessert was really fantastic," she said, walking over to return my credit card. She, like the rest of design, was banished to the glum, cobweb-filled corner of the floor where CEOs were wont to stick their mushroom-growing artsy people. At least three of the designers had to start taking vitamin D supplements, it was so dark back there. "So was the chef."

"Hate that I missed it," I replied.

Fiona shrugged and handed me back my card. "You kind of ran right into him, actually."

I paused. The man with the strong grip. The warm, solid chest. "That . . . was *him*?"

"Absolutely. He's a gem. Really sweet—oh, say, did you end up saving your author from airport hell?"

"Of course," I replied, pulling myself out of my thoughts. "Was there ever any doubt?"

Fiona shook her head. "I envy you."

That made me pause. "Why?"

"Whenever you need to do something, you just go for it. Straight line. No hesitation. I think that's why Drew likes you so much," she added, a bit quieter. "You're an Excel spreadsheet to my chaos."

"I just like things the way I like things," I replied, and Fiona proceeded to tell me about what I'd missed at the restaurant— apparently, someone from Faux had come to the chef about a book (Parker Daniels, Drew guessed), as had Simon & Schuster and two imprints at HarperCollins and one at Macmillan. There would probably be more.

I gave a low whistle. "Drew's got steep competition."

"I know. I can't wait until this is all she starts talking about," Fiona deadpanned. She checked her smart watch on her wrist and groaned. "I should probably return to the cave. Movie tonight? I think that rom-com with the two assassins who fall in love is out?"

"Can I take a rain check? I'm still unpacking from the move. Receipt?" I asked, and Fiona dug our lunch bill out of her purse. As she left for the dark and dank part of the floor, I slipped into Rhonda's office to give it to her, though she wasn't there.

Most of the other higher-ups—including Reginald Strauss—had

photos of their families, vacations they took, memories, on their walls and across their desks. Rhonda's was full of photos with celebrities at book launches and red-carpet events, and achievement awards stacked her shelves where gifts from grandchildren should go. It was very evident what she chose, the life she decided to live, and every time I stepped into her office, I imagined sitting in her orange chair, having lived a life like that, too.

Suddenly, the glass door to her office slid open, and Rhonda Adder, in all her glamour, stepped into the room. "Ah, Clementine! Happy Friday, as always," she announced happily, looking sharp as a knife in a black pantsuit and floral-print heels, her blunt-cut gray bob pulled back from her face with a clip.

Whenever Rhonda came into a room, she commanded it in a way I wanted to. All heads turned. All conversations stopped.

Rhonda Adder was as brilliant as she was magnetic—the director of marketing and publicity, and copublisher, she had started at a lowly PR firm in SoHo, clipping out tabloid rumors and fielding telemarketer calls, and now she planned and coordinated book campaigns for some of the biggest names in the business. She was an *icon* among bookish people, the person they all wanted to be. The person *I* wanted to be. Someone who had her life together. Someone who had a plan, had goals, and knew the exact tools she needed to implement them.

"Happy Friday, Rhonda. I'm sorry I took a long lunch," I quickly said.

She waved her hand. "It's perfectly all right. I saw you handled Adair Lynn's little airport snafu."

"She's really having the *worst* luck on this tour."

"We'll have to send her some flowers once she gets home." She opened a drawer and pulled out a bag of chocolate-covered almonds.

"Will do. I put a lunch expense on the account," I added, setting the receipt and credit card down on the desk. She took a look at both of them and quirked an eyebrow. "Drew's after an author for a nonfiction project."

"Ah. Almond?" She offered me the bag.

"Thank you." I took one out, sat down in the creaky chair opposite of her, and updated her on the afternoon's happenings—the booked podcast interviews, the revised itineraries, the newly confirmed bookstore events. Rhonda and I worked like a well-oiled machine. There was a reason everyone said I was her second-in-command—and I hoped to be her successor someday. Everyone figured I would be.

Rhonda put her almonds away and turned to her computer as I began to get up, our meeting adjourned, until she said, "I saw you rescinded your request for vacation at the end of the summer. Is there a reason?"

"Oh, that." I tried to look unruffled as I smoothed down the front of my crumpled blouse. At the end of the summer, my aunt and I always took our yearly trip abroad—Portugal one summer, Spain the next, India, Thailand, Japan, my passport cluttered with all the places we'd been together over the years. I had taken the exact same week off every August since joining Strauss & Adder, so of course Rhonda would notice when I decided not to go. "I decided that maybe my time would be best spent here, so I'm not going."

Ever again.

She gave me a strange look. "You're kidding. Clementine, you haven't taken a day off all year."

"What can I say? I love my job." I smiled then because it *was* true. I did love my job, and it was a good distraction from . . . *everything*, and if I kept concentrating on the things in front of me, the grief wouldn't catch up with me at two in the morning like it wanted to.

"I love my job, too, and I still took a vacation this year to the Maldives. Had a great massage there—I can give you the number for my guy if you end up going."

Oh, yes, because I could afford that. Well, maybe now that I owned my aunt's apartment, I could. I pushed a strained smile across my face. "I'm fine, really—and besides, *Boston in the Fall* is coming out that week, and you know that author is *so* persnickety. I'd rather deal with him than make Juliette handle—"

"Clementine?" she interrupted. "Take your damn accrued vacation. That's why you have it."

"But—"

"Your request to rescind your request is denied."

"I'm not going on vacation anymore, though," I said, trying not to panic. "I refunded my tickets!"

She gave me a look over her red-frame glasses. "Then you have two months to figure out what else you want to do. Half of our collection is travel guides—borrow one. I'm sure you'll get inspired. You'll need a vacation, after all."

"I really don't think I will."

In reply, she swiveled her chair toward me again with a sigh, and took off her glasses. They hung from a beaded strap around her neck. "Fine. Close the door, Clementine."

Oh, no. Quietly, I did what I was told—albeit a little hesitantly. The last time she asked me to close the door, I found out she fired the marketing designer. I sat down again, a bit gingerly. "Is . . . is there something wrong?"

"No. Well. Yes, but nothing bad." She steepled her fingers and gave me a long look. She wore dark mascara and darker eyeliner around her eyes, and they always made her looks all the more intense. "You are sworn to secrecy, Clementine, until the time is right."

I straightened in my chair. This was big, then. Was it a new book? A celebrity memoir? Was Strauss selling the company? Did Michael in HR finally quit?

She said, "I'm planning to retire at the end of the summer, but I only want to go knowing Strauss and Adder is in good hands."

I didn't think I heard correctly. "You—what? *Retire?*"

"Yes."

I didn't know what to say.

There weren't words enough to describe my profound—sadness? Disappointment? Strauss & Adder without Rhonda was like a body without a soul—a bookshelf without any books. She *built* this company with Strauss—every single one of its bestsellers over the last twenty years came from her.

And she wanted to *retire?*

"Don't give me that look," Rhonda said with a nervous laugh. She was never nervous. So she wasn't pulling my leg. She was telling the truth. "I've done my time! But I'm not going to leave if this ship'll sink without me. I've put too much of my life here," she added, seemingly as an afterthought to her *name* on the business. "However, only you and Strauss know at the moment, and I'd like to keep it that way. Who knows what kind of piranhas the news will attract once it's official."

My mouth was dry. "O . . . okay?"

"In the meantime, I want you to take the lead on most projects and acquisitions this summer, to see how you fare. I'll be in the meetings, obviously, but let's just call it a dry run."

"To see if I can manage with you gone?"

She gave me a baffled look, and then she laughed. "Oh, no, dear, to take my place!"

If I wasn't already sitting down, my knees would have given out immediately. Me—take Rhonda's place? I only half listened as she told me how hard I worked, how exemplary I was, how I was exactly the kind of woman she'd been at my age, and that this was the kind of opportunity she would kill for. What better way to foster the future than to give the future a chance to succeed?

"Well, half of my place. When Strauss and I started the company, I took over for the director of publicity and marketing as well as copublisher because we were so small, but I would not wish that on anyone else. After all, they're not *me*," she added. "Depending on your performance this summer, however, I'm inclined to put your name up for the new director of publicity. You've been here the longest of anyone on the team, so I only think it's fair—not to mention I'd be an idiot not to."

I . . . didn't know what to say.

As it turned out, she didn't expect me to say anything, as she put her glasses back on and returned to her computer. "So, you see, I imagine you'll need to take a vacation before you start your new job—I'll get you the name of my masseuse in the Maldives."

My mouth dropped open. I gave a squeak. My head was spinning from all the information.

"Now, can you send me my meetings for next week? Something tells me Juliette is going to forget. Again."

That was my cue to leave.

I prayed that my legs would work as I pushed myself to my feet. "I'll get that right to you," I replied, and left her office.

First, my vacation cancellation request was denied, and then Rhonda dropped that she might *retire*? And I might take her place as head of the *department*?

I didn't want to think about it.

My cubicle was just across the hall from her door—ten feet,

give or take. It was neat and pristine—the kind of space that Drew called a one-box walkout. Meaning that if I got fired, I'd need only one box to pack all my keepsakes before I left. I wasn't planning on *going* anywhere—I'd been here for seven years—I just didn't have much I wanted to display. Some photos, a few of my watercolor postcard paintings from around the city—Central Park's lake, the Brooklyn Bridge from Dumbo, a cemetery in Queens. I had a bob-blehead doll of William Shakespeare, and a collector's box set of the Brontë sisters' works, and a signed bookplate from an author I couldn't remember and couldn't read the name of anymore.

I sank into my chair, feeling numb and a little out of my league—for the first time in years. Retiring—Rhonda was *retiring*.

And she wanted me to take her place.

My chest constricted in panic.

A few minutes later, Juliette—a petite white woman with braided blond hair, big doe eyes, and cherry-red lipstick—trudged back to her cubicle, red-eyed and sniffling. She sank down at her desk. "W-we broke up again . . ."

Absently, I grabbed my tissue box from under the desk and offered her one. "That's rough, friend."

Home Sweet Home

IT WASN'T THAT I didn't want to take my vacation—I did. Every year for the last seven years, I'd taken that week and I'd flown off to some distant part of the world. I just . . . didn't want to be the girl who kept looking around airports for a woman with an azure-blue coat and a loud laugh, waving her large heart-shaped sunglasses for me to catch up.

Because that woman didn't exist anymore.

And neither did the girl who loved her unconditionally.

No, she was replaced by a woman who worked late on a Friday night because she could, who would rather attend work functions than first dates, who had a spare pair of tights and deodorant in her desk drawer *just in case* she pulled an all-nighter (not that she had yet). She was always the last one in the building, when even the motion-sensor lights thought she'd gone home, and she was happy.

She was.

I finally logged out of my work computer, stood from my chair, and stretched, the fluorescent light above me flickering to life again.

It was around 8:30 p.m. I should get going before security started to make their rounds, because then they'd tell Strauss and Rhonda, and Rhonda had this policy against working late on Fridays. So I grabbed my purse, made sure that Rhonda had everything on her desk for the Monday morning meeting, and left for the elevator.

I passed one of the company bookcases—the ones where people put freebies of extra galleys and final copies. Novels and memoirs and cookbooks and travel guides. Most I'd already read, but one caught my eye.

DESTINATION TRAVEL: NEW YORK CITY

It must have been a newer one, and there was a delicious sort of irony to reading a travel guide about a city you lived in. My aunt used to say that you could live somewhere your entire life and still find things to surprise you.

I thought—for a split second—that my aunt would love a copy, but when I took it off the shelf and put it in my purse, reality hit me again like a brick to the head.

I thought about putting it back, but I felt so ashamed for forgetting that she was gone that I quickly left for the elevator. I'd donate it to a secondhand bookshop this weekend instead. The lone security guard at the front of the building looked up from her phone as I hurried past, not surprised at all to find me working so late.

I walked to the subway station, and headed uptown to the Upper East Side, where I got off the train at my stop and pulled out my phone. It was a reflex by now to call my parents on the walk from the station to my aunt's apartment building.

I never used to do this, but ever since Analea died, it'd become a sort of comfort. Besides, I think it helped Mom a lot. Analea was her older sister.

After two rings, Mom answered with a "Tell your *father* that it is perfectly acceptable to finally move my exercise bike into your old room!"

"I haven't lived there in eleven years, so it's absolutely okay," I said, dodging around a couple looking at Google Maps on their phone.

Mom shouted, making me wince, "SEE, FRED! I *told* you she wouldn't care!"

"What?" my dad called faintly in the background. The next I knew, he was picking up the phone from what I assumed was the kitchen. "But what if you come home, baby girl? What if you need it again?"

"She *won't*," Mom replied, "and if she does, she can take the couch." I massaged the bridge of my nose. Even though I'd been moved out since I was eighteen, Dad hated change. My mom loved repetition. They were a match made in heaven. "Isn't that right?"

Dad argued, "But what if—"

I interrupted, "You can turn my room into anything you want. Even a red room, if you want."

"A red . . . ?" Mom began.

Dad said, "Is that the sex dungeon in that movie?"

"FRED!" Mom shrieked, and then said, "Well, that *is* an idea . . ."

My father said, with a sigh that weighed about as much as all thirty-five years of their marriage, "Fine. You can put your exercise bike in there—*but* we're keeping the bed."

I kicked a piece of trash on the sidewalk. "You really don't have to."

"But we *want* to," Dad replied. I didn't have the courage to admit to my dad that *home* wasn't their two-story blue vinyl house on Long Island anymore. Hadn't been for a while. But it also wasn't the apartment I was walking to—slower and slower by the minute, as if I didn't really want to go at all. "So how was your day, baby girl?"

"Fine," I replied quickly. Too quickly. "Actually . . . I think Rhonda is retiring at the end of the summer, and she wants to promote me to director of publicity."

My parents gasped. "Congrats, sweetheart!" Mom cried. "Oh, we are *so* proud of you!"

"And in only seven years!" Dad added. "That's gotta be a record! Why, it took me eighteen years to make partner at the architecture firm!"

"And it's *just* in time for your thirtieth birthday, too!" Mom agreed happily. "Oh, we are going to *have* to celebrate—"

"I don't have the job yet," I quickly reiterated, crossing the street to the block where my aunt's apartment was. "I'm sure there will be other people in the running."

"How do you feel about it?" Dad asked. He could always read me in this alarming way that my mom absolutely couldn't.

Mom scoffed. "How do you *think* she feels, Fred? She's ecstatic!"

"It's just a *question*, Martha. An easy one."

It was an easy question, wasn't it? I should feel excited, obviously—but my stomach just couldn't seem to unknot itself. "I think I'll be more thrilled when I finally finish moving in," I said. "There's just a few more boxes I have to situate."

"If you want, we can come this weekend to help," Mom suggested. "I know my sister probably left a lot of junk hidden places . . ."

"No, no, it's fine. Besides, I'm working this weekend." Which probably wasn't a lie—I'd find some work to do this weekend. "Anyway, I'm almost home. I'll talk to you later. Love you," I

added, and hung up as I turned the corner and the towering building of the Monroe came into full view. A building that housed a
small apartment that once upon a time belonged to my aunt.

And now, against my will, it belonged to me.

I tried to stay out of it for as long as possible, but when my
landlord said my rent would be increasing in the apartment I leased
in Greenpoint, I didn't have much of a choice—here was my aunt's
apartment, sitting empty in one of the most sought-after buildings
on the Upper East Side, willed to me.

So I packed all my things into tiny boxes, sold my couch, and
moved in.

The Monroe looked like every other century-old apartment
building in this city—a skeleton of windows and doors, having
housed people long dead and long forgotten. A bone-white exterior
with detailed trim work that looked vaguely mid-century, winged
lions chiseled into the eaves and placed at the entrance with missing ears and teeth, and a tired-looking greeter just inside the revolving doors. He'd been there for as long as I could remember,
and tonight he was sitting at the welcome desk, his hat slightly
askew, as he read the newest James Patterson novel. He looked up
as I came in and his face lit up—

"Clementine!" he cried. "Welcome home."

"Good evening, Earl. How're you? How's the book?"

"This Patterson guy never misses," he replied happily, and
wished me good night as I headed for the brassy elevators. My
heart hurt a little, how familiar all of this was—how easy, how
much it felt like home. The Monroe always smelled old—it was the
only way I could describe it. Not musty or moldy, just . . . *old*.

Lived-in.

Loved.

The elevator dinged its arrival to the first floor, and I slipped inside. It was gilded just like the lobby, in brass that needed a nice polish, with fleur-de-lis accents across the baseboard and a cloudy mirror on the ceiling where a tired and blurry reflection of myself stared down at me. Brown hair cut at the shoulders, curling in the summer humidity, and blunt-cut bangs that never quite seemed to look purposeful, but some haphazard job done at 3:00 a.m. with kitchen shears and a broken heart.

The first time I came to stay at my aunt's apartment, I was eight and the entire building seemed like something out of a storybook. Something I'd read about in the cramped library back home—somewhere Harriet the Spy or Eloise would live, and I imagined that I'd be just like them.

Clementine was the kind of name you gave to a quirky children's book character, after all.

The first time I rode this enchanted elevator, I carried a too-big duffel bag with me, the color of cherries, clutching Chunky Bunny—my stuffed animal, which I still had—with all my might. Going somewhere new used to terrify me, but my parents thought I'd be better off with my aunt for the summer as they packed up our house in Rhinebeck and moved to Long Island, where they'd lived ever since. The mirrors on the ceiling were warped even then, and on the slow ride up, I found a spot where the mirrors were uneven and it bowed my face and twisted my arms like a fun-house mirror.

My aunt had said in a conspiratorial voice, "That's your past self looking back at you. Just a split second, from you to you."

I used to imagine what I'd say to that split-second-behind self.

That was when I still believed in all of my aunt's stories and secrets. I was gullible and fascinated by things that sounded too good to be true, a spark of something *other* in the mundane. A mirror that showed your past self, a pair of pigeons who never died, a book that wrote itself, an alleyway that led to the other side of the world, a magical apartment . . .

Now the stories tasted sour in my mouth, but still, as I looked up at my mirrored self, I couldn't help but play along, like I always had.

"She lied," I told my reflection, her mouth moving to my words. If my split-second-past me was shocked by the words, she didn't show it.

Because she already knew, too.

The elevator dinged, and I got off on the fourth floor. The apartments were labeled with letters. In the summers after I first visited, I'd memorized how to say the alphabet backward with them.

L, K, J, I, H, G, F . . .

I turned the corner. The hall hadn't changed in years. The carpet was a faded Persian design, the sconces forgotten with cobwebs. I trailed my fingers down the white chair-rail molding that lined the hall, feeling the rough wood underneath prick at my fingertips.

E, D, C . . .

B4.

I stopped at the door and fished the keys out of my purse. It was almost 9:30 p.m., but I was so bone-tired, I just wanted to go to sleep. I unlocked the door and slipped off my flats in the doorway. My aunt had only two rules in this apartment, and the first was to always take off your shoes.

When I moved in last week, my eyes had wandered over all the tall shadows, as if I expected to see a ghost. A small part of me wanted to—or maybe it wanted at least *one* of my aunt's stories to come true. Of course, none did.

And now I barely even looked up as I came inside. I didn't turn on the lights. I didn't study the shadows to see if they were stranger, if any were new.

She said this apartment was magical, but it just felt lonely now.

"It's a secret," she had said with a smile, pressing her finger to her lips. The smoke from her Marlboro curled out of the open window. I still remembered that day like it was yesterday. The sky had been crisp, the summer hot, and my aunt's story had been fantastical. "You can't tell anyone. If you do, it might not ever happen to you."

"I won't tell anyone," I had promised, and I'd kept that promise for twenty-one years. "I won't tell a soul!"

So she told me in a whisper, her brown eyes glimmering with impossibility, and I believed her.

Tonight, the apartment smelled like it always had—of lavender and cigarettes. Moonlight streamed in through the large windows in the living room, two pigeons nesting on the AC, huddled into their sturdy nest. The pieces of furniture all looked like shadows of themselves, everything still where I last remembered. I dumped my purse by the barstool, my keys on the counter, and I fell onto the velvety blue couch in the living room. It still smelled like her perfume. The entire apartment did. Even six months later, after I'd traded most of her furniture for mine.

I grabbed the crocheted blanket from the back of the couch and curled myself under it, and hoped I could fall asleep. The apartment was foreign to me now, missing something terribly large, but it still felt like home in a way that nothing else ever could. Like a place I once knew, but that no longer welcomed me.

I wished I hated this place that still felt like my aunt could live here. That she could still walk out of her bedroom and laugh at me on the couch and say, *Oh, my darling, going to bed already? I still have half a bottle of merlot in the fridge. Get up, the night's young! I'll cook you some eggs. Let's play some cards.*

But she was gone, and the apartment remained, along with all of the foolish fake secrets she whispered about it. Besides, if this apartment really *was* magical, then how come it hadn't brought me back to my aunt yet, over the hundreds of times I'd come in and out, and in and out, over the last six months?

Why was I still here alone, on this couch, listening to the sounds of a city that kept moving forward, and forward, and forward, while I still mourned somewhere in the past?

It was a lie, and this was just an apartment like A4 or K13 or B11, and I was way, way too old to believe in an apartment that could carry me to a time that no longer existed.

Her apartment.

But now mine.

4

Strangers in a Strange Time

A HAND ON MY shoulder shook me awake.

"Five more minutes," I mumbled, brushing the touch away. There was a crick in my neck, and the pounding in my head made me want to burrow down into the sofa with all the chip crumbs and never return. It was so quiet, I thought I heard someone in the kitchen. My aunt humming. Getting her favorite chipped coffee mug that read F•CK THE PATRIARCHY. Putting on a pot of coffee.

It almost sounded like it used to, when I'd stumble in late at night, head full of wine, too tired (and too drunk) to make it back to my apartment in Brooklyn. I'd always crash on the couch, and wake up in the mornings with a mouth that tasted like cotton and a glass of water on the coffee table in front of me, and she'd be waiting at her yellow kitchen table for me to tell her all about last night's gossip. The authors behaving badly, the publicists lamenting about the lack of datable men, the agent who had an affair with their author, the latest blind date Drew and Fiona hooked me up with.

But when I opened my eyes, ready to tell my aunt about Rhonda's retirement and another failed relationship and the new chef Drew wanted to sign . . .

I remembered.

I lived here now.

The hand shook my shoulder again, the touch soft yet firm. Then a voice, gentle and rumbly, said, "Hey, hey, friend, wake up."

Two things occurred to me then:

One, my aunt was very much dead.

And two, there was a man in her apartment.

With pure unbridled terror, I propelled myself to sit up, throwing my hands out widely. I connected with the intruder. In the face. The man gave a cry, clutching his nose, as I pushed myself to my feet, standing on the couch, my aunt's decorative tasseled pillow of Jeff Goldblum's face raised in defense.

The stranger threw up his arms. "I'm unarmed!"

"I'm not!"

And I hit him with the pillow.

Then again, and again, until he backed up halfway into the kitchen, his hands raised in surrender.

Which was when, in my semi-sleepy state of fight or flight, I got a good look at him.

He was young—in his mid-twenties—clean-shaven and wide-eyed. My mother would have called him boyishly handsome. He wore a dark shirt with an overstretched neckline, a cartoon pickle on the front and the words (PICKLE)BACK ME UP. BRO, and distressed blue jeans that had definitely seen better days. His auburn hair was wild and unbrushed, his eyes so light gray they almost looked white, set into a handsomely pale face with a brush of freckles across his cheeks.

I angled my pillow toward him again as I (ungracefully) dismounted over the back of the couch and sized him up. He was a little taller than I was, and gangly, but I had nails and the will to live.

I could take him.

Miss Congeniality taught me to *sing*, and I was nothing if not a prepared, depressed millennial.

He gave me a hesitant look, his hands still in the air. "I didn't mean to startle you," he said apologetically in a soft Southern drawl. "I take it you're . . . um, you're Clementine?"

At the sound of my name, I held the pillow higher. "How do you know that?"

"Well, I'm actually—"

"How did you get here?"

"The—um—the front door, but—"

"How long have you been here? Have you been watching me sleep? What kind of sick p—"

He interrupted me loudly, "All night. I mean—I didn't watch you *sleep* all night. I was in the bedroom. I got dressed and came out here and saw you on the couch. My mom's a friend of your aunt's. She's letting me sublet the apartment for the summer, and she said I might have a visitor."

That made very little sense. "*What?*"

"Analea Collins," he replied with that same confused hesitance. He began to reach for something in his back pocket. "Here, see—?"

"Don't you *dare* move," I snapped, and he froze.

And slowly raised his hands again. "Okay . . . but I have a note?"

"Give it to me, then."

"You told me—you told me not to move?"

I glared at him.

He cleared his throat. "You can reach for it. Back left pocket."

"I'm not reaching for *anything*."

He gave me an exasperated look.

Oh. Right. I told him not to move. ". . . Fine." I carefully crept up to him and began to reach around to his back left pocket . . .

"And here we find the rare gentleman in the wild," he began to narrate—in a really terrible Australian accent, by the way. "Careful. He must be approached cautiously so not to be easily startled . . ."

I glared at him.

He raised a single infuriating eyebrow.

I snatched the contents out of his back left pocket and quickly moved an arm's length away from him. As I backed away, I recognized my aunt's apartment key. I knew it was hers because it was on a little key chain she bought in the Milan airport years ago when we went after my high school graduation. I thought this key had been lost. And with it was a note, folded into the shape of a paper crane.

I unfolded it.

Iwan,

It's so lovely that this could work out! Tell your mother hello for me and be sure to check the mailbox every day. If Mother and Fucker come by the window, do not open it. They lie. I hope you enjoy New York—it's quite lovely in the summers, albeit a bit hot. Ta-ta!

xoxo, AC

(P.S. If you see an elderly woman wandering the halls, please be a dear and send Miss Norris back to G6.)

(P.P.S. If my niece comes by, please tell Clementine you'll be subletting from me this summer. Remind her about summers abroad.)

I stared at it for longer than I probably needed to. Even though I had countless birthday cards and Valentine's cards and Christmas cards from her stashed in my jewelry box in the bedroom, seeing new words strung together in her looping script made my throat constrict anyway. Because I didn't think I'd ever see any more combinations.

It was silly, I knew it was silly.

But it was a bit more of her than before that remained.

Summers abroad . . .

The stranger brought me out of my thoughts when he said, quite confidently, "Does everything make sense now?"

I set my jaw. "No, actually."

His bravado faltered. ". . . *No?*"

"No." Because Miss Norris passed away three years ago, and a young couple moved into her apartment and threw away all of her antique music boxes and her violin, since she didn't have anyone to will them to. My aunt wanted to save them, but before she could, they were ruined out on the curb in the rain. "I'm not sure what you think *subletting* means, but it doesn't mean you can waltz in just any summer you want to."

His eyebrows scrunched together in vexation. "Any summer? No, I just spoke to her last week—"

"You're not funny," I snapped, hugging the sequined face of Jeff Goldblum to my chest.

He blinked then, and gave a slow nod. "All right . . . let me get my things, and I'll be gone, okay?"

I tried not to look too relieved as I said, *"Good."*

He dropped his hands and quietly turned back into my aunt's bedroom. Inside, I expected to see my full bed on its IKEA black metal frame, and instead caught a glimpse of a blanket I hadn't seen since I'd packed it up six months ago. I quickly looked away. It just looked like that blanket. It wasn't really.

My chest constricted, but I tried to push the feeling down. *It happened almost six months ago*, I told myself, rubbing my sternum. *She's not here.*

As he began to pack up, I turned and paced the living room—I always paced when I was nervous. The apartment was brighter than I remembered, sunlight streaming in through the large bay windows.

I passed a picture on the wall—one of my aunt smiling in front of the Richard Rodgers Theatre the opening night of *The Heart Mattered*. One that I knew I had taken down when I moved in the week before. It was in storage, along with the vase that was now on the table and the colorful porcelain peacocks on the windowsill she'd bought in Morocco.

And then I noticed the calendar on the coffee table. I could've sworn I threw it out, and I knew Aunt Analea had stopped keeping track of the days, but not for *seven years . . .*

"Well, I think that's all of my things. I'll leave the groceries in the refrigerator," he added, a duffel bag over his shoulder as he came out of my aunt's room, but I barely noticed him. My chest felt tighter.

I could barely breathe.

Seven years—why was the calendar set to seven years ago?

And where were *my* things? The boxes I'd yet to unpack that were in the corner? And the pictures I'd hung up on the walls?

Had he moved my things? Put them somewhere to mess with me?

He paused in the living room. "Are you . . . okay?"

No. No, I wasn't.

I sat down—hard—on the couch, curling my fingers so tightly around Jeff Goldblum's face that the sequins began to crinkle. I started noticing all of the little things, now—because my aunt never changed anything in her apartment, so when something went missing or changed, it was easy to tell. The curtains that she'd thrown away three years ago after a cat she brought in off the street peed on them. The Saint Dolly Parton candle on the coffee table that set fire to her feather boa robe, both tossed out the window. The afghan I'd covered up with last night that should've been boxed up and put into the hall closet.

There were so many things that were *here* that *weren't here anymore.*

Including . . .

My eyes fell on the wingback chair the color of robin's egg. The chair that was no longer there. That *shouldn't* be there. Because—because it was where—

"My aunt. Did she say where she went?" I asked, my voice wobbling, even though I already knew. If it was seven years ago, she'd be . . .

He rubbed the back of his neck. "Um, I think she said Norway?"

Norway. Running from walruses and taking photos of glaciers and looking up train tickets down to Switzerland and Spain, nursing a bottle of vintage wine she'd bought from a corner store across from our hostel.

Black spots began to eat at the edges of my vision. I couldn't get a deep enough breath. It felt like there was something lodged in my throat, and there wasn't enough air, and my lungs wouldn't co-operate, and—

"Shit," he whispered, dropping his duffel. "What's wrong? What can I do?"

"Air," I gasped. "I need—I need fresh—I need—"

To leave. To never come back. To sell this apartment and move halfway across the world and—

In two strides, he was over to the window.

Alarmed, I shook my head. "No, not—!"

He threw it open.

What came next was something out of Alfred Hitchcock's *The Birds*. Because my aunt took care in naming everything that she adopted. The rat that lived in her walls for a few years? *Wallbanger*. The cat she adopted that pissed on her curtains? *Free Willy*. The generation of pigeons that roosted on her AC for as long as I'd been alive?

Two blurs of gray and blue darted into the apartment with savage coos. "*Motherfu*—" the man cried, shielding his face.

They came in like bats out of hell, rats of the night, vengeful terrors.

"The pigeons!" I cried. One of them landed with a hard *thud* on the countertop, the other took a round in the living room before landing in my hair. The claws scratched my scalp, getting tangled in my already knotted hair. "Get it out!" I cried. "Get it off me!"

"Hold still!" he cried, grabbing the pigeon by the body, and gently coaxed it out of my hair. It didn't want to let go. I debated whether or not to shave off my entire head in that moment. But his hands were gentle, and it made my panicked heart in my throat beat a little more rationally. "I got it, I got it, there's a good girl," he murmured in a soft, low voice, though I wasn't sure whether it was to the pigeon or to me.

I was glad he couldn't see the blush that inched up my cheeks.

Then—we were free. I scrambled away from the pigeon, behind the couch, while he held it at arm's length.

"What do I do?" he asked hesitantly.

"Release it!"

"I just caught it!"

I mimed throwing it. "*OUT THE WINDOW!*"

The pigeon whirled its head around like the girl from *The Exorcist* and blinked at him. He made a face and threw it out the window. It took flight into the air and left for the opposite rooftop. He gave a sigh. The other pigeon blinked, cooing, as it waddled itself to the edge of the counter and nibbled on a piece of mail.

"Erm, I take it this is . . . Mother and Fucker?" he asked, a little apologetically.

I patted down my hair. "*Now* you remember the note?"

"Could have specified pigeons," he replied, and went to get the other one. It started running the other way, but he clicked his tongue to try and corral it.

I watched with mounting panic.

Seven years ago, I was supposed to go backpacking across Europe with my then boyfriend, but we broke it off just before our departure. I was more bereft about that, in hindsight, than him breaking up with me. Then my aunt had shown up at my parents' house, traveling scarf tied around her head, in heart-shaped sunglasses, a suitcase at her side. She'd smiled at me from the front porch and said, "Let's go chase the moon, my darling Clementine."

And we did.

She didn't know where we were going, and I certainly didn't, either.

We never had a plan, my aunt and I, when we chased an adventure.

Had she said she'd subletted her apartment? I . . . couldn't remember. That summer had been a blur of some other girl without a map or an itinerary or a destination.

"This apartment is magical," my aunt's voice rang in my ears, but it wasn't true. It *couldn't* be true.

"I . . . I have to go," I muttered, grabbing my purse beside the couch. "Be gone by the time I get back. Or—or else."

And I fled.

5

The Time-Share

I STUMBLED OUT OF the elevator, sucking in lungful of breath after lungful of breath, trying to get my chest to loosen up. To get myself to calm down. Breathe.

I was fine, I was fine—

I am fine—

"Clementine! Good morning to you," Earl said, tipping his cap to me. "It's a bit drizzly this morning—is something wrong?"

Yes, I wanted to tell him. *There's a stranger in my apartment.*

"I'm just going for a short walk," I said quickly, flashing him a smile that I *hoped* meant that nothing was wrong, and quickly left into the dreary gray morning. It was already so muggy, the humidity stuck to me like a second skin, and the city was much too loud for nine thirty in the morning.

I'd fallen asleep in yesterday's clothes, which I just realized I still had on. I smoothed down my blouse, tied my hair back into a tiny ponytail, and hoped that the fallout from my mascara wasn't *too* bad. Even if it was, I was sure I wasn't the *worst*-looking person on the block.

This was the city that never slept, after all.

Why didn't I tell Earl about the man in my apartment? He could've gone up there and vacated him—

It's because you believe the story.

My aunt was good at telling stories, and the one she told about the apartment had always stuck to me like glue.

Obviously her apartment had its quirks: the pigeons on the AC refused to leave, generation after generation, the seventh floorboard in the living room creaked for no discernible reason, and under no circumstances were you to turn the faucet and the shower on at the same time.

"And," she had said gravely, that summer I turned eight and thought I knew what made this apartment magical, but I did not, "it bends time when you least expect it."

Like the pages of a book, uniting a prologue with a happy ending, an epilogue with a tragic beginning, two middles, two climaxes, two stories that never quite meet in the world outside.

"One moment you are in the present in the hall"—she pointed toward the front door, as if it was a journey she had lived already, retracing her steps in the map of her memory—"the next you open the door and you slip through time into the past. Seven years." Then, a little quieter, "It's always seven years."

The first time she told me the story, sitting in that robin's-egg blue chair of hers, Marlboro cigarette in hand, she told me only the good parts. I was eight, after all, and my first summer with my aunt stretched wide in front of me. "About twenty years ago, way before you were born, the summer was sweltering, and a storm had rolled across the city. The sky was brilliant with lightning . . ."

My aunt was a great storyteller. Everything she said, she made me want to believe, even while I was figuring out that Santa Claus didn't really exist.

The way she told it, she'd just bought the apartment, and my mom had helped her move in that morning, so cardboard boxes with her things were stacked along the walls, words on the side detailing what was inside in long, loopy handwriting. *Kitchen* and *bedroom* and *music*. She had just ended her career with *The Heart Mattered*, the Broadway show she had starred in. She was twenty-seven, and everyone was baffled as to why she never wanted to act onstage again.

As she told it, the apartment was hollow. It was like a room without books. Her real estate agent had gotten the apartment for cheap—apparently the seller had wanted to get rid of it quickly—and my aunt wasn't one to look a gift horse in the mouth. She went out for groceries (and wine), because she wasn't about to spend her first night in her new apartment, sleeping on the floor on an air mattress, *without* at least a wedge of Brie and some merlot to keep her company.

She returned to her new apartment, but something wasn't right.

There weren't any boxes in the living room. And it was *furnished*. There were plants everywhere, records of old bands suspended on the walls, a huge stereo system with a turntable under the living room windows. She thought she'd walked into the wrong apartment, and so she turned and left—

But no, it was B4.

She went back inside, and all the furniture was still there.

As was a strange young woman sitting on the windowsill, the window open, welcoming whatever breeze would break the sweltering hotness of a New York summer. The humidity just hung in the air, dripping, the sky cloudless of the thunderstorm that should have drenched the city just a few moments before. Her long beige shorts were a size too big, her tank top so loud it should have been in a Jazzercise special. Her blond hair was pulled back into a pony-tail with a bright blue scrunchie, and she was feeding two pigeons on the sill, talking to them in soft coos, until she noticed my aunt and stamped out her cigarette in a crystalline ashtray, her thick eyebrows raised high.

As my aunt used to say—she was the most beautiful woman she had ever met, the sunlight framing her in a halo of light. It was the exact moment she fell.

("You always know," she told me conspiratorially. "You always know the moment you fall.")

The woman looked in confusion at my aunt, and then—

"Oh, so it happened again."

"What happened? What's *happening*—who are you?" my aunt asked, at a loss for words, because she was quite sure she'd stepped into the right apartment. She didn't have time for something like this. The summer heat had already made her irritated, and her flats were soggy from the rain that was now nowhere to be found, and she needed to put her milk away before it spoiled.

The woman turned to her with a smile. "It's a bit odd, but you look like the kind of person who might believe it."

"Do I look that gullible to you?"

Her eyes widened. "That isn't what I meant at all. You just moved in, right? To the Monroe—it's still called that, isn't it?"

"Why wouldn't it be?"

The woman put a finger to her own lips and tapped them. "Things change. I'm Vera," she said, and outstretched her hand. "I used to live here."

"Used to?"

"Technically still do, for me." Vera's smile widened, and she motioned to my aunt's groceries. "You can put them in the fridge.

I was just about to make some summer fettuccine, if you'd like to stay, and I can explain?"

My aunt, flustered, quickly turned and started for the door again. "Absolutely *not*."

So she left again and got the superintendent, who unlocked her door—the same one she had come from, B4, so she *hadn't* gone into the wrong place before—and let her into her small, empty apartment. Her cardboard boxes greeted her. The superintendent looked around for her peace of mind, but he didn't find the petite intruder anywhere, and my aunt couldn't find any of the furniture she'd seen, either. Not the record player, the plants, none of it.

She didn't see the woman again for another few months. By then my aunt was no longer sleeping on the floor, and she had bought a robin's-egg blue wingback chair that she immediately set in the corner of the living room, and her fridge was stocked with wine and cheese, a travel guide for Malaysia open and facedown on the kitchen counter.

She left her apartment for a second—long enough to get a package from the mailbox downstairs—and by the time she unlocked her door and stepped back inside, she found herself in that same strange apartment again, with the records on the walls and the plants overflowing the counters, stacked across the sill.

The same woman, her hair now shorn short, was lounging on a threadbare couch that had gone out of style in the sixties. She looked at her guest over a copy of *Jane Eyre* and quickly sat up. "Oh, you're back!"

The woman—this *Vera*—seemed quite happy to see her, too. Which was odd for my aunt. Most people, after she imploded her career, seemed to only ever look at her with either befuddlement or mild disdain. My aunt wasn't quite sure where to go—what to do. Should she leave again, get the super?

("Obviously I *didn't* this time," my aunt scoffed, and waved her hand in the air dismissively. "He couldn't even fix my *rat infestation*. And I expected him to get a whole person out of my apartment? Absolutely not.")

Instead, my aunt accepted Vera's invite to fettuccine, a meal that was never quite the same twice. Vera never measured any of the ingredients, and watching her in the kitchen was like witnessing a hurricane personified. She was everywhere at once, dragging things, half-thought, out of the cupboards and abandoning them on the counter, forgetting the boiling pot on the stove, deciding on a side salad at the last minute—but oh, what kind of *dressing?*—and all the while she told my aunt this absolutely impossible story.

Of an apartment that sometimes slipped through time—seven years forward, seven years back.

"Like a seven-year itch?" my aunt had asked wryly, and Vera had looked so distraught that she'd even *guess* that.

"No, like the *lucky* number! Seven. It must be lucky, since you're here."

My aunt swore that she had never been flustered her entire life, but at that moment she hadn't a clue what to say. They talked for hours over al dente pasta and wilted salad. They talked until morning was pink across the horizon. They laughed over cheap wine, and when my aunt told this story, you could see the happiness filling her face with youth and love. There was never a doubt in my mind that she loved Vera.

She loved her so much, she began to call her "my sunshine."

And that was where she always stopped in her story—at the big reveal, the wonder and magic of this apartment that slipped through time—and when I was a kid, that was enough. It was a happy ending, and I got to exist in that same space, opening doors, hoping I'd slip, too, into some unknown past—or maybe a *future*. In seven years, would I be successful? Would I be popular? Pretty?

Would I have my life together? Would I fall in love?

Or if I slipped into the past, would I meet my aunt from the pictures of when I was born? The quieter, reserved woman who looked a little lost in those photos, and I never quite understood why.

It took a few years to realize that she had only told me the good parts that first summer afternoon, when she was trying to fill the silence.

I was twelve when she finally told me the sad parts. She told me to pay attention—that the heartbreak was important, too.

The summer evening was cool with a thunderstorm as we ate fettuccine that was never quite the same twice. I knew this story by now, backward and forward, wishing every time I stepped into the apartment it would choose me to whisk away—

"I wanted to marry her."

She said it softly over her third glass of merlot while we were playing a game of Scrabble the night before our flight to Dublin. I remember that dinner so well—the way you do when your brain sticks on a scene and replays it over and over again years after, changing the details just slightly, but never the outcome.

"Finding a person was a little more difficult twenty-odd years ago. We'd met each other somewhere in time so often by then, I could trace the lines of her hands on mine. I had memorized the freckles on her back, drawn them into constellations. The apartment always drew us together when we were at crossroads, and oh, were we at so many—in our careers, in our personal lives, in our friendships. We helped each other. We were the only ones who could." She had this far-off look in her eyes. "I thought I could find her, that it would be easy—that it would be like seeing someone you once knew on a crowded sidewalk, and your eyes meet, and time stands still. But time never stands still," she added bitterly. "A lot can happen in seven years."

She wasn't wrong—in seven years, I'd be going to college. In seven years, I'd have my first boyfriend, my first heartbreak. In seven years, I'd have a passport more worn and weathered than most of the adults I met. I could only imagine what happened in the seven years between my aunt and Vera.

I didn't have to.

It was simple, and it was sad:

When she found Vera in the present, she was different. She had changed, bit by bit, the way years often did, and my aunt, in all her love for new and exciting things, was afraid that what they had in that apartment out of time wouldn't last. She was afraid that it would never be as good as it had been. That a lifetime together would sour, that the second taste wouldn't be as sweet, that their love would grow stale like bread and their hearts would grow cold.

In the end, Vera had wanted a family, and Analea had wanted the world.

"So I let her go," my aunt said, "rather than be burdened with me."

And Vera moved on. Two kids on her own. She moved back to her hometown to raise them. Went back to college. Became a lawyer. She grew and she changed and she became someone new, as time always made you. And she had not looked back.

All the while, my aunt stayed the same, afraid to keep anything too long in fear it might spoil.

She only ever had two rules in this apartment—one, always take your shoes off by the door.

And two: never fall in love.

Because anyone you met here, anyone the apartment let you find, could never stay.

No one in this apartment ever stayed.

No one ever would.

So why would the apartment give me someone *now*? Why not my aunt—the person I wanted to see? Why did it spit me out into a time when she wasn't there, her apartment loaned out to some charming stranger with the most piercing gray eyes?

It didn't matter. He'd be gone by the time I went back. The apartment just made a mistake—or I was going nuts. Either way, it didn't matter because he wasn't staying.

I found myself walking a little farther than I anticipated, over to the Metropolitan Museum of Art. I always ended up here when I was stressed or lost. The timelessness of the portraits, the sweeping colorful landscapes, viewing the world through paint-splotched glasses. I walked through the galleries, and in that time I managed to summon up a little more decorum. And a plan. I got a macchiato from the Italian café across from the Monroe on my way back, and I downed it like a chaser, tossed it into the trash can outside of the building, and marched back toward the last place I really wanted to be.

6

Second Chances

THE WALK FROM THE elevator to my aunt's fourth-floor apartment felt exceptionally long, my nerves beginning to mount—sort of the way my nerves always did when I approached her door ("*your* door," I could hear Fiona say). The dread of going inside, mixed with the uncertainty of whether or not I'd see that stranger again, twisted my stomach. I really hoped he was gone.

I stopped at B4, and the brassy door knocker stared back at me, the lion head forever frozen in a half scream, half roar.

"Okay, the plan is if he's there, chase him out with the baseball bat in the closet. If he's gone, prosper," I muttered to myself as I fished the keys out of my purse. "Don't freak out like you did earlier. Breathe."

Somehow that sounded so much easier than it actually was.

My hands were shaking as I inserted the key into the lock and turned it. I wasn't the superstitious type of person, but the waffling in my head—*Don't be here, do be here*—sounded suspiciously like I was plucking petals off a daisy.

The door creaked open on rusted hinges, and I peeked my head inside.

I didn't *hear* anyone . . .

Maybe he was gone.

"Hello?" I called. "Mr. Murder Man?"

No response.

Though if he *were* a murderer, would he respond to being called one? I was overthinking things. I slipped inside and closed the door behind me. The apartment was quiet, the afternoon light streaming rays of gold and orange through the taffeta-colored curtains in the living room. Motes of dust danced in the sunlight.

I put my purse on the barstool underneath the counter and checked the rooms, but he—and his stuff—were gone.

My relief was short-lived, however, as I took stock of the apartment properly. The calendar was still set to seven years ago. The portraits on the wall were still there, the ones my aunt had taken down, either given away or destroyed, and the ones I'd stored in the hallway closet. Her bed was in the bedroom instead of mine, her books still haphazardly stacked on the shelves in her study, though I was sure I'd put most of them in boxes already.

And then there was the note—the one written on the back of a receipt in long and scratchy handwriting I didn't recognize.

Sorry for the intrusion — I

I turned the receipt over. The date read seven years ago, from a bodega on the corner that had since been turned into an expensive furniture boutique—the kind you'd find in farm-chic makeovers with shiplap.

My chest constricted again.

"No, no, no, no," I begged. The two pigeons sat on the sill, pressed against the glass like they wanted to be inside to watch the show. They looked a bit ruffled from the morning. *"No."*

The pigeons cooed, scandalized.

I set my jaw. Crushed the receipt in my hands and threw it back onto the counter. Grabbed my purse. And left the apartment. The door slammed closed behind me.

Then I unlocked it again, and went inside.

The receipt was still there.

I turned around. Left the apartment.

And shoved my way back in.

Still there on the counter.

"I can do this all day," I told the apartment, and then I wanted to kick myself for *talking to an inanimate place.*

It felt a little like I was talking to my aunt instead. She would be the kind of person to play this *exact* trick on me. We'd always butted heads, even though I loved her. She said I tied my bows too tightly, lived my life too neat, like my parents.

I just liked plans. I liked sticking to them. I liked knowing what was coming and *when* it was coming.

So, yes, this would be the exact kind of thing my aunt would do.

On my sixth reentry, I saw the crumpled receipt and the pigeons watching me like I was some fool, turned on my heels—

And came face-to-face with the stranger.

"Oh," he said, surprised, his pale eyes wide, "you're back already."

I jerked backward, raising my purse. "I swear to *god*—"

"I'm still leaving," he added cautiously, holding his hands up in surrender, "but I forgot my toothbrush, actually."

I frowned. "Oh."

"May I get it?"

I pulled my purse over my shoulder again. "Since you asked so nicely . . ." I stepped to the side, and let him into the rest of the apartment. He had his duffel slung across his body, the airport tag still on the strap. He went into the bathroom to get it while I stood perched at the edge of the living room, picking at my cuticles. He came back out with it triumphantly in his hand.

Maybe when he leaves this time, I'll go back to my time, too, I thought.

"It's a weird thing," he said, waving his toothbrush, "but I have to have it."

"I'm really picky with mine. They have to have the little rubber bits at the edges," I agreed absently, before I remembered that I was supposed to be calling security because he had, in fact, come back. But he'd come back for his *toothbrush* . . .

"Oh, the ones to massage your gums?" he asked. "Those are nice."

"And I hate it when someone just suggests that you use one of theirs they hadn't used—it's not the same."

He threw his hands up. "Right? Not the same! Anyway, now that I have my emotional support toothbrush, I'll be on my way. And if I've left anything else, you can just mail it here," he added, taking a pen from the mug on the counter and jotting down his information on a napkin. He handed it to me. If he noticed the crumpled-up receipt with his note on it, he didn't say anything.

I read his scratchy handwriting. "You're from North Carolina?"

"The Outer Banks, yeah."

"You're a long way from home."

He gave a one-shouldered shrug, more coy than dismissive. "'Travel is about the gorgeous feeling of teetering in the unknown.'"

I cocked my head, the quote familiar. "Anthony Bourdain?"

The right side of his mouth quirked up into a charmingly crooked smile. If it had been any other time, any other place, it might have melted me then and there. "I'll see you around."

"Probably not," I replied.

"Probably not," he agreed with a self-conscious laugh, and saluted goodbye with his toothbrush, and it was adorable.

I lowered my gaze, and it settled on the calendar on the coffee table. *Seven years.*

He started for the door.

I squeezed my eyes shut.

"The apartment always drew us together when we were at a crossroads," my aunt had said of her and Vera. So it must've drawn this man and me together, too. I really didn't care about whatever crossroads I was at—I found myself enchanted by the memory of my aunt on my parents' front doorstep seven years ago, asking me on an adventure, as if time in and of itself was infinite. As if she knew, with that gleam in her eyes, that something was about to happen.

Or, perhaps, it was because of what she'd once told me.

How sometimes time pinched in on itself. How sometimes it bled together like the watercolors I used to paint with.

He lived in a world where my aunt still existed, and if I could stay in that world—however long . . . Even if it was just in this apartment. Even if it was only this once. Even if the next time I left, the apartment sent me back to my time—

In this apartment, she was still alive somewhere, out in the world.

This kind of magic is heartache, I warned myself, but it didn't matter, because a soft, almost dead part of my heart that had bloomed every summer with adventure and wonder whispered back, *What do you have to lose?*

Whatever it was, I spun on my heels and told him just as he reached the door to leave, "You can stay."

He let go of the front doorknob and turned back to me, a curious look in his bright and pale eyes. They reminded me a bit of the shade of clouds just before a plane ascended above them. "You sure?" he asked in that soft Southern lilt.

"Yeah, but—I have to stay here, too, right now," I said, folding his napkin up and sticking it in my back pocket. If I remembered my aunt's stories about Vera, I'd be sent back to my time eventually. "My apartment is kind of"—I paused, wracking my brain for a good lie—"out of commission. It—um. Got infested. With—um." I glanced at the windowsill. Mother and Fucker were huddled on the AC, preening each other after their harrowing morning. "Pigeons."

His eyes widened. "Oh. I didn't realize it could get that bad."

"Oh, yeah. They're called the rats of the skies for a reason." God, I was a terrible liar, but he seemed to buy it with a serious nod. *Seriously?* What were the pigeons like where *he's* from? "So . . . while my aunt's gone, she told me to look after her apartment, and I figured I could stay here a few days while that got sorted out." I finally dragged my eyes back to him. "I'm sorry if I was a bit mean at first. You just surprised me. But if my aunt told you that you could stay . . ."

"Thank you, thank you!" He pressed his hands against each other in prayer. "I swear, you won't even know I'm here."

I highly doubted that, since he was almost impossible to ignore. He just *looked* like a loud kind of person, but he was also mesmerizing to watch. He moved through the world with this air of nonchalance—like he didn't care what anyone else thought. It was infectious. I shifted on my feet uncomfortably, because it was finally beginning to sink in that this was real, and my aunt's story was true. It was exactly what I had wished for for years—opening her apartment, holding my breath, waiting to be whisked away—

Only for it to happen *now*, after my aunt was gone, after I no longer had a heart for impossible things.

Why couldn't I have had an encounter with someone less . . . *enthusiastic*? This man felt like he could exist anywhere and call it home, too much like my aunt, too much like the person I had wanted to be.

"To make up for getting off on the wrong foot," he said, and cocked his head in a boyish way, "can I cook us dinner?"

Us. That surprised me. I felt my chest tighten like a rubber band. I quickly looked away. "Um, sure. I think there's some spaghetti sauce in the pantry?"

"Oh, that's sweet, but I've something else in mind." His grin turned into a smile, and it was bright and crooked and, oh, *no*, so charming, like he had a hundred secrets he couldn't wait to tell me tucked into the corners of his lips. "One of my favorite recipes. I'm Iwan, by the way." He outstretched his hand. He hadn't even taken off his duffel bag yet.

I took a deep breath and accepted his hand. His fingertips were hard and calloused, scars across his fingers, burns on his hands. They were also warm, and his grip was solid, and it melted all the nerves I had had a moment before. This might not be so bad. "Clementine," I replied.

"Oh, like—"

I squeezed his hand a little tighter and deadpanned, "If you sing that song, I might have to kill you."

He laughed. "I'd never dream of it."

I let go of his hand, and he finally slid off his duffel bag, dropping it by the couch, and hurried into the kitchen. I followed him wearily. He pushed up his already short sleeves and grabbed a cutting board from the counter, then spun it around by its handle with a flourish.

This was a terrible idea. The worst idea. What had *possessed* me to do this?

He glanced back at me, standing there in the entryway to the kitchen, and asked if I'd like a glass of water while I waited—or something a little stronger.

"Stronger," I decided, tearing my eyes away from this handsome man in my aunt's kitchen, beginning to feel like I'd just made a grave mistake. "Definitely stronger."

Better Acquainted

I WATCHED FROM MY perch on the barstool as Iwan made himself at home in my aunt's kitchen. My aunt and I usually ate TV dinners or went out, and for the last week since I moved in, I'd gotten takeout from my favorite Thai place. The kitchen was a foreign battlefield to me, somewhere I just cautiously passed through on the way to the bedroom or to get another glass of wine. I could cook the essentials—my mom made sure of that before I left for college, she wasn't going to let her only daughter *starve*—but I'd never been very interested in the art of it all. Iwan, on the other hand, seemed to fit so well there, like he already knew where everything was. He'd taken a worn leather knife roll from his duffel bag, which he put back into the bedroom, and set the knives down on the counter.

"So," I asked, nursing a cheap glass of rosé my aunt had bought before she left for the summer, "you're a chef or something?"

He retrieved a brown bag of vegetables from the refrigerator. I hadn't even realized he had stocked it full of food. The fridge hadn't seen anything besides takeout and leftovers for a week at least. He gestured toward his knife roll. "Did my knives give it away?"

"A little. You know, context clues. Also, please say yes. The alternative is that you're actually Hannibal and I am in grave danger."

He pointed to himself. "Do I seem like the kind of person who would ruin his perfectly acceptable palate with a cut of human tenderloin?"

"I don't know, I barely know you."

"Oh, well, that's *easy* to fix," he said, planting his hands on either side of the cutting board in front of him, and leaning against the counter. There was a tattoo on the inside of his right arm, a country road weaving through pine trees. "I went to UNC Chapel Hill on a scholarship, planning on heading to law school like my mom and sister, but I dropped out after three years." He gave another one of those one-shoulder shrugs. "Worked in a few kitchens while I tried to figure out what I wanted to do, and it was the only place I really felt at home, you know? My grandpa practically raised me in a kitchen. So, I finally decided to go to CIA."

"The Central . . ."

His mouth twitched into a grin. "Culinary Institute of America."

"Ah, that was my second guess," I replied, nodding.

"Got an associate's from there in Culinary Arts, and here I am, looking for a job."

"You're chasing the moon," I marveled, more to myself than to him, as I thought about my own career—four years in college for art history, and then seven working my way up, slowly, at Strauss & Adder.

"The moon?"

Embarrassed, I replied, "It's something my aunt always says. It's one of her cardinal rules—you know, like keep your passport

renewed, always pair red wines with meats and whites with everything else . . ." I counted on my fingers. "Find fulfilling work, fall
in love, and chase the moon."

He bit in a grin, taking a sip of bourbon. "Sounds like good
advice."

"I guess. So, you're, like, what?" I studied him for a beat.
"Twenty-five?"

"Twenty-six."

"*Jeez*. I feel old."

"You can't be much older than I am."

"Twenty-nine, almost thirty," I replied grimly. "One foot's already in the grave. I found a gray hair the other day. I debated
whether to bleach my entire head."

He barked a laugh. "I don't know what I'll do once I start going
white—I won't go gray. My grandpa didn't. Maybe I'll shave my
head."

"I think you'd look refined with a bit of white," I mused.

"*Refined*," he echoed, liking how that sounded. "I'll tell my
grandpa you said that. And anyway, my track record for sticking
things out hasn't been very steady. When I said I wanted to go to
CIA, my mom was beside herself at first—I was one year away
from a business degree—but I just couldn't see myself sitting at a
desk all day. So instead, I'm here." He flourished his hands like it was
a magic trick, but there was a sparkle in his eyes as he said, "There's
an opening at a pretty famous restaurant, and I want to get in."

"As a chef . . . ?"

He was completely serious as he said, "As a dishwasher."

I almost choked on my wine. "I'm sorry—you're kidding?"

"Once I get in, I can climb the ranks," he replied with another
one-shouldered shrug, and dug into the paper bag for the first

vegetable. He took out a tomato, and the large chef's knife from the worn knife roll, the blade sharp, and started to dice it. His cuts were quick, without hesitation, the silver of his blade flashing against the yellowish-white light of the god-awful multicolored chandelier my aunt had "reclaimed" off the street.

"So," he went on as he worked, "now that you know all about me, what about you?"

I blew out a breath through my lips. "Oof, what *about* me? Grew up in the Hudson Valley, and then Long Island, and I've been in the city half my life. Went to NYU for art history, then got a job in book publishing, and now I'm here."

"Have you always wanted to work in book publishing?"

"No, but I like where I am now." I took another sip of my rosé, debating whether or not to tell him the other things about me—the trips abroad, the passport filled with so many stamps it'd impress any lifelong traveler, but every time I showed it to someone they'd get this idea about me. That I was some child of chaos with a wild heart, when, in reality, I was just a scared girl hanging on to my aunt's blue coattails as she spirited me across the world. I sort of only wanted him to see the real me—the me who never left the city, not even to visit her parents on Long Island anymore, the me who went to work and came home and watched *Survivor* reruns on the weekend and couldn't even set aside a few hours to go to her ex-boyfriend's art show.

So I decided not to, and said, "Well, that's me in a nutshell. An art-history-major-turned-book-publicist."

He gave me a weighted look and pursed his lips. He had a freckle on the left side of his bottom lip, and it was almost impossible not to look at it. "Somehow, I feel like you're selling yourself a little short."

"Oh?"

"It's a feeling," he said, grabbing another tomato from the paper bag, and gave another one-shouldered shrug. "I'm pretty great at reading people."

"Oh?"

"In fact, I'm pretty sure I'm halfway to figuring out your favorite color."

"It's—"

"No!" he cried, holding the knife up to me. "No. I'm going to guess it."

That amused me. I looked pointedly at the tip of his knife until he realized he had it angled at me, and then he quickly returned it to the cutting board. "Are you, now."

"It's my one superpower, let me impress you with it."

"Fine, fine," I said, because I was sure he wasn't going to guess it—after all, it was one of the most surprising things about me—and watched him slide the diced tomatoes to the side of the board and then take out an onion to peel it. He was very deft with his hands, mesmerizing in a way I could watch for hours.

"Well?" I asked. "What's my favorite color?"

"Oh, I'm not going to guess it now," he replied coyly. "I barely know you yet."

"There's not much to know." I gave a shrug, watching him dice the onion. "I'm pretty boring. My aunt was the one with all the cool stories."

"Are you and your aunt close?" he asked.

I glanced up from his hands, having not heard the last question. "Hmm?"

He lifted his gaze to meet mine. His eyes were the loveliest pale gray, darker at the center than the edges, so slight you had to get very close to see. "You and your aunt, you two seem close."

The present tense sent a shiver down my spine. It was unexpected and startling, like a douse of cold water to the face. *Right, in his time she's still alive, somewhere in Norway with me, being chased by a walrus on the beach.* It made me feel, for a moment, like she really was still here. Flesh and blood. Like she could waltz into the apartment at any moment and pull me into one of her bone-crushing hugs, and I'd breathe her in—Marlboro cigarettes and Red perfume and hints of lavender from the laundry detergent. *My darling Clementine,* she would say. *What a lovely surprise!*

I swallowed the knot forming in my throat. "I . . . guess we are close."

As he put the chopped onions into a separate bowl, he glanced at me and frowned. "That look again."

I blinked, tearing myself out of my thoughts, and purposefully made my face blank. "What look?"

"Like you're tasting something sour—you had that look before."

"I don't know what you're talking about," I replied, mortified, and pressed my hands to my face. "How do I look?"

He laughed, soft and gentle, and put down his knife. "Your eyebrows crinkle. May I?"

"Uh—sure?"

He reached over the counter and pressed his thumb in the center of my eyebrows, and smoothed the skin out. "Here. Like you're surprised that you want to cry."

I stared at him, a blush rising on my cheeks. I quickly leaned back. "They—they do *not*," I said, mortified. "You're just seeing things."

He picked up his knife again and began to gut a bell pepper. "Whatever you say, Lemon."

I shot him a glare. "It's *Clementine*."

"*Clllllllemontine.*"

"I suddenly hate you."

He mock gasped, dropping his knife, and slammed his hands against his chest. "Lemon, already? At least wait until you taste my food first!"

"Am I getting a fancy dinner tonight?"

He sucked in a breath between his teeth. "Oof, sorry. I didn't bring my fine china. Only my fine knives." And he picked up his chef's knife again. "This one is Bertha."

I arched an eyebrow. "You *name* your knives?"

"All of them." Then he pointed over to his other knives rolled out on the counter and introduced them. "Rochester, Jane, Sophie, Adele . . ."

"Those are just *Jane Eyre* characters."

"They're my grandfather's," he replied, as if that explained everything.

I looked at the one he was using. The handle, now that he mentioned it, did look a bit worn, and the sheen of silver a little dull—but they were clearly well loved, and well taken care of. "Was he a chef?"

"No. But he wanted to be," he replied quietly, and I sensed that it was a tough topic. Was his grandfather still alive? Or had he inherited those knives like I had this apartment?

Though I was *sure* his knives weren't of the time-traveling variety.

"Well," I said, finishing my wine, "it's such a pity that with no fine china, I guess I'll be uncultured for the rest of my life."

He *tsk*ed. "A few of my friends would argue that you can't be uncultured in food because the idea of *cultured* food derives from the gentrification of recipes in general."

The way he said those words, and the severity with which he

said them, was incredibly attractive. My stomach dropped as I briefly wondered, *If he is that good at words, how good is he at—*

"So, I *am* cultured?" I asked, distracting myself.

"You are who you are, and you like what you like," he replied, and there was no sarcasm in his voice. "You are you, and that's a lovely person to be."

"You barely know me."

He clicked his tongue to the roof of his mouth, studying me for a moment, his eyes a shade darker than they had been before. "I think your favorite color is yellow," he guessed, and watched as the surprise trickled across my face. "But not a bright yellow—more of a golden yellow. The color of sunflowers. That might even be your favorite flower."

My mouth fell open.

"I take it I'm close?" he asked in a soft rumble, and the smugness made my toes curl.

"Lucky guess," I replied, and he smiled so wide, his eyes glittered. "Well, what's yours?"

That crooked grin curled across his lips. He *tsk*ed again, clicking his tongue to the roof of his mouth. "That'd be cheating, Lemon," he purred. "You'll have to guess."

Then he pushed himself off the counter and returned to cooking. And just like that, the moment of tension burst like a bubble, even though I still felt heady from how close he'd been.

I grabbed the bottle of rosé and poured myself another glass— I'd need it. I think I'd bitten off more than I could chew tonight. If he was twenty-six now, he'd be . . . thirty-three in my time? Probably renting somewhere in Williamsburg, if he stayed in the city, with a partner and a dog at *least*. (He seemed like a dog person.)

He didn't have a ring on, but a lot happened in seven years.

A lot *could* happen.

My aunt's story was raw in my memory. First rule, always take your shoes off by the door.

Second, never fall in love in this apartment.

I wasn't all too worried about that.

He grabbed a frying pan from the rack and spun it around in his hand—almost clocking himself in the temple in the process. He tried to act like he hadn't just almost knocked himself out as he set the pan down on the front left eye of the stove. "I didn't ask," he said, "but you okay with fajitas tonight? It's my friend's recipe."

I pretended to be aghast, and clutched my imaginary pearls. "What, no split-pea soup for my delicate taste buds?"

"Fuck split-pea soup." Then, quieter, he added, "That's tomorrow night."

Romance in Chocolate

THE FAJITAS WERE, SURPRISINGLY, excellent.

"I'm not sure if I should be happy you're surprised or a bit of-
fended," he muttered, pouring himself another glass of bourbon
(which he had also used to season the strips of steak when he
cooked them).

We sat at my aunt's yellow table in the kitchen and ate some of
the best fajitas I'd ever had in my life. The beef was tender—it must
have been flank or skirt, so juicy it melted in my mouth, with a
back-end bite of that smoky bourbon flavor. The seasoning was
sweet yet spicy, just enough chili powder to offset the cayenne pepper. The bell peppers and onions were crisp, and they kept sizzling
when he brought the pan over and set it in the middle of the table,
along with warm tortillas, sour cream, guacamole, and hot sauce.

He told me he'd learned how to make them from his roommate
at that fancy culinary school of his and that it was a special family
recipe, so even if I loved it, he was sworn to secrecy.

"Someday I'll convince him to open a restaurant—a food truck, at least," he added defiantly, picking at the leftover bell peppers on his plate, "and he's going to thank me."

"Or else!" I joked. I took one last bite of fajita before I realized that I was stuffed and couldn't eat another bit, and I pushed my plate away with a groan. "Okay, I've decided—if you keep cooking like that, you can stay however long you want."

He tore off a bit of tortilla, picked up a piece of bell pepper and steak with it, and ate it. "That's a dangerous declaration, Lemon."

"Dangerous or genius? I've always wanted a live-in chef—like movie stars have. What's it like to just . . . *have* meals prepared for you. Hungry?" And I signaled to our imaginary server. "Please, I'd love some escargot by the waterfall on the pool deck out back."

He snorted a laugh. "You joke, but I know someone who does that in LA," he said. "She hates it, but the pay's good so she stays. I couldn't. They always want the same thing—low carb, low calorie, keto, cleanse, vegetarian, *whatever*—too soulless for me. Not adventurous enough."

"So obviously you want to go work at a restaurant where you have to cook the same thing every day?"

He rolled his eyes. "'The same thing every day,'" he echoed with air quotes, and scooted his chair closer, his eyes bright with passion. The gray was swirling, like the eye of a hurricane, so easy to get lost in, I almost felt like I could. "Lemon, firstly, the menu is seasonal, and secondly, practice makes perfect. How else do you learn how to make the perfect meal?"

That made me curious. What kind of food could make him this passionate? I wondered, leaning against the table, "What makes it perfect?"

"*Imagine*," he began, his voice sweet and soft like butterscotch, "I'm eight and I travel to New York City with my mom, sister, and grandpa for the first time. While Mom took my sister around to some of her old haunts, I went with my grandpa to a small restaurant in SoHo. He was so excited. He'd worked in a denim factory his whole life, but he always wanted to be a chef. He read food magazines religiously, cooked for friends, family—birthdays, block parties, anniversaries, Fridays, any occasion that'd let him. And as long as I can remember, he'd always wanted to go to this one restaurant. I didn't know it then that it was world-class, with Michelin stars hung on the wall. I just knew that my grandpa loved the chef de cuisine there—Albert Gauthier—a genius of culinary sciences. I didn't care, I was eight and getting fed, but my grandpa was so happy. He got some sort of steak tartare"—and his mouth twitched then into a tender and reminiscent smile that reached up into his eyes and made them almost glow, how happy he was—"and I got the pommes frites, and my whole life changed."

"Pommes . . . ?"

"French fries, Lemon. They were *French fries*."

I stared at him. "Your life changed because of some French fries?"

He barked a laugh, bright and golden, and said to my utter surprise, "The things you least expect usually do."

My heart clenched for a moment, because that was something my aunt would say, too. That kind of terrible Hallmark-card platitude.

"And anyway," he went on, sitting back in his chair, "my grandpa never had the chance to open a restaurant, but he loved cooking, and he passed that love down to me." His voice stayed light, but he didn't look at me as he said, "He was diagnosed with dementia last year. It's weird watching this man I've always looked up to—this unstoppable force of a guy—slowly get smaller and smaller. Not physically, but just . . . yeah."

I thought about the last few months with my aunt. How, in

hindsight, she got smaller and smaller, too, like the world was suddenly too big. I swallowed the knot rising in my throat, and curled my fingers into fists under the table, resisting the urge to hug him, although it looked a little like he needed it. "I'm sorry."

"What?" he asked, surprised, and suddenly schooled his emotions into a pleasant smile. "No, no, it's fine. You asked what makes a meal perfect. It's this. Food"—he motioned to our almost empty plates—"is a work of art. That's what a perfect meal is—something that you don't just eat, but something you *enjoy*. With friends, and family—maybe even with strangers. It's an experience. You taste it, you savor it, you feel the story told through the intricate flavors that play out across your tongue . . . it's magical. Romantic."

"*Romantic*, really?"

"Absolutely," he replied, almost reverently. "You know what I'm talking about—a rich cheesecake you dream about hours after. Soft candlelight, a plate of cheese, and good wine. The headiness of a brazen stew. The pillowy promises in a golden loaf of brioche." The passion in his voice was infectious, and I bit back a smile as he painted a picture for me with his words, his hands waving in the air, getting carried away. His joy made my heart ache a little in a way I hadn't ever felt. Not the sad sort of ache—but a longing for something I'd never experienced before. "A lemon pie that makes your teeth curl in delight. Or a piece of chocolate at the end of the night, soft and simple." Then he pushed himself up from the table, went to grab something from a shelf in the refrigerator, and tossed it to me.

I caught it. A foil-wrapped chocolate.

"*Romance*, Lemon," he said. "You know?"

I twirled the chocolate around in my fingers. *No*, I thought, looking at this strange russet-headed man in a shirt with a stretched-out neck hole and frayed jeans, a tattoo of sprigs of cilantro and other herbs across his arm, *but I might like to.*

And that was a dangerous thought.

I'd had memorable meals before, but I couldn't describe any of them as *romantic*—at least not in the way that he did: sprinting through airports with fast food in one hand and a ticket stub in the other, late-night rainy dinners huddled under awnings because the restaurant was too full, pretzels from streetside vendors, croissants from no-name bakeries, that lunch yesterday at the Olive Branch, washing it down with too-dry wine.

"I guess I just never had a perfect meal, then," I said finally, putting the chocolate down on the edge of the table. "I've just always felt so out of my element every time I go to one of those fancy places you're probably talking about. I'm constantly afraid of choosing the wrong spoon or ordering the wrong dish or—something. Pair the wrong wine with the wrong cut of steak."

He shook his head. "I'm not talking about that. A restaurant doesn't have to be fancy, with artfully plated smears of coulis and beurre blanc—"

"What's that?"

"Exactly. It's not important. You can get delicious meals from a mom-and-pop joint just as easily as you can get one from a Michelin-starred restaurant."

"And one requires less Spanx. Or—hear me out—I can just stay home and eat a PB&J."

"You could, though what if it turns out to be your last meal?"

I blinked. "Wow, *that* went dark fast."

"Would you still stay home and eat a PB&J if you knew?"

I frowned, and thought about it for a moment. Then I nodded. "I think so. My aunt used to make me PB&J sandwiches whenever

I came to visit her because she's a terrible cook. She'd always pack more peanut butter onto the sandwich than jelly, so it'd always get stuck right on the roof of my mouth—"

He sat up straight. "That's it! The perfect meal."

"I wouldn't call it *perfect*, but—"

"You just said you'd eat it as your last meal, right?"

He had a point.

"Oh," I gasped, finally understanding what he meant. "It's less about the food, then, and more about—"

"The memory," we finished together. His grin slid into a smile, crooked and endearing, and it made his eyes glimmer.

I felt a blush creeping up my neck to my face again.

"That's what I want to make," he said, resting his elbows on the edge of the table. The sleeves of his T-shirt hugged his biceps tightly. Not that I was looking. I definitely wasn't. "The perfect meal."

It might have been the good food, or the three glasses of wine, but I began to think that maybe he *could*. Who knows—maybe he already had in *my* time. I tried to picture him in a chef's uniform, a white coat stretched across his shoulders, covering up the tattoos sporadically placed across his arms like afterthoughts, and I couldn't get the image in focus. He didn't seem like the kind of guy to play by normal rules. He seemed like an exception.

He unwrapped his chocolate and popped it into his mouth, and rolled it into his cheek to melt on its own. "And how about you?"

My shoulders squared at the sudden question. "What about me?"

"Why'd you want to be a book publicist?"

"I just . . . did, I guess."

He arched a single thick eyebrow. It was a rather infuriating eyebrow, actually. Most of the time, guys would just nod when they heard what I did for a living and move on to . . . literally anything else. "How'd you start?" he asked. "You majored in art history, right? So it wasn't something you always wanted to do?"

"No . . ." I admitted, and averted my eyes and concentrated on a piece of chipped paint on the yellow table, scratching at it to uncover the sandalwood underneath. "I don't know. I guess . . . the summer after college, my aunt and I backpacked across Europe." This year, actually. The summer he was here in this apartment. I didn't know why I was telling him all of this. I thought I had decided earlier that I wouldn't. "I'd been thinking about what I wanted to do my last year of college, and I didn't really want to be a curator, but . . . I loved books. Mostly travel guides. My aunt and I always bought one wherever we went. Just like there's secrets in memoirs and confessions in novels, there's a steadfast certainty to a good travel guide, you know?"

"I feel a similar way about a good cookbook," he replied, nodding. "There's nothing like it."

"There's really not," I agreed, thinking back on when I *actually* decided to be a publicist. "Strauss and Adder publish some of the best travel guides in the industry, so I applied and it turns out I'm really good at being a publicist," I said simply. "So, I schedule interviews and podcasts, I get authors from one city to another, I pitch them to TV shows and radio shows and book clubs. I think up new ways to convince you to read a classic for the twentieth time even though you know it like the back of your hand, and I like it. I mean, I have to like it," I added with a self-conscious laugh. "You don't get paid that well in publishing."

"You don't in restaurants, either," he added, watching me with the kind of rapt attention that made me feel like what I did was actually *interesting*. He studied me with those mesmerizing gray eyes, and I began to think about how I'd paint them. Maybe in layers, navy mixed with a lovely shade of shale. "So, in a way," he said thoughtfully, his eyebrows furrowing, "you create a travel guide of your own. For your authors."

"I . . . never thought of it that way," I admitted.

He cocked his head. "Because you haven't seen yourself the way other people do."

Other people? Or you? I wanted to ask, because it was bold of him to think he knew me from a few hours of conversation and plucking a pigeon from my hair. "I think that's very nice of you to say," I told him, "but it's not that deep. I'm just very good at facilitating the sale of books. I'm good at spreadsheets. I'm good at timetables. I'm good at badgering people long enough and hard enough to get that sought-after interview . . ."

"And what do you do for fun?"

I gave a laugh. "You are going to think I'm the most boring person in the world."

"Absolutely not! I've never met a book publicist before. Or anyone named Clementine," he went on, and put his chin on his hand and leaned toward me, grinning. "So we're already off to a great start."

I hesitated, twirling my chocolate around on the table. "I . . . like to sit in front of van Gogh's paintings at the Met."

That did, in fact, surprise him. "Just sit?"

"Yep. That's it. Just sit and look at them. There's something peaceful about it—a quiet gallery room, people moving in and out like a tide. I actually make it a yearly thing for my birthday. Every August second, I go to the Met and sit on a bench and just . . ." I shrugged. "I don't know. I told you, it's silly."

"Every birthday," he muttered, marveling. "Since when?"

"Since college, actually. I studied him and other Postimpressionist painters extensively, but he always stuck out to me. He was—*is*"—I quickly corrected, trying not to wince—"my aunt's favorite, too. The Met has one of his sunflowers, one of his self-portraits, and a few others." I thought about it. "I've gone for about ten years now. I'm nothing if not a child of consistency and routine."

He clicked his tongue to the roof of his mouth. "You're the kind of person who sticks to the directions on the back of a brownie box, aren't you?"

"Those instructions are put there for a reason," I replied practically. "Baking's a precise art."

He rolled his eyes. "Don't you ever color outside the lines, Lemon?"

No, I thought, though that wasn't exactly true. I used to, just not anymore. "I warned you," I said, downing the rest of my wine, and gathering our plates to take to the sink, "I'm boring."

"You keep saying that word. I don't think it means what you think it means," he said in a very cheesy Inigo Montoya impression, and it was my turn to roll my eyes. The wine had made me warm inside, and relaxed for the first time all week.

"Okay, then come up with another word that means dull and uninteresting, tiresome—"

"Do you hear that?" he interrupted.

I put my plate on top of his and paused, cocking my head to listen. The ghost of a melody drifted through the vents from upstairs. Miss Norris playing her violin. I hadn't heard it in . . . *years*. The strings sounded sweeter than I remembered.

He tilted his head to listen.

It took only a few bars to recognize the melody, and my heart clenched.

"Oh, I know this song!" he said enthusiastically, snapping his fingers. "It's *The Way of the Heart* or *The Matters of the Heart* or—no, wait, *The Heart Mattered*, I think? My mom loves that old musical." He hummed a few notes with the violin, and he wasn't that off-key. "Who's playing it?"

"That would be Miss Norris," I supplied, pointing toward the ceiling. Of all the songs to play, it had to be that one? "She performed in Broadway pits for years before she retired."

"It's lovely. Whenever my mom played this song, she'd put me on her toes and dance me around the kitchen. She's not a big musical person, but she likes that one."

I could imagine a tiny Iwan dancing around a kitchen on his mother's toes.

I said, my eyes trained on the ceiling, "My aunt starred in that musical, you know."

"Really? So she's famous?"

"No, it was the only Broadway show she ever did. Everyone said it was because she was too full of herself to follow Bette Midler or Bernadette Peters. Such a promising young talent, after years of being an understudy, just suddenly abandoning her art? They didn't understand her," I added, a little softer, a little gentler, because my aunt was a lot of things—loving and adventurous, but also messy and human. Something I never really recognized until the very end.

The soft and warm notes from the violin upstairs sank through the ceiling, a love song. I'd seen grainy videos on YouTube of my aunt in the show. She was brilliant, and infectious, in her glittery robes and extravagant jewels, belting refrains with her entire soul. It was the only time I'd ever seen her really—impossibly—happy.

"The truth is," I went on, and I wasn't sure if it was the wine that made me want to talk about her, or the way Iwan listened—closely and preciously, as if my aunt had mattered to more than just me, "she was always afraid that whatever came after *The Heart Mattered* wouldn't be as good. So she did something new instead. I envy that. My entire life I wanted to be like her, but I'm not. I hate new things. I like repetition."

"Why?"

I turned my gaze back to him, studying this stranger I shouldn't have let stay in my aunt's apartment, and all of his questions. "New things are scary."

"They don't have to be."

"How are they not?"

"Because some of my favorite things I haven't even done yet."

"Then how do you know they're your favorite?"

In reply, he stood from the table and offered me his hand.

I stared at it.

"It's not a trap, Lemon," he said softly, his Southern lilt a rumble.

I looked at his outstretched hand, and then at him, and the realization dawned on me. I shook my head. "Oh, no. I know what you're doing. I don't dance."

He began to sway back and forth to the violin and hum the chorus. *For a moment the heart mattered, for a moment time stood still.* My aunt had sang it sometimes as she folded her laundry or curled her hair, and the memory was so raw it stung.

"When was the last time you did something for the first time?" he asked, as if daring me. And if there was one thing I was more than a practical pessimist, it was someone who never backed away from a challenge.

I resisted. "I assure you I've danced before."

"But not with me."

No.

And—despite his insistence—this *was* frightening, but not

because it was new or spontaneous. It was frightening because I *wanted* to, and the Wests never did spontaneous things. That was my aunt. And yet . . . here I was, reaching up to take his hand.

It was because of the wine. It had to be.

A smile curled across his lips as he laced his fingers through mine and pulled me to my feet. His grip was strong, his fingertips calloused, as he spun me in the kitchen. I stumbled a little—dancing wasn't my strongest suit—but he didn't seem to mind. We found a rhythm, one of his hands holding mine, the other coming to rest at my lower back. His soft touch made me gasp involuntarily.

He quickly took his hand away. "Sorry, is that too low?"

Yes. And this is too much. I don't dance in kitchens with strangers, I wanted to say, all of the excuses building in my throat, but at the same time I just wanted to be *closer*, too. He was so warm, and his touch so light and tender, that it made me want him to hold on tighter, steady and sure like he held his knives.

This wasn't like me. And yet . . .

I returned his hand to my lower back, to his surprise, and trained my gaze on his chin instead of his eyes, trying to keep the flush out of my cheeks. But that only meant I could still see the crooked grin that spread across his lips, and as he pulled me closer to him, our bodies pressed together, my skin felt electric. He was solid and warm, and the music was yearning, and my heart hammered brightly in my chest.

We swayed in my aunt's cluttered teal kitchen to a song about heartache and happy endings, and it was so tempting to just let myself unravel. For the first time in what felt like forever.

"See?" he whispered, his mouth against my ear. "Something new isn't always so bad."

The last violin note sang through the vents, and the moment

ended. I came back to myself with sudden, crashing certainty. No matter how I thought about it, this couldn't—*wouldn't*—end well.

I let go of him and stepped back, wiping my hands on my jeans. I felt my stomach twisting itself into knots. The warm feeling in my middle turned icy. "I"—I swallowed the lump in my throat—"I think you got the wrong idea."

First Impressions

HE GAVE ME A confused look. "About what?"

Was it hot in here, or was it just me? "I don't think—we—
this . . ." I just had to go out and say it. Draw the line, because it
very much needed to be drawn. "I'm not going to sleep with you,"
I blurted.

His eyebrows jerked up in surprise. A blush quickly rose across
his cheeks, and he choked on his own breath. "I—I wasn't—no, no,
that's fine. I wasn't thinking you would, Lemon."

"Oh. Well." I averted my gaze. I felt embarrassed. A fool. I
looked anywhere—everywhere—but at him. "Just so we're clear,
then."

"Of course," he replied, quickly recovering. "I'm sorry if I gave
you that impression."

"You didn't! I just—I don't think it'd be a good idea. You're staying at my aunt's place, I'm staying here, too . . ." *Seven years in the
future*, I added in my head. "I just really don't want to complicate
things. Sorry," I added, because I just didn't *do* this. For a variety of

reasons, but mostly because he was *very* handsome, and I was very much attracted to him, and that was the kind of surprise that I did not see coming. Oh, *and* we were separated by seven years.

Nothing good could come out of this.

Rule number two, I reminded myself.

I grabbed our plates and deposited them in the sink—like I should've done instead of dance with him. It was a mistake. Above us, Miss Norris worked her way through a Sondheim. I grabbed a sponge.

Iwan gave a start, rising from his chair. "You don't have to—"

"You cooked," I said, waving him to sit back down. "I clean. That's the rule."

"And what if I want to get some practice in for my future dish-washing gig?"

"If you're that bad," I said, letting the water run for a bit until it got hot, "then I hate to say it, but you might need to start looking for a new profession."

He mocked a gasp. "Rude!"

"Truthful." I put the plates in the sink, and turned back to him fully. "The dinner was lovely, Iwan. Thank you. I almost don't regret not kicking you out of the apartment." His mouth fell open in a question as I went to pull some blankets out of the linen closet. He was still giving me that perplexed look when I returned, two pillows and an afghan under my arms.

"Almost?" he asked.

"Someone has to take the couch," I replied, and decided that it would be me.

He jumped to his feet. "Absolutely *not*."

"Don't pull the 'You're a girl so you deserve the bed' bullshit, please. Gender roles and stereotypes are not my cup of tea."

"I'm not, I'm pulling the 'There's a perfectly good bed in there and we are both adults' card." He put his hands on his hips, as if posing like a dad could get me to comply.

I opened my mouth, but then he gave me a look—the kind that told me to test him if I dared.

I mumbled, "You look like a parent about to go into a parent-teacher conference."

"We can even put a pillow between us," he went on, ignoring me. "You don't really want to sleep on the couch, do you? And you certainly won't let *me* . . ."

No, I wouldn't.

"Just—I'll think about it as I do the dishes," I added when he went to argue again, but then he raised his hands in defeat and bowed out to take the bathroom first.

The thing was, he wasn't wrong. We were both adults and there was a perfectly good queen-sized bed in my aunt's bedroom that we could both sleep in. The couch wasn't doing anyone any favors— it had always been more for looks than actually fainting on, any-way. But that didn't mean I had to like it.

I grabbed my chocolate from the table, finally, unwrapped it, and popped it into my mouth. I smoothed out the tinfoil wrapper. *Your future is here*, it read.

Lies.

I put all my frustrations into washing our plates and glasses and cleaning up. My head was buzzing from the drinks, but the last few minutes had sobered me up pretty well. I drank a glass of water and took two Advil, and as I headed to my aunt's room to pick out some pajamas from my stash in her closet, Iwan opened the bath-room door and stepped out.

I froze.

Because I was staring, very prominently, at his bare chest. It wasn't that I'd never seen a bare-chested man before—it just . . .

surprised me a little. He had tattoos, all black linework in similar styles, sporadically across his body. Besides the ones on his arms, there was another on his rib cage, another just to the left side of his navel. And then there was a birthmark just below his collarbone in the shape of a crescent moon.

I asked, very gravely, "What happened to your shirt?"

"I don't wear one to bed," he replied simply and stepped to the side to let me into the bathroom. "Do you mind?"

Of course, if I was a *nun*. "Oh, no," I said coolly, "you're fine."

"Okay."

Another awkward pause.

Then I asked, "Are you sure you don't want me to sleep on the—"

He rolled his eyes. "If anyone is sleeping on the couch, it's me."

"I refuse. You're my aunt's guest."

He crossed his arms over his chest, and I tried not to stare at how his muscles moved under his skin. The way he held his right shoulder a bit higher than the left. The way I wanted to put my mouth on that crescent-shaped birthmark—"Then we're at an impasse," he said.

"Fine," I muttered, tearing my eyes away from him, and grabbed a T-shirt and a pair of cotton shorts from my aunt's closet, and locked myself in the bathroom. I splashed cold water onto my face, and definitely decided to forget about what he looked like without a shirt on. Not that I had stared at the cut of his muscles as they disappeared beneath his blue pajama bottoms. Not that I scrubbed my face raw trying to get the salacious thoughts out of my head.

Seriously, my *mouth* on his *birthmark*? Ugh.

Even though my aunt was gone, I swore I could hear her laughing at me from wherever she was now.

See, darling? she would say. *You can plan everything in your life, and you'll still be taken by surprise.*

And—worse yet—this was a surprise I was beginning to like. That scared me the most. The way I kept wondering how to paint his eyes—more blue, probably, layered after the diluted gray dried. The way I remembered what his hands felt like in mine, calloused and gentle, how his other hand, as we danced, followed the ridges of my spine down my back, a little too far and not far enough.

Something, something well-laid plans.

And it—all of it, the way I'd paint his eyes, the touch of his hand on my lower back as we danced, his crooked smile, the champagne-feeling of fizzy bubbles in my chest whenever he met my gaze—terrified me.

"One more time," I muttered as I crept out of the bathroom and grabbed my purse and keys. "Try one more time."

There were no sounds from my aunt's room, so I figured Iwan had already gone to bed. If I left, closed the door, and came back—maybe he'd be gone. Maybe the apartment wouldn't send me back to this time again.

So that's exactly what I did.

"Goodbye," I whispered, sort of hating that I wasn't going to say it to his face, but this was for the best. I needed to leave. Nothing good could happen if I stayed.

I opened the door. I stepped outside.

I waited one—two—*three*—

I counted all the way to seven. A lucky number.

Then I inserted the key and turned the lock, and as I held my breath, I opened the door and stepped back in.

And as the door closed, I realized I was in very, very big trouble.

So I crept down the hall to the bedroom and slid onto the left side of the bed. Iwan was already breathing deeply, turned onto his side, the moonlight casting white across his auburn hair, turning the ginger to fire. There were holes in his ear from where, I assumed, he used to have earrings, and the tattoo of a very small whisk behind his left ear, and I realized he wasn't the kind of guy I went for, and I certainly wasn't the kind of girl he'd like. Strait-laced and anxious, a broken and horrible mess with walls so high I'd forgotten what I'd blocked off on the other side.

"Go to sleep, Lemon," he muttered, his Southern drawl thick with sleep.

Mortified, I quickly slipped under the covers, turned my back to him, and waited for either sleep or death to claim me.

10

(Sub)liminal Spaces

MORNING LIGHT TRICKLED IN through the bedroom curtains. My head was fuzzy, the comforter kicked off halfway through the night. I curled my arm around the pillow in the middle of the bed and burrowed my head into it. It was warm, and the apartment was quiet. I'd had such a lovely dream—that I had dinner with a man who could actually *cook* for once. I'd never dated anyone who could do anything in the kitchen beyond grilled cheese. He had a nice smile, too, and beautiful eyes, and I wanted to laugh at myself because I would *never* do half the things I did in that dream. I wouldn't let him stay in my aunt's apartment. I wouldn't dance with him in the kitchen. We wouldn't sleep in the same bed, with a pillow between us.

. . . A pillow that I was very surely hugging right then.

And, suddenly, it all came crashing back to me. I woke up with a start, and scrambled to sit up, grabbing the clock on the nightstand: 10:04 a.m. I looked around. It was my aunt's bedroom. Her monstera plant wilted in the corner, her tapestry from Lebanon on the wall.

Yesterday had been real.

Oh—oh, *no.*

I buried my head in the pillow and took a deep breath.

"Get up," I told myself. Iwan must be around here somewhere. His indentation was still in the bed beside me, but it was no longer warm. When had he woken up? I was such a heavy sleeper, I wouldn't even wake up if an atomic bomb went off. God, I hoped I hadn't *drooled* in my sleep.

I swung my legs over the side of the bed and pushed myself to my feet. His toiletries were still in the bathroom (not that I checked) and his duffel bag was still on the far side of my aunt's dresser (I just *casually* saw it while leaving the room), but he was nowhere to be found.

A lonely, heavy feeling knotted in the middle of my chest as I stepped into the kitchen. He'd put the dishes away this morning, everything returned to where they'd been the night before, though I straightened the wineglasses into neat rows and stacked the utensils on top of each other in the drawers, where he'd haphazardly put them. It was automatic, really, a way to keep my hands busy. The apartment was so quiet without anyone else here, the sounds of the city muted, a dull hum of car engines and pigeon coos and people.

As I opened the bread box to get out a bagel, I noticed a piece of paper on the counter, trapped under a pen, with scratchy handwriting across it.

Gone to get that esteemed dishwashing gig. Coffee's hot! —I

That peculiar knot unwound in my chest at the sight of it. I hadn't known I had wanted to see him again until I realized that I could, and I hated that there was a knot there to begin with. I took the piece of paper, began to ball it up to throw it into the trash can under the sink, but resisted the urge, and put it back. Then I slipped into the bathroom to wash my face and brush my teeth, since my mouth tasted sour from last night's wine. I put on some mascara so I didn't look half as dead as I felt. How did Iwan get *up* so early? He had had almost as much to drink as I had—then again, he was a good five years younger than me, too. And there was a gap between *early twenties* and *late twenties* that only people existing in bodies in their *late twenties* understood. You could still fight god, but you'd have to ice your knees afterward.

By the time the bagel popped out of the toaster, I'd washed my face and pulled my hair back into a tiny ponytail. The coffeepot was still warm, so I took advantage of it and poured myself a cup.

It smelled good, at least.

I slipped onto the barstool to enjoy my breakfast, listening to the pigeons coo on their AC unit, and tried to convince myself that this guy wasn't growing on me.

"Damn it," I whispered because he made really excellent coffee, too.

⸻

HE WAS GONE FOR the majority of the day, and Sundays were usually when I stayed in and caught up on my TV shows—the few that I still watched. Mainly *Survivor* and whatever show Drew and Fiona bullied me into watching, claiming I'd love it. However, my aunt never paid for cable *or* internet, and it wasn't exactly like my phone could connect to Wi-Fi seven years in the future, so I decided to snoop instead.

Just a little.

Just to stave off the boredom.

I wasn't going to at first, but his duffel bag was *right there* in the bedroom, and I kept passing it every time I walked in. Just a little peek, I reasoned, sliding the duffel bag out from beside the dresser. I began to unzip it, but my conscience got the better of me.

It was rude to go through someone else's things, and he hadn't really given me a *reason* not to trust him.

"You can't control everything," I whispered to myself, and pushed down the tendency. "It's probably just clothes and stuff anyway."

But ignoring the temptation was a lot harder than I gave myself credit for, because while he'd told me a lot about himself, I found myself wanting to know . . . *everything*. Where he went to high school. His first crush.

His favorite color.

With one last tempting look at the duffel, I closed the bedroom door behind me so I wouldn't be coaxed into snooping by my own bad thoughts, and went into my aunt's study.

I needed to distract myself.

I could leave the apartment, but what if it didn't bring me back here when I returned? That's exactly what I wanted, and the door was right there, the chance for me to leave . . .

I really should, I realized, because there was nothing keeping me here, and while Iwan was really hot, I definitely wasn't about to break the time-space continuum to be with him. That wasn't how this story went.

Leaving was the best option, but would the apartment just keep sending me back here, again and again? I grabbed my purse and stared at the front door. "We're going to play nice," I told the apartment, grabbed the doorknob, and opened it out into the hallway—

Just as a woman ambled by, walking her ferret on a rhinestone leash. She nodded in greeting, even though her gaze lingered too long on me. "Clementine," she greeted, "nice to see you."

"You, too, Emiko," I replied, pulling my purse self-consciously higher on my shoulder.

"You're certainly fashionable today."

That was when it occurred to me: I still had on my pajamas. A blush rose quickly on my ears. "Yeah, well—uh—just testing my door." I motioned to the door behind me, then inserted the key and pushed myself back inside.

The door closed with a resounding *click*.

And I knew even before I stepped back into the living room that it had sent me back again. The coffee was still warm, the note was still on the counter, and I had exhausted my options. I could go to my parents' tonight, if I really wanted to. Maybe Drew and Fiona could put me up on their couch for an evening. But the thought of admitting defeat tasted sour in my mouth.

I'd always wanted it to magic me away, and now that it had, I kept asking it to take me back.

"Fine," I called to the apartment, admitting defeat. "You win! I'll stay."

It might have been my imagination, but the pigeons on the sill sounded smug as they cooed in reply.

I dropped my purse on the couch again and shuffled back into my aunt's study to find something to do. It still smelled the same as I remembered. Of old books and weathered leather and crinkly paperbacks with broken spines, romances and adventures and fantasies and travel guides, paperweights to picture books. When she wasn't traveling, my aunt read. She pored over stories, drowned herself in words. In the summers between our adventures, she'd build a pillow fort and crawl underneath it, lit with fairy lights and lavender-scented candles in mason jars, and we'd read together. Sometimes I spent entire weekends adventuring with Eloise or solving mysteries with Harriet.

There was something just so reassuring about books. They had beginnings and middles and ends, and if you didn't like a part, you could skip to the next chapter. If someone died, you could stop on the last page before, and they'd live on forever. Happy endings were definite, evils defeated, and the good lasted forever.

And books about travel? They promised wide-eyed wonders. They waxed poetically about the history and the culture of the places, like an anthropologist of once-in-a-lifetime experiences.

On one of our first trips together—I think I was nine at the time—I was bored out of my mind on a tour of some stuffy English castle. The group had been filled with older people, and I was the only kid along on the bus ride. I'd forgotten my sketchbook—I'd loved painting since I was a child (my parents always said that my first Christmas gift was a washable watercolor set)—so I began to doodle on the brochure instead, until my aunt opened her travel guide and pointed to the place we were going, paragraphs upon paragraphs of history on the page, and said, "Why don't you draw on this? It'll make it more exciting."

So that's what I did.

Markers gave way to inks, and then back to watercolors, and it just became a hobby of mine, and I had painted in our travel guides every trip since. The guides lined a bookshelf, from all the different places around the world she'd taken me, their spines cracked and their pages buckled from the watercolors.

It eventually made sense that I wanted to work with books— especially travel books. It was easy work because I already loved it all. The feeling of a naked hardback under my fingers, the smell of new ink, the fresh slice of a page when you dog-eared it, the crinkle of a paperback's spine.

The promise of a secret place only the author knows.

I began to take out a book—a guide to Bolivia—when a tin on

the edge of a shelf caught my eye. It was small, stained with different colors, but I recognized it in an instant. It was my travel watercolor set—one of my older ones, because that year, my aunt had surprised me with a brand-new tin with deeper, richer colors, and I'd painted my way across Amsterdam and Prague. The tin was small—about the size of my palm, with six thumbnail-sized wells of watercolors inside.

The colors weren't flaky like I expected, expired, but just a little dry. With some water, they could come back to life quite easily. There was even a small paintbrush nestled at the top of the tin. I took it, and got an idea. The travel guide to New York City that I'd picked up at work was still in my purse, so I went to get it and gathered a few pillows from the couch (including Jeff Goldblum) and headed for the bathroom. My aunt always joked that I made myself a nest in the tub like a pigeon, but it was really the only place she'd *let* me paint after I accidentally spilled watercolors all over her brand-new rug.

"You can't mess anything up in here!" she had announced, brandishing a hand toward the bathroom. "And anything you can, a little bleach will fix."

I settled into the dry bathtub and dampened my watercolors, waking them up from their slumbers. Most of the wells were almost empty, the last dregs of color clinging to their corners like shadows. Then I flipped to a page of a sight I knew well—Bow Bridge, and the rowboats filled with tourists who sailed under it. Strokes of blues and greens, the creamy brown sandstone of the bridge, pops of white shirts from brightly dressed romantic leads, confessing their love while paddling across the lake.

As I painted, the watercolor hung on the wall—a moon in a sea of clouds—kept me company. I'd painted it for my aunt years ago, and she'd been so delighted she'd taken it to a frame shop that very day.

"You gave me the moon, my darling!" she had said happily. "Oh, what a lovely and impossible gift."

She had always told me to chase the moon. To surround myself with people who would lasso it down in a heartbeat.

It was easy for her. She was the main character in her own story, and she knew it.

And, for a part of it, I think she was the main character in mine, too. Compared to her, I was a shadow. While she went off exploring Milan, I followed after her with a map. While she hiked up to castles, I hung back with the tour guide and made sure to pack a first aid kit. She told ghost stories, and I disproved her by uncovering air vents, and no matter how saccharine those memories were, I was still caught in the sour taste of a world without her.

Eventually, something began to come of my painting. I lost myself in the colors, the whimsical way they bled together. I couldn't remember the last time I had actually let myself paint. Usually I was busy with work, and then when my aunt died, creating hurt too much, because she had always been the one to gift me watercolor sets, to search out beautiful landscapes and plant me down on a bench, and let me paint for hours while she went shopping in thrift stores and tourist shops. She probably should never have left a teenage girl *alone* on a bench on the Seine, or at the Acropolis, or in the garden of a teahouse, but those were some of my favorite memories from those trips: when I saw the world in different shades of blues and greens and golds, blending them together, layering them, finding the perfect shade of azure for the sky.

It felt nice to do something for *me* again. To just *be*.

No to-do lists to keep pushing myself through, no expectations. Just me.

And while I didn't feel like the child who used to curl up in a claw-foot tub to paint, I did feel . . . *safe*.

I still felt alone—I doubted that would change—but I didn't feel like I'd rattle apart. The truth was, I had been isolated for the last few months, ever since Analea died, because it was the only way to keep myself together. My parents had each other to cry on when the grief rose in the middle of the night.

I had no one, alone in an apartment in Brooklyn.

I didn't have anyone to rub my back and tell me that it was okay not to be okay. I had to tell myself as I sat on my kitchen floor in the middle of the night and cried into a pillow so I wouldn't wake up my neighbors.

The past was the past was the past, and it couldn't be changed. Even if I somehow met her here in this apartment seven years in the past, it wouldn't change anything. She would still die. I would still find myself on the floor crying at two in the morning.

And then Nate came along three months later and thought he could fix me, I guess, with a little well-placed love. Except I didn't need to be fixed. I'd gone through the worst day of my life by myself, and I came out the other side a person who survived it. That was not something to fix.

I didn't need to be *fixed*. I just needed . . . to be reminded that I was human.

And dinner with a stranger who didn't look at me like I was broken had been a surprisingly good start.

Burn, Baby, Burn

EVENTUALLY, I STOPPED PAINTING and drew myself a bath.

I sank down into the hot water, the lavender and chamomile from the soap I'd used soft and calming, and I stared up at the crown molding on the ceiling, all of the intricate swirls and gilded patterns characteristic of the Monroe. I must've dozed off at some point, because the next thing I knew the front door was opening, and I heard someone cross the apartment. Their footsteps were heavy. I rubbed my eyes with my pruny fingers.

I sat up in the bath.

Iwan.

I reached for my phone on the stool. Five p.m. *already?*

"Lemon? I'm back," he called, his footsteps coming closer.

"Here!" I replied, trying not to panic. "I'm—um—in the bath!"

His footsteps suddenly stopped. "O-*oh!*"

I winced. *Nice going, Clementine*, I thought to myself. *You should've just said not to come in.* My ears burned with embarrassment. "Don't make it weird!"

He sputtered. "I'm not making it weird, you're making it weird!"

"You made it weird first!"

"I didn't *say* anything!"

"You said *Oh*!"

"Should I have said something different?"

I buried my face in my hands. "Just—just ignore me. I'm going to go drown myself in the tub. Goodbye."

He chuckled. "Well, don't drown yourself for too long. I'm cooking again tonight," he added, and his footsteps faded into the kitchen.

I quickly reached for my towel and pulled myself out of the bath. I heard him in the kitchen, putting things away, as I dried myself off and remembered that I hadn't picked out any clothes. "Shit," I muttered, and opened the bathroom closet to try to find one of her bathrobes. Instead, I found a lovely black satin robe with a marabou feather trim. It was utterly ridiculous—the kind of expensive robe wealthy women in old movies wore, complete with a long cigarette holder and a dead body in the foyer. I snorted, pulling it off the hanger. I'd almost forgotten that she had this monstrosity. A few years ago, it caught fire thanks to her Saint Dolly Parton candle, and she ended up tossing both out the window in a panic. The apartment smelled like melted feathers for weeks.

Well, it was better than a towel, at least.

I shrugged on the robe. It still smelled like her perfume. Red by Giorgio Beverly Hills. So distinctive and intense. She'd worn it for close to thirty years.

As I came out of the bathroom, Iwan glanced over at me, my hair damp, smelling slightly of lavender soap. He opened his mouth. Closed it again. Blinked—quite a few times. Then he said, quite seriously, "Ma'am, I've a very serious question to ask you: Did you murder your husband?"

I fluffed up the boa and adopted a terrible mid-Atlantic accent. "I'm sorry, Officer, I can't recall how my husband died. It must've been the pool boy! I'll have to get a new one."

He arched an eyebrow as he stood by the stove, where he slowly heated a large saucepan, half a dozen lemons on the counter beside him. "Pool boy or husband?"

"I'm not sure, what're your credentials?"

He flicked his gaze down the length of me. "I've a pretty healthy résumé," he replied in that soft, low Southern drawl of his. "And plenty of references."

I *tsk*ed. "For your character, I hope."

The edges of his mouth twitched as it turned into a sort of half smirk, and he really thought he was being suave as he leaned back against the stove—and gave a yelp. "*Sonova*—!" He quickly threw his hand into the air, but he'd already burned the shit out of the tip of his pinky finger, and stuck it in his mouth.

"Are you okay?" I asked in alarm, dropping my awful accent.

"Fine," he said around his pinky in his mouth. "I'm fine. 'Tis only a flesh wound."

I gave him a look and came over, taking his hand out of his mouth to inspect his finger. There was an angry red mark all the way across the inside of it. "We should put butter on it."

"*Butter?*" He sounded incredulous.

"Yes? My mom always does it."

He laughed then, and gently took his hand out of mine. He turned on the faucet and ran his pinky under the cool water. "This'll do just fine, I'd hate to mess up your aunt's Échiré."

It took me a moment to realize—"Her fancy butter has a *name?*"

"It's not fancy if it doesn't have a name," he replied gallantly, turning off the faucet while I grabbed a bandage from the first-aid kit in the medicine cabinet. He outstretched his hand again once he'd dried it, and I wrapped it in a Disney Band-Aid. "Would you like to kiss it?" he asked. "Make it feel better?"

"That doesn't work."

"About as well as butter, I suppose" was his reply.

"Well, in that case . . ." I really didn't like how smug he sounded, and in my aunt's feather boa, suddenly feeling brave, I brought his hand to my mouth and gently kissed the bandage.

His face turned a lovely pinkish-red, from his neck all the way to his scalp, making the freckles across his cheeks glow. And it was also strangely sexy, his curly hair messy from a day out in the city, his tie loosened and askew, dressed in a white button-down that didn't quite fit him, and black trousers that I was sure were a few years old at this point because they were frayed a little at the hems. Whenever I took a closer look at him, he was disorienting in the kind of way kaleidoscopes were, constantly moving and shifting, full of colors and shapes that shouldn't have gone together but did in a way that made it perfect.

He might have been the most handsome man I'd ever seen.

But especially when he blushed.

He swallowed, his Adam's apple bobbing with the difficulty, discombobulated.

I dropped his hand and said, "Butter works, by the way."

"I . . . uh." He looked at his bandaged finger.

"It feels better, doesn't it?"

His gaze fell to my lips. Lingered there. He bent toward me, millimeter by millimeter, and the closer he got, the more of him I drank in, his long eyelashes, the freckles across his cheeks and nose, multiplying by the moment. His lips looked soft. He had a

THE SEVEN YEAR SLIP

nice mouth—a kind one. It was hard to explain why it looked kind, but it did.

But then something made him pull back, second-guess himself, and my stomach twisted a little in regret. He cleared his throat. "Fine, fine. Butter *might* work," he said, busying himself with tossing in measurements of sugar, some sort of corn starch or flour, and salt, and the pinkish tint only remained at the edges of his ears.

Were you about to kiss me? I wanted to ask, and I wasn't sure if I wanted the answer to be no. But instead, I asked, "What's for dinner?"

"Oh, this is dessert," he replied, motioning to the lemons on the counter. "How do you feel about pizza tonight?"

"I think there's a number for delivery on the fridge . . ."

"I meant frozen."

I let out a laugh, though it sounded hollow to my ears. "Are you sure you're a chef?"

"I'm full of surprises, Lemon," he replied, teasing me with another grin, and we were back to before. It was silly to feel disappointed that he hadn't kissed me. This wasn't me at all. And, apparently, it wasn't him, either. "And besides," he added with a wink and shot me charming and—admittedly cringey—finger guns, "I'm making you a dessert tonight, instead."

12

The Moon and More

THE FROZEN PIZZA WAS exactly what it promised to be—it tasted like cardboard with a little bit of plastic cheese on top. And it was delicious in the same way that five-dollar pizzas from the supermarket and cheap wine always were—predictable and solid.

While we waited for it to cook, I had dug out some of my old jeans that still fit from my leftover clothes in my aunt's closet and put on a dark gray T-shirt that I'd lost in Spain two years ago, and he fixed up some sort of pie that smelled of lemons and popped it into the hot oven as we ate.

"How was the interview today?" I asked as I took my last slice. We'd gone through half the bottle of wine already, and picked through most of the pizza.

"Glorious," he said with a content sigh. "It was just like I remembered. They even still had the table my grandpa and I sat at."

"Was the head chef there? The one your grandpa liked?"

He crinkled his nose and shook his head. "Sadly, no. But I

think the interview went well! I was one of twenty-three applicants who made it to the final round."

"For a *dishwashing* gig?"

He picked a piece of pepperoni off his pizza and corrected, "For an opening at one of the most prestigious restaurants in SoHo. It's an institution, of course a lot of people want to work there."

I shook my head. "I can't believe you can't just start as a line cook."

"Maybe if I were more talented, sure," he replied with a shrug, and I didn't believe his false modesty one bit. There was a pie that he'd made *from scratch* in the oven, and I wasn't about to say I was a connoisseur, but I'd eaten my way around the world. I knew good food in the same way anyone who was well traveled enough knew the best pizzas were always in grease-stained hole-in-the-wall joints, the best tacos from tin-colored food trucks, the best falafel from street vendors, the best pasta from family-owned restaurants in the bowels of Rome. Iwan was talented.

The windows were open tonight, and a soft breeze came in from the street, fluttering the gauzy white curtains. The two pigeons that roosted on the AC were cooing in their little nest, Mother and Fucker enjoying the evening.

"So," he said, changing the subject, "what've you been doing all day?"

"Taking a bath," I replied, and when he arched an eyebrow, I sighed and said, "I accidentally fell asleep in the bath. Before that I was . . ." I frowned. "In the tub."

"Just in the tub?"

I hesitated, setting down my last crust of pizza. I wasn't really hungry for it, anyway. There was no reason *not* to tell him, especially after he'd shared so much with me last night. "Don't laugh, but I was always a messy painter as a kid. I'd get watercolors every-where and my aunt would be livid, so she set me up in the bath-room and told me to go wild. So that's what I was doing. You know, before I took a bath."

He seemed surprised—in the best way. "Painting?"

I nodded.

When Nate found out about my hobby, as he stumbled across my landscapes and my still lifes and my portraits, all tucked into my closet, his eyes glowed with the possibility of selling them. Monetizing my passion. "Make it work for you. You're fantastic at it."

But I already worked in an industry that sold art as commodi-ties, and I really didn't want to go down that path. I didn't like painting because *other* people might like it; I liked painting because I appreciated the way the colors blended, the way blues and yellows always turned green. The way reds and greens turned brown. There was a certainty to it all, and when there wasn't, there was always a reason.

And, besides, by the time Nate and I got together, I'd stopped painting entirely.

"Could I see?" Iwan asked, and when I didn't respond immedi-ately, he quickly added, "You don't have to. It's okay. It's something for you, right?" he guessed. "It's private."

I stared at him for a long moment, because that was it exactly. I'd always had to explain it. "Yes. It's for me."

He nodded, like he understood. "Cooking was like that for me. I liked keeping it secret—just between me and my granddad. It felt powerful, you know? This little thing that no one else knew about."

"And if you show it to anyone else, you're afraid it might spoil."

"Yeah, that's it."

"But you did—obviously. Since you cooked for me."

He gave a one-shouldered shrug. "I thought I just wanted it to be a pastime, but then I decided . . . what the hell?"

I looked down at the tiny bit of paint still stuck under my fingernails. "Do you regret it?"

He cocked his head in thought. "Ask me in a few years."

If I find you, I thought, *I will.*

Though I couldn't imagine that he would—there was a certain kind of person who took hold of their passion and never let it spoil. He'd never lose sight of why he wanted to be a chef in the first place.

I admitted, "The painting in the bathroom? Of the moon? It's mine."

He thought, his eyebrows creasing as he recalled the painting, and then his eyes lit up. "Oh, that one! It's lovely. Do you have others around the apartment?"

To that, I smiled and tapped a finger to my lips. "I do. I'll show them to you next time," I said, "if you remember to ask me."

"Deal," he agreed. "They're probably right under my nose."

I thought about the travel guides in my aunt's study. He had no idea. I cocked my head. "You know, it's weird. Today was the first time I've painted in . . . half a year? Yeah, that seems right."

He whistled. "That's a long time. Why did you stop?"

I felt my body tense. "Someone broke my heart," I said softly.

"Oh . . . I'm sorry, Lemon."

I shrugged, and tried to play it off. "It's okay. My last boyfriend tried to get me to paint again, but I just didn't have it in me. I didn't have it in me to do a lot of things with him, to be honest. He said I was too closed-off." I put the words in air quotes. "I didn't even cry when we broke up."

"That doesn't mean you didn't love him."

"It was three months," I replied, dismissing his idea. "I'm sure I didn't. My aunt always said you know the moment you fall."

He studied me for a moment. "Maybe you do."

"Have *you* ever been in love?" And then I asked, trying to joke with him, "Is that why you're *really* in the city? To chase after someone? It's okay," I added conspiratorially, "you can admit it to me. I won't tell a soul."

To which he smiled, crooked and charming, as if he was about to tell me a secret he'd never told anyone else in the world. He leaned toward me. "And if I have?"

I sat up a little straighter. "Do they know?"

"Sadly, yes," he replied. "But alas, pommes frites are a cruel beast, and my body rejects them with . . . *heartburn*!" He dramatically clutched his chest, and I rolled my eyes.

"Okay, I guess I deserved that."

"Mm-hmm." He took my hand and pulled me to stand. "And if you have time to plot out my fictitious love life," he said, pulling me into the kitchen, "you have time to—"

"*Please* don't say dance."

"—to whip some cream for me while I take the pie out of the oven and chill it for a bit."

The dread quickly turned into relief. "Oh, *that*." Then I realized what he'd said. "Wait, *I'm* helping you?"

"It'll be easy, I promise."

Somehow, I didn't believe him. I ruined SpaghettiOs in the microwave, so I didn't have a lot of confidence that I could whip anything. He grabbed my aunt's hummingbird oven mitts and took the pie out of the oven. The scent of lemons exploded into the apartment, warm and gooey and citrusy. He popped it in the quick-freeze and pulled me over to a bowl, and dashed in the ingredients in rapid succession—he had everything premeasured in the refrigerator and chilled, and told me to keep whisking the ingredients until stiff peaks formed. I just nodded and did as I was told, and apparently my whipped cream peaks were beautiful.

"I have no idea what that means," I replied, my arms feeling like Jell-O, as he checked on the pie in the quick-freeze, and he took out the cream, spreading it over the pie.

He grinned, "It means you're a natural."

"At whipping? Or the cream?"

"What is that, a sense of *humor*?"

I laughed and elbowed him in the side. "Shut up."

But he just kept grinning as he took the pie over to the table, and I followed with two plates from the cabinet and two forks. We sat down and I handed him one, and we clinked them together in a sort of cheers.

"You first," he decided, motioning to the pie. "The suspense is killing me. In this recipe, I substitute meringue with whipped cream. It's a twist on key lime, with lemons obviously, with a graham-cracker crust. Simple, really. Arguably too simple, especially without the meringue."

"Why no meringue?"

He shrugged. "The whipped cream has hints of lemon. It's close enough."

". . . Can you not make meringue?"

"Alas," he sighed, and set his head on his hand, "my only enemy. To be fair, I didn't make the whipped cream, either. You did."

"So, you *aren't* perfect?" I mock gasped, reeling away.

He rolled his eyes. "I'd be boring if I was perfect. I've always been bad at meringue, ever since culinary school. The peaks never peaked and I'm wholly impatient. My biggest downfall."

"*That's* your biggest downfall?"

He honest-to-god thought about it for a moment before nodding. "Yes. Yes, it is."

"Huh." Because I was very sure if he found out the laundry list of my flaws, he'd be running for the hills. I twirled my fork around in my fingers and stabbed it into the pie.

Then I scooped up a forkful and tasted it. The warm, gooey acidity of the pie, along with the grittiness of the graham cracker, the sweetness of the whipped cream, with a pinch of lemon zest—it was such a lovely bouquet of flavors and textures. It reminded me of a lemon grove.

He waited patiently. Then, as if true to his word, a bit impatiently. He drummed his fingers on the table.

Shifted in his seat.

Gave a huff.

Finally, he asked, ". . . *Well?*"

I bit the tines of the fork between my teeth, looking from him to the pie, and then to him again. He really *was* impatient, wasn't he?

His face fell. "It's terrible, isn't it? I messed up. I forgot an ingredient. I—"

"You should be ashamed," I interrupted, pointing my fork at him.

In alarm, he grabbed it and took a bite.

"We ate pizza when we could have been having *this* the whole time?" I finished, as he chewed and sank back into his chair, swallowing his bite. "For future reference, I am perfectly okay with dessert for dinner."

He gave me a morose look. "You really had me going there, Lemon." He sighed in relief, and then realized—"So you'll have dinner with me again? In the future?"

"Of course. I'm still waiting for that split-pea soup," I replied nobly, and took another bite. "Why were you so nervous this wouldn't be good?"

"It was my grandfather's recipe—which isn't really a recipe at all," he replied, handing the fork back to me, "so it's a bit different every time."

A bit different every time.

Like Vera's fettuccine.

The phrase was like a gut punch—a reminder of my aunt's second rule. Never fall in love in this apartment.

"He always says food brings people together, and that's really what I love about it." He smiled a little at the memory, though there was this distant look in his eyes. Was that how I looked whenever I talked about my aunt? "How it can be a language all its own," he went on, putting his elbows on the table, his head perched on his hands. "I've had entire conversations with people I've never spoken a word to. You can say things with food that you can't quite with words sometimes."

And there he went again, his passion for this art I had taken for granted turned into poetry. I would read encyclopedias if he wrote them with this sort of wonderlust.

Taking another bite, the sweetness of the cream dancing with the tart lemon, making my teeth curl in delight, I said, "Ah, you're talking about a perfect meal again."

"It all comes full circle," he replied, the edges of his mouth twisting up in a smile. "Universal truths in butter. Secrets folded into the dough. Poetry in the spices. Romance in a chocolate. Love in a lemon pie."

I set my elbows on the table, my head propped on my hands, mirroring him. "Truth be told, I've always found my lovers in a good cheese."

"Asiago is very sassy."

"A nice cheddar's never let me down."

"You go with *cheddar*? That's so . . . like you, honestly."

I gave a gasp. "You mean *boring*, don't you!"

"I didn't say that, you said that."

"I'll have you know, cheddar is a *very* respectable cheese. And versatile, too! You can put cheddar on anything. Not like some of those other *fancier* cheeses, like—like gouda or mozzarella or rock—rocke—"

He tilted his head toward me and whispered, "Roquefort."

"Yes, that one!" I said, pointing my fork at him. "Or chèvre. Or gouda . . ."

"You already said that one."

His face hovered so close to mine as he leaned over the table, I could smell the aftershave on his skin. My stomach was burning. "Or"—My brain struggled to think of another one.—"Parmesan . . ."

"I've always liked cheddar," he finally said. This close, his eyes were more blue and green than gray, growing darker and stormier the longer I stared. I wondered if I could see his future in his eyes, what kind of man he'd be in seven years—but all I saw was a twenty-something a little lost in a new city, waiting to be the person he'd become.

If he liked cheddar, then did he like safe and boring, too? *Me?* No, I was getting carried away. Of course that wasn't what he meant, but he was still so close, and my skin prickled from the heat I felt from his body. His eyes dropped to my lips again, as if debating on whether to take the chance.

And then he asked, his voice barely above a whisper, a secret, "May I kiss you?"

I sucked in a breath. I wanted to and I shouldn't and it was probably the *worst* decision in the world and—

I nodded.

He leaned over the table and pressed his lips to mine. Then we broke away—just for a moment, a sharp intake of breath—and crushed our mouths together again. I curled my fingers around the front of his dress shirt and tugged at his already loose tie. He cupped my face with his hands, and drank me in. I melted into him faster than ice cream on a hot sidewalk. He kissed like he wanted to savor me.

"I fear I have, indeed, gotten the wrong idea," he murmured when we finally broke away, his words hot against my lips, voice deep and hoarse. "Despite my best efforts."

I felt starved—the wild girl I wanted to be but never quite was, the kind who yearned to devour the world, one sensation at a time. The softness of his lips, the hunger there. I wrapped his tie around my hand, drawing him closer to me, and he made a noise in his throat as I pulled him near.

"We both might've gotten the wrong idea," I agreed. "I like it, though. We could try it again?"

His eyes darkened like a hurricane on the horizon, and as I tugged him toward me, he came willingly, and kissed me harder on the mouth, threading his fingers into my hair. His tongue played along my bottom lip, teasing, and he tasted like lemon pie, sweet and summery. My belly burned, ached, as his thumb slid along my jawline, slowly tracing it down toward my neck. His touch was light and soft, the callouses on his fingertips rough against my skin, summoning goose bumps. I shivered. And he smelled amazing—like aftershave and laundry detergent and graham-cracker crust.

I didn't realize how hungry I was for touch, for something good, something *warm and sweet*, until I got a taste.

"Don't fall in love in this apartment," my aunt had warned, but this wasn't love. It wasn't, it wasn't, it wasn't—

The way he kissed me, so thoroughly I felt it in my toes, the way

I pulled him to me, my hand wrapped around his tie, the way I thought about if he was so good with his tongue now, how much better would he be in a few years—

No, this wasn't *love*.

After all, I didn't know what love—romantic love, toe-curling love—felt like. So how could I fall for it?

This wasn't it. It couldn't be.

"You kiss like you dance," he murmured against my mouth.

I broke away, suddenly appalled. "*Terribly?*"

He laughed, but it was low and deep in his throat, half a growl, as he stole another kiss again. "Like someone waiting to be asked. You can just dance, Lemon. You can take the lead."

"And you'll follow?"

"To the moon and back," he replied, and I leaned forward, my hands pressed against his hard chest, and kissed him again. Harder. Over the lemon pie. My insides felt like Pop Rocks, fizzy and bright. He made a noise against my mouth, a growl that rumbled through his chest as his long, long fingers curled further into my hair, his teeth nibbling on my bottom lip—

Suddenly, he pushed the lemon pie aside, wineglasses clattering as they bumped against the wall, and I put a knee on the table, halfway onto it, just to get a little closer. Just a little more. I wanted to press myself into him. I wanted to lose myself in his smell, in his calloused touch, in the way he painted words like poetry.

Romance wasn't in *chocolate*, it was in the gasp of breath as we came up for air. It was in the way he cradled my face, the way I traced my finger over the crescent-shaped birthmark on his collarbone. It was in the way he muttered how beautiful I was, the way it made my heart soar. It was in the way I wanted to know everything about him—his favorite songs, finally guess his favorite color. His mouth migrated toward my neck, feeling my pulse quick and loud at my throat. Pressing a kiss under my ear—

He will never stay, my darling Clementine, I heard my aunt say, crystal clear in my head. I could see her sitting in her wingback chair, remembering Vera. *No one stays.*

"Wait," I gasped, breaking myself away from him. My heart was quick and loud in my head. "Wait—is this smart? *Should* we? This might be a bad idea."

He froze. "What?"

"This—this might be a bad idea," I repeated, letting my hand unwind from his tie. My lips felt tender, my cheeks flushed.

He blinked, tonguing his bottom lip, his gaze still drunk on our kisses. "You could never be a bad idea, Lemon."

But what if you are? I thought, biting the inside of my lip. Because there I was, teetering on the precipice of something. I could tip over and never see the top again, or I could remain perfectly balanced where I was.

And then I looked into his grayish-blue eyes, and I knew exactly how I'd paint them—I'd paint them like the moon. Layers of white, gradually growing darker, with shadows of blue. Now, though, they were like storm clouds out at sea in the golden evening light—

And I was a fool.

". . . Lemon? You have that look again," he said in concern. I snapped out of my thoughts, embarrassment flooding my cheeks. He had come around the table, and knelt down in front of me, his hand on my knee, his thumb gently rubbing circles there. "Lemon?"

"Sorry." I pressed my hands against my face. "I'm so sorry."

"No, no, it's okay." Gently, he tugged my hands away from my face, looking up at me with nothing but concern. What a lovely man. I sank down against him, my face buried into his shoulder, where I—awfully—fit so perfectly. He was so warm and comfortable, and I hated that I loved it. "I'm sorry," I repeated again, because I wasn't sure how else to voice it—how much I wanted this, wanted him, but there were things my heart couldn't handle anymore, still brittle and small, broken from something else that couldn't stay.

I was broken, and I was alone, and I wished he had found *me* seven years ago, instead.

"I'm sorry. I'm sorry . . ."

"Hey—hey, don't apologize, don't be sorry, there's nothing to be sorry for," he said, gently dislodging me from his shoulder so he could look at my face, pushing my hair behind my ear. He cradled my cheek in his warm hand. "It's okay. It's okay, really."

This is where normal girls would have cried, because his voice was so gentle, so comforting. This is where they would have let their heart overflow, and bring down their walls, but my eyes didn't even sting with tears. I think I had cried them all out in the last six months. I think I had run dry. Because as I looked down into his face and his lovely pale eyes, all I could feel was a hollow pit in the center of my stomach.

I wish I could tell you a story, I thought, *and I wish you would believe it.*

But he wouldn't. I was old enough to know that for a fact. Because while he believed in romance, in chocolates, and love over lemon pies, the story of a girl seven years out of time sounded a bit too abstract, even for his ears, and I couldn't bear the thought of the way he'd look at me once I told my story, half pitying, half disappointed, that I had to make up a lie about a time slip instead of telling him the truth.

Instead, I leaned my face against his hand and kissed his palm. "Can we finish our dessert? And talk some more?"

He stood and kissed my forehead. "Of course, Lemon. I would love nothing more."

My heart clenched, because he was so lovely, and I was so relieved—happy, even—that he understood.

He returned to his chair, took his fork, and asked me about my favorite paintings. Why van Gogh? Where did I like to travel? What was my favorite snack? If I could have dinner with anyone, past or present, who would it be and why? And he made me laugh over the rest of the lemon pie, and we drank wine, still with the taste of his lips on my tongue, the memory of the kisses that, for all intents and purposes, never were.

13

||||||||||

Back to the Grind

WHEN I WOKE UP, the bed beside me was empty, and Iwan had left a
note on the counter that read:

Fresh coffee in the pot. — I

He must have already left to see about that dishwashing gig
again—I hadn't even heard him get up. After we finished the bottle of wine the night before, we went to bed, fingers laced together
and foreheads pressed against each other's, the moonlight sharp
and silver, painting soft lines across our bodies, and we talked
some more. About his sister, about his grandfather's dream restaurant, about my parents and their soft, routine way of life. He asked
about the scar slashed through my eyebrow, and I asked about his
tattoos—the bunch of cilantro on his arm for his grandpa (they
both had that gene where it tasted like soap); initials on his torso,
mysterious and faded; a whisk behind his ear because he thought

it was funny, among others. We talked about where I'd traveled, where he'd never been.

"You've *never* eaten at a Waffle House?" he'd asked, aghast.

"My aunt and I passed a few on the road trip we took that one time, but . . . no? Why, am I missing something?"

"WaHos are the best. They never close, and when they do? You know a natural disaster's on its way, so you better get the fuck out of there. Their hash browns are either the best things in the world or so soggy they're soup. It's only the greatest modern tavern experience in the world."

"That can't be true."

"I promise," he replied firmly, "nothing is quite like a Waffle House at two in the morning."

I wondered, vaguely, as I slipped on my blouse, where the closest Waffle House was to me. Would I get amazing hash browns, or greasy soup? Would I find him there, haunting the booths? It made me wonder where he was, really, right now. Seven years later.

"I'll see you later," I told the apartment as I grabbed my purse and keys, and left. Earl was at the front desk reading another James Patterson, and he tipped his hat to me as I hurried out the door.

Now that I was out of the apartment, the city pushed on around me, ever moving forward, and it was so discombobulating at first.

In my aunt's apartment, it almost felt like time stood still.

I was so lost in my own thoughts, between my aunt's apartment and Strauss & Adder, I didn't notice Drew and Fiona in the elevator beside me until Fiona said, looking a bit bedraggled, "You look like sunshine and unicorn farts."

I patted my flyaway bangs down. "I do?"

Drew said, "You're *beaming* with it."

"It's irritating," Fiona added, jabbing the close-door button before more people could jam their way into the elevator. It was already ten strong, and we were scrunched near the back.

My cheeks went pink as I thought about Iwan. And Iwan's mouth. The way he tasted. "I spent all weekend painting, that's all." Not quite a lie.

"Ooh, painting what?" Drew asked.

"That new New York City travel guide that Kate worked on?" I said.

"Oh! I saw one on the freebie shelf. You took it? What did you paint first?"

"Bow Bridge," I replied, and studied the two of them. They looked like the walking dead. "I take it you two didn't have a good weekend?"

"Understatement of the year," Drew muttered, looking at the ceiling. "*We* spent all weekend getting the baby corner ready. And by *we*, I mean I did. This one 'supervised.'" She put the word in air quotes.

"You did great, sweetie," Fiona replied and kissed her cheek.

The elevator opened on our floor, and we fought our way to the front and out into the lobby. Drew split off to her desk while Fiona and I went to the kitchen to fix our morning coffees. It was only when Drew was out of sight that Fiona stepped closer to me and whispered, "I was *worried* about you!"

I gave her a strange look. "Worried? Why?"

She sighed in exasperation and grabbed a coffee cup from the dishwasher. "You didn't respond to *any* of my texts this weekend!"

I stared at her, and then it clicked. "*Oh*—oh, you know my aunt's apartment gets bad reception."

She scrunched her nose. "I didn't realize *that* bad . . ."

I took my phone out of my purse, and lo and behold, I had quite a few messages from Fiona—a photo of her and Drew putting up a forest-themed nursery and getting angry with the IKEA crib. "*Oh*. Oh, I'm so sorry! I didn't even look at my phone. That's a lovely color."

She didn't look like she believed me as she popped a decaffeinated coffee pod into the coffee maker. "It is . . . ?"

"Absolutely—"

"Good morning!" Rhonda breezed into the kitchen, the smell of her perfume strong and her heels loud. "We have a meeting!" she singsonged. "Best not be late!" And she gave me a meaningful look. Right—because starting now, I was on trial. If I wanted to prove myself to Rhonda, that I could fill her shoes, I needed to be at the top of my game. And I would be. This was what I wanted, after all.

Couldn't screw this up.

Fiona eyed Rhonda as she left with her morning breakfast blend, and whispered, "*She's* in a good mood . . . it makes me suspicious."

"She's usually in a good mood," I replied, and Fiona gave me a deadpan look. "What? She is. Better go before that changes."

"Wait—I'm not done interrogating you!"

"You can later," I promised, and quickly fixed myself a cup of coffee, dumped my purse by my desk, and grabbed my notebook and pen before rushing down the hall and into the meeting room.

When we all took our seats, Rhonda jumped at the chance to begin. "I just had the loveliest weekend, and I really hope all of you did, too! Which brings me to my first order of business . . ." She started with marketing design—checking up on the state of ads, whether that new video that would play in front of *Entertainment Weekly* was done, whether they'd fixed the typo in one of the Google ads, etcetera.

I thought about googling Iwan to see if he still worked at that French restaurant, whichever restaurant that was. Maybe I could surprise him. Maybe he'd be sous by now. Maybe he'd won awards.

Or—maybe—he'd gone back home.

". . . Clementine? Did you hear me?"

I sat a little taller in my swivel chair, mortified that I'd been in my own head. "I-I'm sorry. What?"

Rhonda gave me a curious look. "I asked about the media placements for Mallory Grey's books. We don't want her bumping into that last Ann Nichols novel from Falcon House."

"Right, yes." I glanced down at my notes and tried to push Iwan out of my head. The rest of the meeting was just a quick rundown of the week's work. The books that launched on Tuesday, the campaigns we had going for them, the promotions we needed to focus on, the updates on book clubs . . . but in the back of my mind, the question persisted—

Where was he now?

14

Seven Years Too Late

I THOUGHT THAT AFTERNOON I could google Iwan, but I barely had a second to pee because an adult subscription book box decided to feature one of our celebrity memoirs alongside a bar of soap in the shape of an unmentionable, complete with a sucker on the back to *stick it to the bathroom wall*, and I spent my entire afternoon putting out *that* fire.

By the time six o'clock rolled around, Fiona had to drag me away from my computer before I sent another heated email to the book box company, absolutely about to sign it with *Have the day you deserve.* We walked together to the subway, since we were both heading uptown (she had an appointment, and Drew got a migraine halfway through the day, so she'd elected to go home early), and she sat down beside me on a bench as we waited for the subway. A man with an accordion and a drum set at his feet played a jazzy rendition of Billy Joel's "Piano Man," and a few feet away, a rat was nibbling on a crust of pizza.

God, I loved New York. Even the cliché bits.

Fiona said, not looking at me, "Something else happened this weekend, didn't it? I can tell."

"What? No. I just . . . I told you."

"Yeah, you painted and you didn't check your phone all weekend—two things that you *never* do."

She had a point. I chewed on the inside of my lip, debating on whether to tell her. If I knew Fiona, I knew she wouldn't stop asking until she found out, and she was incredibly perceptive. "Okay, so, don't freak out," I began, and took a deep breath, "but I think I met someone this weekend."

That surprised her. She glanced up from her phone. "At the Monroe?"

"He is living in the building for the summer." Not quite a lie. "He's in the city for a job, and we just started talking and . . . he's nice. Talking to him is nice."

She blinked a few times. Resetting her brain. "I'm sorry, did you say you *met* someone? Of your own accord? Has the sky fallen?" she added, perplexed.

I snorted a laugh. "Oh, come on, I can meet people sometimes."

"Yeah, when Drew and I *force* you."

I rolled my eyes. The train pulled into the station, brakes squeaking, and we got up and made our way into the car.

"Have you kissed him? Did you spend the night?" Fiona asked, following me. I made for two empty seats, but a young man in a business suit swooped in before we could take them, and he spread his legs and started playing a game on his phone.

I glared at him.

"Tell me *everything*. Is he cute?" Fiona went on, oblivious.

I continued glaring at the man until he finally looked up, a snarl on his lips, and then saw the pregnant woman beside me. And the other passengers giving him judgmental looks. He shoved his phone into his pocket and closed his legs, and I guided Fiona down into the seat beside him.

"What does he look like?" she asked. "What's his name?"

"Iwan," I replied, holding on to the bar above her, "and we just had dinner together . . . all weekend."

She fanned herself with her hands, blinking back fake tears. "Oh my god! My little Clementine is finally growing up! You might actually fall in *love*!"

I didn't want to think about it. "Okay, that's enough."

"What if you two get married? What if he's your *soulmate*?" She gasped, leaning toward me. "What's his *last name*?"

"It's—" I froze. The train jostled on. And I realized, then and there, that I didn't *know* his last name. "Um . . ."

She stared at me. "You seriously spent the *entire* weekend with him and didn't get his last name?"

Mr. Manspreader beside her smirked, and I shot him another glare. "I'll get it tonight—oh, this is your stop," I added.

She genuinely looked like she was about to skip her appointment to badger me some more, but then she decided against it and gathered up her purse. "You have to tell me *everything* tomorrow—including his name," she said solemnly, but I neither promised nor denied I would as she exited and pointed at me from the platform and mouthed, "I mean it," as the train pulled away.

I waved her goodbye, knowing there was no way to get out of it, and went to go sit in her spot—but the guy had already spread out again. I scowled and moved toward the door instead, and waited to exit at the Eighty-Sixth Street Station.

I couldn't believe I didn't get his last name.

Just a few days ago, if you'd told me that I'd meet a handsome stranger in my aunt's apartment who'd become a not-so-strange friend (*were* we friends? or something else?), I wouldn't have believed you. But now I was wondering what he would cook to-night for dinner, whether he'd gotten the dishwashing job, how his day was. Maybe I could spend weekends at the apartment over the summer learning about the birthmark on his clavicle and the scars on his fingers that kissed one too many knives.

And, maybe by the end of it, I could tell him the secret, that I *did* live in the future. And maybe he'd believe me.

Or—worse yet—I *did* end up telling him, and he didn't believe me, and maybe that's why he never came looking. Because I couldn't ignore the seven years between us, the seven years since he'd met me, and where I was now. He never came looking.

At least not that I could remember.

The train pulled into my station, and I climbed out of the sub-way and got to the Monroe. Earl was at the front desk again, al-most done with the James Patterson novel from this morning. He greeted me with a smile, like he always did, and I left for the eleva-tor and rode it up to the fourth floor.

Iwan looked like he had a whimsical last name—something Welsh, maybe? Since *Iwan* was Welsh. Or was it a family name? And maybe his last name was boring to counteract it?

I pulled my keys out of my purse, trying to rein in my ex-citement.

I unlocked the door to B4 and opened the door quickly.

"How about let's try my aunt's fettuccine tonight?" I called into the apartment, kicking off my shoes by the door.

I stopped a few feet into the apartment. It was dark and silent.

The kind of silence that made my heart twist painfully. The kind I knew all too well in this place.

"Iwan?" I called, and fear mounted in my chest. Because it was the kind of silence that I remembered from just after Analea died. The kind of soulless, unlivable silence that made me want to run away as quickly as I could. The kind of silence that sat with me as I unpacked my boxes. As I put her things away in the closet. I took another step into the apartment. Then another. ". . . *Iwan?*" My voice was softer now. Mostly eaten by my own panic.

This was the kind of silence that was so loud it screamed.

When I rounded into the kitchen, the lights were out and the kitchen was clean, my box of dinnerware from my old apartment set beside the sink, open and halfway unpacked. There were coffee cups still on the drying rack, having never made it to their spots in the cabinets, the napkins in the peacock holder empty. In the living room, everything was orange-yellow with evening light—like a still life portrait, framing the space where a robin's-egg blue chair no longer sat, its impressions still in the oriental rug.

No. No, no, no—

I took a step back, then another, hoping that maybe the apartment would realize its mistake and quickly correct it. But it didn't. And then suddenly, I was running out the door.

I slammed it closed.

My hands were shaking as I unlocked it again and stepped inside.

Dark and silent—and present.

I closed it, and opened it again—and *again*.

On the fifth try, I just stood in the open doorway, and looked into the empty apartment where golden evening light streamed down into an apartment that was no longer lived in, and I knew that was it.

This—whatever this had been—was over.

No more conversations over cardboard pizzas or dancing to a dead woman's violin song in the kitchen or kisses that tasted like lemon pies or—or—

The neighbor across the hall peeked out of her apartment. She was an older woman with thick black hair and glasses. She gave me a worried look. "Clementine, is everything okay?"

No, no, it wasn't, but she wouldn't understand. So I reeled myself in. Cobbled myself back together. I'd taught myself how to do it over the last few months, and I was very good at it. A mason excelling in the art of walled-off emotions. "Fine, thank you, Miss Avery," I replied, surprised at how even my voice was. "Just coming home."

She nodded, and ambled back inside.

I pressed my back against the door to B4 and breathed in, deep, and then breathed out again. My knees felt weak, my chest tight, as I sank down to the carpeted floor. I tried to tell myself that I knew this was going to happen, tucking all of the *what-if*s in my head into a small box—all of the impossible weekends I'd made up, learning about the birthmark on his clavicle and the scars on his fingers that kissed one too many knives.

"It was a perfect weekend," I whispered, keeping my doubt at bay. "Any longer and it would turn out bad. You'd find out that he listened to Nickelback or—or worse."

One weekend was enough.

One memory was plenty.

It *was*.

A wave of grief rose in my chest. I wasn't just going to accept that. I took out my phone and opened my browser, and there on the ancient, carpeted floor of the Monroe, I tried to find Iwan, where he was, where he *could* be. I searched every keyword I could think of—Culinary Institute of America + dishwasher + line cook, North Carolina, lemon pies, Iwan . . .

I scoured every link, every strange Facebook page, and I came up with . . .

Nothing.

It was as if he were a ghost, and I could only think that the worst had happened. That he was gone. That maybe, in fact, he *was* a ghost now, a memory on the far side of some graveyard. And even if he wasn't, even if he was still alive, I was more certain than ever that I'd never see him again.

My aunt had warned me. Rule number one, always take your shoes off by the door. Rule number two, never fall in love.

I bit the inside of my cheek and concentrated on it, and told myself if I cried, then that would be it—I would know what love felt like, and this would be it. And I tried—I wanted to cry. I waited for the stinging in my eyes to turn into salty tears, but it never did. Because I didn't cry over someone I barely knew. That would be silly, and Clementine West was not that.

She did not fall in love.

And she wouldn't start now.

I sucked in a deep breath, steeled my bones, and forced myself back to my feet. It would be okay. It'd be fine. Keep moving forward, keep my eyes straight ahead. I formulated a plan. Made a mental to-do list. Nothing stayed—that was something I should have expected, something I should have remembered.

I was *fine.*

So I turned back to face the door to B4, unlocked it, and went inside the quiet, lonely apartment. I dropped my purse on the counter, changed clothes, and turned on the TV in the living room as I unpacked the rest of the kitchen box and stored it all away in its proper place.

And then I went to sleep in my bed in my aunt's room, my bed frame creakier than hers, the curtains parted just enough to beam in a sliver of silver light from a moon 238,900 miles away. I shut the curtain and ignored it, like I should have from the beginning.

15

Timeless

AND THE SUMMER SPUN on.

Humid June mornings finally gave way to stormy July afternoons, washing into golden-colored evenings, and Iwan had truly disappeared. I kept looking, though, thinking maybe I could find him on the crowded sidewalk or dining at a table in an upscale but unpretentious restaurant in Chelsea or the West Village that might've fit his homegrown personality, but he was always just a bit too far out of my reach. I was looking everywhere for someone who—above everything else—didn't *want* to be found. If he did, then he wouldn't have made it so hard, and I was beginning to wonder how much these last seven years had changed Iwan. I wondered if I'd recognize him on the street.

I wondered if I'd already *met* him, if we'd sat beside each other on a subway somewhere, if we'd shared a joke in a dark bar, if I'd eaten his food, accidentally stolen his seat on a crowded bus.

Maybe it was time to let this go.

So, slowly, I stopped looking as hard.

Besides, my friends were very good at distracting me—well, dragging me into their schemes, anyway.

The hallway of Strauss & Adder Publishers was dark until I moved in my cubicle, and the motion-sensor lights activated. Everyone had left early for the Fourth of July weekend, so I stretched and enjoyed the silence. Summer was always humid in the city, and my aunt's apartment didn't exactly have central air. The window unit worked as best it could, but it never quite shrugged off the heat.

"*Clementine!*" Fiona singsonged, finally dragging Drew out of the bathroom, where they had both been for the last twenty minutes, changing into their fine-dining attire. "Are you ready?"

"We're going to be late," I replied, planting my hands on the armrests of my chair and pushing myself to my feet. Fiona had conned me into a terrible purple dress that made me feel like a grape about to be squashed into wine. "We can just call him and tell him we're not going."

"That's not a bad idea," Drew agreed, fixing her tie. She wore a fresh pink dress shirt with white suspenders and dark-wash skinny jeans. Gone was her tried-and-true tweed jacket and comfortable slacks. The things she did for her wife—the things we *both* did for Fiona. "We can just say we all caught a cold."

I pointed to her. "Exactly."

Fiona rolled her eyes. "We are *going*. This guy is perfectly nice! He lives in our building. He even pays his own rent, which is rare because we live in a building full of hedge fund babies. And you," she added, snapping her gaze to me, "are *going* to have fun."

As I had feared, Fiona hadn't forgotten about our conversation on the subway, and she'd asked about Iwan a few days later. I couldn't exactly tell her that my aunt's apartment decided to stop bringing us together, so I never got his name, and my almost stalkery

googling had resulted in absolutely nothing, so instead I told her
something I now absolutely regretted—

"The timing wasn't right."

She immediately assumed that he was engaged to someone else,
or getting a divorce, or moving to Australia, so she took it upon
herself to do the one thing that best friends were wont to do:

Make me feel better.

So I slipped on my heels and let her drag me to the elevator and
down into the waiting Uber. The restaurant my date had chosen was
on the Upper West Side, a small Italian place that grated your cheese
for you right at your table, and my date in question was—indeed—
incredibly nice. Elliot Donovan had a kind smile. He was tall and
broad, with a head full of curly black hair and chocolate eyes, and he
talked about books, and events he'd gone to at the Strand, and his
favorite authors. Fiona and Drew sat at a table on the other side of
the restaurant, but I could *feel* Fiona's gaze on me the whole time—
and so could my date.

Halfway through dinner, he leaned forward a little and said,
"Fiona is a bit intense, isn't she?"

I shoved a piece of bread into my mouth before I could say anything I'd regret, and instead mumbled after a moment, "She has
her heart in the right place."

"Oh, I'm not disputing that," he replied, but then he took a
deep breath and said, "but I don't think this is going to work out,
is it?"

On paper, Elliot was perfectly good. He was the exact kind of
man I wanted to date—hardworking, with a good job and a decent
book collection. He had a nice sense of humor and a lovely laugh,
but when I looked at the menu, all I could think of was Iwan telling me about a romance in chocolate, a love letter in a string of
fettucine, and I shook my head. "I don't think so. I'm sorry."

"It's okay! I have to admit, I came here hoping it'd be a good distraction," he added in embarrassment.

"There's someone else?"

He nodded. "And you?"

"Yeah, but the timing was all wrong."

He laughed. "That's always the most tragic, isn't it?" Then he glanced at Fiona and Drew's table again—and Fiona had the *gall* to pretend like she was looking at the wine menu instead—and said, "We can pretend for your friend's sake, though, yeah? Give them a good show?"

I smiled. "Absolutely. And then we can pretend to get in a fight at the end of dinner, and never talk to each other again."

"Ooh, I like that idea. What should the fight be about?"

To which I asked, "What is your hottest book take?" Because I knew that a man who was that well-read, who had lived his entire life in the upper crust of society, working on Wall Street, absolutely had a good one.

And oh, he did.

‖‖‖‖‖‖‖‖‖‖‖‖‖‖‖‖‖‖‖‖‖‖‖‖‖‖‖‖

FIONA THREW HER HANDS into the air as we descended into the bowels of the subway. After our fake fight, he'd caught a cab back to his apartment, and Drew, Fiona, and I walked to the subway station. "I can't *believe* you picked a fight over *Dune*!"

"Look, it's not my fault his opinion was wrong," I replied, trying to bite in a grin.

"He was perfect—*perfect*! And then you had to go and pick a fight," she went on, ranting, waving her hands in the air. "I am disrespected! Humiliated! I have to see him in the *elevators* in my building. I'm going to have to look him in the eyes and know that he thinks *Dune* is the best sci-fi book of all time."

Drew shook her head. "The *disrespect* to Anne McCaffrey."

"Look, I will not have some dead man hogging up my shelf space. Real estate in New York is *already* outrageous," I said matter-of-factly.

Fiona narrowed her eyes. "You say that and yet you own four different editions of *Lord of the Rings*."

"I *could* have five," I threatened, and she threw up her hands again.

"Fine! Fine, I'll vet them first, and then we'll try again—"

I grabbed her hand gently, and we stopped in front of the turnstile. There weren't a lot of people in the station at this time of night, and those who were just went around us. "How about let's not?"

Her eyebrows knitted together in confusion. "What do you mean?"

"I'm not really looking right now—I don't *want* to look right now," I amended. "I appreciate all of this, but . . . I'm over Iwan, I promise. I'm really okay alone."

And I meant it. Even though my parents were paragons of a successful romance—they fit each other's quirks and hang-ups like puzzle pieces—my aunt had lived alone almost her entire life, and it wasn't all that bad. Rhonda had a successful life, and she didn't have a significant other, either. They were shining examples that I could do it, too. I just needed to concentrate on work right now, like Rhonda did. Besides, I was tired of this whole dance. It wasn't that I didn't want a partner—I did; thinking about going through the world alone made my stomach drop into my toes—but I didn't really want to look right now.

I didn't want to sit across from another decent man and not feel anything and plot how best to end the date so we never had to see each other again.

Drew pulled her arm through her wife's and added quietly, "She'll find someone when she's ready."

Fiona let out a sigh. "Fine—but until then, you're our third wheel. And you're going to *like* it."

I raised my hands in surrender. "I would love to be your sidecar."

"Good," she replied, though she sounded a little defeated. She looked like she wanted to say something else, but then she thought better of it and dug her MetroCard out of her purse. We rode the 1 downtown to the Q together, and then they got off at Canal to transfer to the R, and I waved them goodbye.

Fiona's heart was in the right place, so I couldn't quite blame her. And besides, the food tonight was pretty good. Not as good as the place Drew had taken us last month—the Olive Branch—but it was nice.

The subway alert announced the doors closing, and I sank down into my seat, finally letting my walls down. My feet hurt in my shoes, and I couldn't *wait* to escape my Spanx.

Keep moving forward, keep my eyes straight ahead, that was the plan. Nothing stayed—that was something I should have expected, something I should have remembered back when I met Iwan.

I was *fine*.

Beside me, two girls bent their heads in to whisper, looking at their phones. "Oh my god, MoxieGossip says he was just spotted in SoHo. Coming out of his restaurant."

"The new one?"

"Yes!"

"Was he *with* anyone?"

"No! I think he's *single* again."

They tittered together, looking at an Instagram story, and I pulled out a pen and the guide to New York City that I had swiped last month and opened it up to the section about the subway. There I began to sketch the girls bent together over their phones, and settled in for the ride uptown.

16

Life Goes On

THERE WAS SOMETHING MAGNETIC about Manhattan in the summer, the way the sun reflected off every mirrored skyscraper window, bouncing off each other like some ancient mirrorball. It was perfect for afternoons standing in line for Shakespeare in the Park, quiet Saturdays at the Cloisters, nights buzzing with light and food and energy. But every year, when the Fourth of July came around, Drew, Fiona, and I packed our bags and headed to the Hudson Valley to escape the tourists and browse all of the delightful little bookstores nestled in quaint towns, and we returned just as the city emptied again, and life spun on.

I had lunch with Drew and Fiona, and I worked late, and then one afternoon, about a month and a half after I met Iwan for the first and last time, in the middle of July, when summer was at its hottest, Drew excitedly leaned in across the wrought-iron table where we sat in the shade in Bryant Park.

"Guess what proposal we got in today!" she said happily.

Fiona and I picked at our grilled cheeses from the food truck parked over by the New York City Public Library's Stephen A. Schwarzman Building. They were warring with a new food truck on the block—a loud yellow fajita truck that had a line that snaked down the sidewalk, and it smelled ridiculously good. Probably not as good as the fajitas Iwan made me a few weeks ago, though. Besides, I had my allegiance to the grilled cheese truck. The grilled cheeses were some of the best in Midtown—gooey and crisp, the sourdough crust crunchy, the meld of cheeses harmonious. Mine had chopped chunks of mushrooms and bell peppers, mayonnaise spiced with a little sriracha, and it was very much bliss. I'd started paying a little bit more attention to the food I ate since Iwan—and the people who cooked it, wondering what their stories were, too.

"Whose?" Fiona asked around a pimento grilled cheese.

"The chef's! You know—the one from the Olive Branch? James Ashton? He's coming into the office tomorrow. He wants to meet with us."

I perked up. "I thought we'd written him off?"

"I almost did. Admittedly, his agent *also* said they were going to a few other imprints . . ." She gave a shrug. "But it's a start! I haven't looked over the proposal yet, but I know it's going to be *amazing*. And *you* should finally read that *Eater* article."

I ducked my head. "Sorry . . ."

I'd tabled the article since that lunch a few weeks ago because life had gotten frantic, and Rhonda had placed a lot more responsibilities on me. Nothing had come out of it at the time, anyway, until now.

Fiona said around a mouthful of grilled cheese, "Oh, Clem, you're going to fall in love with his writing. It's so romantic. His forearms are almost as nice as his face," she added. "They better be front and center on the book cover."

"His forearms or his face?"

"Both."

"*And*," Drew added, reminding us that she was, in fact, a professional, "he writes beautifully. I can just *imagine* what his proposal is going to be like."

I highly doubted I would fall in love with a few well-placed adjectives, but I liked Drew's enthusiasm, and if she managed to nab another author for her list, that was all I cared about. She was so excited to get back to the office to read his proposal, we ended our lunch early and headed back to Strauss & Adder. I thought the afternoon would be quiet. Juliette hadn't broken up with her boyfriend in about a week and a half, and I was on top of all of my emails, so it was a bit of a surprise when Rhonda called me into her office about an hour later and asked me to close the glass door to her office—*again*.

I did, and sat in the hard plastic chair. "Is something wrong?" I asked hesitantly, picking at my nails. Because—again—usually when she closed her office door, something was wrong. The first time, we fired the marketing designer. The second time, she told me she was retiring.

I really hoped she didn't have a terminal disease today.

"What? Oh, no, why would you ask that?" she said in alarm. Then, a bit more seriously: "Should *I* ask that?"

"No! No, absolutely not. No," I quickly replied, waving my hands in front of me. I ate an almond she'd offered me as she sank back into her seat. "Everything is fine. Perfect." There were three dings from my phone. Three emails. I swallowed. "*Mostly* perfect. We're having a bit of a problem with—"

She put up a hand. "Doesn't matter. As you know, we have a meeting tomorrow with James Ashton, who's shopping around his cookbook."

"I think Drew mentioned him, yeah."

"It would be very nice to add him to our list," she replied, and took off her glasses. She set them down on the desk in front of her and added, "Since we lost Basil Ray to Faux."

I sat up a little straighter. "We *what*?"

"He signed a deal with them last week," she relayed, which was possibly some of the worst news we could've had. Basil Ray was one of our top authors—his cookbooks sold so well, we didn't even think twice when he told us to book him in first class and sent us a rider where he requested *only* Diet Cokes, a specific kind of kombucha that had to be imported from South Korea, and vegan-friendly, gluten-free, high-calorie meal options. "To be frank, losing him will be a substantial hit to our finances. Given that, along with some other bits of bad luck, we might be in trouble if we can't find a big book for next summer. I'm not trying to alarm you, I'm just being frank," she added, because she could no doubt see the blood draining from my face.

"Trouble—do you mean, like, for a season or . . . ?"

"Perhaps, Clementine," she said gravely, "but we don't want to take chances. That's why I asked you to close the door."

"Oh," I said quietly.

"I'm gathering a list of other rising stars in the culinary world to approach, but James Ashton would be a shoo-in. He's young, he's quite talented, and he's handsome. We could sell the shit out of his cookbook," she said confidently. "This a pretty rare scenario. From everything I've heard about his agent, this whole *ordeal* is going to be notoriously awful—so I'd like you to take the lead on it with Drew. You're the only one I trust."

Which meant this was my chance to prove myself.

She ate another almond. "I'd like you to look over his proposal and go to the meeting tomorrow with an outline of how you'd go about launching this book. The usual, you know. Drew can email it to you."

"Absolutely, and I can meet with her and formulate a plan of attack."

"Perfect. I look forward to seeing how you nab this chef," she replied.

"Who else has he gone to?" I asked.

"All the big players."

Which meant this was going to be nearly impossible. Strauss & Adder didn't have the kind of money *or* resources that a lot of the larger publishers did, but that just meant I had to get creative. Come up with a marketing strategy he couldn't say no to. I had a lot of work ahead of me tonight. "I'll see what I can do."

"Excellent," Rhonda replied, and sat back in her chair, green eyes glimmering. "This is going to be big for you, Clementine. I can just feel it."

I hoped she was right.

Lost and Found

"START WITH JAMES ASHTON'S article—the one in *Eater*," Drew said as we hurried from work to the subway. It was pouring rain, so we had to dodge large puddles as we descended into the station. "I don't think the proposal really strikes at what he's good at."

"You still want to convince him to write a memoir?" I asked as we swiped our Metro cards.

"More than *anything*—but I'll take a cookbook first if I can get it!" she replied, and waved as she and Fiona hurried off to catch their train.

I headed for the other side of the station, wringing out my hair as I waited for the uptown train. New York was miserable when it rained—but especially when you were caught in it without an umbrella.

I managed to get a seat on the Q and settled in, trying to ignore the strangers touching me from all sides. *This* was another reason I always worked late—I didn't have to contend with rush hour and all the people. Trying to ignore the tourist manspreading to my right, I pulled out my phone and opened the article Drew had sent me a month and a half ago.

Good Food, the article title read. By James Ashton

It was a lovely read—about how there is the art of food, and then there is the art of presentation. The voice was charming, tongue-in-cheek, like a friend telling you a secret over drinks named after dead poets.

At first, I found myself smiling—I could see why Drew loved his voice. It was infectious, his enthusiasm catching. I could do a lot with this, especially if this chef was as charismatic as his writing. The *possibilities* . . .

But halfway through the article, the strangest sensation began to creep down my spine.

The words felt familiar, like a coat someone pulled over my shoulders in the rain. They knitted together into pale gray eyes and auburn hair and a crooked half smile, and suddenly I was back in my aunt's apartment, sitting across from Iwan at that yellow kitchen table, his voice warm and sure—

It is rarely the food that truly makes a meal, but the people we share it with. A family spaghetti recipe passed down from your grandma. The smell of dumplings clinging to a sweater you haven't washed in years. A cardboard pizza across a yellow table. A friend, lost in a memory, but alive in the taste of a half-burnt brownie.

Love in a lemon pie.

The doors dinged and opened to my stop. My head was whirling from the words as I stepped out with the rush of people, scrolling down through the article again, sure I'd missed something. Surely I was mistaken—

And there at the top, a photo finally loaded.

A man in a professional kitchen, dressed in a white uniform, a familiar leather knife roll in his hands. He was older, crow's feet around his pale eyes, but that smile was still so bright and so achingly familiar, it stole my breath away. I stood, staring at the vibrant, glossy photo of a man I used to know.

James Ashton.

No—

Iwan.

Someone shouldered their way up the escalator beside me, snapping me back to reality. It couldn't be him. Couldn't be. But when I got outside, there he was again, on a bus stop ad for a cooking competition, graffiti papered around him. The ad had been there a while. At least a few weeks. My heart rose into my throat as I quickly turned the corner, passing a magazine stand, his face there again on the front of one of them. Reality began to sink in. In disbelief, I went over and picked it up.

NEW YORK'S HOTTEST CULINARY STAR, the headline read.

"You've got to be kidding me," I muttered.

I had been so focused on looking ahead, catapulting myself toward the next step in my plan, the rest of the world a blur so I didn't get hurt—

I hadn't looked around me. Hadn't been part of the world. Part of anything, really. I'd just gone through it, head down, heart shuttered, like a traveler against a torrential rainstorm.

But when I finally stopped for a moment and looked around, he was—

Everywhere.

Another You

"HE WAS RIGHT UNDER my nose," I muttered to my new pothos plant, Helga, as I poured myself a glass of wine.

Here I was, sitting on the floor in front of my coffee table in my aunt's apartment, furiously clicking on every link about a man who was seven years older, seven years farther away, seven years stranger, than the one who had kissed me over a lemon pie.

"Only *now* he's so far out of my league I barely even recognize him. He doesn't even *go* by Iwan. He goes by *James Ashton*. I would never have guessed Ashton," I added, a little morosely, and sank back against the couch, clutching the bottle of wine to my chest. When I'd gotten Helga a few weeks ago, my mom told me that if I talked to it, it'd grow better, but Helga just looked sort of wilty. Probably because I dumped all my emotional trauma on her. "At least he made it, right? He made it. And I found him . . ."

It was a relief, because he wasn't dead, he hadn't gone back home. He'd *made* something of himself, exactly as he said he wanted to, and the more I scrolled through his life, digitally generated across Google, the more I began to wish I'd seen it all firsthand.

In the last seven years, he had been a dishwasher for only a month and a half before he graduated to line cook, where two-time Michelin-starred chef Albert Gauthier took him under his wing. Gauthier . . . wasn't that the chef he'd talked about over dinner? A year later, he was sous chef, being recognized as a rising star, a talent to watch, gathering accolades like some people collected bottle caps. His career trajectory was astronomical. One critic loved his food, and all of a sudden his popularity exploded, and two years ago Albert Gauthier retired and handed over the reins of the restaurant Iwan had started at as a dishwasher. That restaurant?

The Olive Branch.

I remember the broad chest I'd run into on the way out the door.

I bit my thumbnail, skimming the different links and articles detailing his life in a messy, imperfect timeline—

Now that I knew he didn't go by *Iwan*, I found him rather easily on the alumni page of CIA—as a notable chef. With his recognition at the Olive Branch, he'd made quite a name for himself in the culinary world. James guest starred on *Chef's Table* and some Food Network shows; he'd been a frequent guest on travel food shows. And now he was opening up a restaurant all his own at the end of the summer, and I was sure that was going to coincide with this book proposal of his. The name of the restaurant hadn't been announced yet, but I was sure it'd be something about his grandpa, maybe? Pommes Frites?

I smiled a little at the idea.

Somehow, he'd become even more handsome, aged like a

handle of fine bourbon. In the videos online, he was magnetic and polished. If Drew *did* get him, he wouldn't need much media training, which made my job easier.

I thought about that sweet, crooked-mouthed man with a taste for his grandpa's lemon pies that were never quite the same twice, and I decided yes—this was good. This was okay.

I finished my glass of wine, opened his cookbook proposal, and started to make a plan. I was good at plans, good at my job, good at what I did. This was the one thing I excelled in, the one thing I could bury myself under and feel safe with—especially against this one awful thought in my head:

He couldn't remember me, because if he did . . . wouldn't he have tried to find me?

And I wasn't sure I wanted to know that answer.

||||||||||||||||||||||||||||||||||||||||||

AND, AS LUCK WOULD have it, I ran late to the meeting the next morning.

To be clear: it was five minutes until 10:00 a.m., when the meeting was supposed to start, but by the sound of voices on the other side of the conference room door, I was about to be the last one inside. I smoothed down my black skirt, thinking that maybe I should've worn pants. Something that made me look cleverer, bolder. Maybe a different blouse, too—why did I always choose *yellow*? At least no one noticed the stain on the bow from my coffee this morning.

My heart beat quick and sick in my throat. Why was I *nervous*?

You've done this a hundred times before, I told myself. *You're good at this.*

I closed my eyes. Took a deep breath.

And opened the door with a smile.

"Hi, there," I greeted brightly. "Sorry I'm a bit . . ."

Late was what I wanted to say, but the words dropped out of my mouth as I came into the room and caught sight of the man seated at the head of the conference table. I'd rehearsed this moment in the mirror all morning—look pleasant, put-together, smile professionally (don't smile too wide, don't show your gums—act like your life is together, too). Maybe he'd recognize me. Maybe he'd think I looked familiar, and he'd flash that boyish smile of his—

I had it all down to a fine art by the time I got to the subway, going over the scenario in my head until I'd memorized exactly what to say and how to say it.

And all of it, in one split second, failed me.

Because the man at the head of the conference table was not the one I remembered. Curly auburn hair cut short on the side, longer at the top, accenting his sturdy face and clean-shaven square jaw. He'd lost the beard from the Instagram photos, but somehow gained the ability to leave me absolutely speechless. There were bits of the Iwan I knew—a smattering of freckles across his cheeks, a strong nose, soft-looking lips.

I immediately recalled what they felt like on me. The way he'd nipped at my skin, fastened his hands around my waist—

My stomach plummeted into my toes.

But for everything that stayed the same, so much had *changed*. Things I really couldn't know until I saw him in person. Seven years had sharpened his edges, turned stretched-neck T-shirts into a fitted light gray blazer that hugged his shoulders in a sharp cut, Vans into sensible oxfords, dark sleepless circles around his eyes into refined crow's feet, his entire appearance tailor-made. His gangliness had shifted to something solid and muscular, much more fit than the man I'd met over a month ago over a strange summer weekend. The man who kissed me, lips tasting like sweet lemon pie, promising to follow me to the moon and back—

His gaze rose to mine, pale gray eyes, sharp and bright, pinning me to the spot like a moth to a corkboard, and I felt every muscle in my body tense.

Oh, no, I was in *so* much fucking trouble.

The Proposal

"THIS IS CLEMENTINE WEST," Drew introduced me. "Though I think you might've met her for a few seconds last month?"

Last month . . . ? Had she figured out that this was *Iwan*? My Iwan? No, I hadn't told Fiona or Drew any specifics about him, and besides, he looked very different than the man I'd met in my aunt's apartment.

Then it occurred to me, suddenly—

I'd run into him on my way out of the restaurant. That was what she meant.

"Clementine . . . ?" Drew asked, a bit hesitantly.

I snapped to my senses and smiled—*don't show gums, look pleasant*, just like I'd rehearsed. "Oh, hi, yes, sorry. I think we had a bit of a collision, actually, at the restaurant. I'm sorry I didn't get a chance to meet you properly then."

"It's quite all right, we can meet again now," he remarked in that familiar Southern lilt, not unpleasantly. Beside him sat his agent, a shark of a woman named Lauren Pearson, who was, undeniably, one of the best in the business. He still hadn't taken his eyes off me—almost as if he thought I might disappear.

Was he trying to place me—I had that kind of face, really. Someone you might see in a crowd and almost remember.

Do you recognize me, too? I wanted to ask.

No, he couldn't. It'd been seven years. *I* didn't even remember my one-night stands from seven years ago.

Get it together, Clementine.

"You made a good save with that dessert, if I recall," he went on.

"It would've been a shame to wear the dessert out of the restaurant," I replied, and sat down beside Drew, situating my notebook in front of me.

And then the worst thing of all happened, the thing that I had been dreading: he smiled, perfectly straight and perfectly white and perfectly practiced—like mine—and stretched his hand across the table to me. "I'm sure it would've looked stunning on you. I'm James, but James is my granddad's name. My friends call me by my middle name—Iwan."

I accepted his hand. It was rough and warm, marked with scars, so many more from the seven years between us. The last time I had felt those hands, they'd been cradling my face, his thumbs tracing my jawline, gentle, like I was a work of art—

"How would you classify your future publicist? A friend?" I asked, and his agent barked a laugh.

"I like her!" she crowed.

James Ashton's smile turned a little crooked. A small slip in his refined image. "We'll see, Clementine," he replied, and released my hand.

"Clementine's a senior publicist here at Strauss and Adder. She basically runs the entire publicity department when Rhonda's away. Last year, she was recognized as a rising star by *Publishers*

Weekly. Needless to say, any book we have is in good hands with her."

"I have no doubt," Iwan—*James*—replied, and turned to Drew, and as he did, his body shifted and he sat up a little straighter. "Tell me about Strauss and Adder."

So Drew did. She talked about the company's history, our authors, and our work ethic. As she talked passionately about her team, and how we could best serve his career, using a PowerPoint to show other successful book launches and campaigns from over the years, James asked thoughtful questions—about how Drew liked to edit, what was expected from the cookbook, the process of turning a draft into the final product.

I must have been staring at him because his eyes—bright with the light from the PowerPoint—flicked to me. He caught my gaze and held it for one heartbeat, two, as Drew answered one of Lauren's questions. His pale eyes were a perfect and cloudy gray, like my favorite autumn days, perfect for dirty chai lattes and chunky scarves. The way he looked at me made my stomach burn.

He *couldn't* remember me from that weekend. It was seven years ago, and he'd met stars a lot brighter than me.

Then he looked away again, back at the onslaught of numbers and projections, and nodded along to Drew's passionate presentation. The way she talked about her job, her authors, you could tell she loved what she did. She loved helping creative people plant seeds, and she loved watching those seeds bloom into fascinating projects, and her track record so far indicated just that. She mostly dealt in memoirs and historical fantasy, but she truly loved the way he wrote, and his recipes.

"And I want to help you share them with the world," Drew declared, turning off the projector. "I think we could be a really great team."

"Well, that is absolutely lovely," his agent replied, and I couldn't tell whether or not Drew's pitch had endeared James Ashton to us or not. His agent was certainly impossible to read. She made a motion with her hand toward us. "Would you like to start off, James, or should I?"

James sat up a little straighter, lacing his long fingers together on the table in front of him. "I'll start, thank you, Lauren," he began, and his voice was level and cool, and he turned that shale-colored gaze to Drew. "I believe food should be an experience."

I sat up a little straighter, because I knew this part. I knew he was going to talk about love in chocolate and comfort in butter and poetry in spices—and I was excited, perhaps for the first time since seeing him, because it meant he wasn't so different. The best parts of him were—

"Anyone can make a grilled cheese, anyone can make a tomato bisque, and with the right tools, I believe anyone can make it well. It's all in the presentation," he went on confidently. "It's the skill. It's the way you create your culinary art that truly makes for a memorable experience."

I thought about my aunt's peanut butter and jelly sandwiches, always getting stuck to the roof of my mouth, and how the Iwan I knew had told me that was—

"A perfect meal," he said.

No, it wasn't.

I quickly looked down at the printed proposal in front of me. Drew gave me a small smile, and I smiled back and nodded, and hoped I didn't look too confused.

Experience? Skill? What about your memories and stories— what made those foods endearing?

"As you could probably tell from the proposal," he went on, "I'm looking for a publisher who will offer just as much as I'm also able to offer, between my online impressions, media, and connections—all of which are stated in the proposal. The recipe book in question will coincide with my restaurant opening in NoHo. It will detail seasonal specialties and new recipes for those looking for more exciting cuisines, and it strives to capture what makes a perfect meal," he finished, and stole a glance at me.

I couldn't meet his gaze.

"It's a very lovely idea for a cookbook," Drew said, her fingers folding and unfolding the corner of the proposal, "and with the perfect photographer, I'm positive we can make the pages absolutely sing—along with your thoughtful asides at the start of each dish of course. Like you wrote in your *Eater* article."

"I'm glad you enjoyed the article," he replied pleasantly. "I wrote it years ago."

And I wondered if there was anything of that author left in him, because what Drew didn't say, but I could hear between the words, was how . . . out of touch the proposal felt. There was just something so sleek in the pages—almost untouchable. It was all so high-concept and . . . alien to me. He once waxed poetically about comfort foods and yet there was none of that here. Who had dry ice hanging around for a noodle dish? Or spent three days prepping a sauce to dribble on a cut of steak? There was something just so disconnected in this pitch from the man I'd first met, and I'd understood why Drew had told me the article was more important. All of the warmth and care in the piece was at odds with the stilted polish here.

Just six weeks ago—or seven years ago, I suppose—he was telling me with great enthusiasm about his friend's fajita recipe and his grandfather, who never made the same lemon pie twice. *That* was the man who wrote the *Eater* article. Not this one. And his recipes weren't hidden behind a skill-set paywall, inaccessible to anyone who didn't know what *jus* was.

"You look like you have something to say," James Ashton— Iwan—remarked, giving me an unreadable look as he leaned back in his chair, and I quickly schooled my face.

"No, sorry," I replied, and Drew gave me a hesitant look. "That's just my face."

"Ah."

"Well, we have a few other meetings with publishers after this," Lauren said as she gathered up her things, "but we're asking that, if you are interested, you submit your preliminary bid by tomorrow afternoon. This will be a slightly . . . different process than usual."

Drew and I exchanged a strange look. Usually there was a bid—sometimes an auction if there were multiple offers—and Lauren Pearson loved auctions. I figured we'd be going up against quite a few other imprints, so I was confused as to what could be *different*.

Lauren said, "We are going to take all serious bidders on to a second round—a cooking class—in which we'll assess how the publishing teams work together. And just to have a bit of fun. Then we'll take the last and best bid, and we'll decide from there." She laced her fingers together on the table in front of her. "And you might be wondering why we're going through all this trouble."

Yeah, actually.

"And I wish I could tell you more," she went on, clearly enjoying dangling a secret in front of us, "but this is just a preliminary meeting. We'll be looking at all parts of your offer, and so, very likely, as long as a publisher comes to play and has dynamic ideas, they'll be invited to continue on to the second round."

Then she stood, and Iwan—*James*, I had to remind myself— followed suit.

"It was a pleasure to meet you," he told Drew, and shook her hand. "I look forward to perhaps working with you in the future."

"I hope so. I could do so much with you—respectfully," she replied.

He grinned, but it didn't reach his eyes. "I have no doubt."

Drew followed the agent out the door, guiding her to the lobby, and suddenly I found myself alone with the talent. I quickly pulled all my papers together and shoved them into my notebook, wanting to leave as quickly as possible, but it would be rude to leave before him, and he was *certainly* taking his time.

A knot formed in my throat.

"James?" his literary agent called.

"Coming," he replied, and started for the door, but as he passed, he bent toward me, and I caught a bit of his expensive cologne, woodsy and sharp, and he whispered in a deep and delicious rumble, "It was good to see you again, Lemon," before he slipped out of the conference room, and I was left, mouth open, staring after him.

Berried Alive

WEDNESDAY NIGHTS WERE USUALLY reserved for three things: cheap wine and cheese plates at Berried Alive, a small bar down by the Flatiron Building decorated in death motifs that skewed more cute than morbid, and bitching about our week. Fiona called it our "Wine and Whine," though she'd been missing out on the first part of it for the last eight months. Now she picked her way through the cheese plate and lamented about how she missed the taste of a house red. Usually it was just Fiona, Drew, and me, but Juliette had had a particularly terrible week, so we'd invited her along, too.

The wine bar was dead tonight—no pun intended—so we actually managed to get our favorite table in the back in the shape of a skull, and that just *tickled* Fiona. She sat at the top of the skull and cried, "Look, babe, I got a head!" with a cackle, and—not for the first time—Drew looked like she might just walk herself into the sea. We ordered what we always did, cheese plates and cheap house wine, and we started our Wine and Whine session, because it was nothing if not therapeutic, and none of us could *actually* afford therapy.

I, personally, just wanted to burrow into the center of the earth and never come out again. Ever since yesterday, I don't think my heart had—once—calmed down.

"It was good to see you again, Lemon," Iwan—*James*, damn it, he was a potential author—had said. Which meant he *remembered* me.

I knew how to handle a whole host of situations. I knew what numbers to call when my authors were stranded in airports, I knew which journalists to go to first for exclusive scoops, I knew how to make a good first impression, the best words to say to start off on the right foot, but *none* of that was going to help me here.

I kept replaying the meeting in my head, over and over again, trying to pick out the Iwan I knew from the James Ashton seated at the table. The way he just controlled the room the moment the meeting started—it was like I couldn't look at anyone else—was infuriatingly sexy, and at the same time unattainable.

At the table, Juliette was beginning to spiral about the social media campaign that Rhonda had put her on—something involving a TikTok dance that was, above everything else, just a complete waste of time.

"I can't even dance!" she cried, burrowing her face in her hands. "Oh, *why* did she choose me?"

Fiona said, "You could've said no."

"To *Rhonda*?" she asked, aghast. "Clementine can, but I certainly can't, and I like my job."

Which, to be fair, was true, though Juliette was definitely the stronger of the two of us when it came to genius and unexpected campaigns. A year ago—when I was on vacation—Strauss &

Adder had to promote a book titled *I Chart the Stars*, but the marketing designer had left a typo in an ad that ran in the *New York
Times* and, regrettably, on the big jumbotron in Times Square that
made it read I SHART THE STARS. It immediately blew up on the internet, and everyone started making fun of it, but instead of apologiz-
ing and pulling the ads we spent *way* too much money for, Juliette
decided to lean into it with the hashtag #ISHARTTOO. It was only
a coincidence that the main character also suffered from IBS, and
the author, empowered, came out as a person with IBS as well. It
became a whole thing.

And yes, that was the marketing designer Rhonda later fired.

Juliette thought on her feet in a way I absolutely did not, even
though I'd worked as a publicist a little longer.

"Well, maybe you can get that new intern to do it?" Drew
asked, and Fiona agreed.

"Or the new social media manager? Why don't you make this
her problem?"

"I tried," she sighed. "She made it my problem again."

"Well, that's silly—Clementine, what would you do?" Fiona
asked. "Clementine?"

I had my head down, scrolling through Instagram on my
phone. Okay, technically a *single profile* on Instagram. James Ashton's. My phone glowed, full of colors from all of the places he'd
been, the bright yellow of the Sahara, the deep green of Thailand,
the sakura pink of Japan . . . so many different places, soaking them
all in.

Like my aunt.

There were other people on his timeline, too. His agent, Lauren, but also people I assumed he worked with at the Olive Branch.
Further back, there were photos of women, too, grinning as he
kissed them on the cheek, or as they sat on his lap in intimate

poses. Pictures of vacations in the Hamptons and intercontinental trips with exhausted-but-happy girlfriends. None of those women stayed in his feed for long. A few months at most, and then they would disappear, and soon enough another woman would sneak into his life, and another.

Not unlike my relationships, I realized.

"Clem?" Fiona repeated. "Earth to *Clementine!*" She waved her hand in front of my phone.

I quickly slammed it, facedown, on the table. "I'm not looking at nothing!"

Drew said, "Well, that's suspicious."

"Answering a question we didn't ask *and* bad grammar?" Juliette added, sounding a little dubious. "That seems odd."

Fiona agreed, "She's never been good at lying. Gimme that!"

I squawked in protest as Fiona snagged my phone, put in my passcode (since when did she know my passcode?), and gasped as his Instagram came up. I buried my face in my hands.

"*Clementine!* Do you have a *crush*?" Fiona asked slyly, and showed the rest of the table my phone, as if the sudden revelation was *scandalous*.

I immediately popped my head up, startled. "No! Absolutely not! I like my job!" I added, as if I didn't already sound *mortified*. "I just . . ." I pressed my hands against the sides of my neck, knowing I was turning every shade of red imaginable, and all of my friends looked at me expectantly, because I wasn't one to go stalking anyone's Instagram pages. Ever.

Fiona shook her head. "Clementine *never* has a crush," she said, and Drew nodded sagely.

"She must be sick," Drew agreed.

"Oh, what a lovely crush!" Juliette added. "Wait—is that that chef?"

I wanted to die. I couldn't just tell them that I was trying to figure out how someone who wrote such a lovely article in *Eater* could give us such a cold proposal, and I didn't want to undermine Drew and her acquisition. My job was to back her up, so whatever feelings or reservations I had came second to being on her team. So, I ended up with, "Fine. You're right. He's really hot. I hope we get him."

Juliette seemed intrigued. "Oh! Everyone was talking in the kitchen at work about this guy. Something about a weird acquisition process?"

"It's a bit ridiculous, but we're going to play," Drew replied, and ate a chunk of cheddar off the bone-shaped charcuterie board. "Can't afford not to at this point. I'm sure the book will land in the right hands."

"Preferably yours," Fiona said, and took her wife's hand and squeezed it tightly. "We're rooting for you, babe."

I took my phone back from Fiona and shoved it into my purse. "There's no way we won't make it to the next round. Drew's offer was fantastic and we're a great team. I'd be more worried about that cooking class."

Juliette clicked her tongue to the roof of her mouth. "Oh, I can just *imagine* the insurance he'd have to take out for that. Rob always has to insure his guitar."

We gave her a strange look.

"Why?" Drew asked.

She replied, quite seriously, "In case it bursts into flames while he's playing it."

Well, then.

Fiona responded, saving both Drew and me from answering, "If anyone will burn down his restaurant, it'll be Clementine."

"Hey!" I cried. "I might *not*."

She pointed out, "You've admitted that you've put tinfoil in the microwave."

"It was *once* and I was *drunk* and the candy bar was *frozen*," I said defensively, and everyone laughed and agreed that they'd all sell a kidney to be a fly on the wall of that cooking class.

They went on to talk about their current guesses for how long Basil Ray would stay at Faux before regretting his decision and returning to Strauss & Adder. Here, he was a big fish, but over at Faux? Not so much.

"He's not coming back," Drew said to Juliette. "And even if he did, he's exhausted the list of every reputable ghostwriter."

Juliette's eyes widened. "He has a *ghostwriter*? Oh, actually that makes sense. His cookbooks are always so different . . ."

And I found myself zoning out a little again. I smeared a soft Brie on a cracker, topped it with apricot jam, and wondered what Iwan would think of this place. Would he like all the skulls on the wall, the terrible puns on the menu, or would he rake his eyes across the expanse and turn around and leave immediately, because it wasn't somewhere his glossy image would go? Him, James Ashton, drinking house wine and eating the cheapest cheese plate at a death-themed bar with a bunch of gossipers?

I couldn't image him here at all.

And maybe that was for the best.

"*Speaking* of Falcon House," Juliette went on, after Drew mentioned that Ann Nichols had a ghostwriter as well, "I heard that the executive editor over in their romance list now oversees their *entire* imprint—fiction and nonfiction."

Fiona gave a low whistle. "Are they single?"

Everyone gave her a look.

"What? For Clementine!"

"He has a fiancée," I replied absently, just to show that I was, in fact, listening. I snagged another slice of cheddar—my favorite, it never failed me—and added, "Besides, you know me. I don't have time to fall in love."

Broken Doors

THE NEXT AFTERNOON, DREW told me the news. The terrible, awful, infuriating news.

"We didn't make it," she whispered, sitting at the high-top table in the communal kitchen, absently stirring her black coffee, and I knew exactly what she meant—

James and his agent had rejected our offer.

My vision turned red almost immediately. "*What?* But—"

"I know," she cut me off with a heavy sigh. "There's no way we bid lower than Estrange Books, and I heard from Tonya that they are in the next round. He must've just not liked us."

Which was a lie because Drew was impossible to hate, and we had pulled together a hell of a plan to send with our offer. "Well, he's wrong, and he's going to regret it."

"Thanks," she replied, and slipped off the stool at the table. She was trying to act like the decision hadn't gutted her—she was an editor, after all, and she was used to disappointment. But this felt a little different because she *had* gone after James Ashton. She'd pursued him. And under any other circumstances, she would've been the only editor to do so. It was just bad timing, and worse luck. "I think I'm going to go for a walk around the block. Tell Fiona if she comes looking?"

"Sure," I said, a little helplessly, as she left for the elevator lobby. This didn't make any sense. I thought for sure we'd at *least* get to the next round. I paced the kitchen, trying to recall what Drew could've said, what tells there could've been during the meeting yesterday, but she was perfect. Her presentation of Strauss & Adder was spot-on, and her passion for the project had been almost *tangible*. The only other possibility was—

I froze in my footsteps.

Me.

He remembered me, and he didn't want to work with me, and *I* was the reason why he had rejected our offer. A sick feeling settled in my stomach because that was the only possible explanation.

I sank this acquisition. The second I knew it was Iwan, I should've recused myself, but I'd been so hungry to *see* him, and to prove myself to Rhonda that I could handle it . . .

"Shit," I muttered, raking my fingers through my hair. *"Shit."*

<hr />

I WISHED I COULD say the bad luck stopped there, but Rhonda found out that the chef passed on us, and to say she was a little disappointed was an understatement.

She stood by my cubicle, going over his proposal, our plans, and Drew's declined offer with a shake of her head. "It must have been something said in the room. The offer is good—the royalties are ridiculously generous." She shook her head, and instead of handing his proposal back to me, she tossed it right into my trash can. "Rubbish—all of it."

"The agent assured us that everyone would more than likely get into the next round, too."

"Obviously Lauren lied. Back to the drawing board, then. Let's take this as a learning opportunity and move forward."

Then she turned and left for her office, and I resisted the urge to bury my face in my hands. A *learning* opportunity after I'd already been here seven years. This preliminary meeting should have been a cakewalk, and instead it had sealed our fate. I felt humiliated, mostly because I'd been so confident that we *would* make it to the next round.

And I had been the one to blow it up, and that left us without a major player to fill the role of Basil Ray. Fuck Basil Ray, seriously. Did he *have* to go to Faux?

"Learning opportunity," I reminded myself, pulling up Instagram and browsing some of the bigger foodgrammers, ruling out every good-looking guy who came across my feed. They couldn't be trusted.

By the time five o'clock rolled around, I'd plotted four different ways to kill James Ashton and make it look like an accident. I even had a spot on the Hudson saved in my phone as the perfect place to dump his body—not that I would. But thinking about it made me feel better as I gathered my purse to leave.

I knocked on the side of Drew's cubicle gently, and she glanced up from the manuscript she had printed out and was currently taking a red marker to. "Hi," I said softly. "You're going to be okay?"

"It's not the first time I've lost a bid, Clementine," she reminded me, setting down the manuscript, "but thank you for checking in."

I tried not to let my regret show too much, because I was the reason he had passed. He had remembered me, after all. What if he ended up hating me after that weekend, or I had secretly annoyed him, or he didn't want to work with someone he'd kissed, once, a thousand years ago?

I was the reason we lost this book. What if I became the reason Strauss & Adder folded? That was silly, I knew that was silly. Publishers didn't fold because of one failed acquisition.

I was trying not to panic.

Drew glanced at the clock, and gave a start. "It's five already? I can't believe I'm leaving *after* you."

"That's why I asked if you're okay."

"Ha! Oh, thanks. I'm fine. I'll see you Monday?"

"Don't work too late," I said, waving goodbye, and headed toward the elevator lobby before she could see the panic rising in my face. I made my way uptown to the large off-white building with lions in the eaves, and thought that maybe one breaking off and falling on me—a recurring nightmare I had when I was a kid—might actually be a welcome way to spend a few months in a coma before waking up, having forgotten this entire summer, and returning to work blissfully ignorant of James Iwan Ashton.

Today was one of those Manhattanhenges, and as the sun sank between the buildings, tourists and Manhattanites alike crowded the crosswalks, taking out their phones to capture how the oranges and yellows and reds burst from the horizon just beyond the street. I didn't stop as I crossed behind the tourists. The phenomenon was only a few minutes long, as dusk settled across the city like a shimmery tequila sunrise, and by the time I pushed open the doors to the Monroe, it was over.

Earl greeted me as I came in. He was halfway through his next mystery—*Death on the Nile*. I just wanted to get to my aunt's apartment, draw a bath with a bath bomb, and sink down into the water and dissociate for a while as I listened to the *Moulin Rouge* soundtrack.

The elevator was so slow to come, and when I got inside, it smelled a little like tuna salad, which . . . was just as unpleasant as it sounds. I leaned back against the railing, stared up at my warped reflection, and patted down my flyaway bangs, though the day had been so humid my hair frayed out at the ends.

There was no helping it.

The elevator let me off on the fourth floor, and I counted down the apartments to B4. I couldn't wait to get out of this skirt. After a bath, I'd put on some sweatpants, take the ice cream out of the freezer, and watch a rerun of something terrible.

I unlocked the door and trudged my way inside, slipping my flats off at the door—

"Lemon?" a voice from the kitchen said, deep and familiar. "Is that you?"

22

Unsolicited Advice

THE APARTMENT SMELLED LIKE food—warm and spicy—and the soft sounds of a radio hummed through the apartment, playing a tune that'd been popular years ago.

That voice—I knew that voice. My heart swelled in my chest, so much so I felt it might burst.

I took a step in, and then another.

No way. *No way.*

"Iwan?" I called hesitantly—*hopefully?*

Was I hopeful, or was this weird feeling in my stomach dread? I wasn't sure. I took another step down the hallway, slipping out of my flats. What were the odds?

The sound of footsteps rushed across the kitchen, and then a man with auburn hair and pale eyes poked his head out of the doorway.

And the door clicked closed behind me.

Iwan wore a dirty white T-shirt, the neck stretched out, and frayed jeans, so different from the uptight man who had sat down across from me in the conference room, devoid of everything that made him glow. He smiled that kind, lovely smile of his, as if he was glad to see me.

Because he *was*.

Impossible, impossible, this is—

"*Lemon!*" he greeted me happily, and even the way he said my stupid nickname was different. Like it wasn't a secret, but a sanctuary. He threw his arms wide and pulled me into a hug. I wasn't that big of a hugger, but the sudden crush against his chest, the closeness—it made my heart slam into my rib cage. The dread turned into fluttering, terrible, hopeful butterflies. He smelled like soap and cinnamon, and I found myself wrapping my arms around him and holding him tight.

I met you in my time, and you're so different, I wanted to tell him, pressing my face into his chest, but I doubt he'd believe me. *I don't know why you changed. I don't know how.*

And, quieter, *I don't know you at all.*

"You're *such* a sight for sore eyes. And you're right on time for dinner," he said into my hair. "I hope you like japchae."

I stared up at him as though he might as well have been a ghost. My brain was buzzing. The apartment did it again—like it had for my aunt and Vera. But why *now*? Another crossroads?

Iwan frowned, and let go of me. "Is something wrong?"

"I . . ."

I realized I didn't care. He was here. *I* was here.

And I was happier than I'd been in a long time.

"I'm sorry," I blurted, "that I didn't come back."

"Everything work out well with your apartment?"

"What?"

"With the pigeons," he said.

"Oh, yes! Everything's working out fine. I just came to—to check up. To see how you were. I'm sorry I didn't knock first."

"It's fine, it's fine, I was sure you'd be back. Well," he added, with a shy grin, "I was kind of hoping, at least."

We stood there for another awkward moment. Like he wanted to say something, and I sort of did, too. *I missed you*—but was that too forward? *I missed* this *you*—that would've been too weird. I wanted to shake him and ask him if *I* was the reason he passed on Drew's offer, but he wasn't that man.

He wouldn't be that man for years.

Then he cleared his throat and invited me into the kitchen, where he turned down the radio and returned to the stove. The moment passed. I followed him, dumped my purse by the counter, and climbed up on my barstool, as though it were routine. *Was* it routine at this point? This felt comfortable. It felt unreal.

"How've you been?" he asked, picking up the wooden spoon he had abandoned in the pan and stirring whatever was inside.

"Fine." Then, when I realized I'd used that word so often in the last few weeks, I added more truthfully, "Overworked a little, honestly, but I've been painting more." Then I reached down to my purse at my feet, and took out the travel guide to NYC to show him my new paintings. I had finally colored the one with the girls on the subway, and I really liked how they had turned out, bathed in blues and purples.

"Oh, gorgeous!" he cried, and took the guide to flip through and see all of them. "These are really something. I tell you what, someday when I get a restaurant, I'll commission you for a few pieces."

I thought about the Olive Branch and his cookbook proposal. "I doubt they're your aesthetic."

"Of course they are." He closed the book and handed it back to me. "What do you say?"

I was flattered—it was a nice thought. "I don't take commissions, sadly."

"Then how about an exchange?" he replied. "Dinner at my restaurant for the rest of my life."

That was a lovely future he painted. I would've been enraptured by it, if it existed. "Okay," I said, because it didn't exist, "but only if I get my own table."

"Set aside for you every night—best table in the house."

"It's a deal, Chef," I replied, reaching out a hand, and he shook it—his grip firm and warm, fingers calloused. At least his handshake hadn't changed in the future. Except maybe in that meeting room he'd held on for a second too long.

"You're going to regret that," I said, as he went back to his simmering saucepan, and I put my travel sketchbook back into my purse.

"Nah, I don't think I will."

No, he'd just forget about it.

I took stock of the apartment. In the past few weeks since I'd been gone, he'd made himself at home. There were dishes drying on the rack, and a few crumbs on the AC outside, where Mother and Fucker nested. He took two floral bowls out of the cabinet and plated them both with some sort of noodles with vegetables and meat. He brought both to the yellow table and didn't even ask before he took out a new bottle of wine.

"I remembered you liked rosé, so I bought more just in case you came back around," he said, to my surprise, and motioned over to the table. "We can eat."

"Wow, are you trying to impress me?" I joked, slipping off the barstool, and joined him at the table. It was so easy, existing with him. Maybe it was his nonchalant smile, the way it disarmed me like very little else did. Whatever it was, the panic that had set into my bones since the meeting with James, and later the lost bid, ebbed away.

"Ha! Maybe," he relented, and sat down opposite me and poured us both a glass of wine. "Bon appétit, Lemon."

I hung on the way he said my name, like it was something tender. "Can you say it again?" I asked, before immediately realizing how weird I sounded.

"What, *bon appétit*?" He made a face. "I know I suck at French, you don't have to rub it—"

"No, my nickname."

A smirk tugged at the edge of his mouth, and he leaned forward on his elbows and said, "Oh, so you like it now?"

Mortification crawled up my neck. "No. I just—I need to get used to it. Because you *clearly* won't stop." But, of course he didn't believe me. I didn't believe myself, either. "Never mind," I quickly added.

Suddenly, the sharp ring of a cell phone cut through the kitchen.

"Not mine," I told him, because my cell phone didn't work in the past.

"Oh! Sorry," he mumbled, pushing himself to his feet again, and went to go retrieve an old flip phone from the charger on the counter. He really wasn't one for technology, was he? He read the caller ID and his nose scrunched—something he tended to do, I realized, when he was confused. "Sorry, I have to take this," he said, and answered it as he left for the bedroom. "Hey, Mom. Is something up?"

I sat there quietly, looking down at my plate of cold noodles, vegetables, and meat. Should I go ahead and eat or . . . ? I tried not to eavesdrop, really, I did, but the walls in this apartment were paper thin, and the bedroom was just on the other side of the kitchen.

"Yeah, I'm still looking for a place—no, I'm fine, I'm fine," he said with a laugh. "Stop worrying so much, will you? Look, I have a friend over. I'll call you later? I promise." A pause. "I'll let you know. Love you, too. Good night."

As he returned, I tried to pretend like I was doing something— I folded my napkin, unfolded it, inspected the silverware (I didn't even realize my aunt had metal chopsticks), and as he sat down, he asked, "Do my dishwashing skills leave something to be desired?"

"No, no, they're perfect," I quickly replied, putting the chopsticks down. "I just. Um. My reflection in the . . . The walls are thin," I admitted, and he snorted a laugh.

"My mom. She's worried sick. Like mothers are," he added with a roll of his eyes, taking a napkin from the table. "Anyway, she says hello."

"You've told her about me?" I asked, surprised.

"I've told her I've met a *friend*," he replied. "And so of course she immediately assumes we're going to elope to Vegas."

"Wow, that's quite a leap."

"That's my mother." He laughed. "Let's eat?"

"Bone appetite," I said, making him almost choke on his wine as he went for a drink, wheezing a laugh, and I took a bite of food to keep myself from looking too smug. I was starving, as it turned out. The cold noodles were delicious, and the meat was so tender it almost melted in my mouth.

"A good pork shoulder never lets me down," he replied, "and admittedly this is kind of a comfort food for me. It's been a rough few weeks."

"Oh! Your interview!" I gasped, suddenly remembering. He did look a little worse for wear, come to think of it. His hair was greasy and pushed back, and the white T-shirt he wore looked like it'd gone through a lot today, the collar slouching, revealing the birthmark on his clavicle. I immediately looked away from it. "Did you get the job?"

He swallowed a mouthful of food before he struck a pose and said, "I am *officially* their new dishwasher. I just forgot how grueling it was." He showed me his hands. They were dry and cracked already, and when I held his hand, his skin was rough to the touch.

"You need a good moisturizer," I said as he drew them back, and looked forlornly at his nail beds. "Or rubber gloves."

"Probably . . ."

"It'll be okay. It's not like you're going to stay a dishwasher forever."

"No, and cracked hands aside, it's been so cool. I've worked in kitchens before, but there's something about the Olive Branch that just . . ."

"Is that the name of the restaurant?" I ask, even though I already knew.

"Oh, yes! I didn't tell you?" When I shook my head, he gave an apologetic smile. "You should come by sometime. I'll wash your plates really well."

"I am *flattered*, Iwan."

He grinned, swirled his noodles around his chopsticks, and ate another bite. "The head chef is *magnificent*. He knows exactly how to pull the best out of all of his cooks. He runs a tight ship, but I'm looking forward to it," he said, almost reverently, and then he scrunched his nose. "Well, mostly."

I quirked an eyebrow.

"So, there's this line cook position opening up, and I want to apply for it but . . ."

"But what? Do it! Apartments around here are stupidly expensive."

"I know, but I just got hired, so I'm not sure I *should*. I haven't earned it, really, and there's this other guy applying for it, anyway. He preps vegetables. Everyone thinks he's going to get it."

"Which is why," I guessed, "you're not even going to try for it."

"I'm not sure if I should? What if I'm not good enough? What if I make a fool out of myself in front of Chef? I've lucked into this chance to study under my granddad's idol. Grandpa never got formal training, and I want this more than anything. I want to make him proud, you know? And I don't know if—"

I reached over and put my hand on top of his. It startled him into silence, and he looked down at my hand, and then back up to me. I rubbed my thumb gently against his skin. "James Iwan Ashton," I said gently, "you are talented and you are tireless, and you deserve that spot just as much as anyone else."

"I haven't paid my dues—"

"And who decides on what dues you need to pay? If you want something, you have to go for it. No one else will be more on your side than you."

He hesitated.

I curled my fingers around his hand, and held it tightly. "Be merciless about your dreams, Iwan."

He shifted his hand and instead laced our fingers together, his dried and cracked, and mine soft and pale. "Okay," he finally agreed, and turned those lovely gray eyes to me again. "Though I don't think I ever told you my first name."

"Of course you did," I replied quickly, slipping my hand out of his. I returned to my food. "Remember? The first night." I tapped the side of my head. "This brain's like a steel trap."

He chuckled. "I'm sure it is." He tilted his head, debating for a moment. "Did I ever tell you about the restaurant I want to open?"

That piqued my interest, and I sat up a little straighter. "No?"

He perked up like a dog offered a bone. "I haven't? Okay,

okay—picture it: long family-style tables. The walls are red. Everything is comfy, the leather on the chairs broken in. I'd get a local artist to design the chandeliers, hire all my favorite people, put your art on the walls," he added with a wink. "It'll be a place where you feel a bit at home, you know?"

I thought about the dishes in the cookbook he pitched—the noodles on dry ice, the dumplings that needed a commercial steamer, the chili sauce recipe that required rare African Orange Bird peppers—and I couldn't imagine it.

"It sounds like somewhere I'd eat, and I hate eating out at restaurants," I replied. "What would it be called?"

"I dunno. I never really had a name for it." He grinned, slow and melty like butter. "I think I got a few years to figure it out."

Seven, to be exact.

He finished the rest of his wine as I set down my chopsticks, because while there was a little bit left, I couldn't finish it. He motioned to the bowl, and I said, "Oh, yes, please have it."

"I'm nothing if not a gastronomic black hole," he replied, putting my bowl on top of his.

I grabbed my wine and sat back as he finished my noodles. There was an idea slowly forming in my head. "So, I have a scenario for you."

"Go on," he said, his mouth full.

"There's this author, right? At work." I tried to keep it as anonymous as possible. "My friend and I are in this auction—all of the bidders were supposedly going to make it to the next round, but . . . he just turned us down."

His eyebrows jerked up. "Just like that?"

"Just like that. And it's frustrating because I *know* he'd be amazing with my friend." I chewed on my thumbnail, before I realized what I was doing and quickly stopped. "What would you do?"

"Do you know why he passed?"

Because of me, I fear. "I don't know."

"Hmm. That's tough." He began to get up with our bowls, but I slapped his hand away and took the dishes away myself.

"You cooked, I clean, remember?" I declared, and turned on the water in the sink, waiting for it to get warm. He followed me into the kitchen, and as I stood there, he hooked his chin over my shoulder and leaned against me. He smelled like dish soap and lavender, and it took every willful bone in my body not to melt into him like ice cream on the pavement in summer. "Well," he said, his voice rumbling against my skin, "could you go and try to convince him?"

I scoffed a laugh. "Sadly, it doesn't work that way. And to make matters worse, both my friend's and my careers were kind of riding on this. I just don't get it. We *should* have made it to the next round."

"It's a pity he isn't a chef. In restaurants, a good kitchen is a good team. We all work off each other and most of the time it's better if we all like each other, too. My friends have been in places where everyone kept sniping at each other, and it was so awful they quit. *People* are the most important thing in any kitchen."

The *people*? I eyed him. "You really believe that?"

He gave a shrug, like it was a no-brainer. "Absolutely. We don't get paid enough to work somewhere shitty, especially if we have the résumé to go somewhere else."

I turned off the water and stared at him, my brain whirring a hundred miles a minute. Oh my god, that was *it*. All I had to do was appeal to the chef in him—the him who told me *this* exact thing. I'm sure he'd had a shitty time in a kitchen by now; from what I'd read, they're a dime a dozen. It was a long shot—but I believed in long shots.

He hesitated. "What? Is there something on my f—"

Turning to face him, I looked up into his lovely moon-colored eyes, and planted my hands on either side of his face, smushing his cheeks together. "You're a *genius*, Iwan!"

He blinked. "I . . . am? I mean—of course I am."

"A *genius*!" I pulled his face down to kiss him. His lips were soft and warm, startled at first. He barely even registered it before I pulled away. "I'll see you later, okay?" I turned to leave, but he caught me by the hand and pulled me back. His grip was tight—tighter than usual. In a desperate, longing sort of way.

"Just a moment," he murmured, and kissed me again.

This time he was ready for me, his mouth hungry, and I melted into him. I curled my free hand around his shirt, keeping him close. He let go of my hand and, reaching down to grab my waist, suddenly lifted me up off the floor and planted me on the counter. He looked up into my eyes, the bright paleness of his turned stormy. His floppy hair fell into his face, and there were bits of gold in it when the fluorescent lights of the kitchen hit it just right. "Incentive," he growled, and kissed me again and again, quick snaps across my cheeks, against my neck, "so you'll come back a little sooner."

"Did you miss me that much?" I asked, my arms wrapping around his neck.

He murmured against my mouth, "I'd have to lie to say no."

And the worst part was? I wanted to stay. I wanted to stay as he kissed me savoringly, his hands gripping my thighs as he leaned into the kiss. But I could see the time on the microwave behind him, and it was already nine o'clock. If I wanted to make it to the Olive Branch before it closed, I had to leave now.

"I'll come back," I whispered, regretting that I had to go.

He didn't believe me. "Promise?"

"Promise."

Even though it really wasn't up to me, it wasn't a lie *technically*. I would see him again. But if the apartment had brought me back now, I knew it could again—and somehow in my heart I knew it *would*. So he kissed me one last time as I slid off the counter, as if he wanted to seal the promise with his lips, and I knew I had to go then if I wanted to leave at all, because it was getting harder and harder to break away.

Remember rule two, I told myself, and tore away from him. I gathered my purse and what little resistance I had left, and fled before I convinced myself to stay.

23

‖‖‖‖‖‖‖

Main Course of Action

I KNEW IT WAS a bad idea, but I didn't have another. Not if I was going to salvage this.

I hailed a taxi, told the driver to head to the Olive Branch down in SoHo, and found myself in front of the hopping restaurant not twenty minutes later. Without a plan. The doors were all pulled wide, the windows open to let in the evening summer air. The patrons at night were a world away from the ones I'd seen at lunch, all trendy young people in their new glittery fashions, snapping photos of their food while barely eating a bite—and most plates only had a bite on them. I felt more out of place than I had felt in a while, and that almost stopped me from going inside at all, but then I steeled myself, and thought about what my aunt said—

"Pretend to belong until you do."

The hostess stopped me at the front of the house and asked for my reservation name. That was my first hurdle. I didn't have one, obviously, and she wouldn't let me into the restaurant if I didn't. So

I pulled back my shoulders and raised my chin, and pretended with the best of them. "I'm here to see James."

The woman's eyes widened. She gave me a once-over. "And you are . . . ?"

Right, a lot of people wanted to see him these days, and I doubted he'd thought twice about me. Which was odd, seeing as how I still felt the phantom touch of his mouth on mine. "I'm . . ."

No one important—a publicist from a publisher he had rejected. That certainly wouldn't get me in to see him. So I thought quick. What would my aunt do? She'd put on countless hats over the years, pretending to belong somewhere until she did. "I'm a journalist. For—uh—for . . ." My eyes glanced off a magazine pile behind the hostess stand. "*Women's Health*."

I tried not to wince. That was a bad lie.

She frowned, giving me another once-over. "For *James*?"

"In an article about getting women's hearts racing." I was just digging myself deeper and deeper.

"It's a bit late, isn't it?"

"Never too late—that's a journalist's, uh, motto. Is he here?"

She pursed her lips, and then pressed her earpiece and said something into it. She waited a moment, and then nodded. "Sorry, you'll have to come b—Wait a minute!"

I had stepped past her like I had a job to do. Technically I *did*, but not what she was thinking. "You can tell him I'm here," I said over my shoulder, and dove into the dark and decadent restaurant I couldn't afford. She squawked in reply, but didn't make a move to stop me. She had too many other people to greet and seat, and she probably wasn't paid enough, anyway.

I dipped around a server carrying a heavy tray to a large table, and slipped into the hallway that led to the kitchen and bathrooms.

The metal doors to the kitchen swung open, a server rushing out with a tray full of beautifully plated dishes, and I stepped to the side as he passed, catching the metal door before it swung closed. This was it.

"To Mordor," I whispered, and went inside.

An older woman with a teal pixie cut glanced up from plating the latest dish—a fish plate of some sort, and her face scrunched in annoyance. "Kitchen's off-limits," she said, and shouted something behind her—for a sauce or something. She must have been the sous.

Everything in the kitchen was chaos. People shouting "Behind!" as they brought sizzling pans up to the front to plate, or "Corner!" as they turned, heaving dishes into the sinks at the back. It was all very overwhelming, but I made myself stand my ground.

Another server passed me into the kitchen and put down a ticket at the station with the sous, who took it and shouted the order back to the kitchen.

Then she turned back to me and said, again, a little annoyed, "The kitchen's off-limits."

"I'm just looking for—"

She waved at the server beside me. "Get her out of here."

Beside me, the server, a gangly guy in his early twenties, turned and opened his arms to try to corral me back into the hallway. "Sorry, ma'am," he muttered, looking down at his shoes, not meeting my eyes at all.

I tried to bat him away. "Wait—wait—I want to talk to the head chef!"

"Everyone does," the sous replied, not even deigning to look up as she wiped the edge of a hot, plated dish. "You're not special."

Well, *that* was rude. The server grabbed me by the arm, but I tore it away from him. "Look, I just need a few minutes—"

"Do you *see* him here? Out!" she cried again, waving her hand, and the server pushed me out of the kitchen. I'd never been man-handled so apologetically before in my life. He mumbled, "Sorry, sorry, sorry," even as he scooted me out the door.

I stumbled backward into the hallway again, and Mordor closed in a flash of swinging silver doors. "Wait, please, I just need to talk to—"

"Is something wrong?"

The server froze. I froze. My heart slammed against my chest.

He quickly turned to the voice behind me. "Chef," he mur-mured, still looking at the ground. "Sorry. She came into the kitchen asking for you."

"Did she now," he rumbled. I felt my skin prickle.

"Chef Samuels asked me to take her out."

"I hope not permanently."

The server gave a start. "I—uh—"

"It's a joke," he lamented, almost pitifully, and then waved him away. "I have her. You can go back to work."

"Yes, Chef." The server nodded again, and quickly left to tend to his tables.

When the squirrelly guy was gone, I heard the chef rumble, "*You're* not from a magazine."

Turning on my heels, I whirled around to face James Ashton. My stomach folded itself into knots. Just half an hour ago, his mouth was on my neck, his breath against my skin, and now—we couldn't be further apart. "James," I greeted him, trying to keep my voice level.

I hoped this worked.

I hoped Iwan was right.

He was in his chef's uniform, a white coat buttoned down the side of the front, straining his broad shoulders. "Yes, Clementine?"

"You rejected our offer."

"I did, and if that's why you're here," he said carefully, "my decision is final."

My heart plummeted into my toes. "Hold on, hear me out—"

"I'm sorry," he went on, letting his arms fall to his side, and he passed me toward the kitchen. "I really need to get back to work—"

I whirled around on my heels. "Is it because of me?"

He froze in his footsteps, his back to me. My hands were clenched so tightly, I felt my nails leaving indentations in my palms.

"Is it because of me?" I repeated. "Because you and I . . ."

He glanced over his shoulder, and that was all the answer I really needed.

It *was* because of me. My fists began to tremble. I probably should have felt sad that he hated me, but to punish *Drew*? I wasn't sad—I was getting angry. "Hold on, you don't think that's a bit harsh?"

He turned back to me. "No, actually."

"We didn't even do anything," I said, taking a step toward him as he retreated back. "We just kissed—a few times. That's *it*." I took another step, and he pressed himself flat against the wall, framed between a sconce and a still life of a fruit bowl. "And I'm sure you've done more than *that* since then, James."

His pale eyes were wide. "Um . . . well . . ."

"I get it if you don't like me or want to forget about me, but to reject Strauss and Adder's offer because of *me*?" I went on because the Iwan I knew and the man standing in front of me couldn't have been more different, and I didn't care how successful he was now, or how handsome, I had a publishing imprint to save.

"Clementine," he said, and I hated how level his voice still was, how composed, "do you really think we should work together? Do you think that this"—he motioned between us—"would be a good idea?"

"I think you and Drew would work great together! And I think Strauss and Adder would treat your work *so* well. Never mind I am *damn* good at my job, and I *know* I am. I wouldn't let a personal grudge or whatever you have against me affect how hard I will work for you and your books." My hands fell out of fists. "I know my coming here is unprofessional, but you once said that it's the people that make a good team, and everyone at Strauss and Adder is good. They're hardworking, and they're honest, and you deserve that. And they deserve a chance. A real one."

And I wouldn't be here making a fool of myself if it wasn't important. Strauss & Adder needed a big author to fill the vacuum Basil Ray left behind, and if we didn't get one, it would bode very, very badly for my job—and everyone else's job at the imprint. Basil Ray wouldn't be the *reason* Strauss & Adder closed, but I refused to make that old cryptid the nail in this proverbial coffin.

He pursed his lips, hoping I'd break eye contact first, but he finally did, and looked away. A muscle in his jaw twitched. He muttered, "I don't like you using my own words against me . . ."

"Admit it," I said, poking him in the chest, "it's a good move."

He scrunched his nose, the first small crack in his put-together facade. The first small sign of my Iwan. "It's . . . also quite endearing," he admitted, "and a little bit sexy."

I blinked. "*Sexy?*"

To which he replied, his face inches from mine, so close I could feel his words on my skin, "You have me backed up against a wall, Lemon."

. . . *Oh.*

I finally realized how close we were. So close I could see my reflection in the polished buttons of his chef's coat. *Unprofessionally* close. And suddenly, that awful telltale feeling returned. The Pop Rocks in my stomach, how it almost made me feel sick. Heat rose up on my cheeks, and I quickly stepped away, my ears burning hot. "Sorry, sorry."

"I wasn't *complaining*—"

"I'll withdraw myself from the bidding," I interrupted. "I should have in the first place when I realized who you were. That was my fault. Juliette can take my place, she's a lovely publicist and she'll—"

"No, it's okay." With a sigh, he rubbed the side of his neck. The shouts of the front of the kitchen carried down the hall like an echo through a cave. The murmur from the house was loud, the clinking of utensils on tableware, the laughter of friends. Quieter, he muttered, "I thought *you* wouldn't want to work with *me*."

My eyes widened. I looked back at him. "What?"

"That's what I thought. I thought you were just playing nice in the conference room. You weren't exactly friendly in there. You had that look in your eyes. You know, the . . ." And he made a pinching motion with his hands toward his eyebrows. Did he mean my . . . ? "That one! That's the one."

Mortification crawled over me. "I thought *you* didn't want to see *me*!" *You haven't for seven years. You didn't even come looking.* I stepped back and pulled my fingers through my hair. "Oh my god."

"I'm sorry," he agreed, though he looked like he wanted to say something else. "I really did love Drew's energy. She seems like she'd be great to work with."

"She *is*," I insisted. "So you'll reconsider?"

"I . . . will have to talk to my agent," he replied, and scrubbed the side of his neck again—before he realized what he was doing and quickly stopped. Put his hands by his sides.

At least that was better than where we were before. "Fine," I replied shortly.

"All right."

His sous chef poked her head into the back area. She didn't seem surprised at all to find us there. "Chef, stop flirting—we need you in here!"

"Yes, Chef," he replied, and started for the front of the kitchen, but turned back to me and whispered, "I don't like it when we fight, Lemon," and left me in the hall, the sound of his nickname for me like a piece of candy at the end of dinner, sweet and perfect, and I couldn't shake the feeling that maybe—*maybe*—I was in over my head.

An Unwanted Gift

AND THAT WAS HOW Drew found herself floating on cloud nine Friday afternoon. She pulled every cookbook Strauss & Adder had off the shelves like she was a bookworm in a bookstore where everything was free, while Fiona and I sent her YouTube tutorial links and made a list of Netflix cooking shows to binge every waking hour this weekend. The apartment didn't send me back again to him, but maybe it was for the best as I slowly spiraled into a panic about how to hold a knife.

"We might burn down the entire restaurant," Drew said happily, waltzing her way over to Fiona and me at the table in the kitchen. "But at least we're still in the running!"

Fiona was snacking on half of the granola bar that was supposed to go into my parfait. She nibbled at it. "For someone who can't cook, you're certainly going to give it the old college try, babe."

"Absolutely, babe," Drew replied, dumping the stack of books down on the edge of the table, and slid into a seat. "I'm going to burn the fuck out of some tortellini. I don't know how you did it,

Clementine, but you're a miracle worker. As always. The agent said that she jumped the gun before consulting James Ashton."

Fiona added, "What did you do to get him to reconsider?"

I shrugged, stirring up my yogurt. "Nothing, really." Besides trespass into a kitchen and manhandle a prospective client. "I just asked him why, and he changed his mind."

Mostly.

From the mail room, Jerry—our mail guy, a tall man who made the absolute best dump cakes for holidays—rolled out a cart, whistling a Lizzo song. "Mornin', ladies," he greeted, and reached for a package to hand to me. "For you."

"Oh?" I took it and turned the package over to read the name. My world narrowed to a pinprick.

Jerry turned to Drew. "I heard you're in the next round with that chef guy! Congrats!"

They high-fived. "Thanks! I'm going to crash and burn!" she replied happily, and he laughed and rolled his cart on. She took the first book off the pile—*Salt, Fat, Acid, Heat* by Samin Nosrat—and began to read.

"I guess we won't be finishing the baby's nursery this weekend," Fiona said wryly, and Drew gave her a dejected look. "What? You still haven't hung up the wallpaper I bought."

"Babe, I know less about hanging wallpaper than I do about cooking."

"There are fewer ways to screw up wallpaper," she replied matter-of-factly.

Drew glared, and Fiona smiled, and that was their marriage in a nutshell. I set down the package quickly, turning the address side down. "I love doing wallpaper. I can help?"

"Oh my god, really? *Thank you*," Fiona said in relief, and shoved the rest of the granola into her mouth.

"We'll pay you," Drew added.

"A bottle of rosé and I'm yours for as long as you need," I replied, and with one last bite of yogurt, I shoved my plastic spoon into the empty cup and stood. "I should probably get back to work."

I had begun to leave when Drew said, "Hey, you forgot your package."

Fiona picked it up and flipped it over. "I wonder who it's f—Oh." I winced.

Fiona showed Drew the name on the package, and her eyes widened. "Your aunt?" Drew asked. "But . . ."

"It must've gotten lost in the mail," I mumbled.

My friends exchanged a worried look. Sometimes, when my aunt was alive, she'd send packages to my work to surprise me—leather-bound notebooks from Spain, teas from Vietnam, lederhosen from Germany—whenever she went traveling on her own.

But my aunt had been dead for six months.

The package must have been lost in the mail for a *very* long time. She hadn't gone anywhere since last November, when she visited the last place she'd never been—Antarctica. She'd said it was the coldest she'd ever felt in her life, so cold that her fingertips still hadn't warmed in the weeks since she'd come home.

"Is your heater working?" I had asked, and she'd laughed it off.

"Oh, I'm fine, I'm fine, my darling. Sometimes the cold just sticks to you."

"If you say so." I couldn't remember what I'd been doing then—I think I was walking home from work, having just come out of the subway, my nose cold and snow sloshing the ground, but I couldn't quite remember. You never commit a mundane moment to memory, thinking it'll be the last time you'll hear their voice, or see their smile, or smell their perfume. Your head never remembers the things your heart wants to in hindsight.

My aunt said, "I'm feeling restless. Let's go on an adventure, my darling. I'll meet you at the airport. Let's pick the first flight out—"

"I can't, I have work," I interrupted, "and besides, I just bought our tickets to Iceland today for our trip in August. They were a real steal, so I couldn't resist."

"Oh."

"You don't want to go to Iceland?"

"No—no, I do. It's just we've been before."

"But not in August! You can apparently see the sun at midnight, and there's this hot spring I want to try—I hear it's really good for arthritis, so it'll be great for you," I added, and my aunt made a noise in her throat because it was getting more and more apparent that she didn't like the thought of slowing down. She was sixty-two, so in her mind, she shouldn't *have* arthritis. Not at least until seventy. My phone beeped. "Oh, Mom's calling. I'll see you in the New Year—dinner at my parents, you'll be there?"

"Of course, darling," she replied.

"Promise you won't fly off on the next plane out of JFK?"

She laughed at that. "I promise, I promise. Not without you."

And suddenly, I was back to last New Year's morning, my phone ringing and ringing and ringing, as my head pounded. I'd drank too much the night before—too much of everything. My mouth felt like cotton candy, and I think I kissed someone at midnight, but I couldn't remember his face. Drew and Fiona always dragged me to New Year's Eve bashes, and it never failed that every party was all the same kind of awful.

I had felt for my phone on my nightstand, and when I'd finally found it, I unplugged it and answered. "Mom, it's too earl—"

"She's gone." I had never heard my mom sound like that before. High and hysterical. Her voice cracking. Her words forced. "She's gone! Sweetheart—sweetheart, she's gone."

I didn't understand. My head was still sleepy. "Who? What do you mean? Mom?"

"Analea." Then, quieter: "The neighbors found her. She . . ."

The thing no one tells you, the thing you have to find out on your own through firsthand experience, is that there is never an easy way to talk about suicide. There never was, there never will be. If ever someone asked, I'd tell them the truth: that my aunt was amazing, that she lived widely, that she had the most infectious laugh, that she knew four different languages and had a passport cluttered with so many stamps from different countries that it'd make any world traveler green with envy, and that she had a monster over her shoulder she didn't let anyone else see.

And, in turn, that monster didn't let her see all the things she would miss. The birthdays. The anniversaries. The sunsets. The bodega on the corner that had turned into that shiplap furniture store. The monster closed her eyes to all the pain she would give the people she left—the terrible weight of missing her and trying not to *blame* her all in the same breath. And then you started blaming yourself. Could you have done something, been that voice that finally broke through? If you loved them more, if you paid more attention, if you were better, if you only asked, if you even *knew* to ask, if you could just read between the lines and—

If, if, if.

There is no easy way to talk about suicide.

Sometimes the people you love don't leave you with goodbyes—they just leave.

"Are you okay?" Fiona asked softly, putting her hand on my shoulder.

I flinched away from her, blinking the tears out of my eyes. "Yes," I said, sucking in a lungful of breath. Then another. Fiona had the package in her hand, and I took it. I wasn't going to open it. "I'm fine. It's just . . . unexpected."

Drew eyed the package. "It's pretty small. I wonder what it is?"

"I need to get back to work." As I left, I discarded my lunch—and the package—in the trash can, and returned to my cubicle, and drowned myself in work like I used to. Like I should.

Two hours later, when mostly everyone had left the office, I returned to the trash can to dig out the package from beneath four-day-old lo mein and half a tuna sandwich, but it wasn't there. The package my aunt had sent me was gone.

Best in Show

THE REST OF THE weekend and into the next week passed in a blur. The apartment felt empty without Iwan in it. Every time I opened the door, I hoped to find him again, but the present always greeted me, and I started to wonder if it would take me back again at all.

Days passed without much fanfare; Drew and Fiona preparing for their parental leaves as the baby neared, getting everything sorted, until suddenly I found myself sitting in an Uber as it pulled up to the sidewalk in front of the Olive Branch. The sign on the door said that it was closed for the evening for a special event—and that special event? The cooking class. Editors and their teams from all across publishing were supposed to be here. Faux and Harper and some Random Penguins and—rumor had it—the new publisher for Falcon, Mr. Benji Andor himself. Through the open windows, I could see a few people already mingling in the empty dining space.

"So, here's the plan—I do all the cooking, you do the chopping," Drew specified, probably because she didn't trust my cooking skills as far as she could throw me. Which, fair. I also didn't trust them. "And if we come across Parker, we hog-tie him and toss him in the bathroom."

Fiona poked her head out of the passenger seat of the SUV. "Knock 'em dead, ladies!" She gave us the finger guns as the Uber pulled away again, bound for the Lower East Side to drop her off at home.

Drew and I waited until the SUV had turned the corner before she smoothed down the front of her button-down. "How do I look?"

I straightened her medallion necklace and put my hands on her shoulders. She looked about as nervous as I felt. "You are going to kick ass in there."

"*We* are going to kick ass," she reminded me. She pulled her arm through mine, and gave a shiver. "Ooh, I'm finally nervous! Can we back out? Tell Strauss I fucked off into the woods instead? Become a hermit? Live off the land?"

"What happened to the editor who said she'd kill for James Ashton? Also, you'd hate living without instant hot water."

"You're right. I'll just fuck off to a castle in Scotland instead."

"It's probably haunted."

"You like ruining everything, don't you," she deadpanned.

I rolled my eyes and guided her gently in the direction of the front door.

Inside the restaurant, I spied editors from all different publishers, some big names, some I didn't recognize at all. I hadn't been to any mixers in the last however many months—well, since my aunt died, at least—so Drew gave me the 411 on all the different people. There was a table set with glasses of champagne, and we both grabbed one and went to go haunt a corner of the restaurant until it was time to start our culinary journey.

"This is mission impossible," Drew muttered, darting her eyes about the room. "We are deep in enemy territory, two spies in the jungles of—oh, Parker, hi." She quickly straightened as a lanky white guy with too-big glasses and slicked-back hair swaggered up to us. He had what I'd call that guy in your MFA syndrome. Constantly acting like he was the smartest guy in the room, favorite book was something by Jonathan Franzen or—worse—*Fight Club*. The kind of guy who would look at the meme phrase "she breasted boobily to the stairs" and nod and go, *Yes, yes, this is indubitably quality literature.*

He was *that* kind of guy.

"Drew Torres, nice to see you," Parker said with a smile that was probably as genuine as his hair plugs. "Excited for the class tonight?"

"Oh, absolutely. Can't wait to see what we're cooking!"

"It isn't every day you get to learn from one of the best chefs in the industry. Why, just the other week I was talking to Craig over there"—he pointed at the executive editor of Harper or Simon & Schuster or something, a flex if I had ever seen one—"and we were comparing James's ever-changing menu. I'm thrilled he has such a wide range of skills."

Drew gave a nod. "Oh, yes, he's very talented."

"He'll be great over at Faux. We have so many fantastic resources—though, I'm sure Strauss and Adder will try its best, won't it?"

"We're small but mighty," Drew replied, and motioned to me. "Clementine here is one of our senior publicists. She's the mastermind behind a lot of our books' success."

"Ah, Rhonda Adder's second-in-command, I was *wondering* when I'd meet you!" Parker greeted me, extending a hand. "I've heard nothing but great things. I'm surprised she let you out from under that rock where she keeps you!" he added with a laugh.

My smile was strained.

"Well, I'm surprised your publisher let you out from under yours," came a deep, soft voice, and Drew and I both looked over to watch a towering giant stride over. Dark gelled-back hair, thick glasses, his face an expression of artistically placed moles. He gave his fellow editor a knowing look. "You can stop being awful, Parker."

Parker gave Benji Andor a surprised look. "I was just joking! She knows I was joking! Right?"

I told him, "Oh, yes, obviously."

"See? Obviously." Parker slapped me on the shoulder. I tensed, trying not to reel away, when someone on the other side of the restaurant called Parker's name, and he said his goodbyes and wandered over to them. I shivered when he finally let go of me.

Drew said in a mock whisper, "See? He's the worst."

"You weren't kidding."

Benji Andor gave us an apologetic look. "I would say he means well, but we all know he doesn't."

"I would've called you a liar, anyway," I replied before I could stop myself.

"He's someone's villain origin story," Drew agreed, and then cocked her head in thought. "Probably mine, to be honest."

He rumbled a good-natured laugh. "If Parker comes over to bother you again, let me know."

"Thank you, but I think we can handle him ourselves," Drew replied.

"Absolutely, I'd just like to watch," he said with a wink, and after a goodbye, he migrated over to a different corner to stand silently again, like the brooding tree he was.

We didn't have to stand around awkwardly for too much longer, because James Ashton breezed into the restaurant, all smiles and charming dimples, in a button-down maroon shirt and insanely

well-fitting jeans, and I tried to school my face as best I could. I
didn't want him to get the wrong impression of me—*again*.

Drew elbowed me in the side and hissed, "Stop looking like you
want to murder him!"

Apparently, it wasn't working. I groaned. "That's just my face!"

James rounded to the front of the kitchen and clapped his hands
to get everyone's attention. "Welcome!" he greeted. "It's so nice to
see all of your lovely faces. I hope you have all come ready with
open hearts and empty stomachs. Now, follow me back to the
kitchen. I've prepared different stations for everyone so we can
learn how to cook a specialty here at the Olive Branch . . ."

||||||||||||||||||||||||||||||||||||||

DREW REALLY SHOULDN'T HAVE been all that worried about *cooking*. As
it turned out, we weren't the worst cooks in the kitchen—that
honor went, full tilt, to Parker, who, along with his publicist and
marketing director, set their entire station on fire. James rushed
over with an extinguisher and patted him on the shoulder afterward with a laugh.

"Happens to the best of us!" he said.

In this intimate setting, James Ashton was nice and personable,
and he was a very patient teacher, but there was something distant
about the way he smiled at everyone, something guarded whenever
editors asked questions. I kept looking for some crack in his facade
to see the man I knew underneath—like I saw in the meeting
room—but he seemed to have practiced. He wasn't letting anyone
get close, which on one hand was smart and professional—oh, he
was *so* very professional—and it made me wonder how and why
he'd become so practiced and refined.

Despite that, the cooking class was so much fun, I soon forgot
that I'd been worried at all. We ended up getting flour everywhere

as we made ravioli, stealing sips of cooking wine between learning how to reduce the sauce, and we teared up when cutting onions and said our final rights to the chicken as we slit the breasts down the middle. Benji Andor was beside himself at the station next to us, laughing so much he had to excuse himself to sit down and catch his breath. ("I haven't been this winded since a car knocked the spirit out of me.") We had somehow blundered our way through the cooking class, but we knew we weren't going to get top marks for presentation.

And when James Ashton finally came around to our station, he looked moderately entertained by our ravioli. "They look . . ."

Like vaginas. Not that any of us were going to say it.

"Like the Olive Branch's specialty," I said instead, echoing his declaration from earlier, and took another sip of the cooking wine.

Drew wanted to die.

James bit the inside of his cheek, trying hard to keep his professional persona—but there. I saw it. The crack in his image. "How did you even manage this?" he asked only after he was able to look away.

"They kept falling apart," Drew said meekly. "So we just kind of . . . squished them together?"

He nodded, his face earnest. "They'll taste great regardless, I'm sure."

I coughed into my shoulder to disguise a laugh, and Drew elbowed me in the side as James ambled away to go check up on Falcon House. "I can't believe you said they looked like his *restaurant's specialty*!" she hissed.

"They *do*, Drew," I replied. "Would you rather me say they look like vulvas? Each one of them's a little different."

She rolled her eyes and started tossing them into the boiling pot. "You're the *worst*."

I elbowed her back. "You're glad I came."

"Immensely."

The rest of the cooking class went about as well as expected. We finished up our food, and James talked a little about how he ran his kitchen. "A good kitchen runs on excellence, but a great kitchen runs on communication and trust," he said, glancing over to me as I gave him secretive finger guns behind Drew's back. He steadfastly ignored it. "I want to thank you all for coming out tonight. I know this is a bit different than what you normally go through to acquire a book, so I appreciate your willingness to explore cuisine with me."

I wished he sounded a little more enthused, like he had in my aunt's apartment. I wanted to see *that* part of him—the excited, passionate part, but it felt dulled a little in the harsh kitchen lights of the Olive Branch. My heart felt full and heavy thinking about the Iwan waiting for me in my aunt's apartment, and the one here with us now, so different and yet so similar.

He didn't talk about best offers or final bids. He talked about food and technique, and he hoped that we'd all come back to visit him whether or not it worked out.

After the class, he went around and thanked everyone, and we all put our leftovers in to-go bags and exited the restaurant, laughing and picking on Parker for almost setting the entire restaurant on fire.

"I'm a better editor than cook!" was his defense.

And Drew replied, "To be fair, we *all* are."

Outside, a blond woman waited, and she rushed up to Benji Andor when he came out. He bent and kissed her on the cheek, and handed her his terrible ravioli, and they split off toward the subway station. Parker grumbled as he and his team caught a taxi. Drew's Uber came first.

"I can wait for yours," she said, but I waved her off.

"Nah, it should be here any minute."

"Okay." She hugged and kissed me on the cheek. "Thank you for being on my team. I'm not sure what I'd do without you, Clementine."

"You'd still kick ass. Here, you can take mine for Fiona," I added, handing her my food, after she got into the Uber.

"Fiona will love you forever."

"I know."

The car drove away, and soon enough I was the only one left outside the Olive Branch. My Uber was circling the wrong block for the second time, and I began to get the feeling that the driver was about to cancel the ride and flag me as a no-show. I should probably take the train home, anyway, and save my money. Besides, it was such a lovely night. The moon was round and large, framed perfectly between the buildings like the main character in her own film, reflecting off the windows, cascading silvery light into the warm orange of streetlights. For a few hours, I'd been so focused on cooking that I hadn't thought about Rhonda's retirement or the pending disaster that was Strauss & Adder Publishers if we didn't get James. No, *focused* wasn't exactly the right word. My jaw didn't hurt from clenching it; instead, my cheeks hurt from smiling so much. I hadn't had that much *fun* in . . . a very long time. Especially where my job was concerned.

Even before this James Ashton business, I couldn't remember the last time I actually had *fun* at work. I used to—I know I did, I wouldn't have stayed at Strauss & Adder if I didn't—even when I was working myself to the bone. There had been something invigorating about mastering the job, being surrounded by people who loved the same things, but over the last few years . . . I wasn't sure. The job never changed, but I think what I enjoyed about it did. My job used to feel like chasing the moon, and now it just felt like planning out how to give it to other people.

But that *was* what a job you loved was supposed to feel like, right? When you'd been there a while?

As I stood, wondering, watching my Uber take *another* wrong turn, someone came up beside me on the sidewalk.

I glanced over. It was James, having locked up for the evening, swinging his keys around on his first finger. He looked just as pristine as he had a few hours before, and I resisted the urge to scrub my fingers through his hair to make him a little less perfect. I certainly felt like a mess beside him.

"I think we got off on the wrong foot," he said in greeting.

"*We?*" I echoed, turning to him. "Don't drag me into your bad decisions."

He snorted a laugh, and put his hands in the pockets of his dark-wash jeans. They fit him too terribly well, hugging every curve. It wasn't the first time that night that I thought he had a nice ass, after all. Not that I'd *ever* say that to a prospective author. Or say it aloud at all. In fact, I probably should not have thought it in the first place. "Fine, fine," he said, his voice light and warm. "*I* started off on the wrong foot."

"Better." In the app, my driver kept circling and circling. Brad wasn't going to come pick me up, was he?

"You know," he said, and gave a frustrated sigh, scrunching his nose, "this part was a lot easier in my head."

Surprised, I glanced up at him again. "What are you talking about?"

He turned to me then, and I wished he didn't look as handsome as he did in the streetlight, the way the oranges and browns in his auburn hair glimmered, a few streaks of silver at his widow's peak, but he did and I couldn't quite bring myself to look away. It struck me then, how strange it was to see him out in the world and not in a small, cramped apartment on the Upper East Side. He was *here*, real. In my time.

It made my stomach knot in a way I couldn't exactly describe.

"Are you hungry?" he asked.

I inclined my head.

Drew had been snacking all evening, but I'd been so nervous I couldn't eat at all. It was probably a bad idea to cross any sort of professional boundary, but this was just food. It wasn't a marriage proposal or anything. Besides, he was such a mystery to me, I couldn't really resist. And I was, in fact, starving. But maybe not for the thing I thought . . .

I canceled my Uber and asked, "What do you have in mind?"

He pointed with his head down the sidewalk, and tipped his body a little, before he began to walk in that direction, and it must have been the way New York City felt at night—the glow of possibility, shrugging off the heat of the day to bright, glittery evening—but I followed.

Washington Square Arch

MY AUNT USED TO tell me that summer nights in the city were made to be impossible. They were as brief as you needed them, but never long enough, when the roads stretched into the darkness, the sky-scrapers climbed into the stars, and when you tipped your head back, the sky felt infinite.

"So . . ." I began, because the silence between us was becoming a little awkward, "did you plan on what to say *after* you asked me to dinner?"

He flashed me a bashful smile. "Not really. I'm pretty bad at planning."

"Ah."

We walked another block silently.

Then, he asked the worst possible question—"How's your aunt?"

The question felt like a punch in the gut. I put my hands in my pockets to keep them from shaking, and I steeled myself to answer. "She passed away. About six months ago."

"Oh." He rubbed the back of his neck, ashamed. "I—I didn't know."

"I didn't expect you to." We stopped at the next intersection, and glanced both ways before we crossed, but there were no cars coming either way. "It's been seven years."

"And you look like you haven't aged a day."

I leaned back on my heels, and started walking backward in front of him. "Do you want me to tell you my skincare routine?" Because I doubted he'd believe the truth. "I could give it to you in crystal-clear detail."

"Are you saying I look old?"

"*Distinguished* is a much better spin on it."

His mouth dropped open, and he pressed a hand to his chest with a gasp. "*Ouch!* And here I thought we were trying to get off on the right foot."

"You were," I reminded, unable to bite in a grin. I turned on my heels again and waited for him to catch up with me. "I'm joking, by the way."

He pressed his hands against his face, as if he could smooth out the crow's feet around his eyes. "I feel like I need to get Botox now . . ."

"I was joking!" I laughed.

"Maybe plastic surgery."

"Oh, *please*, and ruin your perfect nose?"

"Am I balding, too? Maybe I can just get a new face altogether—"

I grabbed him by the arm to stop him. "I like your face," I told him in good humor, and before I could stop myself, I reached up and cupped his cheek, my thumb tracing over the laughter lines around his mouth. A blush rushed up his throat to his cheeks, but instead of leaning away, he closed his eyes and leaned into the palm of my hand.

My heart stuttered brightly. The skin on his cheek was rough with fine stubble, and as I looked at him—really *looked*—there was so much the same about this man I didn't really know, that it almost felt like I did. But for everything that was the same, there were small bits that were different. His eyebrows were groomed, his hair trimmed neat. I ran my thumb down his nose, feeling the crooked bump there.

"When did you break your nose?" I asked, finally dropping my hand.

His lips twitched into a grin. "It's not nearly as cool of a story as you're thinking."

"So you *didn't* break it in a bar fight?" I asked, mock aghast.

"Sister's wedding about a year ago," he replied. "She threw the bouquet. I was standing too close to the people trying to catch it."

"And you got smacked by one of them?"

He shook his head. "By the bouquet. Had a little silver clasp on it. Smacked me right in the nose."

I laughed. I couldn't help it. "You're *kidding*! Did you at least catch the flowers?"

He scoffed. "What do you take me for? Of course I caught them. My sister and all her friends were livid." We started walking again, and Washington Square Park was just ahead. There was a food truck on the far side, but I couldn't make out the name of it yet.

"So, technically," I realized, "*you're* supposed to get married next."

"That's why they were livid, yes. I haven't been much for commitment."

"Your Instagram tells me as much."

He gasped again. "I'm honored that you *researched* me!"

I pointed to myself. "Publicist. It's my job."

"Sure, sure," he settled, and then gave a one-shouldered shrug. The kind I remembered—and it still infuriated me the exact same way. "Maybe I just hadn't found who I was looking for yet."

I glanced over at him. Studied the lines of his face, how the streetlights cut the shadows of his face sharp. "And who *are* you looking for, James?"

"Iwan," he corrected softly, a thoughtful look flickering across his face. "My friends call me Iwan."

I inclined my head. "Is that what I am?"

I wasn't sure what kind of answer I wanted—that, yes, I was a friend? Or that, no, we shouldn't cross professional boundaries? Or—

Do I want him to say I'm something more?

That was a silly thought, because I'd seen the type of women he had dated, and not a single one of them was like me—overworked nerdy publicists with art history degrees who spent their birthdays drinking wine out of flasks in front of van Gogh paintings.

"Well," he began, "actually—"

Yo Mama's Fajitas

"IWAN! IS THAT YOU?" a man cried from the food truck, startling us both out of our conversation. We'd somehow ended up in front of a bright yellow truck with a highly stylized logo on the side that read YO MAMA'S FAJITAS. A line curved down the sidewalk, mostly college kids and young people taking classes over the summer at the NYU campus nearby.

Iwan . . . ?

Then did that mean—

A larger man waved from the window of the food truck, and James's face lit up at the sight of him. *"Miguel!"* he cried, throwing up a wave. The man abandoned his station and came out of the back of the truck. He was a burly Hispanic guy, with curly dark hair pulled into a bun, the undersides shaved, tawny-brown skin, and a smile larger than life—like you could tell he cracked some really great jokes. They hugged each other quickly—complete with a secret handshake and everything.

"Hey, hey, I thought I wouldn't see you 'til the weekend!"

Miguel greeted him. "What's the occasion? Here to ask for a job?" He wiggled his thick black eyebrows.

"Ready to come work in my kitchen?" James volleyed back.

"In that expensive-ass new restaurant of yours? Fuck that," Miguel replied.

James shrugged. "Worth a shot."

Miguel glanced over to me. "And who's this?"

"This is Lemon," James introduced, waving me over. *Lemon.* Not Clementine. I guess he only used my actual name in professional settings.

I outstretched my hand, deciding not to correct him. I guess I wasn't going to be around enough for his friends to need a full name. "Hi. It's a pleasure."

Miguel accepted my hand and shook it—his grip was hard and firm, and I immediately liked this guy. "Lemon, eh? Nice to meet you. How'd you end up with this guy?"

With?

I gave a start, quickly panicking. "Oh, we're not *together*—we're just—you see, I was waiting for an Uber and it never came and I was just at a cooking class and really I'm his—"

"We've known each other for a while," James interjected, glancing over at me to see if it was a good save. It was. I wanted to melt into the pavement, I was so relieved. "Old acquaintances."

"Yes, that," I agreed, though Miguel seemed immediately suspicious, but before he could ask the *hows* of how we met, the other person in the food truck leaned out of the window and shouted at him: "Hey, asshole! You leave me in here all alone with *this* sort of line?"

To which Miguel turned back and motioned to James. "Isa! Iwan's here!"

"Well, tell Iwan to get in line!" the woman replied, ducking back in through the window. She was a tall and muscular white woman, her honey-colored hair pulled back from her face in a pony-tail, her ears armored with half a dozen earrings, her bare arms filled with so many different tattoos, they melded together in a tapestry. Then, on second thought, she ducked her head back out and added, "Iwan, if you're here to mooch off us again, at least hand out the drinks!"

"He's here with a date!" Miguel replied.

James gave him a betrayed look. "It's not—"

Isa shouted, "Then he better order something—we close at ten *sharp*!"

Miguel's smile grew pained. "I better go help before she plots to kill me in my sleep. Again," he added grimly, and hurried back into the food truck, and took up the next order, and we got in line at the end. A few people glanced back to look at James, though only one or two people recognized him, pulling out their phones to check the images online next to him in real life.

James seemed absolutely oblivious to it. "That's Miguel Ruiz and his fiancée, and better half, Isabelle Martin. We all graduated CIA together."

"Oh?" I had a hunch as I came closer to the truck and read the menu. With a name like Yo Mama's Fajitas, I had an inkling of what they served, but I was pleasantly surprised anyway as I skimmed down the menu. "You did it, then," I said with a grin.

Distracted from taking his wallet out of his back pocket, he asked, "Did what?"

"You bullied your friend with the fajita recipe into opening a food truck."

He had to think on that for a moment, but then he must have remembered, because it dawned on him and he seemed very excited as he said, "I *did* make you his fajitas the first night we met, didn't I? These are infinitely better."

"Oh, I've no doubt."

"Wow, tell me how you *really* feel about my cooking, Lemon."

"I think I just did."

His mouth fell open in a scandalized expression, and I'm sure he would've had something very smart and snarky to say, but we came to the front of the line at that exact moment, and I was thankfully distracted by ordering a chicken fajita, and he a beef one, and two Coronas. He lingered by the food truck as Miguel and Isa prepared our order, looking so much more in his element here than in a pristine kitchen, where he was done up in a chef's jacket, barking orders to line cooks. Here, his shirt was untucked and his hair had become a bit ruffled and droopy from the evening's humidity, as he gave Miguel just a little bit of hell for some knife technique.

"Seriously, look at that knife," James said, *tsk*ing. "That's got to be the dullest thing in that kitchen—and that includes you."

"I've *feelings*, bro."

Isa said while plating another fajita, not missing a beat, "No, you don't. I squashed those years ago."

"From *both sides*? You can both fuck off." But he grinned at them.

James laughed, and, oh, it was *charming*, how easy it was. Like he fit in here, hanging out by the window of his friend's food truck. He turned to me and asked, "Did you know that in the US, a food truck is technically classified as a restaurant? And that because it is, it's eligible for a Michelin star?"

"No, I didn't know," I replied.

Miguel rolled his eyes. "You're not gonna convince me."

"I've done it once already."

"Pfff. You're telling me to get some random highbrow food critic to come over here, eat my food, and tell me what I already know? No, thanks. You can keep your stars." Miguel waved his hand, and went back to his cooktop, and James rolled his eyes.

I asked, because I wasn't quite sure myself, "How do you get a Michelin star?"

He turned to me and wiggled his fingers. "It's a mystery. Well, not *that* much of a mystery, but we never know when a Michelin critic comes into our restaurants. We just know when they're gone. Usually, they come by once every eighteen months or so if you're on their list—unless a restaurant is in danger of *losing* a star, then they can make a surprise visit."

"They sound a bit like a food mafia," I said conspiratorially.

"You're not wrong. To get one star, a critic has to come into a restaurant and like the food enough to award it a star. Two stars, a critic has to come four times. Three stars?" He gave a low whistle. "The hardest of all. Ten visits. Ten consecutive perfect dinners across *years* of work. It's almost impossible, which is why there are only a handful of restaurants that are three-starred." He had this conflicted look on his face, as he spun a silver ring around on his thumb. "Most chefs would kill for three stars."

"And you?"

"I am a chef," he replied, but there was a guarded look on his face. He motioned to the cooktop, where Miguel dipped out a bowl of steak strips, and added a handful of bell peppers and onions. "Miguel and Isa are two of the most talented people I know. They make this look easy, but their food is intricate and incredibly de-tailed. See the steaks? They've been marinating for at least four hours in a mixture of—what is it? Lime juice and . . . ?"

"Yo mama's secret recipe," Isa quipped.

James barked a laugh. "Right, right. The ingredients are fresh, and they change the menu based on what's in season. They have a pumpkin fajita in the fall that just—it blows my mind."

As he talked, I couldn't help but join into his excitement. Like I did in the apartment. He talked too much with his hands, lacing adjectives into the air with his fingers, but it was endearing, and the other people in line couldn't help but lean in to listen.

When he lit up, we were like moths to a flame.

I wished this had been the side of him he'd shown in that conference room, and in that cooking class—everywhere, really, that mattered.

This was the part of him I feared had disappeared, but he'd just schooled it and kept it hidden for friends who wouldn't give up his secret.

"Why are you smiling? Did I say something funny?" he asked suddenly, dropping his hands.

"No, sorry—I just—I missed this." And I motioned to him.

"Me boring you with food?" he asked.

I shook my head. "You being passionate about it."

A conflicted look crossed his brows. "I'm always passionate about it."

Why don't you show it more often, then? I wanted to ask, but I felt that might be a little rude. Besides, seven years made him almost a stranger, so who was I to say anything, anyway? "I know, I just—I missed it. In the"—I waved my hand absently—"seven years. It was a long time."

"Ah." James nodded, biting in a smile that was just a little bit crooked, and the hollow part of my chest ached—the part that had been carved out by grief. It ached for something warm. For something good. For something that maybe, just maybe, could stay. A smile and a bittersweet story over lemon pie.

And I was in trouble tonight, because I smiled back.

"I think it was a little longer for me," he said at last.

My eyes widened.

Suddenly, my phone buzzed, and I quickly tore my gaze away from him and pulled it out of my purse, expecting it to be one of my authors stranded at another airport or convention hotel. It was Fiona and Drew. Crap—I'd forgotten to text Drew and tell her that . . . what, I was out getting dinner with our prospective client?

Maybe not.

EARTH TO CLEMENTINE!!! Fiona texted, along with a slew of emojis I hoped meant that she was concerned and not about to murder me.

Are you murdered? Drew asked. **Do we need to file a police report?**

CLEMENTINE MIDDLE NAME WEST ARE YOU ALIVE, Fiona added. **TEXT Y/N.**

I really loved my friends. I also wished they wouldn't have ruined the moment.

James asked, a little worried, "Is everything okay?"

"Oh, yeah. I just have to answer this." Or else my friends might actually file a missing person's report on me. "My friends. They're a little . . ."

"Say no more," he replied, raising his hands. "I've got the food. You can go find a seat for us, if you want?"

"Sure, thanks." And I quickly left the food truck, which was perhaps for the best because I was getting way too warm standing beside him, and he was looking much too handsome, and that was the kind of line I was not going to cross. I headed for the stone benches in front of the Washington Square Arch, and sat there to wait.

Fiona followed that up with, **Okay maybe don't text. IF YOU'RE THE MURDERER WE'RE COMING AFTER YOU BUDDY.**

Drew added, **YEAH GET FUCKED.**

YOU TELL 'EM BABE

Both of you need to calm down, I finally texted, glancing over at the food truck. Miguel was saying something to James, who looked bashful, rubbing the back of his neck. I wanted to commit that image to memory, put it in a frame in my head, the streetlights bright against his hair, the shadows across his face in blues and purples. I, not for the first time tonight, felt my fingers twitch with the thought of painting him in vivid colors, to capture the moment. To make it last forever.

Immediately, Fiona texted, **HOLY CRAP SHE'S ALIVE. BABE SHE'S ALIVE.**

HALLALUJUAH, Drew added.

Then again, ***HALLILUJIAH**

Then, ****HALLALUDSHGAKJA**

A smile broke out across my lips. **Drew aren't you supposed to be an editor?** I asked.

Drew sent a frowning face.

Fiona said, **Clearly she never had to pirate Rufus Wainwright off Limewire.**

I think I just aged ten years reading that text, I replied, then told them I was out getting dinner with a friend I'd met on the sidewalk—not quite a lie, I figured—and put my phone away as James came over with our food, two Coronas under his arm. I took the beers as he sat down, and he popped them open on the side of the benches.

"To good food," he said, handing me mine.

"And good company," I replied, and we clinked the bottlenecks together, and I made do with painting this summer evening in my head. The night a mix of midnight-blue and purple haze, flecks of pearl, and loud, bright pinks that only I could see, metaphors for how I felt.

The night was warm, and the beer was cold, and the company was, in fact, quite perfect. People strolled under the arch, laughing with each other, and the park made the sky look so wide I could almost see the stars. We chatted as we ate. He asked about my job, and I asked him about his. The new restaurant he was opening took up a good majority of his time, so his sous chef at the Olive Branch was doing a lot of the heavy lifting, and he felt bad about it.

"Was that the chef I met last week?" I asked, recalling the sous who told me to leave the kitchen.

"Iona Samuels," he replied with a nod. "One of the best chefs I have. She doesn't know it yet, but she's going to be the head chef at the Branch once I leave. I can't imagine the restaurant in better hands."

"Is it bittersweet? Leaving a place you've been for the last seven years?"

He gave a one-shouldered shrug. "Somewhat, but it's good for my brand, and my career." It was nice seeing his life pan out exactly the way he wanted it to. It didn't matter what I thought about his glossy life.

I was in so little of it, after all.

"I've worked so much," he went on, "I really can't stop now. Don't really want to."

"You've built something amazing. I bet your grandpa's proud."

He hesitated, and took another long swig of beer. "He passed, actually."

It felt like the wind got punched out of me. "Oh—*oh*, I'm so sorry."

He shook his head. "It's okay, really. It's been almost seven years now. He passed right after—" He stopped himself, and said instead, "A few days after I got my own apartment."

So after he left my aunt's place. After the summer. So soon, though, after he got his job. His grandpa didn't even get to see him become the chef he was today. It was unfair, really. I wasn't sure how to comfort him—or even if he *wanted* comfort. It had been seven years, after all . . . and he seemed to be able to talk about his grandpa a lot better than I could about my aunt. In the end, I just said, "Look at all you've done. You're about to open up your own *restaurant*. You've made him proud."

"I have," he agreed, though there wasn't ego in his voice. There was just . . . a tiredness? Yeah—he sounded tired. "And I've given up a lot to be here. Relationships, friendships, other career opportunities . . . only way to go is up."

I took one last bite of chicken fajita, studying him in the streetlights. "Do you regret it?"

"If I said I did," he replied, looking thoughtful, "would that be a disservice to the past me who dreamed of getting here? Probably." But then a slow smile spread across his lips, honeyed and coy. "Though it's a good thing I don't. But . . ." He hesitated. "I do regret not being there. For you," he added. "When your aunt passed. I regret that."

A knot formed in my throat. I looked away. Anywhere else. "It's fine," I said shortly. "I'm fine."

"No," he mumbled, studying my face, and I knew it looked a little lost, a little broken, "you aren't."

"Why didn't you come find me, then?" I asked abruptly. "Over the last seven years?"

His face pinched, he set down his plate on the bench beside him and started to clean his hands. I imagined he was thinking about how best to break it to me that he didn't care to, that if he wanted to he could have, but he just planted a hand between us, leaned on it as he came in close, and whispered, "Would you have believed me, Lemon?"

Time Well Traveled

"I . . . DON'T UNDERSTAND WHAT you mean," I confessed.

He sighed and leaned back again, looking around the park, to a group of young people taking photos under the arch. "Then let me set the scene. Seven years ago. You're . . . what, twenty-two? I find you, and I'm a stranger, right? Because *you* won't know me for another seven years."

His words caught me off guard, and I almost choked on my beer as I tried to take another sip. What had he said earlier? "I think it was a little longer for me"? "You—you know, then? That . . ."

"Yeah," he replied shortly. "I do."

I wasn't sure what was more shocking: the realization that he *had* thought about coming to find me, or the fact that at some point in the next few weeks before he moved out of my aunt's apartment, I would tell him the truth. I sat up a little straighter at the realization—"I make it back, then, don't I? To the apartment in your time?"

He concentrated on a streetlight. "I don't remember."

I studied his face for a long moment, trying to see if I could tell if he was lying, the set of his mouth, an uncertainty in his eyes, but he didn't betray anything, not even when he caught me staring, and returned it.

"I don't remember, Lemon," he insisted, and I quickly looked away.

Does something happen? I wanted to ask. Something so terrible that he couldn't even tell me? I tried to think back and remember that summer seven years ago, when I went gallivanting off with my aunt at a moment's notice. It was the first and only time my aunt and I stole away for months, charging our phones in cafés and sleeping in hostels. The next year I had a job at Strauss & Adder, and so we planned a trip at the end of summer every year instead. We'd meet at the Met on my birthday, suitcases in hand, and we'd sit and visit van Gogh for a while, and then leave for places unknown.

I didn't remember the day I came home from that glorious summer abroad seven years ago. I remembered taxiing *way* too long on the tarmac in LaGuardia, so long they ran out of complimentary wine, and I remembered dropping my aunt off at her apartment, hugging her goodbye, and being so tired I accidentally caught a taxi with another person already inside.

I frowned.

James reached toward me and smoothed out the skin between my brows with his thumb. He didn't say anything, but he didn't have to, because I figured I had that look on my face again, that distant sour one, like I was sucking on a lemon drop.

"Do you not remember, or do you not want to tell me?" I asked, pulling away from him, and he tilted his head to one side and debated on how to answer.

"Is there a third option?"

"Sure, but what is it?"

He hesitated, and looked down at his half-eaten fajita as if he was trying to figure out how to say what he needed to, and suddenly I got the terrible feeling that it would just make everything worse.

"Sorry," I said quickly. "You don't have to answer that. Wow, I—I really don't know how to carry on a normal conversation, do I? What's your favorite band? Favorite book? Favorite *color*?"

"*Tsk, tsk,* you still have to guess it—oh, no," he added quieter, catching sight of something behind me, and his gaze darkened. "I feel like I'm about to regret this."

"What?" I glanced over my shoulder.

Miguel and Isa were closing up the truck, pulling down their window covering and locking their doors, before heading over our way. I checked my watch. They really *did* close at ten sharp, didn't they?

James said as they came over, "I hope you don't have what I think you have in that brown bag, Miguel."

"*Pffff,* absolutely not. Want one?" Miguel added to me, sliding to sit down beside me, and offered me the contents of the bag. I took out a chip, and it looked to be coated in sugar.

I tasted one. Definitely brown sugar. "Oh, that's good. What is that?"

James arched an eyebrow at Miguel, and took one himself. "Miguel's actual specialty," he told me. "Tortilla chips tossed in cinnamon sugar and something else. Still haven't figured it out."

Miguel *tsk*ed. "Not even Isa knows it."

The dessert chips were lovely and sweet, and had a nice greasy crunch to them. They were quite perfect after the fajitas. I ate another one. "Cayenne pepper?" I guessed.

Taking a handful of them from the bag, Isa said, "He'll never tell you—whether you're right or wrong. My bet is dehydrated sriracha."

"Doesn't have the right kick for sriracha," James mused.

Miguel just looked happy that no one could guess it. "Why's it matter? Do you want to take *all* of my secrets?"

"Might help with his cookbook," Isa said. "God knows he can't do breads."

"I'm not *bad* at them," James replied indignantly, "and chips aren't bread."

She laughed and scrubbed his hair. "Says the guy who almost failed Intro to Breads *twice*."

"And," Miguel added, looking at me, "he wears it like a badge of honor." Then he reached over and pulled James's hair back from behind his ear to show me the tattoo there. The whisk I'd seen before, now faded, the lines a little blurry.

James made a disgruntled noise and slapped Miguel's hand away. "Yeah, don't give away all my secrets."

"*Pffff.*" Miguel waved his hand at James, and leaned into me. "You know how he got that tattoo?"

"It's fucking hilarious," Isa added, slinging an arm around James's shoulder.

"Don't listen to them," James pleaded to me, his hand brushing across mine, too light and lingering not to be purposeful. "They'll tell you nothing but lies. They're liars."

"*Speaking* of Intro to Breads . . . first day at CIA. The three of us were the oldest people there," Miguel said, and James shook his head.

"Oh, no, not that story."

"It's a good story!" Miguel rebutted, and leaned toward me. "Anyway, this guy gets called on by the chef teaching us, and we're all elbow deep in dough, right?"

"I hate this story so much," James groaned, pulling his hand down his face in agony.

"He was asked—Isa, what was he asked?"

She took another chip from the bag. "He was asked what he was doing."

"I was following directions," James mumbled.

"He *says*—to this super-stodgy chef, by the way—'What does it look like I'm doing? I'm beatin' it.' Elbow deep in dough. Flour on his face. Yeast spilled across the counter. Using—what the fuck were you using? A wooden *spoon*? He was pure chaos."

Isa cackled. "And the teacher just looked at him and said, 'Whisk, you *whisk* it.'"

James pointed out, "To be fair, I'd never seen a Danish whisk in my life. Then Isa decided that we'd all go out drinking that night and wound up at a tattoo shop and"—he shrugged—"that's it. That's the story."

To which Miguel and Isa both showed me the utensils behind their left ears, too—a spatula and a ladle.

"Well, now I feel left out," I said. "I want a cooking utensil behind my ear. Which one would I be?"

Isa took another handful of chips from the bag. "Nah, you're not a cooking utensil. You'd be . . . hmm."

"A paintbrush," James said so very certainly.

Miguel asked, "You're a painter?"

"It's just a hobby," I quickly replied. "I'm a book publicist, actually. It's a great job. I work under one of the most talented people in my field, and it's such an honor. I love it."

On the other side of James, Isa asked, "Why do you love it?"

I opened my mouth—and froze.

That was a harder question than I thought.

The thing was, I loved my job, too, but if I was honest with myself? I wasn't sure I was passionate about it anymore—not like Rhonda was, or the person I used to be, six months ago, who just kept climbing higher and higher, and that's all she wanted, but—

I saw how hungry and excited Drew was about the possibility of acquiring James's book, how even as she neared retirement, Rhonda was passionate about her job until the very end, and mostly I just felt . . . tired.

I thought about the last conversation I had with my aunt—"Let's go on an adventure, my darling."

And, honestly? An adventure sounded nice.

"I . . . just do," I ended up replying. "And it helps that my two best friends also work with me. What made you want to be a chef?" I asked her.

"My mom's a renowned pastry chef—excuse me, *pâtissiere*. I grew up in the backs of kitchens," Isa said. "I think my favorite thing, though? The way a fresh croissant smells. Nothing like it."

"Or when you get the perfect blend of salt, acid, and fat . . ." Miguel kissed the tips of his fingers and threw it into the sky. "Makes a dish sing."

"Or the people who come to taste your art," James agreed, and then he pursed his lips, and shook his head. "The truth is most restaurant jobs pay shit. You work terrible hours. While you make great food, you usually eat shit when you get home. Or you're too tired to eat. This business isn't for everyone. If you're not pursuing something worthwhile, then why are you in the kitchen?"

"I can't remember the last time I cooked for myself," Isa deadpanned, a distant look in her eyes.

Miguel threw back the rest of his beer. "I can't remember the last time someone complimented my food."

"I can't, either, and I'm about to open a restaurant, hopefully to critical acclaim, so here's hoping something changes," James added, finishing the rest of his beer, too, and pushing himself to his feet. He grabbed the empty plates and beer bottles, and went to go throw them away. As he left, a sinking feeling began to settle in my stomach.

Isa sighed, eating another chip. "I'm so afraid he's going to burn out."

Miguel rubbed the back of his neck. "I know."

I watched James retreat to the trash can at the edge of the square. "Burn out?"

"Yeah," Miguel told me, watching James kick a can down the sidewalk, then pick it up, and throw it away with the rest of the trash. "I just . . . sometimes think he's doing too much. Not doing enough for himself."

"He wants to make his grandpa proud," I pointed out.

He nodded. "Yeah, well, at what point should he start wanting to do something for himself? If it wasn't his grandpa, it was Chef Gauthier, if it wasn't Gauthier, it was whatever he thought he needed to do to get to the next level. Over and over and over again," he said, rolling his hand to emphasize.

"Maybe it's what he wants to do, too," Isa pointed out.

"Maybe," Miguel replied, "but maybe there's something in doing the thing that brings you joy, too. Even if it's not the thing that gets you a fuckin' Michelin star."

I finished my beer as James returned, his hands in his dark-wash jeans. He sat down hard between us again, and leaned back on his hands. "Okay, enough complaining about work. Lemon, did you know I probably wouldn't have survived CIA without these two?"

"He was *such* a pain," Isa complained, and ate another chip.

I eyed James. "I believe that."

He looked stricken. "*Hey . . .*"

"We have a lot of stories," Miguel agreed.

I took another handful of chips, and told his friends, "I've no-where to be. Tell me *everything.*"

Isa hummed excitedly and hopped to her feet. If James liked to talk with his hands, Isa liked to talk with her whole body. She moved when she spoke, I quickly found out, pacing back and forth, turning on her heels, like sitting still was the bane of her existence. "Well, you are looking at the three top chefs from CIA the year we graduated," she began, motioning to the three of them. "And two of us almost didn't graduate—but not from a lack of trying."

James leaned in close to me and muttered, his voice low and a little playful, "I'll let you guess which two."

"Not you, surely," I replied, and his mouth twitched into the barest grin.

Isa went on, "We sort of all gravitated toward each other, since we were some of the oldest there."

James said, louder, though he didn't lean away from me. Our shoulders brushed, and I felt like a teenager, my heart skipping up into my throat. "I think I *was* the oldest in our class . . ."

"No, no." Miguel waved his hand. "There was that retired ac-countant. What was her name? Beatrice? Bernadette?"

Isa snapped her fingers and pointed to him. "Bertie! She's the reason we went abroad that summer, remember? When we catered for that nude colony on the coast of France?"

James had a far-off look in his eyes, as if he was recounting a war zone. "I wish I didn't."

Miguel went on, "Or the time we almost poisoned the Queen of England."

"We did *not,*" James corrected. "Not even remotely."

But all I took out of that was "You cooked for the *queen?*"

He shook his head. "God rest her soul. It wasn't that big of a deal—"

"Hell yeah, it was! Listen, he never gets excited for anything. It was for a banquet, right? Some real fancy shit, and we'd gotten in on good recs. Though I don't think you were working that kitchen, were you, Isa?"

"No, I was getting drunk down in Shoreditch."

"Right, right." Miguel nodded, remembering. "Well, if it wasn't for that poison taster, no one would've caught it."

"Paprika and ground chili pepper look similar, okay?" James massaged the bridge of his nose, and then said a little quieter, "And I was a *little* hungover."

"Oh my god," I gasped. "You were almost an assassin?"

"Ground chili pepper would not have killed the queen," he replied indignantly, knocking his shoulder against mine. Even through our clothes, he was warm, and this close, I could smell the hints of his aftershave—a woodsy cedar and rose. "Cayenne, on the other hand? Probably."

"That's not even the *fun* story!" Miguel went on, a spark in his eyes. He waxed poetically about some other stories with James, stories of a one-night stand in Glasgow, a meet-cute with a mobster in Madrid that ended in a high-speed moped chase down the Gran Via, traveling as far and as wide as he'd said, far back in my aunt's apartment, he hoped he would.

We talked until our cinnamon-sugar-crusted fingers hit the bottom of the chip bag, and it was a good night. The kind of good night that I hadn't had in a while.

The kind of good that stuck to your bones, thick and warm, and coated your soul in golden light.

Good food with good friends.

By the end of all of it, James was laughing again, his smile easy as he talked about his early days as a line cook at the Olive Branch, and the meat vendor who tried to hook him up with his daughter.

"I think you actually went on a date, didn't you?" Isa asked.

James ducked his head. "*One*. We quickly figured out we were *not* compatible. But she did have a baby goat she dressed up in welly boots. So damn cute," he admitted.

Miguel asked, "Wasn't that the fall after you came to NYC? When you got promoted to line at the Branch?" By then I was so invested I wanted every little dirty, embarrassing thing James Iwan Ashton had ever done or been a part of. "After you met that girl, right?"

Something changed in James's posture then, as we leaned against each other. He went rigid. "Not this story."

"Oh, come on." Isa rolled her eyes, and told me, "He never shut up about her. Not once, not for a second. What was her name? It had something to do with a song, right?"

"A *song*?" I both did and didn't want to know.

"Yeah," Miguel agreed, and started to sing it. "Oh my darling, oh my darling, oh my darling *Clementine*."

Bad Timing

JAMES WALKED ME TO the subway station, though he'd called for an Uber to take him . . . I wasn't sure where he lived, actually, but it most certainly wasn't the Monroe. After Miguel had sung "Oh my darling, Clementine," I thought I'd end up choking on a chip. James had quickly changed the subject to how Miguel had proposed to Isa—in the middle of the food truck, actually, on a rather rainy spring day three years ago. No customers, just them two, and steak that was going to spoil. I would've been charmed by their story if my mind wasn't still reeling from the conversation before.

"He never shut up about her," Miguel had said, just before singing the song, and thinking about it gave me butterflies in my stomach.

He couldn't shut up about her—about *me*.

"Tonight was fun. Thank you for entertaining my friends. They can be . . . a lot," he said, his hands in his pockets.

"If you think *they're* bad, you should hang out with Drew and Fiona," I replied with a self-conscious laugh, because thinking about the four of them in the same room together felt like a panic attack waiting to happen. I stopped just in front of the stairs that led down to the train platform, and he lingered there beside me. Both too close, and too far away.

As if we were both waiting for something to happen.

I turned and asked, trying not to sound too coy, "So, Clementine, huh? How many girls named Clementine do you know?"

His mouth twitched into a grin. His eyes were soft pools of gray. Maybe I'd paint them with watered-down green instead—with bits of yellow and blue, opalescent clouds. "Only the one," he replied softly, and took his hands out of his pockets.

Those butterflies in my stomach turned ravenous. "She must've been lucky, then."

"She's also smart, and talented, and beautiful," he went on, counting my qualities on his fingers, and took a step closer.

This close, he looked so much more handsome than I was prepared for, his thick dark eyebrows trimmed and the freckles across his nose speckling his skin like constellations. His gaze was guarded—and I wished, I wished so terribly, that he was still that wide-eyed man from my aunt's apartment.

I raised my hands to his face, tracing the laughter lines around his mouth, feeling the barely there stubble. I closed my eyes, and I felt his mouth hovering close to mine, and I wanted him to kiss me—I realized that with a pang of dread. I wanted him to kiss me more than I wanted anything in a very, very long time. Being close to him felt like a story I didn't know the ending to—the fizzy-rock feeling in my bones I always got when my aunt smiled at me with all of her teeth, her eyes bright and wild, and asked me on an adventure.

He was an adventure. One I suddenly knew I wanted to take.

Without a shadow of a doubt, I wanted this.

I wanted *him*.

But a second passed, and then another, and the buoyant feeling in my stomach quickly began to sink. I opened my eyes as he shifted away from me, and planted a kiss on my forehead instead.

"And she's supremely off-limits," he finished, his voice against my hair. My heart twisted in the ultimate betrayal. He stepped away from me, a pained look on his face. "Always the wrong time, isn't it, Lemon?"

"Yes," I whispered, my voice tight—because he was right, and I was mortified that he had to be the one to point it out. I couldn't look at him. "I should—I should get going," I muttered, and fled down the steps.

"Lemon!" he called, but I didn't stop until I was through the turnstile and heading toward the subway platform.

I'd almost tossed my career away, and for what? Some quick-hearted feeling that wouldn't stay, anyway? Because nothing stayed.

Nothing *would*.

But what scared me wasn't the fact that I hadn't even thought twice about kissing him—it was that I hadn't cared about my career at all. About what Rhonda would think. About throwing away seven years of overtime and sleepless weekends and papercuts.

That was what scared me most, that the thing that I had been working toward so harshly was something that, in a split second, I didn't even care about.

The train came into the platform, and I got on. I still felt the impression of his hands in mine, and my stomach burned whenever I thought about how close he had been. The smell of his aftershave. The warmth of his body. How he had stopped himself, the almost-silent sigh.

"Always the wrong time, isn't it?" he had asked.

Yeah, I guess it was.

Way Back When

I STEPPED INTO MY apartment, slipping my flats off by the door. Rain pattered against the windows, soft like tiny fingertips tapping on the glass pane. The two pigeons were huddled in their nest on the AC unit, and I was debating whether or not to take a cold shower to scrub off the evening—and all the pesky feelings still humming in my chest, when someone called—

"Lemon?"

I froze. Then, almost disbelieving, I called back, "Iwan?"

Stumbling over my flats, I hurried into the kitchen. And there he sat at the table, a bottle of bourbon and a glass in front of him. He was still in a dirty white T-shirt from work and loose-fitting black slacks. "*Lemon!*" he said with a crooked smile. "Hey, it's nice to see you. What're you doing around this late?"

"I—I wanted to see you," I replied, so truthfully my heart ached in my chest. I just didn't think I could. This man with shaggy auburn hair and pale eyes, who smiled with that crooked and warm smile.

And you never get over me.

I crossed the kitchen, taking his face in my hands as he looked at me, eyes widening in surprise—oh, that wonderful wide-eyed surprise, and I kissed him. Roughly and hungrily, wanting to tattoo the taste of him into the gray matter of my brain. I'd wanted to do this all night. Run my fingers through his auburn hair, hold tight to his curls. Press against him so hard I felt him against me.

He tasted like bourbon, and his five-o'clock shadow was rough against my skin.

"Why so hungry, Lemon?" he asked, coming up to gasp for air, his curiosity a little heartbreaking, as if he suspected that I had ulterior motives. That I couldn't possibly want to be here kissing him.

"Aren't you?" I asked, and that seemed to be answer enough for him, because, yes, he was. Yes, I knew he would be. Of course I knew he would be. The way he'd looked at me all night, studied me, as if he wanted to drink me in, as if he thought he never would again—I *knew* that look. It was the look my mom gave my dad. That my aunt gave that far-off memory that sat like a sour candy on her tongue.

I knew that look so fucking well, I recognized it the moment he lifted his head from the table when I walked in, from the moment he called me Lemon with that hopeful disbelief.

He reached up and tangled his fingers into my hair, drawing me into another kiss. Slow and sensual, his hands cradling my face as his mouth pressed against mine, muttering soft affirmations against my lips. His tongue skimmed along my bottom lip, and I leaned into him, the feeling of Pop Rocks in my chest. He smelled so *good*, like wildness and soap and *him*, that made me hungrier for more.

"You seem to always visit right when I need company," he murmured.

"Company—or me?"

He leaned back a little, looking up at me with those beautiful stormy eyes—like clouds before autumn's first snow. "You, I think," he replied, his voice soft and sure, and it melted the horrid wall I had built up around myself, and I kissed him again, to savor those words on my lips.

His hands were gentle as they cupped my face, slowly drifting downward toward my blouse, undoing the buttons one at a time with those nimble, long fingers of his. As he did, his kisses trailed from my mouth to my neck. I made a noise that sounded more feral animal than sexy as he scraped his teeth across the line of my throat toward my shoulder. He spun us, so I pressed against the table instead, and he lifted me up on it, scooting the bottle of bourbon out of the way. His tongue flicked against the skin at my collarbone, sucking, and then his teeth sank into it.

I felt myself prickle with gooseflesh, and I gasped.

"Too much?" he asked, looking up at me from under his lovely and long eyelashes, his gaze drunk on me.

No, the opposite.

"More," I begged, feeling heat rise up on my cheeks.

"I love the way you blush," he murmured, kissing the hills of my breasts as he undid the top buttons of my blouse. "It drives me mad."

I never considered how I looked when I blushed. "Tell me."

"It's a lovely color," he started, his breath hot against the skin between my breasts, as he laid me back on the table, his knee anchored on the edge, his hands planted on either side of me. "It starts right here"—he planted a kiss just below the center of my collarbones—"and it creeps up"—a kiss at the base of my throat—"and up"—another against the side of my neck—"and up." Another on the edge of my jaw. On my right cheek. "And it drives me crazy when I know I'm the cause."

I felt my skin flush at the—very true, honestly—assumption, my heart slamming against my rib cage. A slow grin crossed that terribly crooked mouth of his.

"Like now," he purred, and kissed my blushing cheeks. The way he handled me was so tender, so honest, it was—quite frankly—erotic. I had been romanced before—of course I had, you didn't travel the world and not fall for a handsome man in Rome or a smart-talking traveler in Australia, a Scotsman with a deep-throated growl, a poet in Spain—but this felt different. Every touch, every brush of his fingertips across my skin, had a weight to it. A reverence.

Like I wasn't merely some girl to kiss and remember fondly in ten years, but someone to be kissed in ten years.

In twenty.

But, of course, that didn't happen, that *couldn't* happen, because I already knew how this ended.

He kissed the furrow between my brows. "What are you thinking, Lemon?"

My fingers trailed down his chest and curled up under his shirt. I was thinking that I wanted to get out of my head. That I wanted to enjoy him, *here*. I was thinking how selfish that was, knowing what I knew, knowing this couldn't ever work out. I was thinking how my aunt had been smart to set up that second rule, and I was thinking how thoroughly I was going to break it.

I traced the tattoo on his stomach, a small running rabbit. Gooseflesh rippled across his skin at my touch. "How many do you have?" I asked instead.

He inclined an eyebrow. "Ten. Do you want to find them?"

In reply, I pulled his shirt the rest of the way off, and he dropped it to the kitchen floor, and I traced another tattoo on his hip bone—a wishbone. "Two."

Initials on the left side of his torso. "Three. Four," I added, kissing the bunch of herbs gathered on his left arm, tied with a red string.

One on the inside of his other arm, of a road filled with pines. "Five."

"You are impressively good at finding them," he murmured as I slid off the kitchen table, and pulled him slowly into the living room. He kissed me again, nibbling my bottom lip.

"I never back down from a challenge," I replied, and turned him around, planting a kiss on the butcher's knife on his right shoulder blade. "Six."

The seventh one was on his right forearm, a radish halfway sliced, falling apart.

Eight was small, so easily overlooked on his wrist, a constellation of dots that formed Scorpio. Of *course* he was a Scorpio.

"It's getting harder," he taunted.

"Is it, now," I replied, and he realized what he'd said and barked a laugh, this time blushing himself, and I tugged him down the hall, kissing him as I pushed him onto the bed and climbed on top of him. He was, in fact, extremely aroused by my game, and that was very thrilling. Number nine was tucked just above his collarbone, his crescent-shaped birthmark below. It was a line of a heartbeat, and when I nibbled against the skin there, he made a noise that sounded, a little, like he was coming undone.

He murmured, "Pity you won't find the last one."

Of course I would. I was nothing if not an attentive listener. I gently turned his head to the side, hearing his breath catch, and pushed back the hair that curled around his left ear, planting a kiss on the whisk hidden there. "Ten," I whispered. "So what's my prize?"

He scrunched his nose. "Would you take a dishwasher?"

"Someone once told me it's the most important role in the kitchen," I replied.

"He might never make much of himself."

"Oh, Iwan," I sighed, taking his face in my hands, "I don't care. I like you."

And there it was.

My aunt's rule broken; my perfect plan shattered. I knew Iwan wouldn't be a dishwasher forever, and even if he was, it wouldn't have mattered—dishwasher or chef or lawyer or no one at all. It was the man with gemstone eyes and the crooked smile and the lovely banter that I felt my soul crushing for.

Those lovely pearl eyes darkened to storms, to tempests, as he seized me by the middle and shifted me off him and onto the duvet. He pressed against me with his weight, dragging his hands up my thighs, under my skirt. "I'm going to take off your blouse," he said, his fingers finding their way to the buttons on my shirt, undoing the rest of them one by one with those long, nimble fingers of his. I wanted them elsewhere. "I'm going to kiss every part of you. I'm going to commit every piece of you to memory."

"*Every* piece?" I asked as he reached back and unclasped my bra.

"Every"—he muttered as his mouth explored my breasts, his fingers following my curves downward, tugging at my skirt, slipping beneath my underwear—"lovely"—

I tensed in a gasp as his fingers toyed with me, my hands finding purchase in his messy hair.

"—*piece*," he growled, and slipped his fingers into me, stroking me, as his tongue danced across the bare skin of my breasts. I squirmed beneath his weight, but he held me firmly and murmured sweetly, like chocolate, his words tart and coy like lemons, affirmation after affirmation into my hair. I was never the kind of woman to fall in love with a voice, but when I came, he pressed his mouth against my ear and rumbled, "Good girl," in the exact way that made me lose all sense of self-preservation.

My aunt had two rules in the apartment—one, take your shoes off by the door, and I'm certain I'd forgotten to do that at least once.

So at least once I could break rule number two as well.

Just once.

But, unlike with shoes, all you need to do is fall in love once, though, to be ruined by it forever. "Birth control?" he asked between kisses.

I had to think for a second. "Um, yeah, but—"

"Hold, please." He peppered a trail of kisses down my body, and planted one on my inner thigh, before he left to get something from his wallet, then came back into the bedroom, slipping out of his trousers. He tore the condom wrapper open with his teeth—which was *so* much sexier than I thought it could be—and put it on before he slowly, savoring me, slipped himself inside of me, murmuring psalms of my body as he traveled it, and I knew I was falling. The kind of falling that would hurt when I hit the ground. The kind of falling that would shatter me into pieces.

So I kissed him, feeling bright and reckless and brave, and I fell.

⸻

THE NEXT MORNING, MY mouth felt like I'd swallowed an entire pack of cotton balls—and then I remembered: *bourbon.* The empty bottle was still on the nightstand, and my pink lace panties were draped from the lampshade.

Classy, Clementine.

Beside me, someone groaned. I was so used to waking up alone, I hadn't realized that Iwan was still in the bed beside me until he rolled over and kissed my bare shoulder.

"Mornin'," he mumbled sleepily, and stifled a yawn against my skin. His voice was slurred and deep fried in the morning, and adorable. "How're you?"

I pressed the palm of my hand against an eye. My head felt like it was full of sand. "Dead," I croaked.

He laughed, soft and rumbly. "Coffee?"

"Mmh."

So he rolled over and began to get out of bed, but the space he left felt so cold all of a sudden, and I quickly grappled for him around the waist and pulled him back to bed. He fell on the mattress with a chuckle, and I curled up against his back, shoving my freezing feet against his.

"Your feet are freezing!" he yelped.

"Deal."

"Okay, okay, just let me—hang on," he said with a sigh, and turned onto his back. "I didn't take you for a cuddler," he added, not unkindly.

"Five more," I mumbled, laying my head on his chest. His heart thrummed quickly in his rib cage, and I listened to him breathe in and out. The apartment was quiet, and the morning light split into golds and greens through the glass artwork hanging up over the window behind the bed.

After a while he said, "I think the pigeons from the living room have been staring at us since sunrise."

"Hmm?"

He pointed up at the window, and I looked up. Sure enough, Mother and Fucker were sitting there on the sill of the window. I sat up in bed, making sure to keep the bedsheet wrapped around myself, and squinted at them. "How long do pigeons live in the wild, you think?"

He considered it. "Probably about five years, why?"

"Just wondering," I replied dismissively, and returned my gaze to the two on the sill. They *did* look the exact same as the ones from my childhood. One had blue feathers around his neck like a collar, the rest of him speckled white and gray, and the other looked a bit oily, with streaks of navy plumage that reached all the way down to the tips of their feathers. Come to think of it, I couldn't remember what the pigeons before them looked like, or if they'd had babies. I'd always assumed that they nested in the winter, and a new couple took their place every year, but now I was beginning to suspect something very different, and they reminded me—quite clearly—that I wasn't where I was supposed to be, either.

I waved my hand at them. "Shoo, shoo! Go away," I said, but they didn't take flight until I drummed my knuckles on the window. Then they just flew around to their normal perch in the living room. "My aunt hated those birds," I said as I settled back against him, and closed my eyes.

He shifted a little. "Lemon?" he asked after a moment.

"Mmm?"

"Why do you refer to your aunt in past tense?"

I froze. The first thing that popped into my mind was to pretend to be asleep. Not say a single thing. My second instinct was to lie. *What're you talking about? Past tense? Must be a slip of the tongue.*

What would a lie hurt? To him, she was still alive. To him, she was gallivanting off with her niece, sneaking into the Tower of London and day drinking in Edinburgh and being chased halfway across Norway by a walrus.

To him, she wouldn't die for quite a few years. She wouldn't even think about it. She was still alive, and the world still held her in it.

So this is where you find out, I thought, and my voice was tight as I whispered, "You won't believe me."

He frowned. It was a peculiar frown, eyebrows furrowed, the left side of his mouth dipped a little lower than the right. "Try me, Lemon."

I thought to tell him. I wanted to—I did. But . . . "She's never home long enough for me to ever see her," I found myself lying. "She goes traveling a lot. She likes new places."

He thought about that for a moment. "I can see the allure of that. I'd like to travel."

"I used to all the time with her."

"What stopped you?"

"Work. Adult things. A good career. A stable relationship. A home." I sat up in bed and gave a shrug, wrapping the comforter around me. "I had to grow up someday."

He wrinkled his nose. "You must think I'm nuts, then, to start a new career halfway to thirty."

"Not at all. I think you're brave," I corrected, and kissed his nose. "People change their lives all the time, doesn't matter how old you are. But . . . can you promise me something?"

"Anything, Lemon."

"Promise me you'll always be you?"

His eyebrows knitted together. "Well, that's a weird thing to ask."

"I know, but—I like you. Just the way you are."

He laughed, a soft rumble in his throat, and kissed my forehead. "All right. I promise—only if you promise something, too."

"What?"

"Always find time to do what makes you happy—like painting, and traveling, and fuck the rest."

"How poetic."

"I'm a chef, not a writer."

"Maybe you'll be both someday. And right *now*, what's going to

make me happy is a shower. Maybe it'll help with this hangover."
I began to scoot out of bed, but he pulled me close to him again
and kissed me. I loved the way he kissed, like I was something to
savor—even with morning breath. "This also makes me happy," I
added.

He smiled against my mouth. "The happiest."

Eventually, I peeled myself away from him, gathered my
clothes, and left for a shower.

When I came back out, he was already dressed.

"Let's go out today," he said as I came out of the bathroom,
drying my hair with a towel. He was sitting on the fainting couch,
his eyes closed and arms behind his head, the window open to let
the pigeons eat some popcorn on the sill. I glanced at the microwave clock—it was already one in the afternoon. "You can show
me around the city. Ooh—and you can bring your watercolors. I
can watch you. Where do you like to paint?"

I gave it a thought. "Tourist traps, mostly."

"Central Park, then? Or is there another one you like more?
Prospect Park is beautiful."

"Well . . ."

He sprung up from the couch. "Let's do it. Before the day's
gone. It's so pretty outside today. Let's lounge, and I can bring a
book, and you can do your watercolors."

"W-wait," I said in a panic, as he disappeared into the study,
and came back with my tin of watercolors and a book, and took my
hand. "My hair's still damp. My head's throbbing. I don't have any
makeup on!"

"You look beautiful just as you are," he replied, pulling me
across the living room. He grabbed his wallet from the counter.

"That's not the *point*."

And yet I still let him lead me to the front door. *I can't leave this apartment*, I wanted to tell him, but he wouldn't believe me. Then again, I hadn't tried to leave this apartment *with* him. Maybe . . .

I could have stopped him if I really wanted to. I didn't. His excitement was infectious. He spouted off places he'd like to check out—the deli from *When Harry Met Sally*, some other movie-specific restaurants. He wanted to try a hot dog in the park, a pretzel, maybe some ice cream.

"Do they actually allow you to rent rowboats in Central Park?" he asked, sliding on his shoes, and I put on my flats. His hand around my wrist was tight with excitement, until I took his fingers and laced them through mine instead.

There, much better.

He smiled as he led me to the door, his eyes bright with the possibility. "We'll go everywhere. Find some of the greasiest pizza in New York. We'll—"

And the second he opened the door, he vanished, leaving only the warmth of his fingers through mine, and then even that faded, and I stood in my aunt's dark apartment in the present, and looked at my empty hand.

Letters to the Dead

AFTER I TRIED TO go back four—no, five—times, I finally gave up and realized that the apartment wasn't going to send me back to him today, and decided to go run some errands. I locked the door and shoved my keys into my purse as I headed out of the building. I didn't want to stay right now, with the feeling of Iwan's hand still in mine. At the front desk, Earl closed his latest James Patterson novel and waved to me. "Oh, hello, Clementine! Summer really blows up thunderstorms in a blink, don't it?" he said as I came up to the revolving door and looked out into the dreary gray rain. I was glad I didn't look that hungover, though I felt it in every bone in my body. "You know, I remember when you and your aunt would come down the elevator and race into the courtyard and come back in soaking wet." He shook his head. "It's a wonder you never caught your death out there."

"She always said dancing in the rain made you live longer," I replied, though it was silly and certifiably untrue. It was a nice thought, even if it turned out to be false.

"I'll have to try it someday," he replied with a laugh. "Maybe I'll live forever!"

"Maybe," I conceded, and leaned against the desk to wait out the storm. Whenever rain would begin to drum on the windows, wherever my aunt and I were—it didn't matter if we were home, or in some foreign place—she would grab my hand and pull me out into the rain. She would stretch out her arms and tilt her head back to the sky. Because that's what life felt like, she'd always say.

That's what life was for—

Who else could say they danced in the rain in front of the Louvre?

"Come on, my darling Clementine," she urged, coaxing me into the downpour in front of Paris's famous museum, the great glass pyramid our dance partner. Then she raised her hands over her head and closed her eyes as if to channel some divine power. She struck a pose and began to shake her shoulders. "You only live once!"

"What? No, stop," I begged, my shoes squeaky, my pretty yellow dress already soaked through. "Everyone is looking!"

"Of course they are, they want to be us!" She grabbed me by my hands and threw them up, and spun me around the cobblestones, a waltz against sadness, and against death, and grief, and heartache. "Enjoy the rain! You never know when it will be your last."

That was the thing about my aunt, she lived in the moment because she always figured it'd be her last. There was never a rhyme or reason to it—even when she was healthy, she lived like she was dying, the taste of mortality on her tongue.

I used to love the way she saw the world, always as one last breath before the end, drinking in everything as if she never would again, and maybe I still loved bits of that.

I loved how she spent every moment making a memory, every

second living wide and full, and I hated that she never thought—never once entertained the idea—that she would have another dance in the rain.

The confused looks of the tourists in the courtyard of the Louvre melted into wonder as she pulled them—all strangers—one by one into the storm. A violinist who had sought shelter under the brim of a newspaper stall lifted their instrument to their shoulder and started playing again, and kids ran out to join us, and soon everyone was spinning around in the rain.

Because that was my aunt. That was the kind of person she was.

The melody of an ABBA song sang over the violinist's strings, a yawp about taking chances, about falling in love, and we danced, and the next day I'd caught a cold and spent the rest of the week in the apartment we'd rented, surviving on brothy soup and club soda. We never told my parents that I'd gotten sick, only that we'd danced in the rain.

I never told my parents the bad bits, anyway.

Maybe if I had . . .

The rain began to let up as Earl said, "Oh, I think you've got something in your mailbox."

My mailbox. It felt so jarring to hear. It was supposed to be my aunt's, but I had the keys now, and any letters addressed to her had gone unanswered for the last six months anyway. She didn't get much mail anymore, after I'd closed her bank account and credit cards, but sometimes there would be a piece of junk mail, so I went over to the row of golden mailboxes and took out my key.

"What is it?" I asked as I opened it.

He shrugged. "Just a letter, I think."

A letter? My curiosity was overtaken by dread. Perhaps a letter returned to sender, address unknown. Perhaps it was junk mail in disguise. Or maybe—

I unlocked the mailbox and took it out. It looked like junk—like everything else that came for her—until I noticed the hand-written address in the corner.

From *Vera*.

My heart leapt into my throat. Vera—my aunt's Vera? The Vera from her stories? Black spots crept into the edges of my vision. My chest was tight. This was too real, too quickly.

"Clementine?" I heard Earl say. "Clementine, is everything all right?"

I tore my eyes away from the letter, and shoved it into my purse. "Fine," I replied too quickly, and tried to steady my breathing. "I'm fine."

He didn't believe me, but the rain had let up and sunshine poured onto the street between the clouds, and it was my chance to leave.

"Have a good day, Earl." I waved to him as I slipped out of the revolving doors and into the hot and muggy Saturday afternoon to take a walk, and try to clear my head.

<hr/>

THAT EVENING, I CALLED Drew and Fiona to dinner for an emergency meeting. Drew wanted to try this new Asian fusion place down in NoHo, but when we got there, the line was out the door and the wait to be seated was at least an hour. Fiona didn't want to wait an hour, and Drew hadn't thought it'd be so busy on a Saturday evening that we'd have needed to reserve a table, since it was new and no one had heard about it yet. Turned out, *Time Out* had written a killer review for the place a few days ago, so now everyone wanted to try the sriracha egg rolls.

"Maybe there's somewhere else around here," Drew muttered, pulling out her phone, but it was prime dinner time and I was sure almost everywhere would be relatively busy. The muggy afternoon had given way to a warm and summery evening, clouds rolling across the orange and pink sky like tumbleweeds.

"Maybe somewhere with outdoor seating?" Fiona asked, looking over Drew's shoulder to skim Yelp.

I tilted my head back in the sunlight, waiting for them to decide where to go, since I wasn't all that picky, and Fiona had the most dietary restrictions out of all of us. They were arguing over whether or not we should just cut our losses and skip over to another restaurant in the West Village since Fiona didn't want to keep wandering aimlessly, when I spied a familiar bright yellow truck at the far end of the street, parked exactly where it had been last night—at Washington Square Park.

Catering to the summer college crowd, as usual.

I said, "How about fajitas?"

They gave me a confused look. Drew said, scrolling through her phone, "Where is that . . . ?"

"What's the rating?" Fiona added.

I turned them around and pushed them down the sidewalk. "Trust me, where we're going, we don't need ratings."

They tried to argue with me until they caught sight of the food truck and the line curling down the sidewalk. Most of the people in line were either students from NYU or tourists who found themselves down by the Washington Square Arch, drawn in by the smell of grilled meats and nineties pop songs.

"This place sounds *delicious,*" Drew said as Fiona found the food truck's Instagram handle and took a photo to tag them. "How'd you know about it?"

I had dinner with James Ashton last night, who just so happens to be a not-so-old flame of mine—it's complicated—and his friends own this truck is what I would have said if not for . . . everything. Though I figured if I *did* say that, then it would just open up a can of worms, and Drew would start asking questions about how I knew James Ashton, when I met him—things that I couldn't exactly lie about because I *actually* met Drew and Fiona seven years ago, and they would have remembered a guy like James back then.

So a somewhat truth it was.

"Don't get mad, but James actually showed me this place last night after the cooking class."

Drew's eyes widened. "The chef?"

I nodded and Fiona gasped, "*Clementine!*"

"It was just dinner! We were both still a little hungry, and my Uber failed to pick me up and . . . anyway, the people who own this food truck are his friends."

Drew seemed a little hesitant, something I understood because, let's face it, if the other imprints found out that I'd been spending time with the author outside work functions, it would look . . .

Well, there would be rumors, to say the least.

In PR, any publicity was good publicity, but not in this case. In this case, it would look highly unprofessional, and Drew knew I wouldn't sacrifice my career that way. At least, I hoped she did.

As we waited to order, Fiona asked, "So, why did you call for an emergency meeting?"

"Oh!" I'd almost forgotten. I reached into my purse and drew out the letter. "I got this in my aunt's—in my mailbox at the Monroe," I quickly corrected.

"A letter?" Drew muttered, and then her eyes widened when she read who it was addressed to. "Your aunt?"

"Who's Vera?" Fiona added.

"Vera was a . . . she and my aunt dated thirty-something years ago. My aunt never talked much about her, but Vera was very, very important to her." So important that she chose to let her go instead—afraid that what they had could only get worse. Because people changed over seven years, and Analea and Vera were no different. It was like how Iwan had changed into James. How I would change in the seven years to come. "I don't know what to do. Should I return it to sender or just keep it?"

"It's dated only a few days ago," Fiona noted. "I don't think she knows your aunt is gone. Maybe you should tell her? In a letter back to her? Or, since you have her address, in person?"

"But what would she say?" Drew asked, and then shook her head. "I'd just return it to sender."

"But what if they were in love?"

"Then why wouldn't she know that Analea's dead?"

I listened to them argue back and forth, looking down at the long and loopy handwriting that belonged to a woman I'd only heard about in my aunt's stories. A woman who had gone through much of the same thing that Iwan and I were currently navigating. My aunt had told me her side of the story, and I'd just assumed that Vera had disappeared and gone to live her life, but this letter proved otherwise. They'd still kept in touch, years later.

Why didn't my aunt ever say so?

"Clementine?" Drew knocked her shoulder against mine, a little worried. "We're almost to the window."

I quickly put the letter away again. "Right, right, thanks."

"What are you going to do?"

"I dunno," I replied truthfully.

Fiona wove her arm through mine. "Well, whatever you choose, we'll be with you."

That meant a lot, and I squeezed her arm tightly.

When we stepped up in line, Miguel's eyes instantly lit up. He threw his arms up and said, "Hey! Long time no see! So good you came back for more, eh, eh?" He asked with a wiggle of his eyebrows.

"Couldn't stay away."

Isa said, leaning out the window, "And who're your friends?"

"Fiona and Drew." I motioned to them, and they waved politely. "This is Miguel and Isa."

"Pleasure," Miguel said with a wave. "I love meeting new friends."

"Lemon here told us a bit about you," Isa agreed.

Drew and Fiona gave me a strange look. "Lemon?" Drew asked.

"A nickname," I quickly replied. "Can I get a chicken fajita and . . . ?" I looked to them for their orders, and they said what they wanted. "And a bottle of water."

"No beer?" he asked.

The thought of it made me green. I was still feeling the effects of last night's drinking. Iwan could absolutely drink me under the table. "Water is perfect."

"Fine, fine, bottles are around the side in a cooler," he said, and I began to take out my card to pay, but Drew waved her hand to shoo me off.

"I've got it."

"But—"

"Seriously, our treat. Two more bottles of water, though."

"Gotcha." He nodded, and keyed it into his tablet. Drew finished paying as I went around to the side of the food truck where Miguel said the waters would be. There was a man sitting on the cooler.

I froze.

He quickly righted himself. Even with a baseball cap pulled low over his curls, I recognized the crescent-shaped birthmark on his collarbone between the open neck of his dark Henley. *Oh.* "James?" I asked.

His eyes widened. "Lemon?"

"What are you doing here?" I asked, because if Drew and Fiona saw him, they would *immediately* assume that I took them here so that I could see him. And I was sure they'd never let me live that down.

He seemed perplexed. "They're my friends! I hang out here sometimes."

"Don't you have a restaurant to run?"

"Usually . . . ?" he replied hesitantly. "I'm in the process of prepping my new restaurant for a soft opening. Isa and Miguel are going to help me with some last-minute touches later. What are *you* doing here?"

"I brought my friends to try your friends' food."

"Friends . . ." His nose scrunched as he thought—and then he sat up straight. "They're here?"

". . . Yes?"

Drew called from the front of the truck. "Everything all right, Clementine?"

I replied, "Fine! The cooler's just—uh—cold!" And I waved my hand for him to open the cooler he was sitting on and get the waters out. "Why're you acting so strange?" I murmured to him.

Miguel called, "Iwan should be back there. Get him to get them!"

James and I locked eyes. "Thanks!" I called back, as James muttered under his breath and plunged his hands into the icy water, and took out three bottles. He handed them to me.

"I'm not acting *strange*," he replied, and then I realized what was off—

"Oh my god, you're *hungover*—we didn't even drink that much last night!" I replied. Well, *he* didn't drink very much. The him seven years ago drank me under the table.

"You don't look so great yourself," he replied wryly. We both looked a little green around the gills, to be honest. He glanced behind me, debating on whether to say hello to my friends. "I'm sorry, I don't think I'm in fighting shape to meet them right now."

"You've already met Drew, it's just her wife you haven't."

"Ah, the editor—yes, I think it might be best if she doesn't see me hungover," he reasoned with a nod. "Would that be okay?"

It was adorable that he asked. "You get one Get out of Jail Free card."

"I'm taking it," he replied somberly. "I'll be sure to make it up to—" His words caught in his throat. Then, without warning, he reached toward me, brushing my hair to the side, and his pale eyes grew dark and stormy. He pursed his lips together, and I didn't understand why until—

"Seems like you had a good night, too," he joked.

And then I realized. "Oh my god," I gasped, quickly reeling away, and pulled down my hair to cover the bruise there. Well, the *hickey*. I'd tried hard to cover it with concealer this morning, but it must have worn off throughout the day.

"Had another date after dinner last night?" he egged me on. "Was it hot?"

I gave him a silent look. He didn't understand for a moment, and then his eyes widened, and he pressed his fingers against his mouth.

And all he said as he remembered was—

"*Oh.*"

I cleared my throat. "It was, in fact."

"Was what?" His eyes were a little dazed.

I replied, "Hot."

He groaned, then, and pulled his hands through his hair. "You can't do that, Lemon."

"You asked."

He sounded absolutely destroyed as he replied, "I *know*. It drives me crazy." His face pinched. "For me it was seven years ago, and for you it was last night."

"Technically this morning, too," I corrected.

He made a pained noise in his throat. "Of course, how could I forget?"

"I'm not sure, really. It was very good sex." I inclined my head a little, studying this man standing in the shadow of his friend's food truck, hungover for—what I suspected—was the same reason I was: each other. Though I was very certain I had more fun last night than he did.

He rubbed his face with his hands. "If this was to get back at me for turning you down last night—"

"Oh, don't worry, you didn't."

"You know what I mean," he growled. Right—he thought I went back to the apartment last night, and had sex with his past self to make his present self jealous.

I rolled my eyes. "Well, you're wrong. The apartment does what it wants to *when* it wants to—it's not my fault you want nothing to do with me now."

He took a step closer, close enough I could kiss him, if I dared. "Nothing to do with you?" he whispered, incredulous. "I remember how you taste, Lemon, the sound of your breath as I held you." I felt my skin getting hot even as I pressed a water bottle to the side of my neck and looked away. "I remember the way you counted the tattoos on my skin, the shape of your mouth, the way your body felt when you came for me," he muttered, gliding his fingertips across my furiously red cheeks. "And I still fucking love the way you blush. It drives me crazy."

My mouth fell open. Heart hammered against my chest. He didn't look like James for a moment, but Iwan, my Iwan, looking out from a face seven years stranger. And I thought he was going to bend down, to steal a kiss, but he stepped away and quickly climbed into the back of the truck as Drew turned the corner.

"Hey," she said, our food in her hands, "is everything okay?"

"Fine!" I squeaked, quickly turning around. The sooner we left, the better. "I got the bottles of water! We should go."

Drew gave me a confused look. "Okay . . ."

"Onward! Let's go sit by the fountain," I said, quickly herding her and Fiona away from the food truck. I glanced behind me when we'd crossed the street, and saw James climbing out of the back of the truck. Then he pulled his cap low and left the opposite way.

Off-limits, I reminded myself, turning back to my friends. *He's off-limits.*

Second and Final Bid

I SPENT THE REST of the weekend deep-cleaning my aunt's apartment and sketching Mother and Fucker in the NYC travel journal section titled "Wildlife." The apartment didn't send me back to Iwan—though I wished it would have. Painting was an easy way to distract myself, at least until I started to clean out my purse and found the letter from Vera again. The address was on the Upper West Side. So close—just across the park from the Monroe—but an entire world away.

The longer I lived in my aunt's apartment, the more I could see why she'd kept it. Why, after her heartbreak with Vera, she hadn't sold it, and instead traveled the world to stay away. There was a possibility in the sound of the lock clicking open, in the creak of the hinges as the door flung wide, a roulette that may or may not bring you back to the time when you felt happiest.

Analea had said that romance across time never worked, but then why was Vera still writing to her? I wanted to open the letter, to read the contents, but that felt too personal. It wasn't my business to read whatever was inside, and I doubted my aunt would want me to. The most I could do was return it, and ask Vera in person.

When I arrived to work on Monday, Rhonda was already in her office, looking more worn out than usual. She had shrugged out of her blazer already—something she usually only did after lunch— and had exchanged her heels for the sensible flats she kept stowed in her bottom desk drawer.

I knocked on the glass door, and she glanced up. "Ah, Clementine! Perfect timing."

"Early start?" I asked.

"I couldn't sleep, so I thought I might as well get some work done."

Which meant that she had thought of something in the middle of the night that kept her awake, so she came into work early to get it done. Her entire life's work was this imprint, she poured her entire life into it. Her hobby was reading, her downtime spent brainstorming new strategies for the next big book, her social circles peppered with the directors of other imprints. That should be me, too—I *wanted* it to be me, but there was an itch under my skin that was growing by the day. A feeling like I was in a box too small, a collar too tight.

And I was afraid of it, because I'd spent so long trying to find somewhere permanent to stay.

"By the way," Rhonda went on, tapping her ballpoint pen against a notepad on her desk, "have you decided what to do about your vacation?"

"I think I'll just be around the city," I replied, knowing she was asking to make sure I was actually going to take it. I was—against my will.

She nodded, though from the bend of her shoulders, I could tell that she was relieved. "Good, good. With the transition, you might need to be on call."

That made me pause. "The transition?"

"Yes." She didn't look at me as she spoke, neatly organizing her pens in her tray. "As I said, Strauss's splitting my job into three—copublisher, director of marketing, and director of publicity. I'm nominating you for the director of publicity, but he wants to interview outside of the company as well. Something about *healthy competition*," she added deadpan.

"Oh." I nodded. "I mean, that makes sense. I've only been here seven years."

Finally, my boss looked at me, and her face was pinched. I recognized the expression—she was angry. Not at me, though. "And you are one of the most talented people I've met in a long time. I will fight for you until the end, Clementine, if this is what you want."

"Of course it is," I replied quickly, hoping the words could be the salve for the itch under my skin. "I want this."

Rhonda's red lips quirked into a smirk. "Good. I expected nothing less. Strauss might want to hire someone else, but there are two people at *Strauss and Adder*, and I have just as much weight as he does. You," she went on pointedly, "just have to nab James Ashton."

"Oh, that's all?" I asked, trying not to sound too panicked. "As easy as catching the moon."

"Go get 'em," she cheered.

I returned to my cubicle, where there was so little privacy I couldn't even scream into my donut neck pillow I had tucked under my desk for days when I took cat naps in the stock room. I already knew the imprint and my career were riding on the acquisition of James Ashton. She didn't have to remind me.

Breathe, Clementine.

If I wanted the career I had been working toward for seven years, I had to do this.

No matter what.

I sent a few emails and followed up on some podcast interviews, and slowly my eyes strayed to the landscape watercolors I'd painted years ago, hanging on the corkboard beside my monitor. The Brooklyn Bridge. The pond in Central Park. The steps of the Acropolis. A quiet tea garden in Osaka. A fishing pier. Snapshots of places I'd been, and the person I'd been when I painted them.

That restless feeling under my skin returned, more terrible than ever.

The painting of a wall of glaciers had hues of purple and blue, from the summer I turned twenty-two—the Clementine from Iwan's time—fresh off a heartbreak with her boyfriend. I should've seen it coming, but I did not, and I was an utter mess afterward. I'd graduated, and went back to my parents' house on Long Island, and holed myself up there to waste the summer away while I applied to curation jobs I wasn't sure I wanted.

My boyfriend and I were going to go on a backpacking tour across Europe, but obviously that didn't happen when he dumped me and decided to take a tech job in San Francisco, and I almost refunded my airline tickets—until my aunt caught wind of it and refused to let me.

"Absolutely *not*," she said over the phone. I was lying in my bedroom in my parents' house, staring up at the ceiling filled with boy bands from my youth. All of my things were in boxes in the hallway, moved out of my ex's apartment in a whirlwind of twenty-four hours. "We are going to take that trip."

I sat up, startled. "*We?*"

"You and me, my darling!"

"But—I didn't plan for us to go. Half the hotels I have booked have one bed and—"

"Life doesn't always go as planned. The trick is to make the most of it when it doesn't," she said matter-of-factly. "And don't tell me you don't want to sleep butt-to-butt with your dear old *aunt*?"

"That's not what I'm saying, but you must have something else to do. That trip you were talking about, the one to Rapa Nui—"

"Nah! I can postpone it. Let's go backpacking across Europe!" she said decisively. "You and me—we haven't done it since you were in high school, remember? Just one last time, for old times' sake. You only live once, after all."

And whether or not I wanted to say no, Aunt Analea was the kind of force of nature who wouldn't let me. I could have thought up any excuse, found any reason to stay home and wallow in self-pity, and it wouldn't have mattered. My aunt showed up the next morning with her bags packed, in the blue coat she always reserved for travel, and large sunglasses, a taxi waiting on the curb to take us to the airport. Her mouth twisted into a smile so big and so dangerous, I felt my heartache break way to something else— excitement. A longing for something *new*.

"Let's go on an adventure, my darling," she declared.

And, oh, did I realize then, that I had the thirst for adventure sown into my very bones.

I missed that girl, but I felt her coming back now, little by little, and I didn't quite hate the thought of something new anymore. The longer I sat here, in this small cubicle, the more I began to wonder what, exactly, I was working toward.

I thought it was the idea of Rhonda, a woman surrounded by framed bestseller lists and accolades, quite happy where she was, and I imagined myself in her orange chair. What I would look like. I'd need to throw my whole self into it. As many hours as I'd worked, I knew Rhonda put in more. Made herself available to our authors, to their agents, to her staff, every waking moment. She wore her job the way she wore her Louboutins. To be as good as I wanted to be, I'd have to do that, too. I'd trade my flats for heels, buy a set of blazers, be the kind of person everyone expected me to be—

Someone like James, I supposed.

I wanted that. Didn't I?

My phone vibrated, and I glanced at the text message from Drew.

It's in! Second and final offer!! Send good vibes, she said with a praying-hands emoji.

YOU GOT THIS BABE! Fiona replied.

James and his agent invited us to the soft opening of his new restaurant on Thursday. Move Wine & Whine to then and there?? Drew asked.

Sounds good, I texted, and Fiona gave a thumbs-up.

I turned my phone to silent, and went back to work. It was out of my hands. Whoever James chose was who he chose. There was nothing I could do about it now.

Everything would run its course—come into my life and then leave again, because nothing stayed. Nothing *ever* stayed.

But things could return.

That reminded me of something. I pulled out my phone again and added, **Would you two like to go with me to deliver the letter?**

What Never Was

VERA LIVED ON EIGHTY-FIRST Street, between Amsterdam and Broadway, in a four-story walk-up the color of cream stone. According to the address on her letter, she lived on the third floor in 3A. Fiona and Drew stood on the sidewalk behind me for support, though Drew still believed I should just mail the letter back instead.

"What if she doesn't want to see you?" she asked.

"I'd rather find out in person if someone I've written letters to over the last thirty years died," Fiona argued, and her wife sighed and shook her head.

I understood where Drew was coming from—perhaps it would have been easier to just send back the letter. My aunt and Vera's relationship wasn't my business, but because I knew the story, I felt . . . obligated, I guess. To finish it.

I had heard so much about Vera, she almost felt like a fairy tale to me—someone I never thought I'd meet. My hands were clammy, and my heart raced in my chest. Because I was about to meet her, wasn't I? I was about to meet the last piece of my aunt's puzzle.

I took a deep breath and scanned the buzzer box. The names were smudged—almost illegible. I squinted to try to make out the numbers at least, and pressed the buzzer for 3A.

After a moment, a quiet voice answered, "Hello?"

"Hi—I'm sorry to bother you. My name is Clementine West and I have the letter you sent my aunt." Then, a bit quieter: "Analea Collins."

There wasn't a response for a good long moment, so long I thought that maybe I wasn't going to get a response, but then she said, "Come on up, Clementine."

The door buzzed to unlock, and I told my friends I'd be back in a minute.

Then I took a deep breath, and steeled my courage, and stepped into the building.

Pursuing Vera felt like opening a wound I had sutured together six months ago, but I had to. I knew I did. If she and my aunt had kept in touch over the years, then why hadn't Analea ever mentioned it? If they had stayed friends, why didn't it work out? I thought Analea had cut ties with Vera, like she had with everything she loved and refused to ruin, but apparently there were more secrets to my aunt than I had originally thought. Things she kept hidden. Things she never let anyone see.

I used to want to be exactly like my aunt. I thought she was brave and daring, and I wanted to build myself like she'd built herself. My aunt gave me permission to be wild and unfettered, and I wanted that more than anything else, but ever since she passed I'd recoiled from that. I didn't want to be anything like her, because I was heartbroken.

I was still heartbroken.

And now I had to tell someone else, someone who also loved Analea enough to write her letters thirty years after their time ended, exactly what I never wanted to hear again.

I stopped at apartment 3A and knocked on the door. My aunt had told me about Vera, about what she looked like, but when she opened the door I was immediately struck by how much she reminded me of my aunt. She was tall and thin, in a burnt-orange blouse and comfortable slacks. Her grayish-blond hair was cut very short, her face angular for a woman in her late sixties.

"Clementine," she greeted, and suddenly pulled me into a tight hug. Her arms were thin, so it surprised me how strong she was. "I've heard so much about you!"

Tears prickled in my eyes, because she confirmed what I had wondered—whether this letter had been a fluke, or if it was another line of conversation in a long history of correspondences back and forth over years and years. And it was the latter.

Analea had kept in touch with Vera, and they had talked about me.

She smelled like oranges and fresh laundry, and I hugged her back.

"I've heard a lot about you, too," I murmured into her blouse.

After a moment, she let go and planted her hands on my shoulders, getting a good look at me from beneath her half-moon glasses. "You look just like her! Almost a spitting image."

I gave the smallest smile. Was that a compliment? "Thank you."

She stepped back to welcome me into her apartment. "Come in, come in. I was just about to make some coffee. Are you a coffee drinker? You have to be. My son makes the *best* coffee . . ."

What my aunt had failed to mention, however, was that Vera had a very slight Southern accent, and her apartment was filled with pictures of a small Southern town. I didn't look at them too thoroughly as I came into the living room and sat down, and she fixed us two cups of coffee and sat beside me. I was a little numb, everything a blur. After so many years of hearing stories about this woman named Vera, here she was in the flesh.

This was the woman Analea had loved so much she let her go.

"I was wondering when I'd be able to meet you," Vera said as she sat down beside me. "It's a surprise, though. Is everything all right?"

In reply, I reached into my purse and pulled out the letter she'd sent my aunt. It was a bit crinkled from battling with my wallet, but I smoothed it down and handed it back. "I'm sorry," I began, because I wasn't sure what else to say.

She frowned as she took the unopened letter. "Oh," she whispered, realization dawning, "is she . . ."

There were things that were hard to do—complicated division without a calculator, a hundred-mile marathon, catching a connecting flight at LAX in twenty minutes—but this was by far the hardest. Finding the words, mustering them up, teaching my mouth how to say them—teaching my heart how to understand them . . .

I would never wish this on anyone.

"She passed away," I forced out, unable to look at her, trying to keep myself tied tightly in a bow. Together. "About six months ago."

Her breath hitched. Her grip on the letter tightened. "I didn't know," she said quietly. She looked down at the letter. Then up at me again. "Oh, Clementine." She reached for my hand and squeezed it tightly. "You see, I recently moved back to the city. My son has a job here, and I wanted to be near him," she rambled, because it felt better than lingering on those words—*she passed away*. She swallowed her sadness and said, after a moment, as she gathered herself back together, "May I ask what happened?"

No, I wanted to reply, but not because I was ashamed. I wasn't sure if I could talk about it without crying.

It was why I didn't talk about it at all—with anyone.

"She . . . she hadn't been sleeping well, so her doctor prescribed her some medicine a while ago. And she just . . ." For all the times I'd rehearsed this, they all failed me now. I didn't know how to explain it. I was doing a bad job. "The neighbors called for a wellness check on New Year's Day when she wouldn't answer the door, but it was too late." I pursed my lips, screwing them tightly closed as I felt a sob bubble up from my chest. "She just went to sleep. She took enough that she knew she wouldn't wake up. They found her in her favorite chair."

"The blue one. *Oh*," Vera's voice cracked. She dropped the letter and pressed her hands against her mouth. *"Oh, Annie."*

Because what else could you say?

"I'm sorry," I whispered, pressing my nails into my hands, focusing on the sharp pain. "There's no easy way to talk about it. I'm sorry," I repeated. "I'm sorry."

"Oh, honey, it isn't you. You did nothing wrong," she said—

But I did, didn't I? I should have seen the signs. I should have saved her. I should have—

And then this woman whom I didn't know wrapped her arms around me and pressed me tightly into her burnt-orange blouse, and it felt like permission. The kind I hadn't let myself have for six months. The kind of permission that I'd been waiting for, as I sat alone in my aunt's apartment, and grief welled up so high it felt suffocating. The permission I thought I'd given myself, but it hadn't been permission to cry—it had been a command to be strong. To be okay. I told myself, over and over, I had to be okay.

And finally—*finally*—someone gave me permission to come undone.

"It's not your fault," she said into my hair as a sob escaped my mouth.

"She left," I whispered, my voice tight and high. "She left."

And she broke my heart.

This woman who I didn't know, who I'd only ever imagined in my aunt's stories, held me tightly as I cried, and she cried with me. I cried because she left me—she just left, even as I chased her, her coattails fluttering, just out of reach. She left and I was still here and there were so many things she hadn't done yet, or wouldn't ever do in the future. There were sunrises she'd never see and Christmases in Rockefeller Plaza she'd never complain about and layovers she'd never catch and wine she'd never drink with me again at that yellow table of hers as we ate fettuccine that was never the same twice.

I'd never see her again.

She was never coming back.

As I sat there crying into Vera's shoulder, it felt like a wall had suddenly come down, all of my pent-up grief and sadness washing away like a broken dam. After a while, we finally pried ourselves apart, and she got a box of tissues and dabbed her eyes.

"What happened to the apartment?" she asked.

"She gave it to me in her will," I replied, then grabbed a few tissues and cleaned my face. It felt raw and puffy.

She nodded, looking a little relieved. "Oh, good. You know it was mine before she bought it? Well, not *mine*—I only rented it from this stodgy old man who overcharged for it. He passed away, so I had to move out, and his family sold it to your aunt. I don't think they ever knew what it did."

That surprised me. "They didn't?"

"No, they never lived there, but the renters knew. The man I took the lease over from warned me. He'd figured out the hard way. He thought someone else had a key to the apartment and was coming in and rearranging his things! It was only after he got her name that he realized the woman who kept breaking in had passed almost five years prior." She shook her head, but she was grinning at the memory. "I almost didn't believe him until it happened to me, and I met your aunt!"

She didn't seem much like the Vera in my aunt's stories. This Vera was more put-together, wearing a string of pearls, looking as pristine as her simply decorated apartment. And if little things were different, maybe some of my aunt's story was, too. "Why didn't things work out?" I asked, and she gave a one-shouldered shrug.

"I can't tell you. I think she was always a little afraid of a good thing coming to an end, and oh, we were a good thing," she said with a secret smile, her thumbs rubbing against the wax seal on the back of her letter. "I never loved anyone quite like I loved Annie. We kept in touch through letters, sometimes every other month, sometimes every other year, and we talked about our lives. I'm not sure she ever regretted letting me go, but I wish I would've fought a little more for us."

"I know she thought about it," I replied, remembering the night my aunt told me the whole story, the way she'd cried at the kitchen table. "She always wished it had ended differently, but I think she was afraid because . . . the apartment, you know. How you two met."

Her mouth screwed into a coy smile. "She was so afraid of change. She was afraid we would grow apart. She didn't want to ruin it, so she did what she did best—she preserved it for herself. Those feelings, that moment. I was so mad at her," she admitted, "for *years*. For years I was angry. And then I stopped being so angry. That was just who she was, and it was a part of her I loved with the rest of her. It was how she knew how to live, and it wasn't all bad. It was good, too. The memories are good."

I hesitated, because how could they be good when she left us? When the last taste in our mouths was lemon drops? "Even after . . ."

Vera took my hand and squeezed it tightly. "The memories are good," she repeated.

I bit my bottom lip so it wouldn't wobble, and nodded, wiping my eyes with the back of my hand. The coffee she'd brought was cold by now, and neither of us had touched it.

My phone buzzed, and I was sure it was Drew and Fiona asking if I was all right. I probably needed to get back to them, so I hugged Vera and thanked her for talking with me about my aunt.

"You can come back anytime you want. I have stories for days," she said, and escorted me back toward the door. Now that my head wasn't spinning, I took note of the pictures that lined the hallway.

Vera was in almost all of them, standing beside two children of varying ages—a boy and a girl both with a headful of auburn hair. Sometimes they were toddlers. Sometimes they were teenagers. Fishing at the lake, elementary school graduation, the two kids sitting on a smiling old man's knees. They both looked very much like Vera, and I realized they must be her children. There was not another person in the photos, only ever the three of them. And I couldn't stop looking at the boy, with his dimples and pale eyes.

"My youngest called us the Three Musketeers when she was little," she said when she caught me staring at the collage of pictures, and it felt like I heard her through a tunnel, and she pointed at a photo of a beautiful young woman in a wedding dress beside a smiling dark-haired man. "That's Lily," she said, and then motioned to the picture of a face I knew too well.

A young man with a crooked smile and bright pale eyes and curly auburn hair, in a floral chef's apron as he cooked something over a well-loved stove. He stood beside a shorter old man with his back curled over, wearing a similar chef's apron that read I AIN'T OLD. I'M WELL-SEASONED, his eyes the same bright pale gray. I stared at the photo in bittersweet awe.

"And this is Iwan," she went on, "with my late father. Iwan really loved him."

"Oh." My voice was tiny.

She smiled. "He's opening up a restaurant in the city. I'm *so* proud, but he's been so stressed lately—I sometimes wonder if he's doing all this because he loves it, or because of his grandpa."

I stared at the photo of the man I knew—Iwan with his crooked and infectious smile. It must have been taken just before he moved to NYC. And suddenly, something clicked, looking at that photo. Of all the things that had changed in those seven years, the most prominent was the look in his eyes. There was unabashed *joy* there.

And I wondered when that left.

"Maybe you'll meet him someday. He's very handsome," Vera added with an eyebrow wiggle.

"He is," I agreed, and thanked her again for letting me cry on her shoulder, and with one last hug, I left and met my friends out front on the sidewalk, who both declared—rather immediately—that I looked like I needed a drink.

They had no idea.

All Too Well

FOR THE REST OF the week, I wondered how I could've missed the signs.

Not that it was apparent. Thinking back on it, Iwan *had* said that Analea was a friend of his mom's, but I'd never asked for her name. It made sense, when I thought about it, that my aunt would offer her empty apartment to someone's child she *knew*. Not only knew, but knew intimately well. I doubted that Iwan knew his mom's history with my aunt, just like I hadn't—he would have brought it up.

Had the apartment known who Iwan was? Was that why it brought us together at these crossroads?

My fingers felt restless—so restless that I brought a tin of watercolors to work and sat over in Bryant Park at lunch and painted the crowds I saw. When I returned to work, I went to quickly wash the paint dried on my fingertips.

"I like that you're painting again," Fiona commented on Wednesday, as we lounged on the green grass in Bryant Park, on one of Drew's blankets from her office, and I washed the Schwarz-man Building in golds and creams in my travel guide's Best Free Tourist Stops. "The yellows are pretty."

"Almost lemony," Drew agreed, lounging on the ground beside Fiona, her hands behind her head. "I've been meaning to ask for a while, but—what made you start painting again?"

I shrugged. "I dunno, I just picked it back up," I replied, cleaning my brush out in a bottle cap of water, and choosing a rusty orange for the edges of the building, "and it makes me feel happy."

Drew hummed in thought. "I can't even remember what makes me feel happy . . ."

"Reading, babe—*ooh*," Fiona held her belly, her face pinching. "Oh, that was interesting."

Drew sat up straight in alarm. "Is everything okay? Something wrong?"

She waved her off. "I'm fine, I'm fine. It was just a weird feeling."

I gave her a hesitant look. "Like baby-coming weird?"

"I'm not due for another week," Fiona replied, as if that would stop it, but for the rest of the day she was fine—and she'd absolutely *scoffed* at the idea of starting her maternity leave early. ("What, and futz around the house all day? No, thank you, I'd go insane.")

So when Thursday rolled around, I brought a dress to the office and changed in the stall after work, and together with Drew and Fiona we caught a cab to James's new restaurant. It was a soft open-ing, reserved for invites-only, to celebrate the launch of hyacinth—all lowercase, by the way, in a loopy handwriting script.

We met Juliette outside, dressed in a stylish cream blouse tucked into baggy brown trousers, a belt at the waist. Her hair was done up into two buns, a knockoff Prada bag on her arm that looked so real I could *almost* believe it if she didn't tell me exactly where to get one myself. Beside her, I looked . . . a little underdressed and casual, in a pale purple knee-length dress with a bow at the collar, and for the first time since my last date with Nate—

"Heels?" Juliette gasped. "Oh my god, you're wearing *heels*! And you're so *tall* in them." She quickly dug out her phone and snapped a photo of them. "This is going right into my Stories! We have to remember this occasion."

I groaned. "I wear heels sometimes!"

"When you want to impress someone," Fiona noted.

"Our future author, obviously," I volleyed back.

Drew put her hands on her hips and practiced her calm breathing. "Speaking of which, if any of you make me look bad tonight . . ."

Juliette said, with a salute, "We'll be on our best behavior! Though someone might have to tell me which fork to use if there's more than one . . ."

I looped my arms through Drew's and Fiona's and said, "Don't worry, I'll be wrong too."

And together we opened the heavy wooden door and walked inside.

On the ride over, I imagined what his restaurant would look like—maybe it looked like the one he talked about over cold noodles. Long family-style tables and crimson-red walls, comfy and warm, the leather chairs broken in. Local artists would be on the walls, the chandeliers this amalgamation of sconces and candelabras.

A table set aside for a woman he met over some far-off weekends in a distant memory.

"Set aside for you every night—best table in the house," I remember him saying.

A conversation I was sure he'd forgotten, even though I kept the same travel guide tucked into my purse as we stepped into his restaurant.

It was bright—that was the first thing I noticed—almost

impeccably so, with polished white marble tables and off-white sconces with the slightest blue hue. The chairs were stools at best, the ceiling bare to new silver plumbing, somewhere between a warehouse and a half-finished department store. It felt like a place where if you made a mistake, it'd be on a pedestal for all to see. My heart sank a little because this wasn't Iwan's dream at all.

It was James's.

The hostess quickly recognized Drew from a photo on her clipboard and ushered us to a special table. A few other familiar faces were already here—Benji and his fiancée, Parker and his wife, and two other editors who had been at the cooking class. We sat down at one of the larger tables, the chairs uncomfortable and cold, and I felt so out of place it made my skin itch.

Pretend like you belong here until you do, I thought to myself.

"This place is so fancy," Fiona said, as our server brought out our menus—which were all the same, detailing a list of seven courses. Fiona had a special menu for her dietary restrictions as a pregnant person. Our server also brought us a bottle of wine—

"Compliments of the chef," the server said, uncorked the red, and poured us each a glass.

When she was gone, Drew picked up her glass and held it up. "To a good evening, whether or not we get the book."

The rest of us clinked our glasses to hers. The wine was dry and a little sour, and suddenly it felt like I was back at that first lunch at the Olive Branch, feeling out of place, swinging my arms wildly to find my footing.

My friends commented on the restaurant, the menu, the other people seated at the tables. I was half listening to Juliette talk about a new campaign she was putting together with the social media coordinator when a familiar face walked into hyacinth—Vera Ashton.

The hostess quickly took her to be seated at the best table in the restaurant, and she smiled as she sat down, and marveled at the décor. I excused myself from the table to go say hello.

"Oh, Clementine!" she cried, clasping her hands together. She was dressed in a sage-colored pantsuit, pearls in her ears. "It's so unexpected to see you here. Lovely, isn't this just *lovely?*"

"It is," I replied in greeting. "How are you?"

"Good! Good. I thought this was a soft opening, what brings you here to Iwan's—excuse me, *James's*"—she said conspiratorially— "restaurant? He hates it when I call him Iwan in public. Something about his image. A bit silly, but he'll figure it out."

I wasn't so sure, seeing this restaurant. "I actually work for one of the publishers he's thinking about signing with." I motioned back to my table. "I just wanted to come over and say hello."

"Oh, what a treat! He'd be wrong not to choose you—Oh, there's Lily and her husband," she added, looking behind me, and I barely had time to look before a petite woman in a flowery dress, her auburn hair long and wild, came up to the table. It startled me how much she looked like Iwan, from her light-colored eyes to the freckles across her cheeks. She gave me a hesitant smile, as did her husband, and I quickly realized I was blocking the chair she was to sit in, and stepped out of the way. "Lily," Vera said, motioning to me, "this is Clementine. Do you remember my stories about Analea? This is her niece."

"It's nice to meet you," Lily said pleasantly, as her husband sat down beside her. "Wasn't Analea who Iwan stayed with that summer?"

"In her apartment, yes," Vera confirmed. "I heard she was going abroad, so I phoned her up and asked if my son could stay there for the summer. He got a job at his grandfather's favorite restaurant, and seven years later, look where we are! All because Analea let him stay there for free." *That* I didn't know. Vera laughed, shaking her head. "Isn't it strange how the world works sometimes? It's never a matter of time, but a matter of timing."

It was, wasn't it.

"I just sort of wish he had more comfortable chairs," Lily said with a laugh. "Grandpa would've *hated* these."

"I'm sure he would've appreciated the thought," Vera replied amicably. "Clementine, would you like to join us? We have an extra chair."

"Oh, no, I should get back to my table, but it was really great to see all of you—and to meet you, Lily. Have a good night," I said in goodbye, and started back for my table.

The kitchen in the back was hidden behind frosted glass that shifted, a little, like an opal, depending on the light. Behind it, shadows went back and forth. I set my mouth into a thin line, looking at the perfect white marbled tables and the clean lines, and the dishes that came out to waiting tables, circles of white with small bite-sized pops of color on them. At the tables sat influencers and celebrities, people I knew of tangentially in the culinary world from researching James. Tastemakers. Critics. People he *should* be seen with. People he wanted to impress.

I returned to my table, but there was someone already in my seat. A man in a pristine chef's uniform, broad shoulders and crisp hair, a whisk hidden behind the curls around his left ear.

James looked up at me as I approached, and gave me a perfect smile. "Ah, hello there. I was just here to welcome everyone to hyacinth."

Juliette said, "It's so bright, I should've brought sunglasses."

"You're going to give copy editors a heart attack with that name not capitalized," I added.

"Maybe I'll start a new trend, Clementine," he said evenly with that perfect white smile of his. He stood and pulled out the chair for me. I sat, a hard lump forming in my throat. "It was a pleasure seeing all of you again—and meeting you, Juliette. Please enjoy your meal, and I hope it's memorable—perhaps even perfect."

Then he left for the next table, and my friends began to talk about the dishes on the menu—almost all of them were iterations of recipes in his proposal but heightened to fit this elevated space.

Around me, the gossip from other tables talked about how he'd earned a Michelin star for the Olive Branch, how he won the James Beard Emerging Chef award. They talked about his presentation, his dishes, his attention to detail, how he was hungry—always hungry—for more. How that made him a rising talent.

How people were excited—starved—for more.

As much as my heart ached, it was hard *not* to be proud of him.

Even though his closest friends, Isa and Miguel, were nowhere to be found.

Our server began to bring out our plates.

The first thing was a fish soup—black bass in flower blossoms. They were all bite-sized, though that was what a *tasting menu* was, a bunch of smaller plates, enough for a mouthful and an evocative conversation about the flavor of the caviar.

There was trout liver with fresh apples and fatty, caramelized butter.

Duck ragù.

Amaranth toast with smoked roe and tartar sauce.

A single cornbread hush puppy with a smoky yolk and nobs of pickled corn.

Pig's-blood flatbread.

Yogurt with marshmallows.

Ice cream with caramel drizzle.

And finally, there was a whisk of lemon-flavored meringue on a crumbly graham cracker. It was supposed to be his new rendition of a lemon pie, but as I ate it, all I could think about was the dessert Iwan and I shared at my aunt's kitchen table.

He had said meringue was his downfall—he couldn't be good at *everything*, he'd be boring if he was perfect—and yet the bite I took was good. The graham cracker crumbled in my mouth.

I didn't realize I had tears in my eyes until Drew asked, "Is everything okay?"

Yes, it should have been. Yes, because this dinner was excellent in every way that it needed to be to impress every publishing team here. Every celebrity, every influencer. It was delicious.

Perfect, even.

And yet I couldn't get the photo I had seen on Vera's wall out of my head, of Iwan and his grandfather in a too-tiny kitchen, wearing mismatching aprons, with flour on their cheeks and that crooked, terribly perfect smile. Perfect because it *wasn't* perfect.

Perfect because it wasn't trying to be. He was just himself.

"Excuse me," I told my table, wiping my mouth, and quickly left for the restroom. The door was locked when I got there. I cursed under my breath and stood outside, waiting. The sign above the door was in the same lowercase loopy handwriting.

My chest felt tight.

My aunt had quit her career because she was afraid she'd never be better than who she'd been in *The Heart Mattered*, and Iwan was the opposite. He kept trying to be better, to earn everyone's respect, to impress people with perfect—or nothing.

Did he realize what he'd given up, though?

I should have been proud of him—I *was* proud of him—but . . .

"So, how was it?"

Startled, I spun around, and Chef James Ashton stood behind me, fresh out of the kitchen where his team worked like a well-oiled machine. I caught glimpses of them through the circular window in the door, faces pinched, working toward the kind of perfection I didn't understand.

"It's . . . quite a restaurant," I told him, motioning out toward the dining area.

His perfect grin grew tight. "You don't like it."

I swallowed the knot in my throat. *Oh, no.* "I didn't say that."

"I can see it on your face."

I glanced back toward the dining area, the clanking of silverware and the murmuring of voices, the gasp as plates came, sighing dry ice off them. We were secluded in our own little world back here.

"I'm sorry, James," I said quietly.

His face didn't give anything away, but he asked, "Why don't you ever call me Iwan?"

It was a question I really didn't know how to answer until just then, looking up into those guarded gray eyes, pools of shale that only needed a single layer. I stepped up to him, and placed a hand on his solid, warm chest. I wanted to kiss him, and I wanted to shake him, and I wanted to bring out the man I sometimes saw between the cracks, but I couldn't. All I could do was give him the truth.

"I used to have lovely dinners with a man named Iwan, who told me that you could find romance in a piece of chocolate and love in a lemon pie," I began, and confusion crossed his brow.

"Those dishes wouldn't have impressed anyone, Lemon. I was a dishwasher then. I didn't know better."

"I know, and the food was delicious tonight. The—um—the fish thing? It was really great. I'm sorry, I don't know the actual name of it," I added quickly, hoping it didn't annoy him. "It was very good. Are you happy with it all?" I asked, waving my hand toward his new restaurant, and all of its sharp edges and blank white walls. The way it tried to be something new, and ended up being nothing at all.

"Why wouldn't I be?" he replied, and there was an edge of frustration in his voice. "Of course I am." He gestured toward the dining area. "Everyone out there looks like they're enjoying themselves—they're having excellent food."

"Then close your eyes—what do you hear?"

"I'm not going to do that."

"Please."

"Lemon—"

"*Please.*"

He breathed out through his nose, but then he closed his eyes. "I hear utensils on plates. I hear conversations. The AC squeaking—I need to fix that. There, are you happy?"

"Just keep listening," I told him, and to my surprise, he did. After a moment, I asked, "Do you hear anyone laughing?"

"I hope they aren't."

"I don't mean at *you*, I mean with each other." I glanced out again at the restaurant, strangers on uncomfortable chairs, shifting awkwardly as they took photos of their food and sipped wine or champagne as they scrolled through their socials.

Slowly, he opened his eyes, and looked out toward the dining area, too, a strange look on his face, searching across the tables as if he could prove me wrong. And when he couldn't, he said, "I'm doing something new here. Something *inventive*. Something people want to see—something they will talk about." He pursed his lips and darted his gaze back to me. "I'm giving people a perfect meal—you know this is my dream. This is what I've worked for."

"I know," I tried to explain, but I was quickly losing him. "I'm just asking you not to lose who you are—"

"Who I *was*," he volleyed back, and I winced. "What do you *want* from me, Clementine?"

To be the man who smiled at me with that crooked mouth over frozen cardboard pizza. The kind of guy who told jokes across cold noodles. The person who told me about his grandfather's lemon pies, how they were never the same twice. "You're so out of touch with everything you were," I said. "I mean *dry ice* for *pasta*?"

His nose scrunched. "Cold noodles."

Like he made for me the other week. I tried again, "A deconstructed *lemon pie*?"

"Every bite tastes a little different."

Like the kind of pie his grandfather made. "But they're not the same—they're things that made you who you are," I tried to reason. "They *made* you—"

"And if I was still that dishwasher, would you be here? *Competing* for my cookbook? No. No one out there would be here."

The realization was like a bucket of ice water. My throat felt tight. I looked away.

"I'm still me, Clementine," he said. "I'm still trying to make my granddad proud, to make the perfect meal—and I know how to now. I studied under the man who made it. I know *exactly* what made it perfect—"

"It was your grandpa, Iwan," I interrupted, and the sharp look froze, and then slowly slipped off his face, until he looked like he'd lost his grandfather all over again. I reached up to try and take his face in my hands, but he moved away.

My throat stung as tears came to my eyes.

"I'm sorry—"

"Change isn't always bad, Clementine," he said, his voice solid but stoic. His jaw worked as he tried to find the right words.

"Perhaps instead of wanting me to stay the exact same person you met in that apartment, you should let yourself change a little, too."

I drew my hand back quickly. "I . . ."

Behind him, the silver doors to the kitchen swung open, but instead of a server coming out with another round of intricately styled plates, it was—Miguel? His hair slicked back, in a maroon suit, a glass of champagne in one hand.

He was here, after all?

Miguel said, smiling, "I was wondering where you'd gone off to! Isa's about to get into that 2002 Salon Blanc back there—Lemon! Hey! Iwan, you didn't tell me she'd be here."

James pursed his lips together, and I looked away, trying to find some excuse to leave, because I had misjudged him, apparently. More than I thought.

Suddenly, shouts came from the dining area. We glanced back toward the mounting chaos, and I paled when I realized that it was coming from my table. Drew was helping Fiona to her feet. Juliette was in a sheer panic, as she searched the restaurant for me, her phone in her hand, calling an Uber. She found me and held up her phone.

"IT'S COMING!" Juliette cried.

It . . . ?

James didn't understand. "Coming? What's coming?" he asked, and I realized a second before he did. "Did her water break?"

"I have to go," I muttered, and he didn't stop me. As I hurried back toward my table, I felt something warm slide down my cheeks, and I wiped my tears away.

I grabbed the phone out of Juliette's hand and my own purse as we left. "The Uber's five minutes away."

"I'll flag it down!" Juliette announced and hurried out the door.

"We really don't have to go that quickly . . ." Fiona was saying, but no one listened. Drew was clearing the way as she led her wife out of the restaurant.

I glanced back one last time at James, and the rest of the unfamiliar faces, and that itch under my skin was so bad now it burned. I didn't want to be here—because he was right about one thing. Clementine West, a senior publicist at Strauss & Adder, wouldn't have noticed Iwan at all if he'd just been a dishwasher. She wouldn't have chased after him so hard if accolades hadn't peppered his résumé. She was good at her job, and she was looking for a talented chef to fill a space in her imprint's roster. She was Rhonda Adder's second-in-command, and that came above all else. Someone steadfast. Someone solid.

But Lemon, overworked and exhausted Lemon, loved that crooked-mouthed dishwasher she'd met displaced in time, and she came to work with watercolors under her nails on accident, and she took travel guides from the free bookshelves near the elevators, and she had an itch under her skin, and a passport full of stamps, and a wild heart.

And in figuring out who I wanted to be, I thought I ruined Drew's chances of getting this book. I ruined a lot of things, it seemed, while I tried to be something permanent—but in the end, I was the one who left, out of the heavy wooden door and onto the sidewalk, where Juliette had flagged down the black SUV.

"You chose the *carpool* option?" Drew accused her.

"I panicked!" Juliette cried.

We loaded into the SUV beside a flustered couple who looked to be going on a date themselves, and I didn't look back as I closed the door, and we set off.

Two Weeks' Notice

THE LABOR AND DELIVERY floor of New York Presbyterian didn't expect an entourage of well-dressed twentysomethings rushing in after their friend, only to be turned away at the door by an overworked nurse and told to stay in the waiting room. Juliette and I did, and we claimed a corner of the beige room to wait it out. We could have gone home, probably, but that never crossed our minds at all. We sat there and we waited, because Fiona and Drew were as much my family as my parents—we saw each other more often, anyway. We complained over wine together, and we spent New Year's and Halloween and the odd government holidays together. We celebrated birthdays and death days, and they were the first people I called when the worst day of my life happened.

It was only natural that we were together for the best days, too.

So it was no surprise that *I* was in the waiting room. Juliette, on the other hand, was new.

"You can go, you know," I told her, but she shook her head.

"No way, I stick things through," she replied. I wanted to point out that she really didn't have an obligation to Fiona or Drew, but then I thought better of it. If she wanted to be here, who was I to say no?

After an hour, I stretched and checked my phone. It was almost 10:30 p.m. Juliette was nervously scrolling Instagram while I sketched in my travel guide, outlining the waiting room in the section titled Quiet Reprieves. The sleepy sofa. The tired-looking chairs. The family on the other side, the dad having gone back with his wife, the grandparents hunched in chairs to wait, two kids watching a Disney movie on their dad's phone.

"Crap," Juliette muttered, pausing at a photo.

I sat down and cracked my neck. "What is it?"

She sighed. "Nothing."

I glanced over at her phone, anyway. "Is that Rob?"

"He had a show tonight," she replied, but that wasn't what was wrong with the photo. He was kissing another woman. "She's probably a groupie," she said, as if to explain it away. "He's very good to his fans."

I gave her an appalled look. "*Really?*"

". . . It doesn't matter. He'll make it up to me," she replied, putting her phone to sleep and shoving it into her purse. "It's fine."

But it wasn't. I turned to her and gathered her hands in mine. "We're friends, right?"

"I should hope so. You see my private stories on Instagram, and if we aren't friends, I really need to reconsider that."

I couldn't help but laugh. "We're friends, so I just want to tell you: fuck Romeo-Rob."

She blinked at me. "What?"

"*Fuck Rob*," I repeated. "You are way too smart and way too beautiful and way too successful to have some D-list guitarist from a no-name band treat you like you're replaceable. You aren't."

"He plays bass, actually . . ." she muttered.

"Fuck him! Why do you keep getting back with him if he makes you so miserable?"

Her eyes widened and she opened her mouth, and then shut it again, glancing at the family on the other side of the waiting room, who had covered their children's ears, scandalized. I didn't care, this was my movie moment.

I went on, "I get it, he's hot. He probably gives you the best sex of your life. But if it doesn't fill you with tinglies to be around him every second you're around him—if he doesn't make you *happy*—then what the hell are you doing? You only live once," I said, because if I'd learned anything about living in a time-traveling apartment, no matter how much time you get, it's still never enough. And I wanted to start living my life like I was enjoying every moment that I had it. "And if you do it right," I said, remembering the way my aunt laughed as we sprinted to catch our connecting flights across the airport, how she flung her arms wide at the top of Arthur's Seat and the Parthenon and Santorini and every hill with a beautiful view she came across, as if she wanted to embrace the sky; the way she always took her time to decide what she wanted on a menu; the way she asked everyone she met for their stories, absorbed their fairy tales, and chased the moon.

"If you do it right," I repeated, "once is all you need."

Juliette was quiet for a long moment, and then her face scrunched in tears. "What if I n-never find anyone else?"

"But what if you *do*?" I asked, squeezing her hands tightly. "You deserve to find out."

With a sob, she flung out her arms and pulled me into a tight hug, burrowing her head into my shoulder. I was not expecting it, so I stiffened at the sudden contact, but if she noticed, she didn't let go, because she held on as she cried into my shoulder. I wrapped my arms around her awkwardly, and patted her back.

I didn't know that no one had ever told her that she deserved more. I didn't know that she had been thinking about calling it quits for a while. I didn't know how unhappy she had been. How miserable. She said she hadn't realized it until I said she deserved better.

A cold, hard realization curled in my stomach, because as she finally let go of me and told me that I was right, I thought about my small cubicle, the paintings of landscapes I hung up across my corkboard, and the piles of travel guides I had stashed in my desk drawer. I thought about coming home to my aunt's small apartment, and catching the train every morning, and planning someone else's adventures in an Excel spreadsheet for the rest of my life.

And I realized that I was unhappy, too.

The waiting room doors swung wide, and Drew swooped in, a smile so wide and bright, it was contagious, and whatever answer I could've had was erased by that moment. "Come on, come on!" Drew said, grabbing us by our wrists, and pulling us to our feet and out of the waiting room and down the hall. "You have to meet her! You *have* to. She's amazing."

And Penelope Grayson Torres, born at eight pounds and ten ounces, was, in fact, amazing. Even when she spit up all over me.

||||||||||||||||||||||||||||||||||||||

THAT MONDAY MORNING, RHONDA'S office was warm and quiet as I came in and set the letter down on her desk. Work was quiet without Drew and Fiona, but they'd be gone on maternity leave for the next few months, and I hated that I'd be gone by the time they came back. A soft pop playlist hummed from Rhonda's speakers as she lounged back in her chair and flipped page after page of a bound manuscript, her glasses low on the bridge of her nose. She glanced up at me, her eyebrows knitting together in confusion at the letter. "What's this?"

The end, the beginning.

Something new.

"I realized something over the summer," I began, twisting my fingers nervously, "and it was that I'm not very happy anymore. I haven't been in a while, but I didn't know why until an old friend came back into my life."

Rhonda sat up a little straighter, taking the letter and opening it.

"I'm sorry that this comes as a surprise—it was a surprise to me, too. I'm not sure what I want to do," I went on as she read the resignation letter, her face growing grim, "but I don't think it's this. Thank you so much for the opportunity, and I'm sorry."

Because I felt like I had wasted her time for seven years. For shaving off parts of myself, over and over again, to squeeze into the expectations I thought I needed to set for myself. I was never going to wear heels and blazers—I didn't want that anymore, and it was scary to think about, but a little thrilling, too.

I couldn't look at her as I turned to leave, but as I did, Rhonda said, "I didn't find out who I wanted to be until I was almost forty. You have to try on a lot of shoes until you find some you like walking in. Never apologize for that. Once I found mine, I've been content for twenty years."

"You barely look a day over fifty," I remarked, and she threw her head back with a laugh.

"*Go,*" she said, waving my letter at me, "and have some fun while you're out there."

So I did just that.

Even though I had two weeks to shift my duties to Juliette, and to help Rhonda start the hiring process for my replacement, I packed up my cubicle into one box—Drew always did call it a one-box walkout—and realized that a part of me, subconsciously, always knew that I wouldn't be here forever. I didn't clutter my desk with things from home. I didn't decorate my corkboard with photos of friends and family. I never even changed the wallpaper on my computer.

I was simply here.

And that wasn't enough anymore.

With my resignation turned in, work was strange. Juliette and I would eat at Bryant Park on the grass, and I slowly started handing off my authors and off-boarding, and we kept Fiona and Drew updated on all the workroom gossip.

After hyacinth's soft opening, Drew didn't hear back from James and his agent until the following Tuesday—and even then it was just to inform us that they would be making a final decision soon, but couldn't quite specify *when*. Things, apparently, had been so busy with final preparations for the official opening of the restaurant that they didn't have time. I didn't have the courage to tell Drew that I was sure I'd fucked our chances pretty thoroughly—I was sure he hated me. Or at least never wanted to see me again—but Drew was so busy with her newborn that I doubt she gave James a passing thought.

And if James *did* want to see me, he knew where I lived, though it seemed even the apartment didn't want me to see him again.

Tourist Season

THE WORST PART OF quitting my job, however, was figuring out how to break it to my parents, who excelled in everything they did. My parents, who never quit anything. My parents, who had instilled that same ethic in me.

My parents, who demanded that they celebrate my birthday this weekend, like they always did.

My parents, who I said yes to because I loved and didn't want to disappoint them.

And I feared I would anyway.

"Oh, *sweetheart*!" Mom called, waving me over to the table where she and Dad sat, even though I could walk to the table blindfolded by now. They came into the city for my birthday weekend every year. They asked for the same table in the same restaurant on the same Saturday before my birthday, and they always ended up ordering the exact same food. It was the sort of tradition that went back as far as I could remember—a ritual at this point.

We would get lunch at this adorable little diner over on Eighty-Fourth Street called the Eggverything Café, where my mom would order the number two—two pancakes, two eggs sunny-side up, and two burnt sausage links. Not cooked, but *burnt*. And my dad would get the egglet supreme, which was just an omelet with bell peppers and mushrooms and three different kinds of cheese, hold the onions, and a cup of decaf coffee. I used to play a game where I never got the same thing twice, but after coming here for almost thirty years, that was an impossible endeavor at this point.

If my aunt was the kind of person who always tried something new, my parents excelled in the monotonous mundane, over and over again.

It was kind of their charm. A little bit.

As I came over to their table, Dad stood and gave me a big bear hug, his beard scratchy against my cheek. He was a big man who was spectacular at hugs—the back-breaking kind. He picked me up and spun me around, and when he set me down, the floor tilted a little. "Daughter!" he cried, and his voice bellowed. "It's been forever!"

"Look at you! You look so tired," Mom added, grabbing my face and planting a kiss on my cheek. "You need to get more sleep, young lady."

"It's been a weird few weeks at work," I admitted, as we all sat down for lunch.

"Well, now you're here! And as the birthday girl, you aren't even going to *think* about work for the next"—Mom checked her smartwatch—"four hours at *least*."

Four?

"Don't look so enthused," Dad added wryly because a long-suffering look must've crossed my face. "You never come see your parents, so we always have to make the long trip to the city to see you."

"It's not *that* long," I told them. "You live on Long Island, not in Maine."

Mom waved me off. "You should come visit more often anyway."

The server remembered our faces, and she knew by now what my mom and dad ordered, and she looked at me expectantly, ready for me to try something new, but as I browsed the menu, I realized I'd tried everything on it already. "How about the blueberry waffles?"

Her eyebrows jerked up. "Didn't you have that last time?"

"I'll try it with that Vermont maple syrup you have," I amended, "and the largest coffee you can get me." She jotted it down on her notepad and flitted away.

My mom made small talk by commenting on the new upholstery on the train seats on the ride here, and how the construction on their stretch of the LIE was taking *forever*, and how she had to change to a new doctor who knew nothing about her medications— Mom was very good at complaining. She did it often, and with great gusto, and my dad had learned early on to just nod and listen. Mom was a universe apart from her sister. They were opposites of the same coin, one tired of new things, the other searching for them wherever she went.

My stomach had laced itself in knots, because at some point today they were going to ask about my job, and at some point—

"So," Dad said, "how's the book thing going?"

Too soon. It came too soon. "I, um—"

The server brought our food out, which immediately distracted my parents, and thankfully they went on to talk about how there must have been a new chef in the back, because Mom's eggs were *not* cooked the way she remembered. I picked at my blueberry waffles, which seemed fine enough, especially slathered in Vermont maple syrup. My parents asked about how the apartment was doing, and I asked them about Dad's bird condominium (a series of birdhouses all stacked together like a designer resort—I told him that he'd find himself overrun with pigeons if he built it, but he didn't believe me until, lo and behold, he was overrun with pigeons).

After we'd finished eating, Mom excused herself to the bathroom, and Dad scooted his chair a little closer to me, stealing my last bite of blueberry waffle. "You know your mom didn't mean it—that you look tired."

I flipped my butter knife around and glanced at my reflection. Anyone could see that my parents and I looked related—I had Dad's reddish nose, his soft brown eyes, and my mom's frown. I never really had much of Aunt Analea in me, though maybe that was why I tried to be so much like her. "I don't look *that* tired, do I?"

"No!" he replied quickly, from years of Mom pinning him in that trap herself. "Absolutely not. That's why I said you didn't. You look happy, actually. Content. Did something good happen at work?"

I tilted my head, debating on an answer. I guess this was as good a time to tell him as any. "Actually . . . I quit my job."

Dad's mouth dropped open. He blinked his big brown eyes. "Erm . . . do you . . . have an offer somewhere else?"

"No."

"Then . . ."

"Yeah." I looked away. "I know it was a stupid decision, but . . . I sort of realized over this summer I wasn't all that happy where I was, and I know it wasn't smart, but the moment I turned in my two weeks', I felt this knot in the middle of my chest come undone. It was a relief." I glanced back at him, hoping that he could understand, even though he'd never quit anything in his entire life.

He thought about it for a good half a minute. That was really what I loved about my dad. He was kind and patient. He evened out my mom, who was loud and quick and bombastic, so I always liked to tell my dad big news first before surprising Mom. "I think," he finally said, choosing his words carefully, "that nothing lasts forever. Not the good things, not the bad. So just find what makes you happy, and do it for as long as you can."

I set down my butter knife, and put my napkin over my plate. "And if I can't find that?"

"You might not," he replied, "but then again, you might. You don't know what the future holds, sweetheart." He scrubbed my head like he did when I was little, and gave a wink. "Don't think too much about it, yeah? You have some savings . . ."

"And I can sell Analea's apartment," I added quietly.

His eyebrows shot up. "Are you sure?"

I nodded. I'd been thinking about it for a while. "I don't want to live there forever. It just feels too close to her, and I'm tired of living in the past."

Somewhat literally, too.

He gave a shrug and sat back in his chair. "Then there you go, and your mom and I will be here if you ever need anything—Ah! My love!" he added with a start when he realized that Mom was standing behind us and probably had been for a while. "How, haha, how long have you been there?"

She towered over us, and turned her sharp gaze to me. Oh, no. "Long enough," she said cryptically.

Dad and I gave each other the same look, a silent pact that we'd dig up the other person if Mom decided to dump one of us in an unmarked grave.

Then Mom sat down in her chair, turned to me, and took my face in her hands—her fingers were long and manicured-pink to match the flowers on her blouse—and said, "You *quit* your *job*, Clementine?"

I hesitated, my cheeks squished together between her hands. "Y-yes . . . ?"

She narrowed her eyes. Before she retired, she was a behavioral therapist, and she employed a lot of those skills to handle my father and me. Then she let go of my face, and gave a tired sigh. "Well! *This* certainly wasn't a plot twist I was anticipating."

"I'm sorry—"

"Don't be. I'm glad," she added, and took my hand in her cold ones. Her hands reminded me of Aunt Analea's. Mom and I never really saw eye to eye, and even though I tried to be like her, I ended up being more like her sister. "You're finally doing something for you, sweetheart."

That surprised me. "I—I thought you'd be angry."

My parents gave each other a baffled look. "Angry?" my mother echoed. "Why would we be that?"

"Because I'm quitting. I'm giving up."

Mom squeezed my hands. "Oh, sweetheart. You aren't giving up. You're trying something new."

"But you and Dad always find a way to make something work. You do things over and over, even when it gets hard." I blinked back tears that stung in my eyes. Of course I'd find myself having a midlife crisis in the Eggverything Café, where all the servers wore splattered egg graphics on the fronts of their shirts and had egg puns on their name tags. "I feel like a failure for not being able to just push through."

"You aren't. You're one of the bravest people we know."

Dad agreed, "Hell, you had a conversation with a stranger in a cab and decided to be a *book publicist*. That's braver than anything I could do. I spent ten years deciding to be an *architect*."

That was true. I had caught a cab with a stranger from the Monroe the day I came back from that summer abroad, and he asked about the book I was carrying—it had been the travel guide I'd painted in all summer abroad.

Mom said, "You will be happiest when you're on your own adventure. Not Analea's, not whoever you're dating, not everyone who thinks you should do what you're supposed to do—*yours*." Then she clapped her hands together, and signaled for the server to bring us the check. "Now! We are *almost* done! Who wants to get celebratory birthday ice cream after this from the cart out front of the Met and go for a walk in the park?" she asked, her eyes glimmering, because it was the exact same thing we'd done for— well, you know. I tucked their words into the soft matter of my heart, and I followed my parents to get frozen ice cream sandwiches, and we walked through the park on this glorious golden Saturday at the beginning of August, pretending like it wasn't too hot and too bright, even though we'd done it a thousand times.

There was something nice about doing it again, sitting at the same park benches, feeding the same ducks in the pond, so well-worn and natural. Not safe, really, because each trip was different, but familiar.

Like meeting an old friend seven years later.

The Last Goodbye

AFTER I SAID GOODBYE to my parents at the train station, I went home. To my aunt's apartment.

To *my* apartment.

Change wasn't always a bad thing, like my aunt had convinced herself to believe. It wasn't always a good thing, either. It could be neutral—it could be okay.

Things changed, *people* changed.

I changed, too. I was allowed to. I wanted to. I *was*.

There were some things that stayed the same—the Monroe, for instance. It always sort of took my breath away as I came up to it, looking like it should be the main character in some whimsical children's book series about a little girl. Maybe her name was Clementine. The building always had a door greeter, an older gentleman named Earl, who knew everyone's name in the building, and always told them hello. The elevator always smelled like someone's forgotten lunch, and the mirror on the ceiling always looked back at you a split second too late, and the Muzak was always awful.

"You'll be okay," I told the reflection, and she seemed to believe it.

The elevator let out on the fourth floor. I couldn't remember how many times I'd rolled my suitcases down this hall, my wheels catching every knot and dent in the carpet. My passport would be in my hand, a flurry of travel guides tucked into my backpack. Seven years ago, I would have been just coming home from our European backpacking trip, tired and in desperate need of a shower, the rest of my life stretched before me like the good parts of a novel that the author had yet to write, and didn't know how.

I had a degree in art history, something that really didn't have a single path to take. I had thought about applying to be a curator. I'd mulled over becoming a gallerist. Perhaps try a graduate program. But none of it really ever caught hold of me. I figured nothing would. I had spent all summer painting through a tattered old copy of *The Quintessential European Travel Guide* that I'd swiped from a secondhand store in London, etching sceneries above recommended tourist traps and restaurants.

I had dropped my aunt off at her apartment, so tired my feet were numb, and hailed a taxi out front, not knowing someone else had just slipped inside. I'd opened the door and slid in, only to find the stranger looking at me with this bewildered expression.

He'd said I could take it, but I said he could, and we ended up finding out that we were both heading down toward NYU anyway, so why not go together and split the fare. The weight of my future had spread out in front of me now that I was on the ground again, in a city where I had to find a job and a future career and—all I could think about was *The Quintessential European Travel Guide*, and the mallet-hammer logo, and an idea began to form. He told me about the apartment he was about to rent with two of his friends, and how he was excited to be able to stay in the city. And then he asked me—

"How about you?" I couldn't remember what he looked like—distressed jeans and a plain white shirt—but the day was mostly a blur. I'd met so many faces over the last few months, they all tended to blend together.

Even the ones that'd change my life.

"I think I want to work with books," I told him, surprising even myself. "Is that weird?" I added with a self-conscious laugh. "I don't know the first thing about book publishing! I must be crazy."

And he smiled, and thinking back on it, I could almost remember his face then. The crookedness of his mouth. His kind eyes. And he said, "I don't think so. I think you're going to be amazing."

It was that germ of an idea that, a few weeks later, had me applying to every job I could find in publishing. Everything that I was remotely qualified for. I just needed a foot in the door. I just needed a chance.

The next thing I knew, I was at a preliminary interview in a conference room at Strauss & Adder, sitting across from a woman so sharp and so bold, it was like she was made for red lipstick and leopard-print heels. And I knew instantly then that I wanted to be just like her—exactly like her. Someone who had their life together. Someone successful. Someone who knew themselves.

But in trying to be Rhonda, I'd never stopped to think about what parts of myself I'd shaved away.

I guess, sort of like James.

We had grown up, and grown apart, in different ways.

I came to a stop at apartment B4. My apartment. I took my keys out of my purse and turned the lock. I felt a hush of cool air as it opened—and my heart slammed into my chest. There was that feeling again. So slight, almost a figment of my imagination. The tingling of time across my skin as I stepped through the doorway, and into the past.

The apartment was dark, save for the golden afternoon sunlight streaming through the living room windows. Mother and Fucker were preening themselves on the AC. Everything was tidy, blankets folded and pillows puffed.

The blankets weren't mine. And my aunt's wingback chair was in the corner.

The apartment had brought me back again.

I quickly checked my phone for the date. Seven years ago, we'd be coming back today. Had I already missed him?

But when I turned into the kitchen, he was sitting at the table. In distressed jeans and a white T-shirt, the neck hole stretched out, and suddenly the man in the taxi came into focus. When he left, I'd meet him outside on the sidewalk. I'd catch a cab with him, and it made my heart ache at the realization that we had crossed each other, time and again, like ships in the night.

He looked up—and recognition lit his gray eyes. "Lemon . . ."

My body reacted before I could, and I hurried across the kitchen, and he pulled me close, burrowing his face into my stomach.

"Are you real?" he mumbled because I had disappeared in front of his eyes the last time he saw me. Every day I came back into the apartment, I'd hoped it'd bring me back so I could explain, but it never had.

I combed my fingers through his hair. I memorized how soft it felt, how his auburn curls hugged my fingertips. "Yes, and I'm sorry. I'm sorry I didn't tell you."

He leaned back a little, and looked up into my face with those lovely pale eyes. "Are you a ghost?"

I laughed, relieved, because, yes, I was and, no, I wasn't, because it was complicated, because I knew what this feeling was now, warm and buoyant, and kissed him on the lips. "I want to tell you a story," I replied, "about a magical apartment. You might not believe me at first, but I promise it's true."

And I told him a strange story, about a place between places that bled like watercolors. A place that felt, sometimes, like it had a mind of its own. I only told him the magical bits, the parts that clung to my bones like warm soup in winter. I told him about my aunt and the woman she loved across time, and her fear of good things going sour, and I told him about her niece, who was so afraid of something good that she settled for safe, that she shaved off so much of herself to fit the person she thought she wanted to be.

"Until she met someone in that terrible, lovely apartment who made her want just a little more."

"They must have been very important to her," he replied softly.

I ran my fingers down his face, memorizing the arch of his brows, the cut of his jaw. "He is," I whispered, and he kissed me, long and savoring, like I was his favorite taste. I wanted to burrow myself in his touch, never come out again, but there was a part of me that tugged back to the present, where I belonged.

"But why seven?" he asked after a moment, his eyebrows furrowing. "Why seven years?"

"Why not? It's a lucky number—*or*," I added teasingly, "maybe it's the number of rainbows you'll see. Maybe it's the number of flights you miss. The number of lemon pies you'll burn. Or maybe it's just how long you'll wait before you find me again in the future." I began to pull away when he grabbed my middle and drew me back in.

"I'll never have to wait for anything if I never let you go," he said earnestly, holding tightly to my hands. "We can stay here—forever."

What a lovely thought. "You know we can't," I replied, "but you'll find me in the future."

His eyes grew steely. "I can find you now. Today. I'll search everywhere. I'll—"

"I wouldn't be me, Iwan."

Seven years ago, I would have been terrible for him. Twenty-two and fresh off my first real heartbreak, having gallivanted off with my aunt all summer, kissing every foreign boy I met in shadowy bars. Love wasn't something that I looked for, it was something I made, over and over again, to try and forget the guy who broke my heart. I barely remembered his name now—Evan or Wesley, something middle-class and suburban, driving an eco-friendly car, with his eyes set on law school.

Seven years ago, I was someone else entirely, trying on different hats to see which one fit best, which skin I was comfortable with sharing.

Seven years ago, he was this bright-eyed dishwasher with soap under his nails, wearing overstretched shirts, trying to find his dream, and in the present, he was glossy and sure of himself, though when he smiled, the cracks showed, and they were cracks that most people probably didn't want to see. But I loved them, too.

That was love, wasn't it? It wasn't just a quick drop—it was falling, over and over again, for your person. It was falling as they became new people. It was learning how to exist with every new breath. It was uncertain and it was undeniably hard, and it wasn't something you could plan for.

Love was an invitation into the wild unknown, one step at a time together.

And I loved this man so much, I needed to let him go. This him. The one in my past.

Because the one in my present was just as lovely, though a little bit worn down, but also a little bit *more*, and I felt so silly now because I'd been comparing him to this man I had met in the past. I'd imagined he'd be just like this Iwan, only older. But we all change.

"But then who will I be in seven years, when you find me?" he asked, unsure, as if he was afraid of the person I'd meet.

But there was nothing to worry about.

"You," I told him, bending down to press my forehead to his, soaking in every detail of this Iwan of before, this boy who hadn't yet had a broken heart, who didn't know the words to those kinds of songs yet. I wanted to hug him. I wanted to wrap him up in a blanket and ferry him through all of it. I wanted to be there for it—I wanted to be there for *him*. But I wouldn't. Not for a long while.

"You are going to travel the world," I said. "You're going to cook widely and you're going to absorb cultures and foods and stories like a sunflower drinks in the sun. And I think people will see a spark in you, and your passion for what you do, and someday you'll make recipes people will write about in magazines, and you'll host guests from all different walks of life, and you'll make good food, and they'll fall in love with it. With you."

A smile played across his lips. "So you *have* met me in the future."

"Yes," I replied, and I memorized the way his cheek felt scratchy with five-o'clock shadow, the soft furrow in his brows as if he was trying not to cry.

"And *you*," I whispered, a promise to him, "are going to be amazing."

38

Ghosts

WE KISSED FOR THE last time, before the clock on the microwave turned over to five, and he muttered that he had to leave. He told my aunt he'd be out by four, and he was already an hour behind, and he still had to go to work for the evening shift and get to his new apartment—"I took your word for it, and I bullied my friend— you know, the one who told me that fajita recipe?—into moving to the city with me. We're subletting a place in the Village."

So, he was going to be living in the completely opposite direction of where I would for the next seven years—above a Greek restaurant in Greenpoint—before taking over my aunt's apartment. "I think it might work out," I replied, biting in a smile.

"Yeah? I'll take your word for it."

We stood awkwardly for a moment longer at the door. And then I planted my hands on his chest and pushed him back.

"*Go*," I said. "You'll see me again."

"Will I be as handsome as I am now? Balding? Oh, I really hope I'm not balding."

I laughed and shoved him again. "*Go.*"

"Okay, okay," he said, grinning, and caught my wrist one last time. He kissed the inside of my hand, and looked me over as if he wanted to commit me to memory. "I'll see you in a few years, Lemon. You promise?"

"I promise—and, Iwan?"

"Yes?"

"I'm sorry."

He frowned. "For what?"

But I just gave him a smile, though it was a bit embarrassed, and a little sad, because when I did meet him again, I'd be so caught up with wishing he was who he'd been that I failed to see who he had become. He would see me again, but I was quite unsure if I would.

This was it. This last moment with my wrist wrapped in his hand, the afternoon light streaming in through the windows, bright and stagnant in a way only August light could be, that made his hair shimmer with reds and blonds.

I think I love you, I wanted to say, but not to this Iwan.

He kissed me one last time, in goodbye, and left to go catch a cab that he would end up sharing with a girl who wasn't quite sure who she wanted to be, and wouldn't know for years. They'd trade small talk, and he'd learn a secret, and then they would say goodbye in Washington Square Park.

The door closed, and I half expected the apartment to catapult me into the present, but the kitchen was quiet, and the pigeons cooed on the windowsill, and so I stood there for a long moment, my eyes closed, and existed one final moment in a time when my aunt was alive.

When she first died, I thought about what it'd be like to pack up my life and leave. Race my sadness across the world, and see who won. But I could never run far enough, not really.

I missed her every day. I missed her in ways I didn't yet understand—in ways I wouldn't find out for years to come. I missed her with this deep sort of regret, even though there was nothing I could have done. She never wanted anyone to see the monster on her shoulder, so she hid it, and when she finally took the monster's hand, it broke our hearts.

It would keep breaking our hearts, everyone who knew her, over and over and over again. It was the kind of pain that didn't exist to someday be healed by pretty words and good memories. It was the kind of pain that existed because, once upon a time, so did she. And I carried that pain, and that love, and that terrible, terrible day, with me. I got comfortable with it. I walked with it.

Sometimes the people you loved left you halfway through a story.

Sometimes they left you without a goodbye.

And, sometimes, they stayed around in little ways. In the memory of a musical. In the smell of their perfume. In the sound of the rain, and the itch for adventure, and the yearning for that liminal space between one airport terminal and the next.

I hated her for leaving, and I loved her for staying as long as she could.

And I would never wish this pain on anyone.

I walked through her apartment one last time, remembering all the nights I spent on her couch, all the mornings she cooked me eggs, the fingernail polish on the doorframe to mark my height, the books in her study. I ran my fingers over the spines full of faces we'd met and stories we'd heard.

Of all the people, all of the experiences, all of the memories, that loved me into being.

I heard the door open, and I stepped out of her study. Had Iwan forgotten something? "Iwan, if you forgot your toothbrush again . . ." My voice trailed off as I stared at the woman in the kitchen doorway, dressed in her traveling clothes.

She dropped her bags, her face stretching in confusion, and finally wonder. Then she smiled, bright and blinding, and threw out her arms. My heart swelled with grief and joy and love. So much love for this ghost of mine.

39

I Knew You When

I SAT DOWN ON one of the benches in front of van Gogh with a flask of wine and three of my best friends, and we all passed it around, sharing sips, as they sang happy birthday to me, and gave me presents. A romance book from Juliette—"It's the latest Ann Nichols! I got it early, don't tell anyone."

And Drew and Fiona, they gave me an elegant and beautiful passport holder.

"Because you should use it," Fiona said with a smile.

I hugged them all, thankful to have friends like these, who were there for me when I didn't need them, and running toward me when I did. Usually, we'd all just celebrate birthdays at our local Wine and Whine haunt whichever Wednesday was closest—that's how we celebrated everyone's birthday—but they knew I'd come to the Met on Wednesday instead, since it was my birthday and I was nothing if not my parent's child of routine, and they'd accosted me on the steps, completely unexpected. I thought I wouldn't see Drew and Fiona for another week at least, but they decided to bring

Penelope along, and she was napping surprisingly blissfully in a wrap across Drew's front. My aunt and I used to visit van Gogh before we set off on our trips, but there was no trip this year, though it was still nice to go and sit, like I used to in college, and drink a little wine, and listen to my friends comment on the pieces of art as if any of us knew what we were talking about.

"I like that frame," Juliette said. "It's very . . . stark."

"I think it's mahogany," Fiona pointed out, before Penelope Grayson Torres made a noise that probably signaled to Fiona that something was amiss, because she took the baby from Drew and said, "I need to go find a bathroom. Drew?"

"I think there's one this way. We'll be right back," Drew added, getting up with her wife.

"Take your time," I replied, and they left down the hallway. Juliette grabbed a map that had been abandoned on one of the benches, and she mentioned that she hadn't been to this museum in a while.

"You should go explore. I've been here so many times, I think I have all the plaques memorized," I replied matter-of-factly, and that seemed like a great idea to her, because she set off for the Sackler Wing, leaving me to my own devices.

Finally alone, in the quiet surrounded by tourists, I settled down on my bench, and looked up at the van Goghs, sandwiched beside other Postimpressionist painters of that era, Gauguin and Seurat. Even though people tried to be quiet as they moved around Gallery 825, their footsteps were loud and shuffling, echoing across the wooden herringbone floor.

I closed my eyes, and breathed out a breath, and I missed my aunt.

She always said she loved van Gogh's work, and maybe that was why I loved it as well. And knowing what I knew now, maybe she liked van Gogh's work for other reasons, too. Maybe she liked how he created things while never knowing his own value. Maybe she liked the thought of being imperfect, but being loved anyway. Maybe she felt some sort of kinship with a man who, for his entire adult life, warred with his own monsters in his head. Vincent van Gogh's last words were, after his brother comforted him by telling him he would get better from the self-inflicted gunshot wound to the chest, "*La tristesse durera toujours.*"

The sadness will last forever.

It wasn't a lie. There was sadness, and there was despair, and there was pain—but there was also laughter, and joy, and relief. There was never grief without love or love without grief, and I chose to think that my aunt lived because of them. Because of all the light and love and joy that she found in the shadows of everything that plagued her. She lived because she loved, and she lived because she *was* loved, and what a lovely lifetime she gave us.

I didn't realize Drew had returned until she cleared her throat, her hands behind her back suspiciously—as if she was hiding something. Fiona wasn't with her. "Hi, sorry. I didn't want to give this to you with everyone else around . . ."

"What is it?" I asked.

"I really hope you won't be mad at me, but . . ." She revealed a package, and handed it to me. "When you threw it away, I . . . fished it out of the garbage. I was trying to figure out the right time to give it to you and, well . . . there's never a right time, I guess."

It was the same package that I'd thrown away—the one from my aunt that had gotten lost in the mail.

I took it, running my hands over my aunt's crisp handwriting.

"I'm sorry if you're mad but—"

"No." I blinked back tears in my eyes. "Thank you. I regretted throwing it away."

She smiled. "Good." Then she stooped down and hugged me. "We love you, Clementine."

I hugged her back. "I love you all, too."

She kissed my cheek, and began to leave again, but I stopped her for a moment. "Did you ever hear back? About James Ashton?"

Did I mess it all up? But I was afraid to ask that part, because I hadn't heard one way or the other what ended up happening to that auction. I think it wrapped up today. He probably went with Faux, or Harper, or—

A sparkle lit Drew's eyes and she nodded with a smile. She sat down on the edge of the bench and took my hands tightly, and said, "We got it! I heard just before we came here to surprise you."

My shoulders relaxed with relief. "You got it."

"We have some things to work out in the contract, but he's ours."

"He's yours," I corrected.

Her smile faltered a little. "Strauss and Adder won't be the same without you."

"It'll be just as good, and he will shine with you, I just know it."

She perked at that. "You're right, and you should say it *louder*."

So I did. I stood and pointed to Drew and shouted, "Attention everyone!"

Drew paled. "No, wait, stop—"

"Please give a round of applause for Drew, the most thoughtful, lovely book editor you'll ever find!" I shouted, while Drew tried to shush me, and clawed at me to sit down again. The attendant in the room gave me a tired look. "And she just won her dream book at auction!"

There was a round of sparse applause as Drew pulled me back down onto the bench, her face red in a blush. "Shush! Stop it! What's come over you, do you *want* to get kicked out?"

I laughed and promised, "I'm going to celebrate every good thing that comes your way."

The room attendant, who had begun to walk over to us, decided that we weren't worth it, turned, and left for her perch by the doorway again.

Drew said, "You're a menace."

"You love me."

"We do," she agreed, and her eyes flicked down to the package again. "Come find us when you're done?"

"I promise."

"Okay, good." And she left again to go after Fiona.

When she was gone, and the quiet crept into the gallery again, I stared down at the package on the bench beside me. It was small, about the size of a postcard, so I could see how it could've easily gotten lost. There were half a dozen different customs stamps on it, detailing its long and harrowing journey. It felt almost impossible that it'd come back to me, but it had.

My fingers slipped under the brown packaging paper, and I finally tore it open. It was a travel guide—to Iceland. *Ævintýri Bíður* by Ingólfur Sigurðsson. When I put it into Google, it translated to *Adventure Awaits*.

And she had tucked a letter into it:

To detail our trip next year! I found it in a darling little used bookstore in Canterbury, England.

Love, AA

My mouth twisted as tears came to my eyes. She had been planning it even though, in the end, she wasn't quite sure she wanted to go.

I closed the letter and tucked it back into the book for the trip I would never go on, and turned my eyes back up to van Gogh.

I would never know if she meant to leave or not, whether it was accidental or intentional, but I chose to believe that in another universe, we were boarding a plane to Iceland, she in her powder-blue traveling coat, her hair pulled up into a scarf, ready to tear through all the romance novels she'd loaded onto her kindle, and I'd be painting scenes in *Ævintýri Bíður*.

I liked that story. It was a good one.

But . . . so was this one. A little sadder, but it was mine, and while Iceland was no longer on the agenda, adventure still awaited, so I opened to the first page, and took out my pencil, and began to sketch the family with the young child across the room. Her parents held her hand as she pulled them from one painting to the next, counting the birds in each of them. If they didn't have a bird, she'd say, "None!" and move on, so naturally I sketched a flock of pigeons behind her.

I'm sure my friends were all dragging each other through the Met, looking at the suits of armor and the sphinxes and the Rembrandts, while I sat happily and let my heart pour out into the pages.

I didn't notice the man who sat down beside me until the little girl came up to him and asked, "Do *you* like birds?"

"Most of them," he replied warmly, "though I'm still unsure about pigeons."

"I love pigeons!" she gasped, and turned to her parents. "Momma, Daddy, let's count the pigeons in the pictures next!" Before she dragged them off to the next room, which—I knew from experience—held quite a lot of paintings with birds in them.

The man beside me leaned forward, his hands on his knees, as he looked up at the paintings. He wore a soft lavender button-down, sleeves rolled up to expose the tattoos across his arms, placed like afterthoughts. I glanced over at him—

"Iwan?" His name was a whisper, afraid I was mistaken. Though, he didn't look as put together as before. His auburn curls were wild, his shirt crumpled. But then he looked over at me, those pale eyes so lovely a gray, I knew how to paint them now—in shades of black and white and creams and golds and blues, pearlescent and soft. And then he smiled at me, that same crooked smile of the man I'd met in that small apartment on the Upper East Side, where time crashed together like opposing waves.

I had just opened my mouth to congratulate him on choosing Drew, the only right choice, trying to make it sound as sarcastic and playful as I could, while trying to disguise my regret, the cracks in an impending heartbreak, when he said, "Happy Birthday, Lemon."

"What?" I gave a start.

He pulled up a small bouquet of sunflowers. "Happy birthday."

I took them hesitantly. He'd remembered my favorite color. Of course he had, because he was still the same person—thoughtful and kind. Like he'd always been. For everything that changed, something stayed the same. "I'm sorry," I said. "I shouldn't have said anything the other week—especially not at your *opening*."

"Perhaps," he replied, folding his hands together. We sat there quietly for a moment, looking at the paintings. Tourists migrated around us, the gallery a soft rush of murmurs.

"How did you know I'd be here?" I asked after a moment.

He gave me a sidelong look. "You said you would be. Every birthday." He gave a small laugh. "You have no idea how many times I debated coming here any other year. Just sitting down beside you, wondering if—maybe—you'd recognize me."

"From the cab?" I asked.

He nodded. "But I was always a little too afraid. And then when you walked into that book meeting . . ." He clicked his tongue to the roof of his mouth and shook his head. "I tried to look so cool for you."

"You accomplished that. Maybe a little too well," I added.

He chuckled, and turned to me. "Would you . . . like to go to dinner with me? I know this restaurant down in NoHo. It's changed a little recently."

"I don't know . . . Is it good?"

"It's decent," he replied, and then after a thought, he added, "I hope."

A grin broke out across my face. I couldn't help it. "Well, then, I guess we need to go see for ourselves," I said, and he stood and outstretched his hand to me, and I felt a familiar kind of thrill curl through my body as I accepted his hand—the kind of feeling I got when I rushed after my aunt through airport terminals, fast and breathless, the world spinning.

It was the feeling of something new.

40

Chase the Moon

"CLOSE YOUR EYES," HE said as we got out of the Uber in front of his restaurant. The afternoon had sunken into a beautiful golden evening, and the light through the streets reflected off the windows of the restaurant, so I couldn't see inside.

"Why? Are you going to kidnap me?" I replied, and he rolled his eyes and put his hands over my eyes so I wouldn't look. "Do you need my safe word? It's *sassafras*."

"Walk forward—watch your step," he added as I stepped over something, and into the restaurant. I heard the door close behind me. The restaurant was cold and quiet—we were the only ones in here, by the sound of our footsteps as he led me further inside.

"Is it a pony?" I asked. "Ooh—are you finally cooking me *split-pea soup?*"

"Can you just be serious for one minute? This is important. Stand there," he added, placing me in an exact spot on the floor. I chewed on my bottom lip, trying not to smile too wide. "Okay," he said, "three . . . two . . ."

He let out a deep breath.

"One."

Then he took his hands away.

Soft rustic chandeliers hung from the ceiling, casting golden light down across the deep-mahogany tables, most of them small, where lovely bouquets of beautiful violet hyacinths sat in glass vases, interspersed with softly flickering candles. The walls were a verdant sage color—not crimson, but crimson didn't really fit him anymore, anyway—peppered with a menagerie of art pieces, all hung in varying frames and in different sizes across the walls.

He hurried over to a chair and scooted it out. "It'll take a bit to break them in," he said as I sat down, and he pushed me in, "but I think we have the time."

"Is this *actual* leather?"

"Pleather, but don't tell the critics," he added with a wink. Then he took a menu on the table, and handed it to me. It looked almost exactly like the menu I'd seen here nearly two weeks ago. Except there was one difference. Two, actually, and of course I said the one he *wasn't* referring to: "You capitalized the name?"

He gave me a look and pointed down at the dessert. "I'm going to make the goddamn lemon pie. The dry ice noodles are staying, though," he added, a little quieter.

The edges of my mouth twitched into a small smile. I liked the lighting in here now, it turned everything hazy and lovely. Romantic. "I think that's a good trade," I replied, still looking at the menu. Smiling at it, really. Because he'd also added another dish. *Pommes frites.* "Huh? What did you say?"

He knelt down beside me, a hand on my knee, so that we were eye level with each other. He was just so handsome, I wanted to trace the lines of his face, I wanted to sketch the sharpness of his jawbone, I wanted to paint the color of his hair. This scene would go in the section of the travel guide labeled "Scenic Spots" because I wouldn't get tired of looking at his face for years—decades. I wanted to watch it age, I wanted to see what kind of wrinkles knitted into his smiles.

"Is this what you imagined?" he asked, turning his gaze across the restaurant. "After you reminded me that what made that meal perfect *was* my granddad, I looked around, and I started to wonder which parts of this restaurant were me."

I shook my head. "It was all you, every second of the way. I was wrong."

"Not completely," he replied, and pulled me to my feet again. "The chairs were a bad idea—they were way too uncomfortable."

"They were," I admitted in relief.

"And the lighting was too bright and unforgiving—like I put everyone in a spotlight. But," he added, "unlike the dishwasher seven years ago, I know that I like the idea of small tables—they're intimate—but perhaps the white was a little too arrogant." He pulled me into the middle of the restaurant and stood behind me, wrapping his arms around my middle, his chin on my shoulder, as he slowly turned me to a blank space on the wall in the middle of the restaurant. "It's for you, if you ever find the inspiration to put something there."

I pressed my fingers tightly around his at my waist, my lips pressed together as tears stung at my eyes. "Really?" I whispered, and felt him nod against my shoulder.

"Really. All my life, I've wanted to make a place that felt comfortable—it's what I always worked toward. A place where people can come, and eat perfect meals with their granddads, and feel at home. This Hyacinth is me. Not the me from seven years ago, not the press release version of me—but me. And you helped me remember that, Lemon."

I turned in his arms, and looked up at this lovely man, a blend of an idealistic dishwasher and an experienced chef de cuisine, part little boy whose perfect meal was a plate of French fries, and part man who made the most delicate lemon pies.

"And I love," he went on, "how every piece of this restaurant now tells a story—how the ambiance is the narrator. And this story is about the past"—he pressed his forehead against mine—"meeting the present."

"Or the present meeting the past," I reminded.

He brought my hand up to his lips and kissed it. "And the present meeting the present."

"And"—I smiled, reminded of that girl sitting in a shared taxi—"the past meeting the past."

"I think I'm in love with you."

I blinked. "W-what?"

"Clementine." And the way he said my name just then felt like a promise, a vow against loneliness and heartache, and I could listen to the way his tongue wrapped around the letters of my name for the rest of my life, "I love you. You're stubborn, and you worry a little too much, and you always get this crease between your eyebrows when you're thinking, and you see parts of people they don't see in themselves anymore, and I love the way you laugh, and the way you blush. I loved the woman I met in apartment B4, but I think I love you a little bit more."

I swallowed the knot in my throat. My heart felt bright and terribly loud in my ears. "You do?"

He snagged my chin, turning my face up toward his, and whispered, "I do. I love you, Lemon."

I felt like I could float right off into the sky. "I love you, too, Iwan."

He leaned close, the smell of aftershave heady on his skin. "I'm going to kiss you now," he rumbled.

"Please."

And he kissed me there, in the stolen moments of a Wednesday evening, in a restaurant that felt like his soul, and his kiss tasted sharp and sweet, like the beginning of something new. I smiled against his mouth, and I whispered, "And here I thought you'd find romance in a piece of chocolate."

He rumbled a laugh. "A girl I once met swore she'd had it in a good cheddar." His hands sank down to my waist, and he began to sway me a little, back and forth, to the sound of some invisible song. "What would you like tonight, Lemon?"

I kissed him again. "You."

"For *dinner*!" He laughed, throwing his head back, and then he said, a bit softer, "*Then* you can have me."

"You won't judge me?"

"Never."

"I want a PB&J."

He laughed again, bright and golden, and kissed me on the cheek. "Okay." And he pulled me into the immaculate kitchen and made me a peanut butter and jelly sandwich from some leftover ends of a loaf of freshly baked bread, grape compote, and natural peanut butter. The bread was soft, and when I kissed him, he tasted like grape jelly, and he told me about the new chefs in his kitchen, and asked me, "What are you going to do with the rest of your life now, Lemon?"

I cocked my head and debated while he leaned over and took a bite of my sandwich. "I don't know, but I think I should make sure my passport is good."

"You're going to travel?"

"I think I might. And, I don't know, maybe chase the moon."

He leaned over, since we were both sitting on the countertop, and kissed me gently on the lips. "I think that's a great idea."

I put the rest of my sandwich down, and curled my fingers

around his collar, feeling the heat from his skin on my cold fingers. In all honesty, I was hungry for something else entirely. "Do you want to come back to my apartment?"

"Only," he replied, as a crooked grin curved his lips, "if you can guess my favorite color."

"Well, that's easy," I said, and leaned in close to whisper the answer in his ear.

He barked a laugh, his eyes glittering.

"Am I right, James Iwan Ashton?" I asked, already knowing that I was. At first, I hadn't been all that sure what his favorite color was, but it turned out that he'd been saying it this entire time, repeating it, over and over, every time he called my name.

Because his favorite color was the same as mine.

||||||||||||||||||||||||||||||||||||||

THE MONROE WAS QUIET that evening. The sky was bright with the last dredges of sunlight, throwing pinks and blues across the horizon, as I led Iwan into the twelve-story building where stone creatures held up the eaves and neighbors played musicals on their violins. Earl was at the front desk, reading Agatha Christie, and he perked up with a wave, and returned to it as we hurried to the elevator.

"You have no idea how many times I walked past this building hoping I'd catch a glimpse of you," he said as we slipped inside. "I was half afraid that man would recognize me eventually."

"It's a wonder we never bumped into each other after the taxi," I agreed. "What would you have done?"

He bit his bottom lip. "Plenty of things that are probably frowned upon in polite society."

"Oh, now I'm *very* interested—Look up," I added, and when he did, I whispered to him, and my mirror-self whispered to his a half second later, and his eyes widened at the words. He gave me a look

as color crept up his collar and tinged his cheeks, making his freckles almost glow. I watched him run his tongue along his bottom
teeth, mouth slightly parted.

"Really," he mumbled.

I gave a shrug. The elevator door opened onto the fourth floor.
"Maybe," I said, smiling a secret sort of smile, and pulled him out
of the elevator and down the hall. We passed rows and rows of
crimson doors with lion-head door knockers. In front of the door
to apartment B4, he pulled me close and wrapped me in his arms
and pressed my back against it, and snagged my mouth with his.
He kissed fervently, as if he'd been waiting for a drink for years.

"I never got over that," he murmured, breaking away just long
enough for a breath.

I slid my hands up his chest. "What?"

"How well you kiss. Over the last seven years," he went on,
resting his forehead against mine, "I went on so many dates, I
kissed so many people, I tried to fall in love again and again, and
all I could think about was you."

I wasn't sure what to say. "All seven years?"

"Two thousand five hundred and fifty-five days. Not that I was
counting," he added, because clearly he had been, and that made
the butterflies in my stomach awfully happy. Seven years—seven
whole years.

I whispered, "At least you don't have to wait a day more."

He smiled, wide and crooked. And he pressed his lips to mine
again. Softly, savoring. "No," he murmured against my lips, planting another kiss on the corner of my mouth. "But the wait was
worth it, Lemon."

"Say it again?" I murmured, because I still loved the way he said
my nickname in his soft Southern drawl.

I felt him smile against my mouth, as his hand came up to

cradle my face, and he kissed me again, as if he couldn't get enough of it, and quite honestly I could spend the rest of my life being kissed *by* him. His mouth lingered against mine, deeper this time, hungrier. He leaned in, his hands traveling to my hips. I ran my fingers down the line of buttons on his shirt before I slipped them between two of them near his stomach, brushing my fingertips along his skin. I could get lost here in this moment, no travel guides, no itineraries.

Until I remembered—"We're still in the hallway."

"Are we?" He kissed my cheek.

"We are."

Another kiss on my temple, on my nose, returning to hover against my mouth. "I guess we should get inside."

"Probably." And I pulled him in to kiss him again, and then I unlocked my apartment door, and we fell in, a mess of arms and limbs. We kicked off our shoes at the door as it closed behind us, and pushed each other down the hall. He slid his arms behind my back, and lifted me up. I wrapped my legs around his middle, pulling him closer. My fingers curled into his ginger hair. He was like a brandy I wanted to drink on a clear summer day, a golden afternoon I wanted to get lost in, an evening over cardboard pizza and lemon pie that was never the same twice—

He sat me up on the counter of the kitchen, trailing kisses down my neck.

"The plant's new," he murmured, glancing at the pothos on the counter.

"Her name's Helga. She won't mind."

He laughed against my skin. "Good." He nibbled my shoulder, his fingers slipping under my skirt, and unzipped it, tugging it off me, and then he undid the buttons of my blouse, and planted a kiss between my breasts.

I undid his buttons one by one, tracing the crescent-shaped birthmark on his collar before I kept going—and then I paused. Felt over a new tattoo I'd never seen before. My eyebrows furrowed. "When did you get this?"

He looked down at the tattoo, and then sheepishly back at me. "About seven years ago. It's a bit faded now—"

"It's a lemon flower."

"Yes," he replied, looking up into my eyes, searching them. He'd gotten a lemon flower tattooed over his heart.

"What do you tell people, when they ask about it?"

His shyness melted into a smile, warm and gooey like chocolate. "I tell them about a girl I fell in love with at the right place but the wrong time."

A knot lodged in my throat. "And what are you going to tell them now?"

"That we finally got the timing right."

"A matter of time," I whispered.

"A matter of *timing*," he proposed, and kissed me again, before his mouth trailed down my stomach to my underwear, until he pulled them down, and I curled my fingers around his auburn curls as he said soft devotions to me right there in my kitchen. He was so tender as he planted his hands against my thighs, and spread my legs wide, and, oh, I really loved this man. I loved this man as he kissed the rest of me, and carried me to my bedroom. As he took time to learn about the scars on my knees from when I fell as a kid, as he traced his fingers, calloused and warm, across the freckles on my back, and kissed the scar on my right eyebrow from a close call with a piece of glass. He pushed my hair back gently and kissed me so deeply I finally realized what my aunt meant when she said you always knew the exact moment you fell—

I did, too.

Sort of.

I fell for every kiss he planted on me, but I'd fallen days, weeks, months, before. I fell a little in that taxi ride with a stranger, and I fell a little more when I asked that stranger, seven years later, to stay. I kept falling, tumbling, not realizing I wasn't on solid ground anymore, as we had dinner and laughed over wine and danced to violin musicals, as we ate late-night fajitas in the park and walked on glittery sidewalks made of recycled plastic, tripping headlong into something so deep and terrifying and wonderful I didn't realize I had fallen at all until he came to sit beside me in front of a painting of a dead artist, and told me he loved me.

He meant it as his fingers memorized my body, as he discovered how we fit together again, and he was *so* much better at it all than he was seven years ago. Like, impeccable game, sir. I suddenly had no qualms with all the women I remembered from his Instagram. They were a lot of practice and I was absolutely reaping the benefits. He wrapped his hands around mine, and as we moved together, he said my name as if it meant something all its own—a spell. Maybe the start of a recipe. *For disaster? No, I won't even think it.*

He nibbled the side of my neck, just under my ear, and I pressed myself up against him, trying to be closer than we ever could go. I wanted to enter into his bloodstream, meld into his bones, become a part of him with everything that I was—

"I have dreamed of this for years," he murmured, kissing the dip of my neck. "I dreamed so much of you."

"How's reality?" I asked, myself around him, never wanting to let him go.

"*Fuck*, so much better."

I laughed and kissed him, and then he moved faster as our heartbeats rose, and there was no more talking as we fell, harder and harder, toward each other, coming together in the right place at the right time in the right moment, and I loved him. I loved his scars and the cooking burns on his arms and the stupid whisk tattoo behind his ear. I loved how his auburn curls hugged my fingers, and I loved that he had three strands of gray hair.

Only three.

I was probably going to give him more.

And we laughed, and charted each other's bodies down to our cores, maps of places that were familiar and yet new, and the night was good, and my heart was full, and I was happy, so happy, to fall in love on a night like this, where I felt like I had finally caught the moon, and more.

And We Stay

ON THE FOURTH FLOOR of the Monroe on the Upper East Side, there was a small, cluttered apartment I loved.

I loved it because in the mornings a perfect slant of light draped itself across the kitchen, spilling golden egg yolk across the table and tiled floor, and in the stillness of 10:00 a.m., motes of dust glittered across the air like stars.

I loved it because it had an elegant claw-foot bathtub that was the perfect size to curl oneself inside and paint. I loved it because books spilled off the shelves in the study, and half-dying devil's ivy curled around busts of long-dead poets. And in the evenings, I remembered my aunt sashaying through the living room, her hair up in a colorful scarf, wearing her favorite "I murdered my husband in cold blood" robe, a martini in one hand, and all of life, grabbed by the horns, in the other.

I loved it because there were marks on the doorway leading into the bedroom, where every summer my aunt measured my height and marked it with a different shade of fingernail polish.

And I loved that apartment because I loved seeing Iwan in it, humming along to nineties pop songs as he danced around the kitchen, from cutting board to stove to sink, stealing glances at me with those glittering gemstone eyes. I could almost imagine wanting to come back to those moments, again and again, just to remember how he smiled and called me Lemon in his soft, rumbling voice.

Even as we packed everything into boxes, I loved this apartment. As I kissed my fingers and planted them on the wall, and said goodbye, for the first and the last time, I wanted to stay here forever, but Iwan took my hand and led me through the front door and into some bright unknown.

Nothing stayed—or so I had always thought. Nothing stayed and nothing lingered.

But I was wrong.

Because there was an apartment in the Monroe on the Upper East Side that was full of magic, and it taught me how to say goodbye.

And it was no longer mine.

That didn't matter, though, because I carried all of the good moments with me, the walls and the furniture—the claw-foot tub and the robin's-egg blue chair—and the way my aunt danced me around the living room, so no matter where I was, I would always be home.

Because the things that mattered most never really left.

The love stays.

The love always stays, and so do we.

Acknowledgments

Every book is a process.

As I'm writing this, *The Seven Year Slip* is in copyedits, which just means it's at the very beginning stages where it goes out to early readers. Writing acknowledgments at this stage always feels like a little bit of a guessing game—you see, *The Seven Year Slip* doesn't come out for another six months as of right now, so I'm not quite sure who all to thank yet, and as people come and go, I'll miss a few names.

Publishing is an ever-changing landscape, both working in the industry and writing in it, but for the moment, these are the people who have championed *The Seven Year Slip*—and my previous novel, *The Dead Romantics*.

This novel, in particular, wouldn't be what it is today (or six months from now, really) without the dedication and support of my talented editor, Amanda Bergeron, who took a look at all my jumbled ideas, and helped me mold them into this glued-together clump of dead trees you're holding.

I'd also love to thank my agent, Holly Root, for always being so incredibly present with me. She's one heck of a partner for all of my creative endeavors. Thank you for saying yes to all my harebrained ideas.

To the team at Berkley: Sareer Khader, Danielle Keir, Tina Joell, Jessica Mangicaro, Craig Burke, and Jeanne-Marie Hudson. My copyeditor, Janine Barlow; and Alaina Christensen and Christine Legon and Daniel Brount; my proofreaders—Michelle Hope, Megha Jain, and Jennifer Myers; and the sales team; the marketing designers; the booksellers and librarians and readers—thank you for making my career such a delight.

Vi-An Nguyen, the cover you designed is lovely, and thank you also to Anthony Ramondo for a stellar look for my romance novels.

To my friends and critique partners—Nicole Brinkley, Katherine Locke, Kaitlyn Sage Patterson—thank you for being my guinea pigs time and again.

And this might seem a little silly, but I also want to thank my cat, Paprika (Pepper, my lovely Pepper), who's sat at my feet for almost all of my novels so far, a steadfast companion in a career that is, often, a solitary thing. She's sick right now, and I'm not sure about the future, but for the moment, she's lying on my bed, and she's here.

There's a magic to that, when I read these acknowledgments in the future, and I remember this moment. My cat on my bed, coffee cooling on the desk beside me, piles of laundry mounting in my basket. A gift from me to me.

Speaking of which, last of all, I'd like to thank myself. Because I *did* it. I wrote a novel. It doesn't matter how many I've written before this, or how many I'll write after—it's still a wonder I wrote this one. I did something I didn't think I could do. I put the Technicolor fluff in my head into ink-colored words on the page. It's a wonder.

I hope this feeling never goes away.

THE
SEVEN
YEAR
SLIP

ASHLEY POSTON

READERS GUIDE

EVERY BOOK IS A time capsule.

Who I am right now—as I'm writing this six months before *The Seven Year Slip* finds its way onto shelves—isn't the person I'm going to be when you read this. Books are like a magical apartment in that way, capturing a singular point in time when an author writes a book that maybe, someday, a future you will visit and read.

Who I was at the beginning of writing this book isn't the person I ended up being at the end. I look back on those earlier drafts, and it does feel, a little, like glancing through a window back at a person you knew intimately—how they take their breakfast, and their favorite restaurant spots, and the worst day of their life—already knowing what'll come next.

Grief is a weird thing. It can be a monster on your shoulder. It can be a friend sitting with you at the table. It can be a memory in a smell—the soft, delicate notes of floral perfume. Grief can find you in the middle of the night as you roll over to go back to sleep. It can even find you in your dreams.

And grief—what it looks like, how it whispers, how you respond—is different for everyone.

When I look back on the first draft of *The Seven Year Slip*, trying to pinpoint the exact shade of grief Clementine felt for her late aunt, I could see that I was close, but it was the sort of feeling, the sort of life experience, I had to imagine.

And then, suddenly, on a bright blue day at the end of March, I didn't have to anymore.

It's so strange when your life suddenly stops—when the worst day happens—and the world just spins on without you. My grandfather died by suicide, and I had a book due. My grandfather didn't even leave a note, and I had interviews to schedule and videos to film and events where I needed to smile. My grandfather was dead, and I had to answer questions on a book about grief and funerals—and yeah, I know how ironic it sounds.

When I look back on that first draft of *The Seven Year Slip*, I think—mostly—about how . . . nice . . . I wrote it all. A comfort and a warm hug, and at the same time it said nothing at all.

So, after a few months, I rearranged my writing space—because I couldn't sit in that chair at the end of that table like I had the day my mom called me sobbing, because I still visit that moment in my nightmares—and I wrote a second draft of *The Seven Year Slip*. I wrote a draft that was much more divorced from my feelings than I'd ever written before, because I myself didn't want to sit too long with that grief. I could have changed the story. I could have pried the aunt out of the bones of this book and written something new—my editor would have let me, she's so lovely and so understanding—but *I* don't think I could have.

So, finally, I tried again.

The last time. This time.

It becomes the book in your hands.

I wish I could say that I wrote about suicide correctly or perfectly, but I know I didn't. I'm messy, and I'm prone to purply language, and I try to meet this terrible experience with love and thoughtfulness, because even though I'm heartbroken, I love my grandfather.

This book is very personal to me in the exact ways that feels raw and too telling.

I'm not the person I was when I finished that first rose-colored draft of *The Seven Year Slip*, and by the time you read this, I won't be the person I am after I put the last period in this sentence. A book is a time capsule. No matter how much I change, or will change, or will learn, this book will be stagnant. It'll exist here, forever unchanged, along with the pieces of me that I put into the pages.

I know I will be different in the future, and every time you come back to this book—*if* you come back to it, ever again—you'll be different, too. I think there's a little bit of lovely magic in that. The magic of a memory. A piece of creativity born from the person you were, once upon a time. The art stays the same, but you change, and as you change, so does what the art means to you—even as it allows you a window into who you once were and the people you once loved, and still love.

It changes, but in little ways, it all stays.

Everything stays.

If you or a loved one is experiencing thoughts of suicide, please contact your national suicide prevention foundation at 988 (in the US).

DISCUSSION QUESTIONS

1. Grief is difficult to manage, but especially sudden and traumatic grief. How does Clementine cope with hers? How does Iwan?

2. The apartment can only travel seven years into the future or past—would you travel seven years into either your future or past? And if so, who would you want to meet there, and why?

3. My family has the story of my great-grandma's "dumpling sweater"—the sweater she always made her homemade dumplings in. Rumor has it, the sweater still smells like dumplings and her soft floral perfume to this day. Do you have a food or recipe that reminds you of home?

4. Iwan claims that food is a universal language—do you agree with him?

5. At the end of the book, Clementine sets off on a new adventure after she realizes that she has changed since she began her publishing career. Have you ever thought about changing careers? Why, and did you?

6. In the culinary world, it's easy to say that Michelin-starred restaurants are the best—but we all know that one dive bar we'd kill for. What are some of your favorite restaurants, and why? (Don't be shy, drop the names!)

7. Do you think a chef who invents new recipes and flavors is more talented than the chef who perfects an old, but exquisite, recipe?

8. Clementine has a love for art and artists, but most specifically Vincent van Gogh. Is there a piece of art that moves you? (Book, painting, film, comic—they all count!) And if so, why?

9. If you had a plane ticket to anywhere in the world, where would you go? And where do you think Clementine went?

BOOK PAIRINGS FOR *THE SEVEN YEAR SLIP*

- *Salt, Fat, Acid, Heat: Mastering the Elements of Good Cooking* by Samin Nosrat.
- *Kitchen Confidential: Adventures in the Culinary Underbelly* by Anthony Bourdain.
- *The Anthropocene Reviewed: Essays on a Human-Centered Planet* by John Green.
- *The Princess Bride* by William Goldman.
- *This Is How You Lose the Time War* by Amal El-Mohtar and Max Gladstone.
- *Garlic and Sapphires: The Secret Life of a Critic in Disguise* by Ruth Reichl.
- *Everything I Need I Get from You: How Fangirls Created the Internet as We Know It* by Kaitlyn Tiffany.
- *Every Heart a Doorway* by Seanan McGuire.

ASHLEY POSTON is the *New York Times* bestselling author of *The Dead Romantics*. A native of South Carolina, she lives in a small gray house with her sassy cat and too many books. You can find her on the internet, somewhere, watching cat videos and reading fan fiction.

CONNECT ONLINE

AshPoston.com
HeyAshPoston
AshPoston